After the ship landed, Captain Tom Javik and his crewmate looked out the open hatch. The ship was surrounded by walking, talking fruits, all dressed in three-piece suits and carrying briefcases. Oranges, lemons, apples, kiwis, they all clamored around the ship hysterically, piling on top of one another to reach the hatchway.

Finally, one creature reached the top, where he pressed a business card into Javik's hand. Javik read:

"Wily Watermelon, Attorney at Law..."

Berkley books by Brian Herbert

SIDNEY'S COMET
THE GARBAGE CHRONICLES

THE GARBAGE CHRONICLES

Being an account of the adventures of
Tom Javik and Wizzy Malloy in the faraway
land of catapulted garbage.

BRIAN HERBERT

BERKLEY BOOKS, NEW YORK

THE GARBAGE CHRONICLES

A Berkley Book / published by arrangement with
the author

PRINTING HISTORY
Berkley edition / January 1985

ISBN: 0-425-07450-1

INTRODUCTION

During most of the previous decade, Winston Abercrombie was Garbage Thrust Commandant for the American Federation of Freeness. It was a crowded world, with no room for graveyards or garbage dumps, so the AmFeds used electromagnetic catapults to hurl bodies and trash into deep space. But Abercrombie did not follow the prescribed program.

He catapulted hundreds of thousands of full garbage cannisters to the remote planet of Guna One, secretly intending to retrieve them for the creation of a massive and illegal recycling industry. This glut of merchandise would have destroyed the new-product-based AmFed economy, setting Uncle Rosy's Thousand Year Plan on its ear. Fortunately, Abercrombie's diabolical plan was discovered in time by the Black Box of Democracy, Uncle Rosy's watchdog agency. Abercrombie fled before apprehension, presumably to Guna One.

Captain Tom Javik has been assigned to scout Guna One and report on any unusual activities there, bringing back Abercrombie if he can be found. Javik would prefer another assignment—investigating a mysterious, comet-like body which has been skywriting over New City for the past eight months. But Javik is in no position to argue.

Just before leaving on his mission, Javik is joined by a miniature talking comet who calls himself Wizzy. Wizzy claims to have magical powers, and indicates that he is the offspring of the skywriter.

As Javik's ship hurtles across space at hyper-light speed, he finds himself attracted to a female member of his crew, the transsexual, Marta Evans. Repulsed at the thought of such a tryst, Javik gulps a sexual sublimation pill. But Evans pursues him aggressively. Her principal weapon of seduction is a mento-activated brassiere, a device she can snap open by sending a thought command from her brain-implanted mento transmitter to a sensor in the bra.

Poor Javik. Even with all of his pills, he is no match for this. . . .

ONE

My observation is that there are two sorts of comets: one wandering, the other magical. None of the accepted scientific premises can be applied with respect to the behavior or physical makeup of a magical comet. Let those little minds obsessed with rules and categories stew over this one!

> Scrawled note found on
> Uncle Rosy's bedstand
> after his death

On the afternoon before the birth of the new magical comet, Tom Javik was escorted down a brightly painted sixth-floor corridor in Building B of the Bu-Tech Space Center. All the latest promotional colors were represented here in bright geometric shapes on the walls, ceilings, doors, and floor. The corridor was awhir with moto-shoes, as silver-uniformed government workers bustled to and fro.

"This has been redecorated since I was here last year," Javik said, smelling fresh paint. He glanced down at the oriental man rolling at his side. The small man wore silver-colored nylon pants and a matching top, with canary yellow stripes down his sleeves and legs. An octagonal blue lapel tag indicated rank: "G.W. 1000." This meant he held one one-thousandth of a job. He rustled as he moved.

"Haven't you heard?" the G.W. said, not looking at Javik.

"Bu-Free came in this week and redid the whole wing."

"Bu-Free? What the hell are Freeness people doing in Bu-Tech? Are they setting up a giveaway?"

"Who knows? Here's your briefing room." He stopped at a purple and gold door and mentoed it, sending a thought command from his brain-implanted transmitter to a receiving unit in the door. The door slid open without having been touched.

As Javik rolled into the room, he was forced to narrow his eyes in sunlight which slanted across the floor. "Say," he said, "this looks like the same briefing..." Javik fell silent when he noticed the G.W. guide was leaving. The door slid shut behind the guide.

Javik was certain it was the same briefing room he had been in the year before. But it had been painted more brightly, with colorful geometric shapes like those in the corridor. And the galactic model was gone, having been replaced by a floor-to-ceiling CRT screen. The screen was dark, save for the words "Faith, Consumption, Freeness," in white letters at the center.

Wonder what they've got in mind for me this time? Javik thought, noticing a G.W. standing by the wall to his left.

The G.W. rolled forward to greet Javik; he was so similar in appearance to the guide that he might have been his clone. "Good afternoon, Captain," he said crisply. "I am Leonard Nakato." He touched hands limply with Javik in a Bu-Health-approved method of handshake. As much as practical, the expenditure of calories was to be confined to Bu-Health gyms. It was another Job-Support policy, based upon the centuries-old teachings of Uncle Rosy, founder of the American Federation of Freeness.

Javik returned the salutation. Then: "I was told to report for a presidential assignment. Is this the right room?"

"Yes," Nakato said, revealing a slight oriental accent. "Come with me, please." He pulled Javik's white-uniformed arm gently, then released it when the men began to roll side by side toward the CRT screen.

When they stopped in front of the screen, Javik saw his own reflection in the dark glassplex: tall, muscular, and in his late thirties, with gold captain's epaulets on the shoulders of his Space Patrol uniform. "Is the President going to speak with me by video hookup?" he asked.

Nakato mentoed the screen, causing the words "Faith, Consumption, Freeness" to fade. A large roulette wheel appeared on the screen, surrounded by what looked like green felt.

Deciding that this was the aerial view of a gaming table, Javik felt his lips mouth the word "What?" without making a sound.

"Mento the wheel," Nakato said. The window shade on Javik's left snapped down, making the screen image clearer.

"I'm not here to play games," Javik said. "Who's going to brief me?"

Nakato nodded at the CRT screen. "This is an assignment wheel," he said.

"What?"

"Bu-Free's idea. Some of their people were looking for things to do, so they got permission to set this thing up. You are to mento-spin it. The wheel will stop at the number indicating your assignment."

"I should be talking with a general," Javik said, "or at least a presidential aide." He turned to leave. "I must have the wrong briefing room."

Nakato checked a small clip pad that had been in his tunic pocket. "You *are* Captain Thomas P. Javik?" he asked.

"I am."

"Then this is the right place. You are to mento the wheel."

Javik turned slowly to face the screen. He closed his eyes and rubbed the fingers and thumb of one hand across his cheekbones.

"Captain Javik?" The voice was impatient.

Javik opened his eyes and mentoed the wheel. He felt a click in the back of his brain as his thought command was accepted by the CRT roulette wheel.

The wheel spun in a silent blur.

"Round and round she goes," Nakato said, "and where she stops . . ."

The wheel slowed, then stopped. A red pointer was over the number fifteen.

Nakato mentoed a pen to make an entry on his clip pad. The clear plastic pen floated out of his tunic pocket and moved across the paper without being touched. Then the pen floated back into the pocket.

The wheel faded, being replaced by white letters and numbers against a carmine red background:

ASSIGNMENT 15
GUNA ONE

"This is a search and scout expedition to Guna One," a pleasant woman's voice said, "largest planet in the Aluminum Starfield. It was the landing region used by the arch recycling criminal, Winston Abercrombie. When he was Garbage Thrust Commandant for the Federation in the nineties, Abercrombie catapulted hundreds of thousands of full garbage cannisters to the region, intending to retrieve them for his own diabolical scheme. If successful, he would have undermined the AmFed economy with a glut of recycled goods, thus putting millions of manufacturing people out of work."

"Public enemy number one," Nakato said. "He's never been apprehended."

"Abercrombie may be on Guna One," the woman's voice said. "No one is certain. Your assignment is twofold: First, see if there is any unusual activity in the region. Second, locate Abercrombie and bring him back for trial. More details are provided in a briefing tape on board your ship."

The screen darkened. Then the original white-lettered message reappeared. The window shade snapped open, filling the room with sunlight.

"I'd rather go to the Columbarian Quadrant," Javik said. "That's where the garbage comet originated."

"The what?"

"The garbage comet." Javik's voice reflected irritation. "It's been writing the same sky message for more than eight months: 'We are not your garbage dump!'"

"Oh?" Nakato looked up at Javik with a blank expression.

"It's only the biggest cosmic mystery ever," Javik said. "And you don't know anything about it?"

Nakato shook his head.

"Look, I deserve the Columbarian assignment . . . if there is one. I was the one sent to stop the comet last year, you know. I feel . . . well . . . responsible for it being here."

Nakato was unresponsive.

"Maybe I could find out what caused it," Javik said. "I hear a hundred missiles have been fired at the thing, from behind Bu-Tech-made clouds. But the comet's too quick. Hell, it has the capability of moving five, maybe six times the speed of light!"

"Your assignment cannot be changed," Nakato said. He slipped the tiny clip pad back into his pocket.

"*Is* anyone going to the Columbarian Quadrant?" Javik asked.

"I don't know."

"What *do* you know?" Javik asked. His deeply set blue eyes flashed angrily.

"You leave tomorrow," Nakato said, unruffled. "Report to Robespierre at nine A.M. Field sixteen."

Javik seethed, but he held his tongue. He recalled the many quarrels in his career and all the hot water into which they had gotten him. He was on the comeback trail now, fortunate to hold the rank of captain. The fights flashed across Javik's brain in a blur of fists and faces.

"I'll be there," he said.

At shortly past midnight, two magical comets hung in the ionosphere over New City, trailing delicate jet-ray tails of light across the deep blue starcloth of space. These were especially fiery comets, one large and brilliant blue, the other much smaller and cosmic pink. As the larger magical comet watched proudly, a tiny white nucleus with no visible tail emerged from the pink nucleus of its mother. The baby comet gasped for air and cried.

Anxious glances were exchanged between mother and father.

Reluctantly, the mother passed her newborn child to its father. Now the tiny white nucleus burned next to the father's brilliant blue fireball.

Words drifted across rarefied air as the cosmic pink comet spoke. "I wish he didn't have to go so young," she said.

"You know it's necessary," said the blue, his tone deep and mellifluous. "We've discussed it thoroughly."

"*We've* discussed nothing! You did all the talking—and the deciding!"

"Now, dear . . ."

"Don't you 'now dear' me!" the cosmic pink comet snapped, flaring an angry, hot shade. "I should have as much to say in this matter as you!"

The blue comet began to flash electrically. "There are laws," he said, his voice reaching a crescendo. "*Now go, woman! We will speak of this later!*"

Dutifully, the smaller comet bowed her nucleus. "Yes, Sidney," she said, trying very hard not to show the sarcasm which often irritated him. Demurely, she turned ninety degrees and sped off into deep space, trailing six magnificent plumes of cosmic pink gas.

I've never seen her more lovely, Sidney thought.

Any Earth inhabitant watching the sky at that hour would have seen a great blue comet dropping toward Earth, with a tiny white flame burning next to its nucleus. And had this observer been outside, oddly enough he would have felt cool. For the Great Comet was an electric fireball now, so cold that it left a layer of frost on the building tops below.

"Papa!" the baby comet cried out. "Papa Sidney!"

Sidney spoke tenderly to his child: "You are a new life force, son, with emotions much like those of a fleshcarrier. Physically, however, you resemble no other creature in the universe."

The baby comet cried softly.

"For the present, you have lungs, a heart, and other organs. Gradually, however, these will evolve into higher states. The emotions are different: They will stay with you always. There will be problems, but you will grow much wiser in only a few days."

"What are emotions, Papa?"

The Great Comet stopped its descent now, dimming and hovering a few kilometers above the surface. Below, New City twinkled like a distorted reflection of the universe.

"They are strong feelings, son, which will cause you to behave in certain ways. You must learn to control your emotions, but do not become callous in the process. Retain some vulnerability. This is perhaps the most important part of being alive."

"I do not understand."

"You will have to discover such things for yourself. Find the fleshcarrier Tom Javik. He will help you. And you will help him." The Great Comet glowed orange now, imparting warmth to the baby.

"I don't want to go, Papa! I'd rather stay with you, roaming the universe!" The little comet felt himself shaking all over. Mercuric perspiration ran down the sides of his molten rock body. He felt weak. "I have so many questions to ask you! Where did you and Mama meet?"

"On a singles flight to the Jahuvian mountain planets—one of the most romantic places in the universe."

"And she ensnared you?"

"I was a willing captive. There's one more thing you should know: Avoid water on your outside surface. Too much of it neutralizes your magical powers."

A great gust of wind blew all the mercuric perspiration from the little comet's body. Then the caressing warmth of his papa soothed him. The little comet wished he could stay in this place forever. It was so secure, so peaceful. He narrowly opened the yellow cat's eye on top of his body, trying to see his papa. But he saw only a warm orange glow.

"I will not dry you again," the deep, mellifluous voice said. "Go forth now, and do what is meant for you."

An irregularly shaped piece of molten material fell from the Great Comet's nucleus. It tumbled toward Earth.

"Don't leave me here, Papa!" the little comet cried out.

"Remember my words, son!"

"But Papa!"

"Become a Great Comet yourself! Make all creatures love and fear you! Place them in awe!"

The magical comet Sidney pulled away now, rising quickly toward the heavens. Soon he was out of Earth's atmosphere and traveling away at many times the speed of light. He became a speck in the distance, blending with the background of space.

The dense chunk of material comprising the little comet's body glowed bright red as it spiraled swiftly toward New City. Then it dimmed to a flicker and hardened, floating down on a cushion of magical air. With a dull thud, the piece fell to the skatewalk just outside the entrance to Javik's condominium building.

Tom Javik padded out of the bathroom module in his robe and slippers, crossing his unit to the kitchen module. He wore unmotorized slippers, the illegal type frowned upon by Bu-Health. The kitchen module was small, with black and gold foil-fleck walls, a mirrored floor, and a black plastic table by the window. A conveyor counter still had the dirty plastic dishes from dinner on it. Javik mentoed the conveyor, causing it to squeak noisily as it carried the dishes into a disposa-tube on one end. Machinery inside the wall whirred.

As he paused to examine an electronic letter on the table, the faint notes of a rock waltz reminded Javik of an old tune he and Sidney Malloy knew. For a moment, he thought of the way sounds and smells could bring back old memories.

The stereo system fell silent at his mento command. He looked out the window. From the 261st floor Javik could see the sparkling lights of downtown New City on the other side of the lake. Somewhere beyond the opposite shore in that cluster of government office buildings was the White House office tower.

Sid used to work there, Javik thought.

He looked down at the text of the blue-bordered letter with unfocused, bleary eyes. He closed his eyes and rubbed them, then looked back at the letter:

RE: MALLOY, SIDNEY
     YOUR INQUIRY OF 18 OCTOBER, 2605
REGRET TO INFORM THAT MALLOY HAS NOT BEEN SEEN SINCE 30 AUGUST LAST YEAR. IS PRESUMED LOST IN DEEP SPACE. KNOWN TO HAVE COMMANDEERED THE SHAM-ROCK V."

Eight months ago! Javik thought, staring at the cottage-cheese-sprayed ceiling. He let out a deep, exasperated breath. *Sid's gone for good.*

Javik pictured his sleek black and silver space cruiser, smiling softly as he thought of Sidney at the controls. *Didn't realize Sid had it in him,* he thought.

An overwhelming sensation of guilt hit Javik. He dropped his head and stared down along the blue and white striped front of his robe. "Poor little fellow," he whispered. A haunting, recurring feeling hit Javik that it was his fault for not reaching the cruiser in time to accompany Sidney.

If only I'd made it, he thought. *But Sid died well. That's some consolation.*

Javik shook his head, still staring down. *Nine hours to blastoff,* he thought, reading the illuminated green face of his wrist digital. *I should try to sleep.*

He pulled at the little pouch of fat under his chin, then leaned on the table and stretched his long frame. His muscles ached. In the window reflection he saw that his hair was tousled. He knew it was overdue for a trim and would be much worse after the mission.

"Wonder how much extra weight's in my hair," he mused.

Javik straightened and thrust both hands in his robe pockets.

Staring at the floor all the while, he shuffled his way to the videodome in the living-room module.

The dome was orbit orange plastic, with a sliding black door that opened at his mento-command. He slid into one of two soft bucket seats inside, mento-flipping on the set.

The screen lit up all around, giving Javik the illusion that he was seated in a racing car barreling down a straightaway.

Too hectic, he thought, changing the channel.

Javik finally settled on *The Yippee Hour,* a rockem-sockem game show. Javik became a member of the studio audience now, seated between two immense fat ladies.

Contestants came and went with astonishing speed, all departing with their arms full of bright, shiny consumer products. One man with a stick-on blond mustache became so ecstatic at his winnings that he knocked his mustache off his lip. Undaunted, he left it on the floor.

A volley of commercials accompanied each new contestant. Javik dozed off and blinked awake several times. Once, with heavy-lidded eyes, he watched seven chubby men in pineapple suits do a modern dance step while singing the virtues of Piney Pops fruit tarts.

"Cute little fellows," Javik muttered. "Cute little fellows." he dozed off again.

On the skatewalk outside, the little comet righted himself and used the yellow cat's eye on top of his body to look around. "Gracious!" he said, in a squeaky voice. "Now let me get my bearings." He felt an unidentifiable emotional rush which made him shake.

It was shadowy on the skatewalk, illuminated faintly by a street lamp. A midnight moto-shoer whisked by, oblivious to the little coal-shaped visitor who lay below.

The comet flickered, then whirled around in several complete circles. When the moto-shoer had disappeared into the dark distance, the comet brightened, flickering bright red for a moment to call upon his imprinted data banks.

"There!" he exclaimed, pulsating light as he focused his cat's eye on the synthetic marble face of Javik's building. He scooted partway up the building's entrance ramp, traveling only a hair's breadth above the surface. An undersized, barely discernible red tail flashed like sputtering rocket exhaust from his rear end.

Being young and undeveloped, the little comet had to stop only halfway up the ramp, panting heavily. "Uh oh!" he squealed, out of breath. He tumbled down the ramp, arriving in roughly the same spot from which he had begun.

After several deep breaths, the neophyte comet was ready to try again. "Up we go!" he said, taking a deep breath. "Up we go!" He scooted up the ramp, and this time nearly reached the top. But once again he tumbled back to the skatewalk, where he lay for several minutes, wheezing and coughing.

"Oh dear! Oh my! What a terrible thing!" The little comet was quite upset. "Papa Sidney flies across the heavens, but I'm stymied at the tiniest slope."

A brilliant blue light flashed overhead. The little comet focused his gaze upward and saw his papa streak by, alternating his mighty nucleus between blue and white. The Great Comet made a graceful turn, then zipped away, disappearing beyond the building tops. The buildings were silhouetted for a moment in the waning light of the comet. Then it became dark again.

He really is leaving me here, the little comet thought. *All alone*.

On the next try, he struggled to the top of the ramp. Then he scooted along a slick marbleite surface to double sliding doors. Through the glassplex of the doors a faintly illuminated lobby could be seen. The lobby had a red plastic and chrome couch, with a matching side chair and table. Pictures of flesh-carriers and government buildings were arranged on two walls.

The entrance doors were electric-eye-activated, and this presented no small problem for the comet. He saw how to activate the system, but noted to his chagrin that the seeing eyes were a full meter and a half above him. So he hopped as high as he could. That was all he could think to do. He jumped perhaps half a meter on the first try and three-quarters of a meter by the fourth attempt. After that, however, the height of each effort decreased. He grew very weary.

The little lump of stone took a deep breath and spun around several times. "So weak," he said sadly. "So weak." He looked up at the night sky, still half expecting assistance to arrive from that direction. But all he saw over the building tops was a twinkling, unconcerned night blanket, dotted with silvery stars.

Without warning, a moto-shoer bore down on him from less than a meter away. A skate wheel hit rudely, knocking him through the building entrance just as the electric eye doors swished open.

"Son of a slut!" the fleshcarrier man who was moto-shoeing said, falling to one knee. "What the Hooverville was that?"

The comet scurried behind a planter, then peeked around to watch as an angry, wavy-haired man searched the entrance area. Finding nothing, the man soon abandoned his effort.

As the moto-shoer rolled to the elevator bank, the comet flew along behind, ever so silently. Presently the man and his stealthy pursuer boarded an elevator.

Two-sixty-one, the comet mentoed as the doors closed, using a knowledge of elevators imparted to him magically by his fireball father. Feeling no click in his brain, the comet quickly realized why. *I have no mento transmitter!* he thought. *Papa Sidney had one when he was human.*

The elevator rose swiftly.

Only fourteen minutes, thirty-one seconds old, the comet thought. *And already I'm facing another crisis!*

The comet was very upset at this latest development. He had no idea which floor the man had selected. Faint, incomplete thoughts touched the comet's consciousness. Something about a new autocar, cheerful thoughts.

What is this? the comet thought. Then he realized with a rush of excitement that the thoughts were not his own. They came from the fleshcarrier standing next to him! The comet's pulse quickened.

What floor did you order? the comet wondered. *What floor?*

But this thought was nowhere in the man's mind now. Other thoughts became more clear, however. All concerned new consumer goods purchases the man and his permie were contemplating.

Time was running out quickly. The elevator rose rapidly through the building's core, completely oblivious to the pressing concern of the little visitor from another realm.

Ah, here we are, the man thought, transmitting brain waves to the comet. *Floor two-sixty-one*

The elevator doors whooshed open.

Now what am I doing here? the man wondered. He mentoed the correct floor into the elevator's computer, unaware of the little magical comet at his shoe tops who was scooting out at floor 261.

That was a stroke of luck, the comet thought as the doors shut behind him.

It may very well have been more than that, although no concrete evidence has been found to support such an assertion. This was a building of 450 floors. Even the most foolhardy gamesman would not have bet upon such an occurrence.

Still, it happened.

The little comet scooted along a beige-walled corridor decorated with pictures of fleshcarriers and government buildings. He rounded a corner. Through a large window at the end of the hallway he saw something bright and pink flash in the sky over the city. Whatever it was disappeared in the blink of a cat's eye.

The little comet found himself at Javik's synthetic walnut door. *Maybe I can squeeze under,* he thought, seeing a slender band of light beneath the door.

In an attempt to get through the crack, he reached about halfway. But he was irregularly shaped, like a lump of coal, with a big bump on his back that held his eye. The bump would not pass through.

Darn, he thought, wishing he could think of a stronger word. He flipped over and over, trying different angles of entry. Then he looked for wide spots under the door. He squeezed and squeezed and squeezed some more. But he could not get through.

"Dad blast it!" he said, feeling better about this selection of words. He began to glow bright orange. Then he whirled and hopped about angrily, throwing a first-rate tantrum. At the height of his rage, he smashed headlong into Javik's door. Then he hit it again. And again.

Crash! Thud! Kaboom!

This caused a good deal of racket in the hallway, despite the comet's very small size.

A brunette woman in the unit next door opened her door to peer out. "What's going on?" she asked. She cinched the belt of her bathrobe and ventured into the hall on moto-slippers.

Crash! Kathump! Thud! The little comet continued to pummel Javik's door.

The woman jumped back, startled. The comet was flashing a brilliant rainbow array of colors.

"What's this?" the woman asked. She ventured closer. Then a little closer. All the while, the angry comet continued his onslaught against the door, falling back intermittently for wild, whirling spins.

Now the woman was only a few centimeters from the curious little creature. With a tentative smile, she reached down, saying, "A toy?"

The comet smashed into her shinbone.

"Ow!" the woman yelled. "Ow! Ow!...Harold!" She hobbled and rolled back to her condominium, squealing in pain and calling for her permie.

Javik's door opened. A sleepy, robed Tom Javik stood with one unmotorized slipper off, looking down at the whirling little fireball.

Before Javik could react, the comet darted through his legs and into the condominium.

"Hey!" Javik yelled.

Turning his head, he saw an orange light flash through his arch-ceilinged entry hall. The intruder disappeared into Javik's living-room module.

Fully awake now, Javik mento-slammed the door and ran for his bedroom module. "Service pistol," he mumbled.

Seconds later, holding his automatic pistol, Javik tiptoed into the living-room module. This room had champagne-colored carpeting, with specks of orbit orange in it, matching the orange of the centrally positioned videodome. The walls matched the floor, and this often made Javik lose his sense of perspective. He looked under two padded chairs and the couch. Then he tiptoed toward the videodome, feeling deep pile carpeting with his bare foot.

"I am not a threat to you," a tiny voice said.

Javik whirled in the direction of the sound. He saw what looked like a lumpy, dark blue stone hovering in the arched doorway. The stone's surface was rough and irregular, with the exception of a clear agate dome crystal that jutted out of its top. Javik heard buzzing and saw a faint, exhaust-like glimmer of blue light on the other side of the stone.

"My name is Wizzy," the stone said. "I came up with that name just now, sensing your fleshcarrier need for such a reference."

Javik glowered.

"Papa sent me to see you. I'd rather be somewhere else, though."

"Papa?"

"Papa Sidney. He says you and I should help one another. . . . Oops!" Wizzy fell to the carpet with a dull thump. Then he glowed red and let fly a barrage of curses that would have made any nonsynthetic flower wilt. The expletives made him feel better.

"Where'd you learn to swear like that?" Javik asked. "That was good. Damned good."

"The words just came to me. Like an inspiration."

Javik smiled. "A real religious experience, eh?"

"My data banks use a rare red star crystal . . . embedded in my nucleus . . . to absorb energy waves from every source." Wizzy continued to glow dimly red. "I am receiving your data at this moment. You are an expert in foul language, I presume?"

"Kind of. Yeah. I guess I am."

"Perhaps you would prefer that I leave?" Wizzy changed to dark blue and scooted a meter down the hallway toward the front door.

"Hold on a sec," Javik said. "What the Hooverville is going on?" He pointed his pistol down at Wizzy.

Wizzy settled to the floor, where he rocked back and forth. "Guess I need more strength to hover like that," he said. "I'm just a baby, you know."

"No, I don't know! Is this a gag?" Javik looked around warily, sighting around his apartment along the barrel of his gun.

Wizzy laughed nervously. For the first time, Javik noticed a dimly glowing yellow cat's eye in the agate dome on Wizzy's topside. There seemed to be no mouth on the device. "This is difficult for me," Wizzy said. "I have not yet acquired social graces."

"I'll say! Barging in like that!"

"You're supposed to instruct me, I believe."

"In social graces? *Me? Ha!* What a laugh. You and I should go to the same school, pal."

"Uh, I think Papa also wants you to explain my emotions to me. He says they are very important."

Javik continued to glance around warily. "I don't like this," he said. "Smells like a Colonel Peebles trick . . . but he's dead."

"You want me to leave, then?" The little comet moved farther down the hallway. "I shouldn't bother you."

"Hold on," Javik said. He walked past Wizzy and knelt

beside him. "You look like a Bu-Tech surveillance unit," he mumbled, studying Wizzy's irregular surface.

"Oh no! Nothing of the sort!"

"A final security check before my ship takes off?" Javik touched Wizzy's surface. It was lumpy and cool.

"No."

"It *is* a classified mission."

"I said *no*. That's not it at all." Spying a chunk of aquamarine crystal on a charcoal-tinted glassplex hall table, Wizzy flew over for a closer look.

Javik shivered. He drew his robe shut at the neck.

"Pretty one," Wizzy said to the crystal. "Do you have a boyfriend?"

The crystal remained silent and motionless.

"So you're a male meckie, eh?" Javik said. "Well forget it, pal. That's just a meteor fragment I picked up in the Hepfer Droids."

"Speak!" Wizzy demanded.

There was no response from the crystal.

"Hmmmph!" Wizzy said haughtily. "Just another pretty face." He focused his cat's eye on Javik.

Javik leveled his pistol at Wizzy, saying, "You wanna know about emotions, eh? Let's start with fear, then. You got any of that?"

"I presume so. What is fear?"

"It's when you worry about your own skin."

"Skin." Wizzy glowed red again, calling upon his data banks. "Ah . . . epidermis. But I have nothing like that."

"You try to act smart, but you know what I think? I think you're dumb."

"I am not! I am wise now, with the inherited data banks of my parents. Papa Sidney says I will grow wiser each day!"

"Shit! What in the hell are you?"

Wizzy nudged the piece of crystal and dropped to the tabletop for a rest. "You remember Sidney Malloy?" he asked.

"Sure. But what—"

"That's my papa."

Javik's head snapped back in surprise. "Your *papa? Ha!*"

"He is! Papa Sidney's in deep space."

Javik lowered the gun. "Sid died last year . . . never returned from our mission."

"Oh, he's very much alive. Let me assure you of that. And

I sense Papa wants to see you again someday. But he's quite busy now with assignments from the Council of Magic."

"Magic, huh," Javik said, scratching his head. "Where do you fit in?"

"I've already told you that. You and I are supposed to help one another. I would prefer not being here, but Papa said—"

"Papa said, Papa said! I don't care what your goddamned papa said!"

Wizzy flashed an angry shade of orange. "Now look here, Thomas Patrick Javik!"

Javik became introspective. He laid the gun on the floor. "I was thinking of Sid before falling asleep," he mumbled. "Is this a dream?"

"I sense an answer to that question," Wizzy said.

"And that is?"

Wizzy buzzed across the hallway and slammed into the knuckle of Javik's hand.

"Ow!" Javik groped for the pistol with his other hand.

Wizzy knocked it beyond Javik's reach. "Does that answer your question about a dream?"

"Yes!" Javik said. "Yes!" He shook his wounded hand, wondering if he should lunge for the gun.

Wizzy laughed mischievously. Then his yellow cat's eye darted around in surprise. "That sound I just made," he said. "What was it?"

"What?" Javik snapped. "What-what-what?" His hand throbbed.

"The odd noise I made. Ha-ha-ha! Like that."

"Laughter," Javik said with a sneer. "You were laughing, idiot!"

"This laughter—it has a purpose?"

"It makes a person feel good, you little S.O.B.!"

"S.O.B.?"

"Son of a bitch. You're a son of a bitch!"

"That would be S.O.A.B. No, S.O.B. must be something entirely different. Like 'Sweet Old Boy.' But I'm not old, not at all old."

Javik fumed.

"You seem very confused. I think I'll laugh again. A ha-ha-ha! That feels very good, indeed. Ha-ha-ha!"

Javik shook his sore hand. The pain was subsiding. "Damn, but that hurt," he said. Out of the corner of one eye he looked at the automatic pistol. It lay several centimeters away, just beyond his grasp. *Maybe if I lunged . . .*

"Don't even think about it," Wizzy said.

The pain was almost gone now. Javik shook his hand and flexed the fingers, still eyeing the gun.

"Your weapon probably couldn't harm me, anyway," Wizzy said. "I am young, though, and uncertain of my powers."

Should I go for the gun? Javik wondered. *Could be an Atheist trick. Spying on my mission . . .*

"You still don't trust me," Wizzy said. "Now you think the Atheists sent me."

Startled, Javik blurted, "How did you . . . ? Oh, my energy waves . . . from my brain?"

"Uh huh," Wizzy said. "I know all about your mission: You're to scout Guna One, checking for unusual activity in the landing region of garbage catapulted there by Winston Abercrombie. You're to bring him back, too, if you can find him."

Javik felt that his jaw must be scraping the floor.

"It's the Abercrombie recycling crime you're investigating. Isn't that right, Captain Tom?"

Javik stared at the table legs and chewed at his lower lip. "That doesn't prove anything," he said. "Atheist operatives are everywhere."

"What about this? You remember the big reunion at the Sky Ballroom . . . where they discovered Papa Sidney was a cappy? And the time you went to see him in therapy detention?"

Javik's sea blue eyes opened wide. "I remember those things," he said. He looked at Wizzy and nodded like an old man, with his chin continuing to bob up and down.

"'You and me on an important mission together'—that's what you said to Papa."

"Sure, I said that. But you could have gotten it from my thoughts."

"You weren't thinking about it in my presence, Captain Tom. Not reasoning this out too well, are you?"

"It's not up to me whether you can go. You'll have to be cleared with mission control."

"Impossible. They'd think you were nuts. Just for checking. It might cost you the mission."

Javik pursed his lips. "I need this assignment. It's the comeback trail for me."

"Then believe what I said. I *can* help you."

"I don't know."

"Don't believe me, then. I could care less. I'm just here because Papa—" Wizzy saw Javik's eyes flash angrily.

"All right," Javik said. "You're coming along." *I don't like this creep's personality,* he thought. *But something tells me—*"

"Maybe I don't like you either."

"Huh? Oh."

"You've made a wise decision," Wizzy said. He yawned, using unseen mouth muscles.

"What did you say your name was?" Javik asked. He opened his hand and extended it.

"Wizzy. Wizzy Malloy." The little comet hopped on Javik's open hand.

Javik felt a tingle in his palm and heard a barely audible hum. It resembled the purr of a meckie cat. Wizzy was heavy— far heavier than he appeared to be. "Wizzy, eh?" Javik said with a smile. "Is that because you're a wise stone?"

"It's a name. That's all."

Javik wondered how the dark blue stone on his palm could be Sidney's son but not human. And he did not understand where Sidney was at that moment.

"Papa Sidney is flying," Wizzy said, referring to one of Javik's unspoken questions.

"He has a ship?" Frustrated at the lack of privacy, Javik felt his heart skip a beat.

"In a sense, yes. A very large ship. But I'm too weary to explain now." The cat's eye dimmed and closed. Soon Wizzy was breathing deeply, expanding and contracting on Javik's hand. The rolling rumble of snores followed.

"Well I'll be," Javik said, rubbing an itchy eyelid with his free hand. He placed Wizzy on the couch. Obtaining a hand towel from the linen-closet module, he laid it gently over Wizzy's clear agate top.

"Concentrate on happiness," Javik said softly. "That's the biggy—the emotion that's eluded me."

It was an overcast morning at the northeast corner of Robespierre Field, with a thick layer of Bu-Tech-made clouds overhead. Javik stood with his two crewmen beside other clusters of crewmen near their cream-colored, AmFed-marked ships.

Gray-uniformed ground crews were making final adjustments to the ships, chattering back and forth as they worked.

Javik felt in the side pocket of his Space Patrol jumpsuit. Wizzy buzzed contentedly in there, and felt warm to his touch. Javik considered the reason for the Bu-Tech clouds: placed there at President Ogg's orders to conceal the skywriting comet's embarrassing activity from AmFed citizens. *We AmFeds like to think we can control everything,* Javik thought, bemused. *But here's something beyond the power of our technology.*

Javik felt a chill wind as he removed his hand from his pocket. He mento-zipped his jumpsuit all the way to his neck. Glancing to his left, he focused on the buxom figure of co-pilot Marta Evans. Clad in a white and gold Space Patrol jumpsuit like his with ribbons across the chest, Evans had short yellow hair with big Venusian curls. She held her helmet with both hands in front of her waist.

He stared at her chest. *Amazing, the things surgeons can do,* he thought.

She caught his gaze, smiled.

Javik looked away and grimaced. *Stinking transsexual,* he thought. *Why couldn't they have sent along a real woman, or even a meckie, instead of this . . . thing?* Recalling the killer meckie that had been sent with him on the last mission, he shuddered.

Beside Evans stood the other crewman, the freckle-faced, red-haired science officer, Vince Blanquie. Blanquie was fat and soft. He shook noticeably.

Evans whispered in Javik's ear, "He's on withdrawal."

"Huh?"

"Video games. He's hooked. They made him cold turkey it, I hear."

"No mention of that in his dossier," Javik husked.

Evans shrugged. "My source is unimpeachable," she said. *I hope they left the sex-change operation out of my file,* she thought.

A meckie buzzed nearby. Javik turned to see it service the cluster of crewmen who stood at the base of an adjacent space cruiser. *Rings and necklaces,* Javik thought.

Moments later, the meckie stood in front of Javik, fitting a two-jeweled ring on the third finger of his right hand. "These were rush-packed," the meckie said, showing synthetic nervousness. "Hope they work okay." The meckie draped a language-mixer pendant around Javik's neck, then moved on to Evans.

Javik studied the ring. It was tita-gold, bearing two rectangular stones, one white and one turquoise.

"White for shower, turquoise for change of clothes," the meckie said to Evans. "It's called a wardrobe ring."

Evans grunted.

While attending to Blanquie, the meckie said, "Your necklaces are more powerful than older models. They can locate a common language denominator for up to five hundred beings within a fifty-meter radius. Less people, more radius—and vice versa."

After the meckie moved on to another crew, Javik lifted the necklace pendant. It was octagonal and ruby red, with four rainbow-hue stylized faces on it: one round, one square, one triangular, one rectangular. Javik knew they were representative of different cultures and races that might be encountered in deep space. He touched a button on one side, causing the faces to spin in a blur. The mechanism beeped and flashed a green light, indicating it was operating properly. Javik shut it off and tucked it beneath his shirt.

"The President!" Evans said excitedly.

Javik glanced quickly at Evans, then followed the gaze of her large olive green eyes to the west. Autocopter One banked over the General Oxygen Factory, then began its descent toward Robespierre Field.

The craft was white, with the red, yellow, and blue markings of the American Federation of Freeness. Javik saw a large presidential seal on the underside and smaller ones on each side of the cabin. The copter descended rapidly and set down in a cloud of dust. As it had dark-tinted windows, Javik could not see the President. Javik smelled dust and rubbed a speck out of one eye.

Presently, President Euripides Ogg short-stepped from the copter to a lift, followed by two aides. The lift dropped slowly.

President Ogg was an immense, hulking black man in a bright yellow leisure suit with green lapels. He brushed his hand through a wave of long, golden hair that he combed straight back from a widow's peak. The aides spoke to him nervously and constantly, one in each ear. The President and his aides moved quickly to a stage that had been erected for the occasion.

"He looks tired," Evans said.

Javik heard low tones from the clusters of crewmen nearby.

As President Ogg reached the top of the stage, Javik watched the aides brush dust from the President's suit. Then Ogg rolled to the microphone.

The crews fell silent.

"I'll make this short and sweet," Ogg said, addressing the crewmen. "Get out there and find where our catapulted garbage went!"

"Yes, sir!" the crewmen responded. Javik felt the patriotism of the moment as he spoke in unison with the others.

"And when you find it," President Ogg continued, "see if the garbage can do us any goddamned harm!" He coughed.

"Yes, sir!"

One of the aides was a tall blond man whom Javik recognized as Chief of Staff Billie Birdbright. Birdbright leaned close to Ogg's ear and whispered something.

Ogg nodded, looked flustered. "Uh," Ogg said, returning to the microphone. "I mean, report back any unusual activity."

"Yes, sir!"

Without warning, a great wind swept across the field. Javik shuddered and closed his eyes as dust blew in his face and filled his nostrils. He smelled grit and sulfur. He tried to open his eyes, but a blinding flash covered the sky.

"The comet!" someone yelled.

Javik opened his eyes to slits and held his hands over them. Through his fingers, he saw an immense blue and orange fireball streaking horizontally across the sky, disrespectfully shoving aside the Bu-Tech clouds.

"Be careful, Papa!" Wizzy squealed, peeking his head out of Javik's pocket. "There's water in those clouds!"

"What are you talking about?" Javik asked.

"Water can be terrible for a comet," Wizzy said. "Papa is taking a big risk!" After a moment's thought, he added, "Papa Sidney is very large, however. Perhaps a few clouds are of no concern to him."

Javik pushed Wizzy back in the pocket and zipped it shut. A muffled cry came from the pocket. *Sid's a comet?* Javik thought.

On the stage, President Ogg was very agitated. "Get away!" he screamed at the comet, jumping up and down and waving his arms wildly. "Get away!"

Without Javik noticing it, his pocket zipped open. Little Wizzy leaped out and dashed across the asphalt landing field in the same direction taken by the Great Comet. "Wait, Papa Sidney!" he called out. "Take me with you!"

Javik slapped his hand against his pocket. It was flat empty. "Uh oh," he muttered. *Wizzy's a comet too?* he thought.

Wizzy tried to fly high, but kept falling back to Earth. This made him look like a rock skipping across the landing strip. Soon Javik could not see or hear him.

"What came out of your pocket?" Evans asked, looking at Javik.

Javik did not respond. He watched the tail of the Great Comet disappear, leaving a gaping hole in the cloud cover. The sun appeared, pushing the long shadows of the scout ships across the field. Javik felt warmth on his cheeks.

Wizzy mentioned a Council of Magic, Javik thought. *So that's it? Magic?*

President Ogg continued to wave his arms until the Great Comet had gone. Then he turned to face the crewmen, saying angrily, "That will be all, gentlemen." He turned hastily and left the stage with his aides.

Javik saw Chief of Staff Birdbright break away from the President. Birdbright rolled toward the clusters of crewmen. "Which crew is going to Guna One?" he called out.

"Here, sir!" Javik yelled, raising his hand.

Birdbright was all business as he approached Javik, leaning forward and carrying a very stern expression.

When the Chief of Staff arrived, he and Javik exchanged salutes. Then Javik compared their heights. *He's a bit taller than I am,* Javik thought.

Birdbright's smoke gray eyes met Javik's gaze. "You are in charge?" Birdbright asked.

Javik straightened. "Yes, sir."

"As you must be aware, Captain, your mission is unique. The other crews are on random searches, but you..." Birdbright paused and rubbed his dimpled chin thoughtfully.

"I understand, sir. The arch criminal Abercrombie catapulted garbage to Guna One intentionally—planning to set up a recycling station there."

"Lower your voice!" Birdbright rasped. "We do not appreciate that word!"

Javik lowered his eyelids in shame, cursing himself inwardly for his faux pas.

"The 'r' word!" Birdbright whispered, nearly touching noses with Javik.

It doesn't seem so horrible to me, Javik thought. *I'm tired of being beaten to death with this Job-Support thing!*

"'It's not fair to repair,'" Birdbright intoned. "'It's not nice to use twice.'" Javik saw Birdbright's eyes glaze over from the profound truth of the mantras.

Nodding dutifully, Javik thought, *Anyone who thinks 'Jobs Are Sacred' never pulled garbage-shuttle duty!*

"Abercrombie may be on Guna One," Birdbright said. "He's never been apprehended, you know."

"We'll be alert, sir."

Birdbright stared at Javik with the overbearing scrutiny of one knowing he is in a superior position. "Very well, Captain," he said.

They exchanged salutes again.

Moments later, as Autocopter One lifted and sped away, Javik wondered what lay in store for him. *Gawd,* he thought. The immensity of his assignment hit him. *This is big stuff!*

"What jumped out of your pocket?" Evans asked.

"A meckie toy," Javik said. "Sent by a friend to amuse me."

"Well, here it is back," Blanquie said.

Javik barely had time to cup his hands before Wizzy leaped onto them. Wizzy's dark blue body felt cool.

"Papa's gone," Wizzy said dejectedly. "I'm on my own."

"Aw Cha-rist," Javik said, seeing crewmen from other ships approaching.

"I'm sorry," Wizzy said. "My emotions . . ."

Javik stuffed Wizzy in his pocket and zipped it shut.

"What you got there, Tom?" one asked.

"Cute little gadget," another said. "Bring it out, Tom."

"It talks?"

"Leave me alone, guys," Javik said. "It's nothing. Nothing at all."

Gradually the crewmen dispersed.

Javik looked up at the patch of blue sky. The Great Comet came into sight for a moment, a far-off orange fireball heading out to deep space. Soon it became a tiny dot of orange light.

Javik felt something rustle at his side. Looking down, he
saw Wizzy peeking out of the top of the pocket, watching the
comet. Wizzy's cat's eye was bright orange now, as was the
rest of his lumpy body. Javik felt Wizzy's warmth against his
side.

The same shade of orange as the comet, Javik thought. *Wizzy
could be a chunk of it.* Electrodes flashed wildly in Javik's
brain. *Sid? Was that you out there, Sid?*

Far across the galaxy, in a cavern beneath the surface of
Guna One, a blue female meckie studied symbols and cartoon
pictures that had been scratched on a recently discovered limestone wall. This was an unnamed Earth-catapulted meckie, like
all others on the planet, with a brass "REBUILT" plaque on her
torso. Being rather standard in appearance, she had no head
and a flashing blue dome light on top. Numerous dents and
abrasions marred her rivet-covered surface.

Lord Abercrombie stood in the doorway of the cavern, looking in. "Anything more?" he asked, his bearded half face wrinkled inquisitively beneath a thistle half crown. "It's been two
weeks now since we found these drawings." Lord Abercrombie's half body, split from his forehead to the ground, was
draped in a floor-length, rust-colored caftan. The caftan hung
oddly at the split, in a straight dropoff due to his left side
having disappeared entirely into the Realm of Magic. Abercrombie knew it had not really disappeared. It was there but
not there at the same moment. It was chilly in the cavern, and
he inserted his only hand in his pocket.

"It's history," the meckie said in a voice that sounded like
a gargle, evidence of an unsolvable mechanical defect. She
half turned toward Abercrombie while pointing at a series of
six cartoon squares on the wall. "There were three magicians
here before you. One was a giant amoeba, and another a plant
creature with wide philodendron leaves. The third was humanlike, but with a duck-billed face."

"Really!" Lord Abercrombie said. His eye flashed intently
as he glided to the wall. Rubbing his fingers over the carved
pictures and symbols, he asked, "All became soil-immersed?"

"Yes. That is what it means to be a magician here—becoming one with the soil, one with the planet."

"But they're all gone. Where did they go?"

"I haven't been able to figure that out. Most of the symbols are strange."

"But you were a linguistics assistant," Lord Abercrombie said. "You, of all meckies, should be able to interpret such things!" He scratched his nearly bald half pate, feeling a few strands of baby soft hair there.

"Earth linguistics is a different thing," the meckie gargled. "I did find one familiar symbol, however. Here." She touched the wall.

Lord Abercrombie leaned close to study the symbol. It was a circle with four tangential triangles spaced evenly outside the circumferential line. Jagged lines inside the circle touched each triangle, looking like bolts of lightning between the triangles. "What is it?" he asked.

"Well, without the circle it's the symbol of magnetics." She moved her hand along the wall. "See here? It's beneath each of the three magicians."

"Hmmm. Yeah. Magnetics, huh? Maybe they used magnetics somehow in their magic."

"Could be."

"What about the circle? What does it mean?"

"I don't know."

"And the cartoons?"

"Maybe something funny was going on," the meckie said.

"Well, nothing seems very funny around here to me. Any incantations there, or magical potion recipes?"

"None that I've been able to figure out yet."

Lord Abercrombie put his hand on his hip. "Some kinda history here, eh? Well, add my story to it."

"That's a good idea, Lord. There are sharp pieces of obsidian on the floor here, evidently used by others to carve on the wall."

"Good."

"I don't draw very well, Lord. I will need artistic programming."

"Report to Servicing for that."

"Yes, Lord Abercrombie." The meckie paused for a moment, then said, "If I'm to portray you accurately, however, I will need to know more about you."

"Such as?"

"You're kind of a confusing personality, Lord. You wanted

to set up a recycling base here, using the Earth-catapulted gar-bahge as raw material. Then you were going to ship the recycled products back to Earth."

"That's right."

"But you had all that trouble with Uncle Rosy and his say-ermen. You were forced to hide here, beneath the surface. You managed to set up a system of getting gar-bahge down here to your recycling facility, and now you've got caverns full of recycled products—so much stuff you hardly have room to move around."

"So?"

"What are you going to do with all the stuff? Is it supposed to stay here forever, proof to yourself and to no other human that recycled goods could be manufactured?"

"Yeah, I guess that's right." Lord Abercrombie's eye stared at the dirt floor. He focused on a piece of obsidian. "The work kept me busy, I suppose. Maybe I held out a hope that some big shot from Earth would come here and beg me to go back, saying Earth needed my expertise to set up a recycling industry there."

"All right. But what about your obsession with creating planetary disasters? You spend half your time in the Realm of Flesh, and half soil-immersed in the Realm of Magic. In flesh, most of your time is spent with that old Earthian disaster control equipment, trying to create earthquakes, floods, hurricanes, and the like. In magic, that's all you do: Every waking instant is spent trying to impose your will upon the elements."

"Well, it's been something to do. It can get kinda dull around here. Haven't I told you that before?"

"It's power, isn't it? You want to feel absolute, dominating power over the planet and all its inhabitants."

"Could be. I don't know. Say, I don't need to be psychoan-alyzed by a meckie! Just put what I tell you on the wall!"

"Yes, Lord."

"Tell how Uncle Rosy's evil sayermen came after me, and how I was fortunate enough to find the Sacred Scroll of Cork. Show that the scroll led me to this place and instructed me in the ancient methods of soil immersion."

"Okay, Lord. Shall I also relate your difficulties in magically inducing disasters? After all, you have only come up with one magically willed rockslide in four years of soil immersion."

"I've been *here* four years," Abercrombie said, irritated.

"Only half of that time was spent immersed."

"Pardon me, Lord."

"Give me a break, historian."

The meckie picked up a piece of obsidian and placed it on a wall ledge. "What about your fleshy half, Lord? Should I show you and those old rebuilt meckies working with patched-together Earthian disaster control equipment?"

"I don't know."

"You *have* created some dust storms with the equipment, Lord. An earthquake, too. And three floods."

"Yeah, but the atmosphere goes haywire each time I get something going real good. That damned reverse rain, coming right up out of the planet!"

"That *is* a big problem," the meckie said. "We shouldn't dwell on the negative, I suppose."

"Make it heroic," Abercrombie said. His brow furrowed.

"Guess I'd better not depict your indecision, either, Lord. You know, the way you're halfway between the realms of Flesh and Magic, afraid to commit yourself to either one."

"Leave all that out too."

"There isn't much you're permitting me to say about you, Lord," the meckie gargled.

"Just show me getting here," Lord Abercrombie snapped. "Then leave a lot of blank space. My story isn't over yet."

TWO

Cork: Called Guna One by the AmFeds. A planet abandoned by soil-immersing magicians aeons ago. Declared unfit by the Council of Magic for the safe and efficient practice of magic. Unusual magnetic and ionic conditions encountered there.

From the *Encyclopaedia of Magic*, one of the microdata books kept in Stone 31–12

"See if the garbage can do us any goddamned harm!"

With these urgent words from President Ogg on his mind just minutes after takeoff, Captain Tom Javik mentoed the speed toggle on the chrome and white plastic dashboard. The scout ship *Amanda Marie* accelerated through the stratosphere, stretching to reach the limits of Earth's atmosphere. The licorice smell of G-gas wafted under Javik's nose.

"We're clear," Evans said moments later as they reached space. She glanced to her left at Javik.

"Speed twenty-seven thousand k.p.h. and beginning hyper-acceleration," Blanquie reported. He sat behind Javik and Evans at a midships science officer's console.

Javik mentoed course coordinates into the ship's mother computer—simply "Mother" to the crew—causing the ship to bank gracefully. The *Amanda Marie*'s E-cell-powered ion engines emitted quiet blue flames, which Javik saw on the console screen between him and Evans. Looking at Earth, he saw that the hole in the gray cloud cover below was sealed now, evidence of the continuing tug of war between Bu-Tech and the Great Comet. The idea of Sidney as a comet seemed ludicrous to Javik. At the same time, it frightened the hell out of him. Gyros whirred as the ship's gravitonics system kicked on.

Wizzy buzzed out of Javik's pocket and flew around the cabin, examining each article of equipment with a child's fascination.

"That's Wizzy," Javik said, with a nod over his shoulder. "A newfangled flying meckie." Javik retreated inwardly to his thoughts: *If Wizzy is Sid's boy, and Sid is a comet . . .*

"Hi, Wizzy!" Evans said, cheerily.

Spotting a mirror on a half bulkhead behind Javik, Wizzy hovered in front of it to admire himself. "Does my tail look longer today?" he asked, directing his cat's-eye gaze at the back of Javik's head.

Javik shot Wizzy a quick backward glance. "I dunno," he responded, noting that Wizzy's tail was silvery and translucent, his rock body pale and golden. *Wizzy is a friggin' comet!* Javik thought, as he faced forward. *I'd better take him aside . . . keep it from the crew.*

"Hmmm," Wizzy said. "The silver is nice."

"I'd like a word with you, Wizzy," Javik said, mento-unsnapping his safety harness.

"It is a beautiful tail, Wizzy," Evans said. "Kinda like on that big comet."

Gotta move quickly, Javik thought.

"Ain't like no meckie I ever seen," Blanquie drawled.

Javik swung his long legs out from under the instrument panel. "Did you hear me, Wizzy?" he snapped.

"Watch me change colors," Wizzy said, paying no attention to Javik.

Javik chewed nervously on his lower lip as Wizzy's tail and body switched colors. Now the tail became a sputter of gold light, with a lumpy, silver body. Wizzy's yellow cat's eye darkened, matching his tail.

A brilliant flash of orange light off the starboard bow diverted Javik's attention. A fraction of a second later, Wizzy was perched on the dashboard beneath the curved windshield, looking out at the return of the Great Comet. Wizzy did not speak this time. He, like the others, watched in awe.

The Great Comet approached fast, causing Javik to squint in the increasing orange-hot glare. He mentoed for a collision report.

"Comet-like body at fifteen thousand three hundred kilometers," Mother said, using a mellow, computer-synthesized voice. "Not on a collision course with this ship."

Spinning on his chair to look out his side window, Javik saw the comet swoop below them to Earth, pushing away part of the cloud cover and creating another opening. Through the new hole, Javik saw the soft brown and green tones of Earth. Feeling his pulse quicken, he wondered, *Will it hit Earth this time?*

Wizzy let out a little squeal of excitement. He was on the sill of a side porthole now.

Suddenly the Great Comet rose and veered off, beginning a series of loops and swirls as it trailed a stream of white smoke.

"W," Javik thought. *It made a "W"!*

"A message!" Evans said.

Javik glanced to his side at the co-pilot's seat, focusing for a moment on Evans's robust chest. It seemed automatic to look there, with the eyes homing in like smart missiles on their target. This time, however, Javik looked away quickly before she caught him.

He heard Evans rustle, and sensed her looking at him.

Javik's face felt hot. He fumbled in his jumpsuit for the titanium pillbox. Leaning away to conceal the box, he selected a brown sex-sub pill and a clear water capsule. Hurriedly, he swallowed the pills and replaced the tin. Cool water molecules expanded in his stomach. He waited for the sexual sublimation to take hold.

"What'd ya take there?" Evans asked.

Javik did not answer or meet her gaze. Closing his eyes, he felt a warm, satisfied feeling soak into his bones. Inaudibly, he sighed.

Evans snickered. It was not a loud snicker. But Javik heard it just the same.

He wiped beads of perspiration from his brow.

"Warm, Captain?" she asked, noting a scar on the bridge of Javik's aquiline nose. His deeply set blue eyes darted around like those of a cornered animal.

Feigning interest in a digital weather screen, Javik cursed himself for the continuing moments of weakness. *Evans is a transsexual!* he thought. *If the guys ever heard I dabbled like that, I'd be the laughingstock of the . . .*

Evans rolled to a midships porthole to get a better view of the comet. Javik pictured her attractive features in his mind's eye: soft, creamy skin, with smooth, rounded cheeks and a small nose that turned up slightly at the tip. Long black lashes and dark eyebrows overhung the eyes.

"We are . . . not . . . your . . . garbage dump!" Evans read, squinting to read the skywriting. "That same message for more than eight months! What does it mean?" She turned to look at Blanquie.

Blanquie winked at her.

The gaze of Evans's large olive green eyes darted away like a timid fawn under pursuit by a buck.

"I think I know!" Wizzy said, in a tiny voice. "I think I know!"

"Shutup, Wizzy," Javik snapped.

"Well!" Wizzy huffed.

Javik watched the Great Comet speed off into deep space. A parallel with guerrilla warfare struck him: This comet was employing hit and run tactics. But Javik sensed the comet did not have to flee. It was playing games with the AmFeds.

If that is Sid, Javik thought, bemused, *he's getting even with the bureaucrats now . . . making them run around . . . embarrassing the bastards.*

"Damn, that thing's fast!" Blanquie said. "Just a pinprick of orange light now!"

Rolling to Wizzy's side, Javik spit out a terse command: "Come with me."

But Wizzy remained on the sill of the porthole. "Just a minute," he said, glowing red. His voice became hollow and faltering: "I sense trouble ahead . . . Davis Droids . . . signal intermittent."

"Davis Droids," Blanquie said. He flipped the selector on his CRT screen. "Here it is," he said. "Directly in the target of Abercrombie's garbage shots. Not much land mass there. Twenty million kilometers this side of Guna One, in the same Aluminum Starfield with the Guna planets."

"Wizzy," Javik said. "I want you—"

"Begin searching for garbage in the droids," Wizzy said.

"Is that meckie an official part of this crew?" Blanquie asked.

Irked, Javik snatched Wizzy from the sill and moto-shoed aft.

"See here!" Wizzy protested. "Put me down!"

"Shush!" Javik said. He rolled into the bathroom and slammed the door. "Keep it down," Javik husked. "Or by God, I'll flush you into outer space!" He held Wizzy over the unlidded toilet.

The gravitonics system whirred noisily here. A wall plaque beneath a Patterman gravitonics indicator read:

> CAUTION!
> Do not use bathroom
> if gravitonics
> inoperable

Seeing the toilet, Wizzy understood Javik's threat. He almost told Javik to go ahead, but reconsidered. It was cold out there. And a long way from Papa Sidney. "But the signals I'm receiving," Wizzy said. "We must heed them!"

"I'll be the judge of that," Javik said, smelling a chemical odor from the toilet. "You're comets, aren't you? You and Sid . . ."

"There's no secret about that."

"Some kinda magic? I mean, comets with personalities aren't your everyday sort of thing."

"You've got it."

"Good magic? I mean, uh . . ."

Wizzy laughed. "It's not witchcraft. Trust me."

Javik's expression was very intense. "I don't want my crew disrupted with this sort of information. They're flaky enough as it is, and I need their undivided attention to duty."

"All right."

"Keep it between you and me. As far as everyone else is concerned, you're a meckie. A comet-like device some Bu-Tech pal of mine thought up to be cute. You got it?"

"Sure. No problem."

"It's yessir from now on," Javik said, holding Wizzy close to the toilet bowl. "That or I flush you."

"I understand!" Wizzy snapped. He glowed orange-hot.

"Ow!" Javik yelled. He dropped Wizzy and blew on his hand. "Why, you little . . ."

Wizzy hovered in the air. "Let's get something straight, shall we?" he said. "Don't play big-time operator with me, fella. I know your background—the girls, the fights, the whole bit."

Javik continued to blow on his hand.

"You're a trashman."

Javik's eyes flashed angrily. "This assignment isn't like garbage shuttle duty. This is important. *Really* important."

"You're still chasing trash."

"Yes, but on a larger scale." Javik rubbed the palm of his burned hand. "You saw the President back there."

Wizzy laughed. "Large-scale trash? Trash is trash in my data banks." He had become dark blue again, with a short green tail.

"Just remember what I told you," Javik said tersely. He jerked open the door and rolled into the cabin. Mother's computer voice was completing a course projection for Evans. Then it fell silent.

"Check those droids," Wizzy shouted. He flew by Javik, alighting on a wall-mounted oxygen tank behind the captain's chair.

Javik seethed as he rolled forward.

"Sounded like a fight back there," Evans said, watching Javik slide into his chair. "Amazing, the way they can build personalities into meckies now."

Javik glowered as he stared out the windshield. His hand still hurt.

"Ogg's cloud cover isn't working worth a damn," Blanquie said.

Mento-swiveling her chair, Evans looked aft. Blanquie's freckled face was pressed against one of the portholes. His soft, round body seemed inappropriate for the rigors of Space Patrol duty. "Sure isn't," she agreed.

"Maybe the comet is God," Blanquie said, "just cruisin' around tryin' to decide if Earth is worth savin'."

"Yeah," Evans said. "Like Sodom and Gomorrah."

Blanquie laughed nervously. Then he coughed. "Maybe it's Uncle Rosy," he said, "angry because the AmFeds are off schedule on his Thousand Year Plan."

Javik watched another scout ship speed into space along a different course. Bullet-shaped and cream-colored, with AmFed markings, the other ship was moving faster than the *Amanda Marie*. Javik mentoed a speed increase and felt his ship respond instantly.

"Confirmed," Mother said. "Will accelerate to seventy-five thousand k.p.h. and hold."

"Hey, Cap'n," Blanquie drawled. "What them boys gonna do about the comet?"

"Haven't been invited to any ministerial sessions lately," Javik said acidly. "You can bet they're fuming about it, though. I hear a hundred missiles have been fired at it already. Maybe they're assembling a super-missile right now. Who knows?"

Blanquie giggled. "What if it *is* God?" he asked, looking at Javik's back with a silly leer on his face.

Javik looked around to see the silly expression, then turned forward, shaking his head in dismay. *At least the video game-aholic isn't shaking now,* Javik thought.

Blanquie concentrated on the back of Javik's jumpsuit. Gold captain's epaulets rested regally on the shoulders, with thin, stitched-on gold braids encircling the armpits. Javik's smooth, amber hair gave off a soft sheen.

"Just think on it!" Blanquie gushed. "If we blasted God with a missile!"

Javik saw Evans crack a smile. Out of the corner of his eye, Javik also saw Wizzy, on the oxygen tank behind his chair. "Pay attention to your duties!" Javik howled. "Evans! Blanquie! Think about the mission, damn it!"

Evans straightened, and Javik heard the whir of Blanquie's moto-boots as he returned to his station.

"Looks good so far," Evans said, reading a digital trouble scanner. She thought of the way Captain Javik often stared at her laboratory-shaped breasts.

"Now listen to me, crew," Javik said, his tone terse. "You risk your lives—and mine—every time you forget about duty!"

Blanquie gave an astrogational reading.

I sounded pretty good, Javik thought. *Strange, coming from me.* He stared at his instruments with unfocused eyes. *What sort of assignment do I have here? Is Wizzy going to get in my way?*

"No," Wizzy said in Javik's ear.

Javik started. He snapped his head forward.

"Thoughts create energy waves," Wizzy said. He flew aft.

Javik gazed into space in the direction taken by the Great Comet. It was out of sight now, having blended with the stars and shining planets in the distance. *Damn, Sid!* he thought. *You're big time now!*

Oblivious to the businesslike chatter of the crew, Javik felt a rush of envy for the Great Comet. And he recalled his meeting with Sidney at the Sky Ballroom the year before.

Sid was envious of me, then, Javik thought. Those days seemed like long ago. They were simpler, more innocent days. But Javik did not want them back.

An hour later, from a dark resting place in an aft cupboard, Wizzy surveyed the thoughts of the crew. In the darkness, thoughts inundated him like sounds to a blind man. He practiced identifying them.

This one's from Javik, Wizzy thought. *He feels both attraction and repulsion for Evans. That's interesting.*

Wizzy concentrated on Evans's thoughts now. *Ah,* Wizzy thought. *She wants to hit the sack with our friend Captain Tom.*

Blanquie's thoughts crowded in: *I could turn this console into a video game. With a maze here, and sixteen laser-fired squibs . . .*

Wizzy laughed aloud when he heard this.

"Shutup back there!" Javik barked. He mentoed the mission briefing tape.

"Assignment fifteen," a woman's voice said over a dashboard speaker. "Guna One."

THREE

No one has ever seen proof of the Happy Shopping Ground. I wonder if our Product Failure did really go to such a place!

Whispered words picked up by a Black Box of Democracy detector

It was evening by New City time.

Leaving Mother in charge of all ship's functions, Javik yawned while rolling by Blanquie toward the captain's sleeping compartment. "Fifteen minutes to clothing destruct," Javik said, glancing at his wrist digital. "Has everyone changed?"

"I have," Evans said in a sultry voice. She popped her head out of the hatch of her sleeping compartment, on the deck to Javik's left.

Javik gave her a cursory glance downward. She was staring hard at him. Feeling the effects of his sex-sub pill wearing off, he mentoed his own sleeping compartment hatch hurriedly. Tumblers sounded as the lock was released. He leaned down and pulled open the hatch that was just forward of hers. It squeaked.

"Is Captain Daddy reminding us to change our clothes?" Blanquie drawled. He slouched at his console, a sneer on his freckled face. "Now we have a mother and a daddy on this ship."

"All right!" Javik snapped. "Just forget the automatic de-

36

struct time once. That's all. Just *once*. You'll be standing there in nothing but your moto-boots."

"Now that would be interesting," Evans said, examining her wardrobe ring closely. "Clever little gadget. All the problems of reducing weight in space, and they've still got a device that gives you a regular change of clothes!"

"You're too easily impressed," Javik said. He mento-locked his boots, then stepped on the top rung of the ladder inside his compartment.

"Night, Captain Daddy," Blanquie said.

Javik scowled at him.

"Did you brush your teeth, Blanquie?" Evans asked.

"How about a little co-hab tonight, Evans?" Blanquie asked.

She laughed. "Not tonight," she said.

Javik shook his head in dismay as he stepped down the ladder, pulling the hatch shut behind him. Reaching the corrugated metal floor of his compartment, Javik removed his pillbox from his pocket and slipped it into a wall-hung stuff pocket. It was a tiny room, with barely any walking space around the bed. Mirrored walls and a reflecting, gold-foil ceiling made it seem larger. A single porthole on the outside wall displayed a distant blue nebula with veinlike streaks of pink and green. Corner ceiling fixtures lit the room evenly.

He mentoed a nightshade over the porthole. It snapped over the glassplex.

Feeling a dull, low-level throb of pain in the back of his head around the implanted mento unit, Javik gave it a brief thought. The pain subsided.

Javik stood next to the bed, there being nowhere else to stand in a room of this size. Staring at his wardrobe ring, he mento-concentrated on the rectangular turquoise stone. The stone glowed.

A happy tune sounded from the ring, with a tiny computer voice that sang: "It's fresh-up time! It's fresh-up time!"

Javik hated that tune.

Now his Space Patrol jumpsuit disappeared in a puff of white smoke, leaving him wearing nothing but his moto-boots and his ring. A black thread shot out of the ring, followed by a thread of gold. For a moment, they hung poised in the air, like tiny cobras about to strike.

Checking my size, Javik thought, recalling the demonstration class he had taken.

Now the threads darted around Javik's wrist and up his arm, covering the arm with finely woven black and gold cloth. Over his shoulders and around his neck the threads flowed, forming a braided collar. Then down the other arm, back up the arm and down the torso. He felt the warmth of the pajama cloth take hold.

A white strand darted out of the ring next, and this encircled his waist and thighs to form a fresh pair of underwear. Then two new black and gold threads covered that and his legs, forming pajama bottoms.

It is kinda clever, Javik thought. He sat on the bed, sinking into its synthetic softness. Soon the moto-boots were off and he was under the covers.

"Captain Daddy," he muttered, just before falling asleep. "I'll have to speak with Blanquie about his attitude."

The wall-mounted transcriber worked while Javik slept below decks, making ship-log tapes from his resting brain. In the cabin above, Wizzy sat on the dashboard, rolling the gaze of his cat's eye aft. The chrome and white plastic cabin was empty, with captain and crew belowdecks in sleeping compartments. With his sensitive tympanic sensors, Wizzy heard the low hum of the transcribing machine, despite it being in another compartment.

Through the curving windshield he watched two closely aligned planets come into view, covered by a continuous system of swirling, mysterious clouds. Both planets were mountainous, plunging to high plains of green and thence to wide blue seas. Being so close to the twin spheres, Wizzy absorbed a torrent of animal and geological history from their energy waves, more than enough to whet his appetite for knowledge. But too soon the *Amanda Marie* had sped by and the planets were receding into the distance.

I'll return to explore someday, he thought, feeling the energy waves subside.

Now the faint twinklings of stars, red quasars, and bright planets beckoned to him from far off. He felt a weak signal trying to find its way into the atoms and molecules of his brain. Something about a solar system with three suns, a planet with disturbing activity.

From Cork, Wizzy realized. *The planet Javik calls Guna One.*

Static crackled in his brain, blocking out the Corkian signal. He surmised a meteor storm had intervened, or perhaps a solar flare. Feeling weary, he let his cat's eyelid droop.

Wizzy called upon his cometary data banks, drawing forth information imprinted in him at birth. Papa Sidney's deep, mellifluous voice spoke to him: "Energy waves take a variety of forms, including simple heat waves, radio signals, and microwaves. Your red star crystal sensor is highly adaptable, permitting you to learn from all things. The most ordinary-looking piece of plastic and the most brilliant nova in the universe have something to offer."

He tried for the Corkian signals again, but received no further messages. Staring out the windshield with a bleary, stinging eye, he tried to focus on a cluster of stars dead ahead. *That planet is out there somewhere,* he thought.

Wizzy's gaze wandered sleepily around the cabin, from the blinking instrument panels to the tan gortex, wall-hung survival packs. His eyelid drooped heavily, then opened once, seeing only unfocused images. He dozed off.

Moments later, a loud *clunk* and the rustle of clothing awakened him. Looking groggily toward the sleeping compartment hatches along the floor, he saw that one of them was open.

Marta Evans popped her curly blond head out and looked around. Then she lifted the adjacent hatch. It squeaked open. Wizzy heard voices after she entered that compartment.

Javik turned to one side, scrunching the air pillow between his shoulder and head. Hearing the hatch squeal, he opened one eye in the half-light of his sleeping compartment. A woman's foot was on the bottom ladder rung.

He sat bolt upright.

Evans short-stepped to the floor, looking down over her bare right shoulder at him. She wore a black lace blouse, low-cut, with black bikini panties.

"You!" he husked angrily, smelling lilac perfume. "Get out!" His tone was low and menacing.

Smiling softly, Evans knelt next to him on the mattress. He felt the bed move.

Javik moved away. "I told you to get out," he said. But his voice was not firm, and Javik knew Evans had noticed this. *Where are my sex-sub pills?* Javik wondered, his gaze fleeing frantically.

Kneeling on the mattress with her gaze locked on Javik, Evans mentoed the zipper on the front of her blouse.

Ziiippp! Each side of the blouse parted.

My God! Javik thought, seeing her well-shaped bust. Evans wore a scanty yellow brassiere with tiny black buttons down the front. He looked into her olive green eyes.

She smiled. "Shall I get the buttons?" she asked. "Or would you prefer—"

"Uh, I don't think . . ." Javik coughed. He felt weak.

She mentoed the buttons. Her breasts virtually exploded out of the brassiere as the garment flew open. The breasts were exquisitely formed and impressive. Javik saw no surgical scars.

Javik's gaze locked on hers. He felt his eyes burning with desire. He looked away and felt the tempo of his breathing increase.

"I've seen you watching me," she said.

Javik scowled. Another time he might have laughed at the situation. He had known many women, some as aggressive as Marta Evans. All the aggressive women had mento-activated bras.

Evans removed her blouse and brassiere. Then she leaned close to Javik and pressed her lips against his. Her mouth was soft and warm. She pulled back and said, "I thought you might like some company. It can get lonely in deep space." She brushed a yellow curl out of her eyes.

Transsexual! Javik thought, pulling away in revulsion. "I'm doing fine without you," he said. He reached around her to the wall-hung stuff pocket and located his tin of sex-sub pills. He noticed the pocket floated a little against the wall. "I'll have to adjust the gyros," he muttered, fumbling to open the tin.

She knocked the tin away. It clattered against the wall.

"Hey!" Javik said, leaning across the bed to retrieve the tin. "My ulcer pills!"

She lay next to him and nibbled at his ear. "What sign are you?" she asked. "Pisces?"

"Sparky the Hormone," he said, irritated that the tin was beyond his reach. His glands were beginning to go wild.

"I've never heard of that one," she said.

"Thirteenth sign of the Zodiac," he explained sarcastically. "The sign of natural craving."

"Oh."

Stupid transy broad, he thought. *Won't admit she's con-*

fused. He butted the palm of one of his large hands against her shoulder and pushed her away firmly. Then he glared at her. Evans's green eyes were soft and feverish, reminding him of a girl he had once datemated in an astro-port—the one he almost permied. *What was her name?* he wondered.

Their lips drew close, then touched. Javik pulled her body against his. His lips ran down along her neck to her bust. Her lilac perfume smelled inviting and exotic.

Evans was beginning to breathe hard. She ran her hands through his hair.

Javik moved his hand along the curvatures of her body, from the soft skin of her bust along her waist to her hips. A shudder coursed through his body.

She sighed.

How did they do it? Javik thought. *No surgical scars. Anyone else would think this is a real woman. But I read her dossier.*

He massaged her stomach and pressed his hands against the underside of her breasts. Javik felt curiosity over how a transsexual made love. He knew he had reached the point of no return.

A loud *thump* sounded around the ship.

"What was that?" Javik asked, staring at the black nightshade over the compartment porthole.

"I didn't hear anything," she said.

Thump! the sound was right next to them.

"I heard *that*," she said, sitting up on one elbow.

Crash! This came from somewhere else on the ship.

Javik mentoed the porthole nightshade. It snapped open, revealing a clear view of deep space. A red quasar burned brightly to one side of his framed view. Suddenly a mangled, semihuman face appeared in the porthole, staring in with bulbous, bloodshot eyes. The eyes were unfocused, with death's disorientation. The head was oversized and entirely hairless, having no eyebrows or eyelashes.

Javik felt his heart beat irregularly. He reached for his service pistol, which hung in a holster on the wall. "The engines aren't on," Javik said, just realizing it then. "We aren't moving!"

Evans screamed.

"Topside!" Javik barked, pressing his feet against the moto-boot rack at the foot of his bed. He felt the boots snap on over his ankles.

Evans fumbled around, trying to find her clothes.

Javik scrambled up the ladder and opened the hatch. Looking into the cabin, he saw clusters of the strange creatures against the outside of the windshield and portholes, knocking against the ship. "Hurry!" Javik yelled to Evans. "They're trying to get in!"

Javik felt his hand quiver on the automatic pistol's handle as he short-stepped out of the compartment to the deck. He rolled forward to the command chair. Wizzy was on the dashboard, snoring heavily. Javik knocked him away with the gun barrel and fell into the seat. He heard Wizzy hit the floor and roll. There was a fit of breathing for a moment from the baby comet. Then the snoring resumed.

With bulbous-headed humanoids only centimeters away outside the windshield, Javik mentoed the engines. There was no response. He felt a sharp pain in the back of his skull around the implanted mento transmitter.

"Nine hundred thirty-three possible causes," the ship's mother computer reported. "Complex circuitry. Search commencing."

Switching the pistol to his left hand, Javik slammed down the black manual START toggle in the center of the instrument panel. Still no response from the engines. "Shit," he said. His head ached. *Something's terribly wrong with my mento unit, too,* he thought. *What a place for it to go gunnysack!*

Glancing aft, Javik saw Evans scurry half-dressed to her own sleeping compartment. He was about to yell for her when she hustled out with her service pistol and used it to pound on Blanquie's hatch. "Stations!" Evans yelled. "Blanquie!" Then she rolled forward.

Javik waved his gun menacingly at the creatures on the other side of the windshield. But they didn't react, and continued to pummel the ship with their mangled heads, legs, arms, and bodies. Their unfocused, bloodshot eyes stared beyond Javik. "Where's Blanquie?" Javik asked.

"I called him. Do you think they can get in?" She stood beside her chair.

"Zip that," Javik said, glancing at her blouse.

She mentoed it.

As Javik heard the zipper rise, he wondered how the mento-zipper system worked. He knew from experience that another person could not mento your zipper, but did not understand the technology. He scowled. *I am really low,* he thought, scolding himself. *On a critical presidential mission, and I'm in the sack with a goddamned transsexual.*

Evans pressed a red alarm button on her console. "Blanquie!" she yelled as the siren screamed. "Get out here!"

"Where *is* he?" Javik snapped.

At Javik's mento-command, Mother reported on the ship's mechanical problem: "Still searching. Maximum search duration three minutes, fourteen seconds."

"There's something strange about these creatures," Evans said. She shut off the siren.

"That's news?"

"I mean, they look like dead humans, with terrible wounds. Oh! That one has no arms!"

A hideous, deformed creature with open wounds at its torn and empty armpits pounded its body against the windshield. Javik grimaced as the glassplex flexed.

"His forehead!" Evans said. "What's that on his forehead?"

"I don't know," Javik said, glaring at the instrument panel. "Damn these engines!" He rubbed the back and one side of his head. The mento unit pain had become dull and had traveled around the outside of his skull.

"P.F.," she said, reading the creature's forehead. "Product Failure!" She felt a chill. "Catapulted bodies from Earth!"

Javik heard Wizzy snore fitfully from somewhere on the floor.

"I think we're in the Davis Droids," Javik said. "Asteroids to port and starboard."

"How could they be alive out here?" she asked.

"Forget 'em!" Javik yelled. "And help me get the friggin' engines started! Blanquie! Where the hell are you, Blanquie?" Javik flipped the starter toggle on and off, with no result. "Go back and check Blanquie. Get him out here. Now!"

Evans rolled aft rapidly. She opened the hatch to Blanquie's sleeping compartment and looked in. She screamed. Then she coughed as a rush of icy, rarefied air hit her face.

Whirling around on his chair, Javik saw Evans recoil from the hatch in shock.

Evans slammed the hatch shut and mento-locked it. "The compartment is full of monsters!" she said. "I saw Blanquie lying on the bed with blood all over him." She looked at Javik with terror-stricken eyes. "I think he's dead."

"Jeheezus!" Javik said.

"Could this be the Happy Shopping Ground?" Evans asked, rolling forward. "Are they Product Failure victims?"

"Do you wanna die, Evans?" Javik said. His voice became loud and high-pitched: *"You wanna die?"*

"No sir. I don't." She slid into her chair.

"Then get a hold of yourself. I might as well be alone out here, for all the help you're giving." He mentoed Mother again.

"Three hundred sixty-two possible causes remain," Mother said. "Maximum search duration one minute, twenty-eight seconds."

"Sorry, sir," Evans said. "What should we do, Captain Javik?"

"What's all the commotion?" Wizzy asked in a little voice. He scooted out from under Evans's chair and hopped on the dashboard.

"So you're awake," Javik said. "Finally."

"I was tired," Wizzy said, studying the humanoids with his yellow cat's eye. Wizzy glowed red, calling upon his data banks. "Davis Droids," he said. "I warned you about this place. Nurinium here."

"What the hell is nurinium?" Javik asked.

"An element sprinkled around the universe by magicians," Wizzy said. "It gives inanimate objects life."

Javik shook his head. "Don't believe a word of it," he said, to Evans.

Thud! Barump! The creatures pummeled the ship with extra intensity. The windshield flexed again.

"Show me some of your wondrous powers, Wizzy," Javik said sarcastically. "Or would you rather sleep?"

"Well!" Wizzy huffed. "I'm not perfect! I told you that. And I am only nineteen hours, fifty-six minutes old!"

"All right, all right," Javik said. "Any idea why the engines won't start?"

Wizzy's cat's eye slanted toward Javik. "Creatures in the exhaust tubes," he replied, glowing red again. "Tubes are plugged."

"How the hell could they do that, with the ship going in excess of three hundred thousand kilometers per hour?"

Wizzy laughed, rocking for a moment on the dashboard. He glowed red-orange this time, although his eye remained yellow. "From your energy waves, and those of the ship, I see precisely what happened: One of the ship's E-cells was consumed sixteen minutes ago. There was a delay in switching to a new fuel cell—"

"Shit," Javik said. "And that shut off the engines. I could have solved it easily. Hell, Mother should have—"

"But you were preoccupied," Wizzy said, "and didn't realize the ship had stopped. It shut down in a very bad place."

"Never heard of a Mother failing before," Evans said gloomily.

Javik glared at her. "Thanks for the analysis," he said. "Both of you. Now what?"

"Something plugging the exhaust tubes," Mother reported. "Manual correction required."

Thump! Kathud! The pummeling continued.

"You're the captain," Wizzy said.

"Don't be rude," Evans said to Wizzy.

"The word is insubordinate," Javik said. He waved his gun at the humanoids. They paid him no heed.

Disconsolate, Javik stared down at the deck. Wearily, he set his pistol on his lap. The headache was subsiding. He sighed at the small relief of that.

An aft hatch clanked open.

"They're getting in!" Evans shouted.

Javik looked aft. A creature floated in, then fell to the cabin floor in the pseudo-gravity of the ship.

Evans rolled aft. She skirted the creature, which lay on the deck in apparent disorientation. Gasping in rarefied air over the hatch, she slammed it shut. Then she mento-spun the locking device while creatures in Blanquie's sleeping compartment thumped against the underside of the deck.

"I'm mento-holding it locked," Evans said. "They're trying to force it open again." She heard the ship's oxygen system hum loudly, replenishing the air supply.

Smelling the odor of decaying flesh, Javik studied the creature that had entered the cabin. It was male, wearing a torn Earth T-shirt and blue jeans. An electroplated purple badge was attached to the shirt, dangling next to a rip that exposed a black "P.F." stamp on the chest. Seeing a deep gash on the face, Javik decided this must have been the cause of death. The creature staggered to its feet, waving its arms wildly as it took a step toward Javik. Then it took another step, hesitating and unsteady, like someone who was either afraid or not practiced in walking.

It's not dead now, Javik thought. He aimed and fired the gun.

There was a pistol crack and a flash of orange. The laser bullet missed, ricocheting around the cabin and whistling by Evans's ear. She dropped to the deck, continuing to mentohold the hatch-locking mechanism.

A volley of subsequent shots from the automatic weapon were on target, tearing gaping, bloody holes in the creature's flesh. It continued to stumble ahead, its bloodshot eyes vacuous and long dead. Curiously, the open wounds did not drip blood.

Javik emptied his gun into the creature. But it continued to advance, slowly and inexorably. He looked for another clip. "Shoot it, Evans!" he shouted. "Hurry!"

Before Evans could take aim, the creature was lunging for Javik. Javik repelled it with a swift karate kick to the torso, causing the assailant to fall back on the deck. Slowly, however, the creature sat up and rose to its feet.

Without warning, Wizzy glowed bright orange and flashed across the cabin, slamming into the tattered humanoid. This had more effect than all of Javik's firepower, for the creature slipped and tried to go the other way. Its purple badge clattered to the deck. Cringing at the sight of Wizzy, the creature tried to get away.

Wizzy attacked again.

The creature fell over itself trying to escape. It crawled aft, in full and terrified retreat.

"Over here!" Evans said. "I'll open the hatch!"

Wizzy forced the intruder into Blanquie's sleeping compartment. "I'm going in too!" Wizzy announced. "Close the hatch after me!"

"Right!" Evans said.

"He's afraid of me!" Wizzy said, pausing at the open hatch and displaying obvious pride. "Probably a primordial fear of comets."

"Who cares why!" Javik said, shaking his head. "Just do it!"

"You don't care to understand these things?" Wizzy asked, surprised. "With so much to learn, you would bury your head in the sand?"

"This is no time for philosophy!" Javik snapped.

"Fleshcarriers!" Wizzy huffed. Haughtily, he flew into the compartment.

Evans slammed the hatch shut.

Now there was a ferocious commotion below decks. Javik felt the ship shake and heard shattering glassplex, probably from the compartment's mirrors. Wizzy squealed down there, with all the zeal of an attacking samu-rani warrior.

"He's doing it!" Evans reported, looking along the side of the ship with a prismatic porthole. Creatures poured from the broken porthole of Blanquie's compartment, tumbling in the vacuum of space. Gradually they regained their equilibriums and made their way back to the ship, half swimming, half walking on air.

"Good work, Wizzy!" Javik said.

Evans screamed.

Javik hurried to the porthole with her and saw the reason: Outside, the bloody and battered corpse of Vince Blanquie tumbled in freefall. Then it began to move, swimmingly and dreamlike with its humanoid brethren.

"Blanquie's one of them," Javik said. A chill cut through his shoulder blades.

"Open up!" Wizzy squealed from below decks.

Evans lifted the hatch, allowing Wizzy back in. Then she resealed it.

Wizzy hovered breathlessly in midair. "A . . . burst . . . of strength," he said proudly.

"Not a minute too early," Javik said. "Say, you sound done in." He opened his palm, and Wizzy landed there.

Wizzy breathed rapidly. "I fused a cover . . . over the porthole," he said. "Using titanium . . . from the compartment deck."

Javik felt him breathing, expanding and contracting like any human. "Good," Javik said. "Now I have one more assignment for you."

"Name it," Wizzy said, full of himself.

"The exhaust tubes. Can you clear them?"

"Just command it."

"I command it," Javik said. He tossed Wizzy in the air.

Wizzy clunked ungracefully to the floor. "Hey!" he yelled, surprised. "Give me a moment to get my stuff together!"

"Sorry," Javik said.

Presently, Wizzy entered an airlock on the starboard side of the *Amanda Marie*. Within seconds, he darted into space.

The creatures continued to pummel the ship.

Javik took his command chair and mento-held on the ship's

starter button. With the mento transmission, a sharp pain returned to the back of his skull. Releasing the mento hold, Javik swore and slammed down the black START toggle.

Moments later, he felt the ship rumble as twin ion engines roared to life. He breathed deeply.

"Thank God!" Evans said.

Outside the ship, Wizzy was just exiting the last exhaust tube when the engines turned over. Had the engines started just a fraction of a second earlier, Wizzy might have been blown away into deep space and lost forever. As it was, he had to cling to a deflector fin with magic suction while the ship accelerated.

Some of the humanoid creatures clung to the ship too. But they soon lost their grips and fell back as the *Amanda Marie* picked up speed. Wizzy saw them float aimlessly in the asteroid belt behind the ship.

Inside, Javik was beginning to think of Wizzy. He flipped a dashboard toggle to reverse-thrust the engines. When the ship stopped, he threw the Hi-Tech gearbox into neutral.

Wizzy reentered the airlock, then was admitted to the cabin. He flew in, angry as a Jahuvian hornet. "Hey!" he squealed. "Remember me? I coulda been lost out there!"

Javik apologized, then pushed the toggle to resume acceleration. The *Amanda Marie* surged ahead.

"I'm just the guy who saved your butt," Wizzy said, glowing an angry shade of bright orange. He dropped to the corrugated metal deck, breathing hard.

"I would have gone back for you if you'd fallen off," Javik said. "I just wanted to be sure the engines were running okay."

"Hrrumph!" Wizzy said.

Javik laughed. "In case you're wondering, Wizzy—wanting to learn things as you do—you just displayed the emotion of anger."

"Anger? That is good?"

"Sometimes," Javik mused, glancing back at Wizzy and noting he was still bright orange. "It's gotten me into a lot of trouble, though."

"Is that what I am now?" Wizzy screamed. "Angry? Well, it feels good! Damned good!"

Javik tossed a disdainful look over his shoulder.

"Hrrumph!" Wizzy said again. He scooted aft along the cabin floor. "Must learn more about this anger," he said. Evans watched him disappear into Blanquie's sleeping compartment without another word.

"Some meckie you've got there," Evans said. She tossed the humanoid's purple badge in a disposa-tube. Then she moto-shoed forward, grabbing a half-bulkhead for support as Javik turned the ship.

"Mother, why did you delay in switching to a new fuel cell?" Javik asked, speaking into his dash microphone.

"Unknown," Mother said. "Better have me checked over in the next astro-port."

"That's a long way off," Javik said. "We alternate rest times from now on, Evans. Can't leave Mother alone." He watched Evans slide into the co-pilot's seat.

I'll never go near her again, he told himself, arching his eyebrows thoughtfully. *Never again*.

FOUR

When God created life on Cork, he must have been
in a whimsical mood.

> Report of the sayerman
> team sent in pursuit
> of Winston Abercrombie

Sixty-six hours later, the *Amanda Marie* entered orbit just outside the atmosphere of Guna One. Javik scanned a clip chart
on the wall to his left. "Should be Garbage Central down there,"
he said.

The ship's engines rumbled for a moment, bouncing Javik's
long legs together under the instrument panel.

"You've hardly spoken to me since the Davis Droids," Evans said, squinting in the light of three synchronized Guna
suns. She studied a planet file on the CRT screen, noting that
the combined energy produced by this solar triumvirate was
little more than the output of Earth's single sun.

"That hydraulic line fixed?" Javik asked tersely.

"Mother took care of it," Evans said.

"Took care of it, 'sir,' to you, Evans!" Javik snapped. "Don't
forget it!"

She paused for a moment, then: "Yes, sir." Javik heard
anger in her tone.

Evans clamped an Ego Booster headset over her ears and
mentoed it on. Javik overheard portions of the recorded mes-

sage as it played in her ears: "You are important and incredibly talented. You have many unique qualities."

"Turn that thing down!" Javik said.

She did as he instructed without looking at him.

Javik mento-banked the ship, giving him a clear view of Guna One. This time there was no pain around the mento transmitter, and he hoped it wouldn't bother him again. As he looked through the glassplex side window, he saw that the planet had flowing greens of varying shades, along with browns and blues, much like the colors of Earth. Quite a number of moonlike craters dotted the landscape, apparent evidence of meteor activity. Swirling, misty gray clouds moved rapidly across the surface, providing different views through cloud clearings every few seconds. Feeling the engines vibrate again, Javik glared at his instruments.

Evans removed her headset and stared at Javik. His features were drawn and tired, with hair matted on one side of his head from sleeping against that spot and not combing it out afterward. She took a deep breath, then said, "You might at least be civil."

"Shut up," Javik blurted. He paused. Evans saw his deeply set blue eyes half turn in her direction, seeming to stick their gaze in the vicinity of the windshield's center. His lips moved angrily as he muttered something under his breath.

"You're being rude."

"Just follow orders. Why is this damned thing running rough?"

"I'll ask Mother," Evans said.

"Adjust the engine polarity," Wizzy said.

Looking aft, Javik saw Wizzy resting on the back of Blanquie's chair. "What?" Javik asked.

"Increase engine polarity seven point three two percent," Wizzy said. "Shall I make the adjustment, Captain?"

"No. Where do you get that?"

"Unusual planetary magnetics here," Wizzy said, "caused by rare subatomic monopoles. See those craters down there? This place attracts junk from all over the universe."

"Your meckie is playing science officer," Evans said. Then she spoke into her dash mike: "Mother, what's wrong with the engines?"

"Unable to determine," Mother said, using a mellow computer voice.

"Should program a survival instinct into Mother," Javik

said. "She sounds too calm, no matter what's going on in the cabin." He glanced back at Wizzy.

"The magnetics problem is not revealed by your instruments," Wizzy said. "But I know it to be true."

The ship rumbled again. This time the vibration was worse and continuous.

Javik cursed.

"My teeth are knocking together," Evans said.

"Just try the engine adjustment," Wizzy said. "If I'm wrong, you'll know soon enough."

"Make it!" Javik said.

Wizzy tapped a computer keyboard on the science officer's console. Then he returned to the chair back.

Javik felt the engines smooth out. He nodded with resignation and turned forward. *Is everything Wizzy says right?* Javik wondered. *Even that story of magical nurinium being sprinkled around the universe?*

"This ship needs a science officer," Wizzy said.

"We can get along," Javik said.

"I know the inadequacies of the Theory of Relativity," Wizzy said, "and what happens when G-gas mixes with—"

"Okay!" Javik said. "You've got the job!"

"Science officer, *first* class?" Wizzy asked.

"All right, damn it!"

Wizzy squealed with excitement.

Javik ordered an atmospheric readout from the ship's mother computer.

"Like Earth in many ways," Mother reported, "with nitrogen, oxygen, argon, carbon dioxide . . ." The computer read off other elements, then said, "There are four unknown elements."

Wizzy glowed red to utilize his data banks. "The key unknown is nurinium," he said. "The same stuff I told you about in the droids."

Javik rolled aft and mentoed the science officer's CRT screen. It confirmed Mother's report, listing four unknown elements. Javik tugged at an eyelash and pursed his lips thoughtfully.

"I know what I'm talking about, Captain," Wizzy said. "Trust me."

"Magic?" Evans said. "You're talking about magic?"

"That's right," Wizzy said.

"Assuming you're correct about the atmosphere," Javik said, "and it sounds pretty improbable to me, is it breathable?"

"For some beings."

"Be specific," Javik said. "For humans?"

"Yes. But be prepared for surprises." Wizzy glowed faintly orange, and Javik thought he detected a teasing tone in Wizzy's voice.

"I'm waiting, Wizzy," Javik said.

"As I hinted, odd creatures live down there, Captain." Wizzy chuckled softly.

"Specifically?"

"Let me have a little fun with this. I am only three days, fifteen hours old, after all. Children need their fun."

Javik seethed. "Are they dangerous?"

"Would it matter if they were? You'd land anyway, looking for unusual activities. Could you return to Earth and tell them you were afraid to land?"

"More humanoids?" Javik asked, his breathing labored from anger. He scratched his forehead.

"Some are like that. A minority, however."

"I'm not going to play Twenty Questions with you. If you want to keep your position . . ."

"Be rational, Captain Tom," Wizzy said calmly. "I have bad points, admittedly. But on the whole, you need me."

"Aaargh!" Javik said. Furious, he spun Wizzy's chair.

Resting on the spinning chair back, Wizzy glowed bright yellow. Suddenly the chair stopped rotating.

Javik tried to spin the chair again. It wouldn't move.

Wizzy chuckled. Then he became dark blue again.

"I wonder if Abercrombie is down there," Evans said. "What a dirty guy. He could have ruined the AmFed economy with his recycling. Think of it! Millions of manufacturing and distribution people in souplines."

"Who cares?" Javik said.

"But isn't that why you're here?" Evans asked. "To promote the AmFed Way? The greatest good for the greatest number?"

"Naw," Javik said. He popped a red tintette out of a dispenser on the science officer's console. He lit the tintette and blew a puff of red smoke at Wizzy.

"I didn't know you smoked," Evans said.

"He's nervous," Wizzy said.

Javik laughed uneasily. He thought about flushing Wizzy into deep space, but knew Wizzy was reading this thought. It was a frustrating situation.

"Our Captain Tom is here for personal reasons," Wizzy said. "Promote Number One and to hell with everybody else. Right, sir?"

"Can it!" Javik said. He tossed the tintette in a wall-mounted disposa-tube. Machinery inside the wall whirred. "Punch down to Guna One, Evans," he said.

Evans acknowledged the command and mentoed the blue, T-shaped DIVE lever. The lever flipped down without being touched.

The *Amanda Marie* dropped its nose abruptly toward Guna One and accelerated. As Javik hurried back to his seat, he saw an orange glow in front of the ship. Remembering his mento transmitter headaches, he secured his safety harness manually.

"Entering the atmosphere," the mother computer reported.

Javik monitored the interior and exterior heat gauges. He punched a button to freeze the cooling tiles. A gauge told him that the ship's outside temperature had dropped.

Wizzy fluttered in the air during the descent, then landed on Javik's chair back. Javik heard a buzz in his ears. The buzzing was erratic: first loud, then low, first long, then short.

Wizzy grew very quiet. Then, suddenly, he shrieked in Javik's ear: "Wait, Captain Tom!"

Javik slammed against his shoulder harness trying to get away from the noise. Angrily, he snatched Wizzy off the chair back and held the little fellow in front of his face. The comet was cool but bright red. "Don't ever yell in my ear again, damn it!" Javik barked, setting his jaw. His ears rang.

"Sorry, Captain," Wizzy said. "Stop your descent. I am picking up disturbing, mysterious signals from the planet."

"You didn't care about danger before."

"I understood the other danger. Or thought I did. This is an unknown."

Mother reported the altitude at twenty-nine thousand, five hundred meters.

"Look at all those pockmarks on the surface," Evans said.

Javik placed Wizzy on the dashboard, saying, "I can't make heads or tails out of you, Wizzy."

"A life force," Wizzy said. "Very large, I think. I picked

up similar, weaker signals from deep space. But they didn't repeat, so I forgot about them." Wizzy flew in a confused pattern around the cabin, then landed on the deck.

"We have to disregard everything he's saying," Javik said, to Evans. "He's out of his meckie mind."

Evans nodded.

"My metamorphosis is proceeding," Wizzy said, shaking. "I don't understand the changes." He scooted for cover under the science officer's console and remained there, whimpering.

"You're feeling fear, Wizzy," Javik yelled. "That's another emotion!"

"I want my papa!" Wizzy squealed. He sobbed.

The *Amanda Marie* continued its descent.

Below, in a gray-rock control room cave beneath the surface of the planet, a crew of dented and chipped meckies stood at computer terminals, punching entries into keyboards. The computer hardware looked long in the tooth, having been catapulted from Earth as garbage and salvaged by Lord Abercrombie.

"We've got it going!" a dented red meckie said. She, like the others, carried a brass "REBUILT" plaque on her torso. "Tell Lord Abercrombie we're making a big wind!" she exclaimed. "Hurricane strength!"

"But Lord Abercrombie is soil-immersed now," a silver meckie said.

"Oh, that's right," the red meckie said. "We'll tell him later, then. He'll be very pleased!"

Lord Abercrombie lay buried in the soil, deep in an underground chamber. This was how he spent half of each day, totally immersed in the Realm of Magic. The half of his body that remained human went into dormancy at these times, with no breathing and no fleshcarrier sensations whatsoever.

Abercrombie's head was the planet now. He looked out upon the universe with a billion porous visual sensors, reflecting the stars across the panorama of his magical soul.

The universe is calling to me, he thought, *telling me to join it.*

A torrent of rain poured up out of the ground, filling the atmosphere with water. Clouds formed quickly from this upside-down rain, followed by thunder and lightning. Within seconds a full-blown electrical storm was in progress, with clouds dumping rain back on the planet. When this subsided, more rain rose from the surface, restarting the cycle.

That odd reverse rain again, Lord Abercrombie thought helplessly. *What causes it?*

Thunder boomed across the sky.

At the same time, in the control room. . . .

"Reverse rain in Sector Seventy-four," the red meckie said. "And one hell of a dust storm just ten kilometers south of that!"

"Now our equipment is shorting out," another meckie said.

"Not again!" the meckies wailed in unison. "Not again!"

"I see buildings down there," Javik said. He was looking through the midships magna-scope, manually adjusting it to focus. "One looks like a large stone castle . . . and a number of smaller structures. Long gray strips, too."

"I'm picking up signals again," Wizzy said, glowing bright red. Different this time." He sat on top of the science officer's console. "Messages from the planet's history. An expedition six hundred years ago led by someone named Yammarian. These were not humans. The expedition found evidence of Yanni tribesmen and Bolo herdsmen who once populated the planet. Found cliff habitats, too, and the skeletons of long goats. There was an upheaval here. Can't tell what sort. An earthquake, maybe—or a war."

"Anything else?" Evans asked.

"Don't listen to that stuff," Javik said.

"Not much," Wizzy said. "The Yannis are gone. They left or died during the upheaval."

"Well, they're back," Evans said. "Or someone is."

Wizzy's bright red color faded, then flickered. "I'm losing the signal," he said.

"Look, Captain!" Evans said, pointing across the dashboard to port. "Looks like a big storm heading right toward us! It's coming outta nowhere."

Javik saw swirling, rust-colored particles only a few meters off the side of the ship, along with rain that seemed to be going up. It seemed impossible. The cabin darkened. "See if we can outrun it," Javik barked, trying to get back to his chair. The cabin lights brightened, compensating for the storm's darkness.

The storm hit before evasive action was possible. The *Amanda*

Marie rocked violently, forcing Javik to hold a half-bulkhead with both hands. The cabin lights flickered off, leaving them in semidarkness. Then the lights danced back on.

"How odd," Wizzy squealed. "I saw rain going up—coming from the planet's surface."

"I saw it, too," Javik said. He crawled to his command chair as the ship rocked. Pulling himself up to the seat, Javik snapped on his safety harness. "Hit the thrusters!" he yelled.

"Nothing, Captain," Evans said. She was holding tight to her chair with both hands, trying to mento the thruster rockets. "No response at all."

"I'll bet there's dust in the thruster tubes," Wizzy said. "Now the main engines are sputtering too."

The ship vibrated badly. It rocked to port, dipped its nose, and plunged.

"Going down fast, Captain Tom," Wizzy said.

"I can see that, for Atheist's sake," Javik snapped.

"Altitude fourteen thousand, two hundred meters," Mother reported. "Thruster tubes blocked. Manual correction required."

"Can't tell up from down," Javik said. "Too much damned dust."

"It's a magnetic storm," Wizzy said, glowing red from the red star crystal in his nucleus. "A remarkable battle between the planet and its atmosphere."

"Wonderful," Javik said. He grimaced. "Now we know what it is."

"Eleven thousand, six-fifty," Mother said.

Seeing that the rusty dust particles were thinning out, Evans said, "I think we're dropping below the storm."

"It's moving overhead," Wizzy said, looking through a porthole.

"Checking ship's functions," Mother said. "Still no thruster power. One main engine out."

The *Amanda Marie* rumbled roughly, then fell silent.

"Damn!" Javik cursed. "There went the remaining engine."

Mother confirmed this, then gave the altitude: "Seventy-two hundred meters."

Evans pounded on the instrument panel. "No CRT, accelerometer, or artificial horizon."

"And the para-flaps didn't go out," Javik said. "Aren't they automatic on this ship?"

"I think so," Evans said. She mentoed the flaps.

"Manual operation required," Mother said.

"I'll try 'em," Javik said, releasing his safety harness. He crawled aft along the corrugated metal deck to midships. There he grabbed a large black plastic wheel which was supported by an oblong pedestal. The surface of the wheel was abrasive to provide a gripping surface. Javik horsed with it, but it didn't budge. He cursed.

"Can you get it?" Evans asked.

"No."

"Thirty-nine fifty," Mother said.

"Get over here, Wizzy," Javik yelled. "Can you help me with this goddamned thing?"

"I'll try," Wizzy said. He alighted on one side of the wheel and clamped on with magic suction. With the two of them straining at it, the wheel finally broke free and moved. Then it stuck again.

"Where are all your wonderful powers now?" Javik asked, wiping his brow.

"Three thousand," Mother said.

"Unfortunately, they are inconsistent," Wizzy said. "One moment I feel super, and the next . . . well, quite weak."

"What about now?" Javik asked. They resumed pushing and pulling.

"Not good," Wizzy said. He fell to the deck, short of breath.

"Get up," Javik said. He gave the wheel an angry, mighty push. It moved. He pushed it again, and it moved freely. Now Javik spun the wheel.

"Starboard flap's out, Captain," Evans said, sighting along the prismatic porthole at her side. Glancing at the porthole on Javik's side, she added, "Port flap's out too."

Javik felt the *Amanda Marie*'s nose rise as the para-flaps took hold. The ship continued its descent, but much less steeply.

"Eighteen hundred," Mother said.

Javik looked out a midships porthole and saw a para-flap undulating gracefully outside, like the wing of a great bird. He checked the other flap. It was functioning perfectly too. Para-flaps were massive and white, with scalloped arches on the trailing edges and flotation cups on the undersides. They were awe-inspiring when viewed from the ground, and Javik recalled seeing a sky full of them once, with the sun setting beyond the Rosenbloom Mountains.

Those were good days, he thought, recalling the comaraderie of the corps.

"Fourteen hundred," Mother said.

Javik snapped to awareness. He returned to the command chair, asking, "What do you see, Evans?"

"Long gray strips," she said. "Maybe an airfield. We don't have a heck of a lot of choice." She pressed a yellow lever on her console to drop the landing gear.

Javik breathed a sigh of relief as he heard the gear pop down and lock into place. A green landing light flashed on at the center of the instrument panel. *Thank God,* he thought.

"Looks peculiar down there," Wizzy said. "Don't see any planes or rockets."

"Below a thousand," Mother said. "Final descent."

"I see ground vehicles," Javik said, watching streams of blue and pink flame streak along the gray ground strips.

"Primitive jets, sir," Wizzy said. "Jet-powered cars, to be precise."

"They're staying on the gray strips," Javik said. "So we'll land off to one side."

The *Amanda Marie* vibrated.

"Encountering turbulence," Evans said. "Rough glide."

"I know, I know," Javik said. He guided the steering toggle with one finger, hesitant to mento it.

The *Amanda Marie* hit an updraft, carrying it hundreds of meters from the gray ground strips. They crossed a heavily cratered area and approached a lightly wooded section where Javik saw pale green trees that resembled Sumerian pines.

"Up, baby," Evans coaxed, mento-adjusting the para-flaps.

The para-flaps fluttered desperately, carrying the ship just over the treetops. Now Javik could see a group of colorfully dressed people in a clearing. When the *Amanda Marie* was less than a hundred meters above the clearing, Javik noticed that the people below appeared to be wearing odd costumes—some were dressed like apples, others like oranges, bananas, watermelons.

"They're all dressed like fruit," Javik said.

"Not the bananas," Wizzy said. "Technically, the banana is neither fruit nor vegetable. More accurately, it can be categorized as cereal."

"Useless information," Javik said.

"Not to a nutritionist," Wizzy said.

Javik scowled.

The ship caught an updraft and rose momentarily. Then it dropped again.

"Hold on!" Javik yelled.

Javik and Evans braced themselves as the *Amanda Marie* bumped to the ground rather ungracefully. Javik felt a compression pain in his lower back. He rubbed it.

The ship rocked to one side on the ground, falling against one of the para-flaps. Then it righted itself. Javik heard the drone of electric motors as the para-flaps returned to their compartments.

Evans breathed a sigh of relief. "We're down," she said. "In one piece."

"I sense that our troubles have just begun," Wizzy said.

Javik mentoed the circular exit hatch without feeling any pain. The hatch unfolded from the center out like a camera orifice, revealing distant pine trees seen through dusty air. He smelled grit.

"Hmmm," Wizzy said as dust enveloped him. "Fine dry particles from a complex topsoil sediment, variable in texture . . . part crystalline, part disintegrated planetary mantle."

Javik shook his head as Wizzy went on to analyze the dust in its most minute detail.

A cacophany of cheers arose from outside, followed by the excited, unintelligible voices of many people. Rolling to the open hatchway, Javik commented, "They're dressed like trick-or-treaters." He felt the ship rock.

"What was that?" Evans asked.

Wizzy could be heard in the background, analyzing the entire climatological history of the planet, based upon the particles of dust adhering to the clear agate dome over his eye.

The *Amanda Marie* rocked again, then went back the other way. Leaning out of the circular hatch and looking to one side, Javik saw the edge of a mound of the colorfully dressed natives. *Now, why would they climb on top of one another like that?* he wondered.

The ship rocked once more, and this time it continued going over, in the direction away from the mound of natives. Javik had the answer to his unspoken question: They were toppling the ship!

"Going over!" Javik yelled. "Hold on!"

Wizzy buzzed by Javik and flew out the open hatchway.

The *Amanda Marie* fell on its side in a thunderous crash, slamming Javik and Evans against the interior walls. Then the ship began to roll over and over, gradually picking up speed. This created pandemonium inside, as Javik and Evans tried to get handholds on wall brackets, console bases, chairs, and anything else that was bolted down.

"Why are they doing this?" Evans wailed. She clung to the magna-scope base.

With considerable difficulty, Javik crawled to his command chair and tried to pull himself into it. *If I could just strap myself in*, he thought. But he was not able to get off the deck. Hanging on to the chair, he heard laughter outside and strange words which almost sounded Latin. He decided the language mixer pendant around his neck was not working properly.

Outside, in the afternoon light of three synchronized suns, Wizzy flew unsteadily over the *Amanda Marie*. He was much like a tiny bird who had not yet perfected the art of flying. Below, people dressed in tattered fruit costumes pushed the ship, causing it to roll along a dusty, bumpy surface. Chanting phrases which Wizzy identified from his data banks as Corkian legalese, they guided the ship to a wide path, lined along each side with red, yellow, and blue cylinders which had been partially buried and propped upright.

AmFed garbage cannisters, Wizzy thought, glowing red as he continued to use his data banks.

Through the windshield and portholes of the *Amanda Marie*, Wizzy got glimpses of Javik and Evans clinging for their lives inside. Over and over the ship rolled, down the center of the path.

"Only one thing to do," Wizzy said to himself. He dived toward the people.

As Wizzy neared the throng, he realized they were not humans, and they were not wearing costumes. They were Fruit people, men and women, dressed in shabby, ill-fitting three-piece suits and suit dresses of varying colors and patterns. Each sported a tarnished gold chain across his waistcoated belly, and carried a worn briefcase in the hand which was not being used to push the ship. They looked distinguished to Wizzy, in a peculiar sort of way. He veered off just before hitting them.

The creatures swatted at Wizzy with their briefcases and ducked out of the way. Some yelled ferocious epithets in legalese. They continued pushing the ship.

"This is our chance, lawyers!" Wizzy heard one yell in a high-pitched, squealy voice. "Lord Abercrombie will favor us after such a large offering!"

From his ever-handy data banks, Wizzy pinpointed the language as one of seventeen Corker dialects, a variety which had been sprinkled generously with Aluminum Starfield Latin.

Offering? Wizzy thought. *What terrible rite is this?* He tried to pick up energy waves from the lawyer creatures' brains, but got nothing.

Wizzy dived at the creatures again. Again, they swatted at him and yelled epithets. After seven passes like this, all without success, Wizzy felt extremely tired. In a last-ditch burst of energy, he placed himself on the opposite side of the *Amanda Marie* from the creatures. Using all his strength against that side of the ship, he attempted to stop the crowd from rolling the ship any further.

For a fraction of a second, Wizzy thought he felt the ship hold. But then he realized he was slipping down along the riveted skin of the craft. It rolled over him, followed by hundreds of thunderous, trampling feet. Wizzy was kicked to one side of the path.

By the time Wizzy had picked himself up from the dust, he was behind the mob of Fruits and quite out of breath. Above him on each side towered the red, yellow, and blue garbage cannisters. He tried to fly, but did not have sufficient energy. So he scooted as quickly as he could off the path and up a little knoll overlooking the action.

Upon seeing where the ship was headed, Wizzy squealed, "Oh no!" Below him and perhaps a hundred meters ahead of the tumbling ship, Wizzy saw a huge, gaping hole in the ground.

"Wait!" Wizzy screamed. Panic-stricken, he scooted and fell down the knoll. "I've got to stop them!" he exclaimed.

The *Amanda Marie* hit a smooth downslope and picked up speed, leaving the Fruit lawyers running along behind. Some fell in their anxiety and were trampled by their cohorts.

"No!" Wizzy yelled. "Stop!" He scurried as fast as he could, but this was not nearly fast enough. He knew it was too late. The ship was outrunning everyone.

The *Amanda Marie* hit a bump at the edge of the precipice, then tumbled into the black, cavernous hole and disappeared. Wizzy felt an empty pang in the center of his nucleus.

Ahead, Wizzy saw the lawyers reach the edge of the precipice. The thunder of their feet subsided. They encircled the hole, looking down into it. As Wizzy caught up, he heard them chatter excitedly.

"Favor us, Lord Abercrombie!" they wailed. "Favor us, oh mighty Lord!"

Wizzy darted between the Fruit-lawyers' stubby legs and around their briefcases, soon reaching the edge of the hole. Looking down, he saw only blackness. It made him sad, extremely sad. This was a new emotion to Wizzy, and he did not understand it.

I want to feel better, Wizzy thought. So he laughed boisterously for several seconds. This did not help.

"End our suffering, Lord!" the Fruit lawyers moaned.

Wizzy leaned over the edge to get a better view, clinging there with all his remaining strength. *It worked the last time I laughed,* he thought. *Why don't I feel better now?*

He felt himself shaking, and wondered if this was caused by yet another emotion. Then he realized it was the ground that was moving, not him. He jumped away from the hole.

The Fruit lawyers cried out in terror, bemoaning the fact that Lord Abercrombie still was not pleased with them. Earthquakes were a bad sign. They ran for cover in the nearby piney woods, leaving Wizzy alone by the hole.

Shortly before this, Lord Abercrombie lay far below, immersed in the soil. It was nearly time for him to leave the Realm of Magic once again, returning to his half existence in the Realm of Flesh. Fear tore through him. He wanted completeness, either in magic or flesh. But he could not decide between the realms.

If he chose magic, the planet Cork would be his. *Chief Magician of Cork,* Abercrombie thought, letting the words roll across his pleasure sensors. *Has a nice sound to it. And no fleshcarrier can invade my private place from the surface, not as long as I remain soil-immersed.*

Cork was a planet waiting to be taken. But it seemed too easy, and this troubled him. *Why did the other magicians leave?* he wondered. There seemed no answer to such a question. Perhaps he could learn the answer—if he committed himself this time, not returning to flesh.

He wondered if he needed to commit himself entirely to the

Realm of Magic before he would be able to use magic efficiently for the creation of disasters. In theory, that made a certain amount of sense. He was only pecking away at magic now, on the outskirts of something big. But could he return to flesh if he made such a commitment?

What if being the planet is all there is here? he thought. *A philosophical niche in which I can contemplate my navel . . . vegetating.*

Abercrombie stirred angrily. *God, but I hate vegetables!* he thought. He recalled a recurring nightmare in which his Earthian mother forced him to eat brussels sprouts, those horrid little leafy balls. In the nightmare, his mother smiled in that falsely sweet way—the "It's good for you, dear" smile that he detested.

Cataloguing his enemies, past and present, Lord Abercrombie recalled when the villainous Uncle Rosy had sent six white-robed sayermen to take him back as a recycling criminal. But Abercrombie had stumbled across the Sacred Scroll of Cork, which led him to the Magician's Chamber: his private place. He was relatively safe here.

But I was powerless to prevent the scroll's flight back to Sacred Pond, he thought. *It is vulnerable there. And that makes me vulnerable—unless I choose to seal the surface entrance by remaining soil-immersed.*

He wondered if there might not be better planets. Why should he settle for a third-rate place?

Lord Abercrombie became aware of hordes of little feet scurrying across his surface. They were pushing something along the ground to the sacrifice hole his meckies had dug— a long, cream-colored cannister with red, yellow, and blue markings—

AmFed markings! he thought. His visual sensors probed the cannister as it tumbled across his planetary crust. *An AmFed ship! But what are those stupid lawyers doing? This is not garbahge, you fools!*

Lord Abercrombie felt himself returning to the Realm of Flesh as he thought of the ship. Maybe he could commandeer it to escape in his fleshy form, finding a better fleshcarrier life somewhere else, a life without Earthians pursuing him. But where would he go? On the other hand, he might still function as a magician, despite his frustrations to date. He was learning more about magic each day. Only the day before, he had magically induced a small rockslide. That was progress, his first magically created disaster in four years of trying.

But being a planet seemed so boring most of the time, just staring out on an unchanging universe, with occasional novas, comets, and shooting stars. He longed for action, for the excitement of change. This seemed possible only in the Realm of Flesh. And he longed for conversation with a real person. It had been four years. . . .

His reasoning went in circles, touching each side of the argument over and over, and always returning to the starting point. It was frustrating.

As the AmFed ship tumbled into Abercrombie's maw, he wondered if he could put its computer hardware to use; maybe his meckies could adapt it to improve his outdated Earthian disaster control machinery. He needed to solve the reverse rain problem. At times, the patched-together disaster control equipment seemed to function well, producing nice phenomena, but then the rain would pour from the planet, and everything would short out.

It's got to be in my equipment, he thought. *Some misfunction I haven't discovered yet.*

Then Lord Abercrombie worried about the AmFeds sending warships to investigate the disappearance of an AmFed ship. He knew his magic was as undependable as his technology. He would be no match for sophisticated AmFed weaponry. They could destroy the entire planet.

No, he decided. *I can't keep the ship.*

The *Amanda Marie* hurtled deeper into the sacrifice hole, bouncing off dirt and rocks on the sides. Something fell out of the ship, but Lord Abercrombie did not focus on what it was.

Magnetics, he thought, recalling the symbols on the history wall. He pictured one of the symbols in his mind now: a circle intertwined with the symbol for magnetics. *Circle,* he thought. *Circle . . .*

Lord Abercrombie recalled that the symbols were beneath the pictures of his magician predecessors. *Circle,* he thought. *Could that represent a planet? Maybe the whole symbol refers to planetary magnetics.*

He wanted to consider this further, but began to feel ill, sick to his pleasure sensors. His fleshy hand clutched fitfully out of the dirt, reaching for its survival. He swooned. Suddenly, a monstrous burp echoed through the passageways and caverns of the Magician's Chamber. Lord Abercrombie jumped out of the hole, throwing dirt everywhere.

In sunlight on the planet's surface, Wizzy smelled a peculiar, sulfurous gas which nauseated him. He took refuge behind one of the upright garbage cannisters.

Burr . . . rupp! An echoing regurgitation sound came from the hole, followed by the *Amanda Marie*. A deep voice thundered from the hole: "You stupid lawyers! Incompetent fools! Can't you do anything right?"

The ship was hurled high in the air over Wizzy, along with fragments of dirt and rock. Something white hurtled by too, causing Wizzy's magical heart to sink. *A body?* he thought.

Whatever it was sped away before he could identify it. The ship itself went so high that Wizzy almost lost sight of it. Then, from a distant, tiny speck, it began to grow larger. It was falling back to Cork.

Most of the Fruit lawyers managed to dodge rocks and other debris that pelted the area, but Wizzy saw one hapless banana man squashed flat by a large stone. It was horrible. Other Fruits nursed wounds and looked for their missing property. Briefcases and business cards lay on the ground in disarray.

"Lord Abercrombie refused our offering!" a bottom-heavy pear woman lamented. "Now the curse will be worse! He is furious with us!"

None could dispute this statement. There was a general condition of extreme unhappiness.

Soon Wizzy saw the *Amanda Marie*'s para-flaps go out. *Someone's inside,* he thought, recalling that the automatic system had not functioned earlier. *At least one.*

The ship drifted down gracefully, landing almost without flaw at one side of the clearing. It was badly dented, with portions of riveted skin hanging loose like bloodless wounds.

"Oh my!" Wizzy exclaimed in a voice drowned out in the surrounding commotion. "I hope everyone's all right!"

The crowd ran toward the ship, yelling angry and confused epithets. Wizzy followed, scooting in short bursts and stopping frequently to catch his breath.

A tall pineapple man with scaly brown skin ran past Wizzy at one of these rest stops. This fellow looked quite silly to Wizzy in comparison with the others. He wore bright purple and black checkered shorts that were torn on one side and a faded, royal purple tunic. An immense, leafy green headress grew from his head, on top of which he held on a misshapen helicopter beanie with one hand. "Be calm, my friends!" the pineapple man called out as he ran. "Calm yourselves!"

Ahead, Wizzy could see the open hatch on the *Amanda Marie*. *Pop your head out, Captain Tom*, he thought, staring anxiously at the open hatch. But there was no sign of movement on the ship.

FIVE

The effects of ultra technology often seem identical
to those of magic. This is the point at which the
Realm of Flesh approaches a more perfect, magical
state. Only a knowledgeable observer can spot the
difference.

A Timeless Truth

"We're down!" Evans said, clinging with both hands to the
midships para-flaps wheel. She released her grip. Her palms
were moist.

"Ow," Javik said. A sharp pain shot through his shoulder.
He had been holding fast to his command chair. Now he rose
to survey the cabin. It was in disarray, with clip files, medical
packs, and other items of equipment scattered about. Sunlight
slanted through the portholes on one side. Javik rubbed his
sore shoulder.

Evans rolled to the open circular hatch and looked out.
"Lucky we didn't fall out," she said, watching the crowd of
oddly dressed natives approach.

Javik was at her side a moment later. "Still no response
from the engines," he said, holding his hand on his holstered
service pistol.

"God, it stinks in here!" Evans said. "Some kinda gas in
that hole."

"Sounded like a big burp to me," Javik said.

As the crowd approached, Evans speculated that they looked like a bunch of costume-party goers. "Maybe they're drunk," she said.

"They look like offbeat lawyers," Javik said. "Look at the three-piece suits, briefcases, and gold watch chains." He squinted. "Wait a minute," he said.

"Are those costumes?" Evans asked.

"Exactly what I was wondering. I can't tell."

The crowd became excited upon seeing Javik and Evans. They ran faster, pointing and waving white cards. As they neared, Javik realized they were business cards. And he realized something else.

"They're Fruit people!" Javik exclaimed.

"Frumba hallinon?" an orange woman asked, looking up and extending a business card. She was the first to arrive. Javik noticed a small folding shovel on her hip, secured to her belt.

Others arrived now, an endless variety of Fruit people, all dressed similarly and all waving business cards. "Frumba hallinon?" they asked. "Frumba hallinon?"

"What the . . . ?"

Javik fumbled with his language mixer pendant. It showed a red light. Then it beeped and the light became green.

"Do you want legal advice?" the Fruit creatures asked. They still spoke in their native tongue, but now Javik understood.

"Where are we?" Evans asked. "In Glitterland?"

Soon the Fruits were clamoring to reach the visitors from Earth. Since the open hatch was high off the ground at midships, the Fruits had to pile on top of one another, just as they had done earlier to topple the ship. They fought to be first, pushing and kicking their brethren with complete abandon.

One watermelon man reached the top, where he hung desperately to the hatchway deck. Stretching to reach up, he pressed a business card into Javik's palm. Javik used his mixer to read it as the fellow was dragged down the heap to the ground. The pile fell now, and the Fruits scrambled to rebuild it.

Wily Watermelon
Attorney at Law,
non compos mentis

Javik flipped the card away, and watched the wind take it. Below, the Fruit people were clearing their ranks, allowing a tall pineapple man through. Obviously, he was someone in authority. Dressed differently from the others but carrying a similar folding shovel on his hip, the pineapple man's most distinctive article of attire was a red helicopter beanie with a bright yellow plastic rotor that spun as he walked.

A murmuring passed through the crowd. The Fruit lawyers who had been piling up retreated, nursing their wounds.

When he reached the front of the multitude, the pineapple man extended his arms to each side, gazing up at Javik and Evans. "You there!" he called out in a loud, syrupy voice. "Identify yourselves!" *Drat!* he thought. *This had better not interrupt my plans for tonight!*

Javik gave names, then said, "We are in the American Federation of Freeness Space Patrol. From Earth." He wrinkled his brow, recalling the dancing pineapple man he had seen when he was half asleep in the videodome—just before Wizzy's entrance. Every event after the time Wizzy appeared seemed unreal to Javik. But then he recalled Wizzy slamming into his hand to prove he was awake. *That hurt like hell,* Javik thought.

"I am Prince Peter Pineapple," the pineapple man announced proudly. "Of the Royal Family of Cork." He squinted in the light of three suns which were low in the sky to the west.

"This place is called Cork?" Javik asked. He saw Wizzy scoot up at the prince's feet, panting heavily. Wizzy was dark blue with a thin layer of dust on his body.

"It is our planet's name," Prince Pineapple explained. "Sixth planet in the Triad Solar System."

"We call it the Aluminum Starfield," Javik said.

Prince Pineapple smoothed his elegant leaf headress with one hand. "We know of Earth, you know," he said.

"You do?" Javik said. "How?"

"You sent us gar-bahge."

"I know," Javik said nervously, taking note of the affected pronunciation. "I have been sent to discuss that with you."

"We know you by your gar-bahge, Earthian. And I can't tell you how happy we are to see you."

"Uh . . . we will straighten everything out. I promise you that."

"Wonderful!" the pineapple prince said. "Come down now, Earthians. King Corker would hear of your gar-bahge!"

"Why did your people push my ship in a hole?" Javik asked.

"Those foolish lawyers," Prince Pineapple said, glowering

around. "Our lowest social strata. And there are so many of them! They tried to gain favor with Lord Abercrombie by offering you."

"Offering us? To what?"

"To our planetary God, Lord Abercrombie. It was a mistake, for which I apologize profusely."

The Fruit lawyers hung their heads in shame.

Evans leaned close to Javik's ear and whispered, "Could it be the same Abercrombie, with a new scam?"

"We'll find out," Javik whispered. Then: "We'd better do as they say. Too many of them." He removed the ship's black and white striped Tasnard rope from its wall hook. At his mento-command, the rope secured itself to the base of the science officer's console. A small pang of pain struck at the rear of his head, then subsided.

Evans wrapped the Tasnard rope around her chest and under her armpits. At her mento-command, the rope dropped her gently to the ground.

Javik followed.

"Honored to meet you," Prince Pineapple said, bowing graciously as Javik reached the ground. The prince straightened to face Javik, and his black button eyes wavered nervously. He was a towering Fruit, fully half a head taller than Javik.

"Thank you," Javik said, bowing in return. *Don't trust anyone who won't look you in the eye,* he thought, recalling his commanders' Psych 101 course.

On the ground at Prince Pineapple's feet, Wizzy breathed deeply and loudly. Javik noticed this and saw that Wizzy was accumulating more dust from the motion of feet around him.

Prince Pineapple smiled, revealing puffy white teeth which resembled kernels of white corn. Looking past Javik at the *Amanda Marie,* he said, "You must understand our unfortunate lawyers. Since Decision Coins were implemented for virtually all matters, we have little need of legal advice."

"Seedy-looking bunch," Javik muttered.

"Lawyers hang around this clearing looking for clients," the prince explained. "Rumor has it one attorney found a client here two years ago. It became hallowed ground for them after that."

"I see," Javik said, shuffling his feet impatiently.

Prince Pineapple felt obliged to explain further: "The cannister-lined pathway and sacrifice hole are hallowed for all

Fruits," he said. "It looks like our local dimwits saw your ship and mistook it for a giant gar-bahge cannister. We toss most of our gar-bahge in the sacrifice hole for Lord Abercrombie."

Javik fingered a pimple on the side of his neck.

"They are desperate to win Lord Abercrombie's favor. Poor creatures think they've been cursed." After reflecting for a second, Prince Pineapple added, "Maybe it's true."

"What an odd place this is," Evans said.

"Don't impose Earth standards," Wizzy said from the ground, using an instructor's tone. Breathing loudly, Wizzy glowed softly orange. The dust particles on his surface melted and disappeared. He became dark blue again.

"None of us have been ourselves lately," Prince Pineapple said. "It's this infernal gar-bahge thing, you know. Tremendous pressure over it. The Planet God has been troubled." *To hell with Lord Abercrombie!* he thought. *The foolishness he condones!*

Javik smiled uneasily. He looked back at his ship, noting many dents, torn pieces of skin, and numerous abrasions. It would require a major overhaul to make it spaceworthy again. "How were we blown back out of the hole?" he asked, turning to face the pineapple prince.

"Don't step on me!" Wizzy squealed. A prune man stood on him.

Prince Pineapple hesitated as he focused on Fruit people who were pressing in around them, listening to every word. Some took notes on long clip pads or whispered back and forth excitedly, using their Corkian legalese.

"Move along now!" Prince Pineapple commanded. "Make way!" He waved his arms demonstratively.

Javik noticed now that the prince and all the Fruits had four fingers and a thumb on each hand like any human, except the thumb was on the outside of the hand.

Slowly, the throng moved back.

"Come with me," Prince Pineapple said to Javik and Evans. He guided them toward an opening in the crowd. "It will be dusk soon."

"I'll join you later," Wizzy said. "I need a breather."

Javik held back. "My ship will be safe here?" he asked.

"Your ship is nearly new. New things have no value to our people."

Javik scratched his head thoughtfully. "Is that so? Well, it's received quite a bit of damage. Doesn't look so new to me anymore."

"Hmmm," Prince Pineapple said, studying the *Amanda Marie*. "The damage helps a little. Still, I do not find it very appealing. Perhaps with a few more dents and abrasions..."

"I can't leave my ship with this mob," Javik said.

The prince shrugged. "Very well," he said. "I'll post guards, then. Will that make you feel better?"

"It will."

Prince Pineapple spoke with a cluster of banana man lawyers, instructing them to stand guard over the craft. Then he drew forth a purple and black checkered wallet, removing several creased pieces of paper which looked to Javik like old Earth candy bar and gum wrappers.

Leaning close, Javik verified this. He recognized wrappers from a Big Hunk, a Hershey's plain, and a Juicy Fruit.

Solemnly, Prince Pineapple handed a creased wrapper to each of the banana men. They nodded and stuffed the wrappers in their pockets.

"Juicy Fruits are the most valuable," the prince said to Javik. He slipped the wallet back into his pants pocket.

"I see," Javik said.

When they were out of earshot of the lawyers, Prince Pineapple said: "Poor devils. Our law schools still pump out so many of them."

Evans caught Javik's gaze. She raised her eyebrows.

Prince Pineapple led the way along a rough path which skirted the piney woods. "The sacrifice hole appeared several years back," he said as they reached late afternoon shade. "Lord Abercrombie's metal men dug it. I saw them."

"Metal men?" Evans said. "You mean meckies?"

"I don't know what they're called," Prince Pineapple said. The prince's cadence changed now as they continued along the path. His steps became staccato-quick and inefficient. The big pineapple man was expending a lot of energy but not moving commensurately fast.

Javik and Evans rolled as best as they could on the uneven surface, but tripped several times as their moto-boot wheels encountered stones, twigs, and tufts of dirt. At one point, Javik fell to his knees.

"Hurry now," the prince said, looking back. "The king is waiting." *I must act as though I care,* he thought. *Or the king will suspect . . .*

Javik touched a button on his moto-boots to eject the wheels and wheel frames. He tossed them aside.

Evans did the same, leaving both of them wearing unmotorized service boots. "That's better," she said, testing them on the ground.

"Unusual shoes you Earthians wear," Prince Pineapple said. "Hurry now!"

"More suited to Earth, it seems," Javik said as they resumed their course. He added: "This Planet God, Lord Abercrombie. He is terribly upset at the gar-bahge situation?"

"Oh yes! Indeed he is! And so is King Corker. It is a good thing you arrived now. We could not have survived much longer." *Odd that Earthians would appear just now,* he thought. *By morning, I will be gone, scroll or no scroll.*

"I can imagine," Javik said, scanning the terrain. "You've certainly managed to keep the planet clean," he added. "In view of our garbage, I mean." *I expected to see junk strewn all over hell,* he thought.

Prince Pineapple led them over a sturdy wooden bridge which traversed a dry creek bed. "What wonderful gar-bahge you Earthians have!" he exclaimed. *Oh, the foolishness I must endure!* he thought. *There is more to life than gar-bahge. There must be!*

Wonderful? Javik thought. *Is he being sarcastic?* "They tried landfills on Earth many years ago," he said. "But we ran out of space and had to catapult the stuff." A little light went on in Javik's head now as he put Abercrombie, the sacrifice hole, and the garbage together. *The same guy!* he thought. *What's he up to here?*

Facing a fork in the path just after they left the bridge, Prince Pineapple selected the left path, which led them into the forest. This was a narrow neck of woods, and through streaks of sunlight Javik could see a clearing not far ahead. Beyond that loomed a large gray structure. He heard crowd noises and the roar of powerful engines.

Presently they left the woods, stepping into full sunlight. The terrain was flat here, with a town of low buildings visible beyond the gray structure.

"Wait!" a little voice squealed from somewhere behind them.

"It's your little meckie," Evans said. "Welcome back, Wizzy."

Wizzy came out of the woods, moving along the ground in staggering spurts, resting and then scooting for very short distances. He glowed a dim, sickly yellow which appeared on the verge of extinction. When he arrived, Evans reached down and lifted him to her eye level. He felt warm and wet.

"The little guy's panting!" Evans said. "This is one complex meckie!"

"I have emotions too," Wizzy said proudly. "I am similar to you in many ways."

"Sometimes he forgets he's a meckie," Javik said, scowling at Wizzy. Javik's sea blue eyes flashed angrily.

"You take him," Evans said, handing Wizzy to Javik. "He's all sweaty." She wiped her hands on her jumpsuit.

As Javik accepted Wizzy, a strong gust of wind blew, drying the baby comet's surface. Surprised at how heavy Wizzy was, Javik noticed that his surface felt sandpaper-rough and lumpy. On closer inspection, he noticed little stones, pieces of dirt, and twigs embedded in Wizzy's stony skin. He brushed Wizzy's back, but the debris remained.

"A natural process," Wizzy explained. "I am beginning to accumulate material as my system feels able to assimilate it. That is how I grow in the physical sense." He glowed orange-hot, forcing Javik to let go quickly. Wizzy hovered in midair where Javik's hand had left him. His lumpy body became smooth and molten. Then he cooled, returning to dark blue.

Hesitantly, Javik retrieved him.

"We must hurry," Prince Pineapple said. "The king does not like to be kept waiting . . . waiting . . . waiting . . ." His voice slowed, and his black button eyes rolled upward. Desperately, he dropped to the ground on the seat of his checkered pants. He unsnapped the small folding shovel from his belt. His motions were painstakingly slow.

Three times Javik reached out with the hand that did not hold Wizzy, offering to help. Each time, Prince Pineapple shook his head negatively.

From his vantage point on Javik's hand, Wizzy watched the prince unwrap a slender barbed cord from the shovel handle. Then he removed one shoe and sock and wrapped the cord around his bare foot.

Catching Evans's gaze, Javik shrugged.

By now, Prince Pineapple was quite run down and an un-
healthy shade of pale brown. He unfolded the shovel and dug
in the soil between his outstretched legs. The ground was hard
here, permitting the prince only slow progress.

"Let me help," Javik said, touching the shovel handle.

Weakly, Prince Pineapple pushed him away.

"He is like me," Wizzy said. "I get awfully tired too."

The pineapple prince was leaning on the shovel now, breathing very slowly.

"He's more than just tired," Javik said. "It's like he has a
run-down battery."

"My foot," Prince Pineapple said, looking at Javik. "Help
me get it in the hole."

Javik set Wizzy on the ground and pushed the prince's
stubby leg until his wrapped foot was in the hole. As the foot
touched the freshly dug soil, Javik saw sharp barbs spring out
from the cord, stabbing into the ground like hungry roots.

Presently, the prince's breathing became more rapid. The
rich golden color returned to his face. "I shouldn't have tried
to go so long on my morning charge," he said with a deep
sigh. "Not on such an active day."

"You were right, Captain Tom," Wizzy said, hopping on
the palm of Javik s hand.

"We are Fruits of the soil," Prince Pineapple said with a
serene expression. "Children of Lord Abercrombie."

"That name again," Evans said.

Minutes later, Prince Pineapple's expression became angry
as he pulled his foot from the ground and unwrapped it. "I hate
myself for needing Lord Abercrombie," he said. "We are his
captives, you know, unable to lead our own lives." He wiped
his foot with a moist-pak towelette, then replaced his sock and
shoe.

"What do you mean?" Wizzy asked, jumping to Javik's
shoulder.

Prince Pineapple rose and wrapped the barbed cord around
the handle of his folding shovel. Then he replaced the items
on his belt clip. "Lord Abercrombie does not just give us
nutrition," he said. "With that comes the worst sort of
dogma . . . little statements from him to mold our opinions, to
make us revere him. He even comes to us in dreams! No rest!
He gives us no rest!" The prince grew silent, disturbed with
himself for saying too much.

When they resumed their course on the path, Javik noticed that Prince Pineapple's cadence had improved, having eliminated the wasted motions. One of the three synchronized suns was partially obscured now, having dropped below the horizon formed by the buildings ahead.

Catching up with the prince, Javik held Wizzy out for him to see. "This little lump of stone is Wizzy," Javik said, revealing only a little derision in his tone. "A mechanical unit."

Prince Pineapple glanced back at Wizzy only briefly, for he had more important matters on his mind. *King Corker is already unhappy with me,* he thought. *I must try to please him, just for tonight. Can't have him ordering me into detention. Not when I am so close.*

"I'm science officer on the ship," Wizzy said.

"Oh?" Prince Pineapple said. "That's very nice."

Javik smiled as he followed the prince. "Wizzy thinks he fulfills an important role on the ship."

"Can't you say anything nice about me?" Wizzy asked.

"Well," Javik said with a sneer. "I'll think very hard about that. Maybe I can come up with something, if I take long enough." He placed Wizzy back on his shoulder.

"Hrrrumph!" Wizzy said.

To their left beyond a small meteor crater Evans saw a throng of carrot men and women being led out of cattle chutes. Fruit guards prodded the carrot people with electric sticks, using the power of blue shocks to herd them toward a ramp. At the top of the ramp was an elongated piece of machinery with what appeared to be conveyor strips.

"What's that?" she asked.

"A power plant," Prince Pineapple said. "It's nearly dusk, and extra power is required to run the lights. The Vegetable slaves jog on a treadmill to generate electricity."

"What about solar power?" Javik asked. "With three suns, I would have thought—"

"No need for that," Prince Pineapple said. "This keeps the Vegetables busy . . . and in their places." *It might have been much worse for me,* he thought. *At least I'm a Fruit.*

Javik grunted. He heard boisterous crowd noises and the roar of engines clearly now. The sounds came from the vicinity of the towering gray structure, which was perhaps five hundred meters ahead. Seeing colorfully dressed spectators on top, Javik realized it was the back of an immense grandstand. To one side of the grandstand he saw blue and pink streaks and balls of flame, and heard the *pop-pop* of what sounded like gunfire.

"Many Earthians used to arrive in your gar-bahge cannisters, you know," the prince said.

"I know," Javik responded. "We ran out of burial space on Earth. I will apologize to your king, of course."

"No need for that. We have put the Earthians to good use."

"Oh?"

"I will show you," Prince Pineapple said. "Just ahead."

The path turned toward the grandstand. It was a wood frame thing, with horizontal rows of weathered, rough-hewn boards. In sunlight to one side, Javik focused on a group of male Earth humanoids with the same oversized heads as those in the Davis Droids. They wore glossy blue and pink uniforms and were gathered around unusual-looking land vehicles.

"The atmosphere here," Evans said to Javik, hearing her own words crackle nervously in the air. "Wizzy said it was different."

"Nurinium did it," Wizzy said from Javik's shoulder.

Javik scowled as they walked by. "Looks like they used old Earth parts to assemble these cars," he said. "That one has a DeMartini front end, but the rest looks like shop work."

Evans studied one vehicle as they passed close. It was Windsea blue and white, covered with dents, with mismatched body parts that had undergone extensive welding. The windshield glassplex was cracked, and none of the other windows had any glassplex at all. A large-caliber gun was turret-mounted on the roof, with smaller machine guns on each fender, two guns at the front and two at the rear. Three humanoids were looking in the engine compartment, speaking to one another in loud monotones.

A crowd roar drowned out the voices.

The three bulbous-headed humanoids paused to watch Javik and Evans with bloodshot eyes. Javik noticed they had yellow-stained teeth, like the "before" segment of a videodome tooth-paste commercial. Grape men guards rushed over and prodded them with electric sticks. Blue lances sprung from the tips of the sticks, jolting the humanoids to return to work.

"Those guards are Corkers," Prince Pineapple said. "Highest of the Fruit castes."

Javik counted six legs on each Corker. Grenache purple and rotund, they had plastic containers strapped to their backs.

One humanoid who had just been shocked into action donned a blue and black helmet and strapped it tight around his chin. Then he climbed through the window of the car and slid into the driver's seat. Seconds later, the vehicle roared to life, sending a huge streak of bright blue flame out of the tail.

This caught an inattentive Corker dead center, sending him rolling away. Singed and angry, he sprang to his feet and ran after the car. Another ball of flame sent him reeling.

"Damn fool Corker," Prince Pineapple muttered, watching the car speed away, heading for one of the drag strips. "Those fellows haven't got a lick of sense. Half the time they're out on their feet, drunk on the grain alcohol they carry in their packs. They're born tipsy, you know. I hear fermented grape juice runs through their veins."

"Your king is a Corker too?" Javik asked.

"We call these Earth Games," Prince Pineapple said, disregarding the query. He hurried along the path, adding, "Conceived in one of Lord Abercrombie's dream messages."

They rounded a corner of the grandstand, placing them out of view of the action. On this side the ground was littered with Corker backpacks and other debris. The prince kept looking up nervously at the grandstand. Then he yelled, "Look out!" and pushed Javik and Evans off the path.

A large bottle crashed to the ground where they had been, followed by two plastic backpacks, partially full. Wizzy scurried away from a big splash of dirty-colored grain alcohol.

"It gets a bit rough back here during the games," Prince Pineapple said.

An inebriated Corker approached, weaving from side to side on the path. Short and round with a plastic grain alcohol pack strapped to her back, the grenache purple Corker had peculiar, scaly skin with bumps on it like flattened grapes. As she neared, Javik heard odd sucking sounds. Looking closely, he noticed she was sucking at a tube that led from the backpack to her mouth. Black, brackish liquid dripped down her chin.

Prince Pineapple nodded dutifully to the Corker as they passed. She did not acknowledge the gesture, and instead coughed, hawked, and spit a ball of black phlegm on the ground.

Javik wrinkled his face in revulsion as the Corker passed. "Smelly little brute," he whispered to Wizzy.

Still on Javik's shoulder, Wizzy went into a discourse on the smelliest, most vile things in the universe. After less than a minute of this, Javik stuffed the little comet in his jumpsuit pocket and zipped it shut. From the pocket, Javik still heard Wizzy's muffled voice, saying something about the slime in which Esterian pigs liked to root.

"We must go faster," Prince Pineapple said, seeing shadows lengthen across the path.

They moved more quickly now, crossing a footbridge over a highway of vehicles that were pulled by carrot people. Each vehicle carried a different variety of Fruit person. Javik noticed that some of the carriages were a good deal more extravagant than others, with longer cabs, more silver or gold trim, and longer teams of carrot people.

Wizzy fell silent in Javik's pocket, realizing just then what had been done to him.

Javik asked about the vehicles.

"They reflect status in the Royal Family," Prince Pineapple said. "Every Fruit is a member of the Royal Family. The king has a carriage pulled by one hundred carrot men. No one is permitted to have more."

"I see," Javik said. *I wonder if they call it carrot power,* he thought.

"Carrot people are strongest of the Vegetables," the prince said. "Health fanatics. They make ferocious warriors for the enemy, excellent slaves for us."

"Who are your enemies?" Evans asked.

"The Vegetable Underground," Prince Pineapple said.

"Fruits against Vegetables?" Javik asked, bemused but trying not to show it.

"Since time immemorial," came the reply. "But it is not a perfect system. Even drunkard lowlifes such as the Corker we passed at the grandstand have a good deal of status . . . simply by virtue of their close juice relationship to our king."

They could see the castle now, at the crest of a Vegetable garden terraced hill. "We grow our own slaves," the prince explained.

The Corker castle was massive, constructed of native charcoal stones in the Earthian medieval manner. Imposing ramparts of dirt and stone surrounded the structure, and Javik counted eight guard towers on this side alone, each flying a triangular purple banner.

"What is your position?" Evans asked of the prince.

"Number One Adviser to King Corker. We Pineapples are

extremely intelligent—but not entirely appreciated, I fear."

"How so?" Evans asked, catching up with the prince and walking at his side.

"Important matters do not require brains here. Decision Coins are flipped. Whenever the king asks me for my opinion, I am expected to flip a coin."

"That sounds dumb."

"You think so too?" Prince Pineapple asked, pleased.

"Definitely."

"We pineapples might have taken control of the planet on the First Day . . . if the blight had not hit us. Things would be different today if only . . ." He hesitated.

"What happened?" Javik asked, catching up and walking on the prince's other side. *Planet of the Grapes,* Javik thought, making a play on an ancient, tattered paperback book Sidney once had shown him. It was one of the illegal things Sidney kept hidden in his safe.

"A strange malady," Prince Pineapple said. "Only affecting pineapples. Some say the Corkers . . ." He sighed.

"The blight was intentionally inflicted?" Evans asked. "A power grab?"

"I have said too much," Prince Pineapple said. *And I am supposed to be so intelligent!* he thought, raging inside.

"We will not repeat it," Javik said.

The prince's gaze flitted all over the place, like a moth near light. "I have been fortunate personally," he said, "though recently in disfavor with the king. That's why I'm so anxious to take you straight to his court. He has been most unhappy with me of late." *A half-truth,* he thought, recalling his clandestine plans for that evening.

They reached a section of uphill straightaway lined with high English hedges. Ahead, Javik saw a wide moat and the castle's main drawbridge.

"The Corkers were destined for power anyway," Prince Pineapple said, attempting to change his image to the Earthian visitors. "They are our best fighters, having six legs instead of two like the rest of us. This gives them great individual speed and mobility on the battlefield."

"The ones I've seen don't look so ferocious," Javik said. Glancing through an opening in the hedge, Javik saw a wrinkled old prune woman sitting on a wooden bench. She smiled softly at him. It was an all-knowing smile, a haunting smile, the sort of smile that numbed you with its intensity.

They crossed a drawbridge over a wide, murky moat, then stood at the castle gates. Javik saw watermelon men guards along the wall above. Looking back, Javik was disturbed to see the old Fruit woman staring at them from across the moat. "Who is that?" he asked.

"Just a prunesayer," Prince Pineapple said. "I think you would call her a soothsayer. I've heard the word in the Earthian vocabulary."

SIX

Morovia: A planet dominated by the police magician Lancaster IX. Linked through Dimensional Tunnels 901 and 902 across the universe to the planets Cork and Agrippa.

From *A Magician's History of the Universe*

Standing naked next to the dirt hole in his Soil Immersion Cavern, Lord Abercrombie mentoed the white rectangle on his wardrobe ring, activating a dry shower. The rectangular white stone on his AmFed ring glowed, giving him a low-level electrical tingle through the epidermis of his fleshy half. He watched dirt fall from his body.

Wait a minute, he thought, looking at the back of his hand. *A freckle just fell off too!*

He soon forgot about this and mentoed the ring's turquoise stone. A blue, yellow, and white striped caftan with gold scroll sleeves stitched itself over his half body. Following his form, the caftan covered only his right side. Extending his single foot, he watched a white crew sock and brown patent leather shoe appear there. Then he felt a crown of thistle circumnavigate the outer portion of his nearly bald half skull.

Lord Abercrombie glided regally across the cavern floor, passing cardboard boxes and plastic crates of recycled products, so numerous that he had only a narrow pathway through them. In the rock-lined passageway outside, it was the same, with finished products stacked to the ceiling on each side. He entered a complicated maze of rocky tunnels which he had committed to memory. This led to glassplex tunnels which his meckies had constructed for him. Through the clear glassplex, he could see ancient underground firebat caves and irridescent, multi-tiered waterfalls.

He floated by a wall sign that read "DON'T ABUSE IT! REUSE IT!" In a moment of sadness, he considered how tarnished was his success, limited only to making recycled goods. He had no distribution system. No other human in the universe knew the goods were there.

"I'm not a Job Support criminal!" he yelled into the empty glassplex tunnel. "It *is* fair to repair!" His words echoed down the passageway, heard by no human except himself.

Now he floated by caverns filled with robotics-operated machinery—hundreds of recycling machines forming the heart of his enterprise, each with a hopper on top. He paused to watch a yellow meckie load old clothing into a hopper. Behind the machine a noisy, loose-belted conveyor carried freshly wound spools of recycled thread to the boxing room meckies. Meckies in other rooms recycled plastics, metals, glass, and paper.

But it was quieter now than it had been, with many machines idle. He was running out of raw material.

Presently he entered a wide cavern which had three walls of mirror glassplex. The side opposite the doorway was a black abyss, the opening to the Dimensional Tunnel. Fifteen large trunks on wheels were chained together in a train at the center of the cavern, with a rock-filled dummy chained at the rear of that. A frigid galactic wind howled through this room, causing Lord Abercrombie's fleshy half to shiver.

Pausing to light a lavender tintette in front of the mirror, he used his human eye and the bank of visual sensors on his magical side to study the reflected inner workings of his head and neck: an exposed pink cerebrum and a cerebellum that throbbed as his arm moved with the tintette. There was a clear, glossy surface over the exposed inner parts, through which he saw his open nasal cavity, his half tongue and half mouthful of teeth surrounded on the fleshy outside by an ebony beard. Below that was a split windpipe with a pink, lumpy thyroid gland next to it.

I look like someone sliced me down the middle, he thought. *From my head all the way to the ground.* Lifting his robe with his single hand, he saw one leg hanging oddly by itself, just centimeters off the ground.

Trailing lavender tintette smoke, he glided past the trunks to the edge of the black abyss. Here the wind flapped his robe and howled with an eerie, hostile loudness. He saw the blackest black imaginable from this spot, so dark that Abercrombie knew no artist could ever match its pigmentation. The Dimensional Tunnel was a powerful thing, an awesome thing. Lavender smoke disappeared into the abyss. He tossed the tintette in too.

So many tests! he thought. *And what do I learn from them?*

He considered throwing himself into the Dimensional Tunnel at that very instant. In a wild flight of fancy, he imagined finding the tintette again and smoking it in some strange and distant place.

Surely I would land in a place where my enemies could not find me, he thought. *But what new dangers await me out there?* Throwing himself in the Dimensional Tunnel was but one of his options if he decided to remain a fleshcarrier. In another scenario, he would remain on Cork in his fleshy form, using salvaged Earthian disaster control equipment to impose his will on the planet and its inhabitants. But that reverse rain problem... and planetary magnetics. What did it all mean?

Wearily, Lord Abercrombie trudged to the lead trunk in the train. Grabbing a side handle on this trunk, he used it to pull all fifteen trunks and the dummy toward the Dimensional Tunnel. They rolled effortlessly.

Reaching the edge, he glided to the rear of the procession of trunks and gave them a mighty push. Sidestepping the dummy, he watched the lead trunk disappear into blackness, followed quickly by the others and the dummy.

Fwoosh! They were gone.

He thought of the option being tested here, a scenario whereby the trunks could be filled with recycled goods and a meckie, just enough trinkets and a helper to get him started comfortably in a new place. If he chose flesh. That was a very large "if."

Now he wondered, *Should I ride in front of the trunks? Or at the rear? How about inside one?* He knew there was no way to answer this question with such a limited experiment. He could not see the other end of the Dimensional Tunnel: His laboratory was universe-size. But the experiments gave him time to think. He was considering all the possibilities he could, preparing a mental balance sheet of flesh versus magic.

With his caftan flapping in the wind, he shouted into the blackness of the Dimensional Tunnel, "Is there another place for me out there?" The words barely touched his ears and tympanic sensors before they were gone, sucked into the howling abyss.

He worried about missing a greater opportunity, a higher calling. Maybe there was a beautiful planet waiting for him out there in the Great Beyond.

But what if every other place is taken? he thought. *I might be murdered as an intruder.*

The unknown terror nearly overwhelmed him.

"Why wasn't Cork taken?" he yelled. "Why was this place left for me?"

There was no answer, only the ceaseless, eternal howl of galactic winds.

His human side felt lonely. It was an intense loneliness, as deep and black as the universe itself.

In the box-lined passageway outside, Lord Abercrombie was stopped by a silver and black female meckie.

"Would you answer a question for me, please?" the meckie asked. A white dome light on its top pulsed.

"What is it?" Abercrombie snapped. He was irritated, for there were important matters on his mind.

"You are always speaking of the great joys and benefits of recycling," the meckie said. "But isn't that a new outfit you're wearing? Shouldn't you be wearing recycled clothes?"

"Report to Servicing!" Abercrombie commanded. "A meckie cannot be expected to understand such things!"

The meckie rolled backward, shocked at the outburst. Gears ground. Then, dutifully, the meckie retreated under the weight of Abercrombie's ferocious glare.

Moments later, Lord Abercrombie was in the history wall cavern, watching the blue linguistics meckie carve Abercrombie's story in the limestone with a sharp piece of obsidian.

"I didn't use cartoons, Lord," the meckie gargled. "That is in my artistic program, but I didn't think you wanted humor."

"This is fine," Abercrombie said, studying a straightforward pictorial depiction of him under pursuit by evil, white-robed sayermen.

"I'm getting to the time you found the Sacred Scroll of Cork."

"Good." Lord Abercrombie glided to another section of wall and studied the circle/magnetics symbol which was beneath a cartoon of a plant being. "This circle," he said. "Could it represent Cork?"

"A planet? Sure."

"And the magnetics part . . . Couldn't the whole symbol refer to planetary magnetics?"

"Hmmm . . . Yes. Very possible. Maybe that's what defeated the other magicians. An imbalance in planetary magnetics which prevented their magic from operating efficiently. Come to think of it, that could account for your problems with disaster control equipment, too. Your laser shots can't get around the magnetic disturbances."

"Where do you come off saying such things? You're just an artistically programmed linguistics meckie."

"Uh," the meckie gargled with synthetic nervousness. "I saw a math and science program lying on a table in Servicing—quantum mechanics, geology, advanced math. Kind of a shotgun tape on a lot of things."

Lord Abercrombie glared at the meckie.

"I asked for it, Lord."

"You asked for a program without checking with me first?"

"Yes, Lord," the meckie said timidly. "I'm sorry, Lord."

"Get your metal ass into Servicing," Lord Abercrombie said, shaking his head. "Then get back here and finish this project."

"Yes, Lord." The meckie placed its piece of obsidian on a wall ledge, then turned and whirred out of the cavern.

Rebo had only one name. This was the way it was far across the universe on the dimensionally connected planet of Morovia. One person, one name.

With his head bobbing, he loped on three legs in front of his small band of black-jacketed cutthroats. Dark brown hair covered his bulky body, with one stocky leg at the front and two at the rear—a tricycle arrangement of calloused paws instead of wheels, with a large oval head that jutted forward on a mane-covered neck, a knotlike, knurled chin, and wide, cuplike ears. An arm to each side of the front leg had six slender fingers, which he used on one hand to grasp a long knife. The polished steel blade glinted in low light from the street lamps which burned wearily overhead. This was a tired neighborhood on the Southside of Moro City.

Scraps of paper and a piece of yellow cloth swirled in a warm breeze at Rebo's feet. It was the height of the Morovian summer. He felt beads of perspiration all over his body, culminating in sticky pools of moisture at his arm and leg pits.

Pausing at a street corner, he glanced up to see a curtain move in a third-floor tenement window across the street. Someone was pulling it shut. Rebo dropped his gaze to the main level of the tenement, to Marnus's Flower Shop, one of many tiny mercantile businesses huddling side by side in the tattered block. The flower shop was dark, save for one light at the rear.

"Old Marnus can't hurt us," a woman's voice husked from behind Rebo. "Let's leave him alone." The only female in the gang moved to Rebo's side, brushing against him.

Glancing at Namaba in the low light, he saw her rest on her haunches. With soft, golden-brown hair and a long golden mane, Namaba wore the scaly black obbo skin jacket of the club, with its wide-winged grapple bird insignia across the back. A yellow ribbon with black polka dots adorned her mane.

"Blades!" Rebo said, disregarding her appeal.

With the exception of Namaba, the gang members drew knives and popped them open. Their red eyes reflected on the shiny steel.

Rebo glared at Namaba.

Reluctantly, she slipped a hand into her jacket pocket, bringing forth a pearl-handled switchblade.

Rebo gazed at her with the disdainful, detached stare favored by Southsiders. Impatiently, he grabbed her knife and snapped it open. "It's no good to you closed," he said. His lips parted into a cruel smile, revealing irridescent blue teeth that illuminated the shadows.

"He's just an old man," she said softly.

"He told the other shopkeepers not to pay our standard protection fee." Rebo's voice was cultured. "For that, he dies."

"We don't need to kill him. Why not just rough him up?"

"I need an example. One our people won't forget." The tone was resolute, indicating to her that his mind would not be changed easily.

Namaba knew she was in no position to question Rebo. He had saved her from the laboratory fire, and by Morovian tra-

dition this made him her lifelong master. There was no formal
law decreeing such a thing; it was a matter of maintaining self-
respect. Still, killing an old man did not seem the sort of activity
conducive to nurturing self-respect. Her conscience would bother
her long afterward, perhaps for the rest of her life. Rebo had
told her often that a conscience was nothing for a Southsider
to have. It was a meddling, unnecessary thing. Maybe he was
right.

Rebo's red-eyed gaze moved around the group, and he spoke
the club members' names in his thoughts: Kaff, the big one;
Yott, the lover; Howack, the small one with blond hair covering
his body; Namaba, the sensitive one; and Durl, the crazy one
who never knew when to stop hurting people.

"We rule the night!" Durl exclaimed. His glowing eyes
flashed crazily. He lunged and slammed a heavy chain into the
lamppost.

Rebo laughed. Durl always made him laugh.

Copycat laughter rolled through the group—except for Namaba. Rebo heard the chugging of their steam engine hearts
and heavy, matching breathing. He felt his own cardiopul-
monary system running roughly from the high excitement.

Now Rebo turned his head and bounded across the street.
As the others followed, he heard the clatter of their heavy
chains. He smelled familiar street odors here: raw sewage in
the gutter as he leaped over it, and the garbage of ripe fruit
and meats from a cluster of overflowing trash cans on the
sidewalk. A dog had its head buried in one of the cans.

Rebo kicked this can over for effect, spilling garbage across
the sidewalk and sending the dog fleeing. Rebo liked making
noise, and Namaba had once offered a plausible explanation:
It made others fear him.

Rebo used his calloused front foot to kick in the glass store-
front door, then glanced around as his gang fell in around him,
awaiting instructions. Their irridescent blue teeth and red-pup-
iled eyes reflected readiness. The big one known as Kaff swung
his chain and broke away the remaining spires of glass. Then
Kaff stepped to one side.

Rebo coiled on his haunches, then sprang through the doorway, making a beeline for the back office. Reaching the office,
he found himself in a small room full of books and papers,
with a wide, leafy potted plant in the corner to the right of the
door. It was a Parduvian flytrap plant. The old man had threat-

ened him with it once. *Imagine that!* Rebo thought at the memory. *Threatening me with a plant!* The room reeked of alcohol.

Old Marnus sat at a paper-littered dark mahogany desk in the light of a suspensor lamp, resting his front leg on the desktop. His calloused toes were twisted and yellow, possible evidence of martial arts training. Rebo had learned to look for such things.

Looking in from the doorway behind Rebo, Namaba saw that one of Marnus's hands held a pen, which the old Morovian had been using to make entries on a faded yellow ledger sheet. His body and facial hairs were silver-gray, except the scraggly beard had streaks of black in it which seemed curious to Namaba, like paint drippings on the old flower vendor's face. She touched Rebo's forearm.

Rebo pulled away to swat at a fly that buzzed in his face.

The insect flew away, settling on the large plant in the corner. *Wha-hoosha!* The plant made a powerful sucking noise, drawing the hapless fly into its center. Rebo felt cool air from somewhere.

"I have been expecting you," old Marnus said. The voice was throaty, with a chronic wheeze. He set down the pen with a note of finality, then reached for a brass alcohol flask. After taking a big gulp, he smiled, as though having won a bet with himself that he could swallow the liquid before Rebo made his move. It was common knowledge around the Southside that old Marnus loved to drink. Calmly, he replaced the flask on the desk.

Rebo felt his face flush with anger at the old Morovian's apparent unconcern in the face of obvious peril. His heart did not even seem to be chugging. But Rebo's was. He met old Marnus's defiant stare, then lunged across the room menacingly with his knife extended.

"Rebo!" Namaba yelled. "Please, Rebo!"

The old flower vendor did not flinch.

Rebo paused at the desk's leading edge, still staring. *Have to admire you, you old fool,* he thought. Smiling, he dug the knife into the desktop, flicking off a piece of dark wood. *Must have been a tough one in your day.*

For a fleeting moment old Marnus smiled in a kindly way, and Rebo felt himself returning the kindness with his own expression. They understood one another.

"Can I have him, Mr. President?" Durl asked, moving to Rebo's side. Durl fingered his chain.

"You popped the last one," Rebo said, leaning close to old Marnus and smiling cruelly. "This one's mine." He used the blade of his long knife to sweep the papers off the desk.

Marnus salvaged his flask.

Looking back, Rebo caught Namaba's anxious gaze. She shook her head. Her eyes begged Rebo not to kill. But he knew she would stay with him no matter what he did. It was her Morovian obligation.

Marnus raised the alcohol flask to his lips. But if he made a second bet with himself, he lost this one. Rebo's razor-sharp blade sliced open the front of his neck. The flask clattered to the floor.

The sound of releasing steam filled the room. Everyone ducked as old Marnus's body flew around the room like a discharging balloon, bouncing off walls and furniture. There was no blood, for no blood coursed through Morovian veins. Only air and water.

Presently old Marnus's limp and shriveled form landed on the floor by the desk in a gray woolly bag. His foreleg twitched.

"Search for cash and securities," Rebo barked. He did not know what the word "securities" meant. It was one of those words buried in his brain on this high vocabulary planet.

While the gang pulled open drawers and ransacked file cabinets for hiding places, Namaba knelt over Marnus's lifeless form. The odor of death permeated the room. It made her gag. Tearfully, she rose to her feet.

Rebo focused on the large potted plant in the corner. Namaba saw him staring at it. He moved toward it cautiously, saying, "Maybe the old buzzard hid his valuables in the plant."

A brass plaque on the plant's red brick pot read: "PARDUVIAN FLYTRAP." Crouching, Rebo dug in the dirt with his fingers, stepping around the plant as he did so. He tried to move the plant away from the wall, but it was too heavy to budge. So he reached to the back of the pot and dug there.

"Nothing here," he said, rising to his feet. He studied the central leaves, then inserted his knife blade between them.

The plant whooshed ferociously. Angrily, it seemed to Rebo. And cold air came from somewhere. He pulled his knife away just before the jaws snapped shut.

"Ha!" Rebo exclaimed.

"What are you doing?" Namaba asked, loping to his side. Wiping tears from her face, she said, "You think there's money in this thing?"

"Could be." He slashed at the base of the plant, but was unable to cut through its tough, fibrous skin.

Namaba tried to cut the leaves, also without success. Then she and Rebo tried to rock the pot. It did not move.

"Kaff!" Rebo yelled. "Yott! Give us a hand!"

They all tried to rock the pot, but still it did not budge. Kaff had the idea of pulling open the plant's jaws. Three large leaves comprised the jaws, and they opened easily. While the others held the leaves open, Rebo reached inside.

"It's cold in here," Rebo said. "And I can't find a bottom."

"Try a little deeper," Kaff said.

Rebo climbed up on the edge of the pot and reached way inside. "It oughtta be here somewhere, but I still don't feel it." So he stuck his head in and groped deeper. "It's cold in here!"

Seeing that Rebo's feet were in midair now, Namaba urged him to be careful.

Without warning, there was a loud *Wha-hoosha!* and the plant's jaws snapped shut around Rebo. This clamped the hands of Namaba, Yott, and Kaff between powerful leaves.

"Hey!" Rebo yelled, his voice hollow and distant. "Get me out of here!"

With great effort, Namaba and the others were able to pull their hands free. Then they tugged at Rebo's ankles, trying to free him. He screamed in terror. Namaba tried setting her paws against the pot for traction, but this did not help. Slowly, Rebo was being pulled deeper inside.

"Help me!" Rebo screamed.

"It's dragging him in!" Namaba said, panicky.

Now the rest of the gang joined in the desperate effort to save their club president. But with all their grunting and tugging, it did no apparent good. Rebo continued to disappear, a little bit at a time.

All gave up except Namaba. They told her it was no use. But she held Rebo's ankles, closing her eyes and steeling herself mentally and physically. It may have been her Morovian sense of obligation which provided such determination. But Namaba was the sort who might have done this for anyone.

"Give it up!" Kaff yelled. "He's lost!"

Opening her eyes, Namaba saw that only Rebo's ankles remained visible. Suddenly, the plant made a loud *Wha-hoosha!* sound and pulled Rebo and Namaba inside. The leaves snapped shut.

"They're gone!" Yott said.

"Let's go!" Durl yelled. "We gotta get outta here!"

Stumbling over one another, the survivors of Rebo's cut-throat gang ran away, leaving a ransacked office, the woolly remains of old Marnus, and a mysterious potted plant.

With his eyes closed, Rebo whirled through the bottomless vacuum of the Parduvian flytrap at hyper-light speed. He knew he was moving fast, perhaps too fast for Morovian flesh to survive. Cold air swirled past him, running along his face and down his neck, then along the bumpy length of his body, cutting through the thick hair that covered him. Knives of freezing cold cut into the skin, blades of air so frigid that they seemed hot. It was burning, searing cold. Unbearable cold.

Plates and lances of shadowy blue color raged across his brain, and he absorbed them like metal against ice. Short stretches of blackness followed, and then the frozen storms of shadowy blue returned. He felt the temperature dropping, until it seemed to Rebo that it could not possibly get any colder.

He wanted to shiver. But Rebo had no control over any of his bodily functions. Something pulled or pushed him along a great freezing tunnel. He sensed twinkling vastness all around. Or perhaps he saw dancing lights far ahead in the shadowy blue distance. He was not certain. Although his eyes were closed, he felt able to see something out there, at the dim reaches of his consciousness.

Rebo screamed but heard no sound. His brain fogged over, then contracted and swelled like a great undulating ocean wave. Something held fast to his ankles in a clawlike grip. He tried to shake free but could not. A smell of cleanness snapped his nostrils alive, then faded, leaving him with memories of the stinking filth back home in Moro City.

Now the twinkling vastness ahead focused into distant stars in the shape of old Marnus's face, laughing at him and drawing him inexorably forward. Through closed eyelids, Rebo saw bright green and blue planets in the foreground. Inexplicably, he passed through some of them. Suns flared white-hot like great growling beasts on each side. Worlds and their suns approached quickly and faded. Now the image of old Marnus's face neared, still laughing. Rebo passed right through the image, and then it was gone.

Rebo's body rolled into the shape of a three-legged fetus, then straightened for a time. Soon it resumed spinning, carrying him headlong through aeons or perhaps only seconds. He had no sense of time or space, only the sensation of eternity and vastness all around, pressing in on him and releasing him at the same moment.

Namaba released her grip on his ankles, and for a time they walked together in the vacuum place without touching ground. Then they ran and skipped, frolicking through the universe like young lovers. Presently she took hold of his ankles again and they spiraled over and over into the bottomless maw of the Parduvian flytrap.

A fly? Rebo thought, feeling Namaba's strong grip. *Is that all I am? A miserable speck of an insect?*

Strange, deep thoughts of life, love, and the meaning of existence touched him, but he forced them back. Gang leaders did not need to consider such matters. They were better left to Morovian philosophers, that odd breed who lived in another part of his world.

Before Rebo could sort out these disturbing new thoughts he sensed the warmth of soft yellow and orange colors in place of the harsh, shadowy blue storms. He began to feel warmer, sleepier. Then a tremendous red flash blasted across his eyelids, making him terribly hot, as hot now as he had been cold before. He knew he could not stand more heat. Even so, the temperature rose. To unimagined limits.

With Namaba still hanging tight, they spun at tremendous speed in a huge, clear tube. They spiraled from the center out, ending up in the outer ring. Here their speed slowed, and gradually Rebo was able to see objects outside the ring through the clear tube walls. It looked like a cave out there—an immense underground area with translucent spires and steeples of ice rock.

In slow motion, they passed a great stone chair upon which sat a bearded creature with a split head and body. On each side of the creature art objects were displayed that looked as though they had been fashioned from pieces of scrap: great hunks of iron and ragged, broken slabs of plastic tied together by wire.

The creature's half face was contorted in anger, and he screamed at them as they passed.

"Intruders!" the creature bellowed. Rebo did not understand this word.

Soon they had passed the creature. They picked up speed again, remaining in the outer tube. Objects in the caverns outside became a blur. Moments later they slowed again. Rebo recognized the surroundings, for they were back in front of the half-faced one, passing in slow motion while he yelled at them in a language Rebo did not understand.

"Intruders!" Lord Abercrombie screeched. "No one will steal my domain!" Then he laughed, and his laughter seemed to echo across the universe. Rebo wanted to plug his ears, but could not move his arms.

This recurred perhaps thirty times. Each time the creature laughed, and each time he hurled a menacing epithet at them. Rebo had never seen anything like this in the Southside. Nor had he imagined what the universe outside his world was like. He was not surprised at what he saw, for he held no preconceived notions about how such things were supposed to be.

He became aware of a change. Cool air rushed across his body, and he was no longer in the clear outer ring of the great spiral. Now he flew headfirst through a wide, black tunnel, with Namaba still holding fast. *Up*, he thought, judging from the pressures on his body.

A blinding flash of light forced his eyes shut. He lapsed into unconsciousness. When he awoke moments later, Rebo found himself face down on a dirt surface with his front leg bent to one side. Namaba lay behind him, still grasping his ankles. From the aches in his body, it seemed to Rebo that he and Namaba had been through an eternity together.

Namaba let loose her grip on Rebo and pulled herself up. When Rebo saw her terrified expression, he felt it must be a reflection of his own: a grimace with wide-open, burning eyes that flitted nervous glances in all directions. She was breathing hard, with intermittent gasps. He heard her steam engine heart chug, and felt his own doing the same.

Rebo felt his chest swell and drop irregularly. A great tenseness climaxed inside him and released, leaving him limp and drained—a deep weariness such as none he had ever before experienced. It was worse than the time he had run from the police for two hours with no opportunity to catch his breath.

Steam came out of Namaba's ears.

That was a faraway place, Rebo thought, looking around at the terrain. They were on a wide, dusty path, with the marks of many feet on the powdery surface. Lining the path were cream-colored upright cannisters which had red, yellow, and blue markings. He remembered seeing cannisters like them before. Two had landed in Moro City the year before, right in the middle of Nelson Park. The police had arrived quickly to take the cannisters away, and Rebo had never heard of them again.

In the low light of dusk, the gaze of her red eyes met his. He followed her gaze to the edge of a cavernous black hole that was around twenty meters to Rebo's left. He surmised that they must have traveled through it to reach this place.

"Where do you think we are?" Namaba asked. The question seemed ridiculous to Rebo. How could either of them know?

Rebo felt perspiration forming on his hair-covered body. Rising to all threes, he removed his club jacket. He became conscious of a stream of opposites during the moments of his journey: freezing and heat, cleanness and filth, seconds like aeons, speed and tremendous, painstaking slowness. As he set the jacket on the ground, he felt his breathing become slower and more even.

Namaba's terrified expression changed to one of curiosity. Beyond the cannisters she saw that they were in a large clearing, surrounded by a thick forest of pine trees.

Their jutting heads moved in unison to watch a white glider plane fly gracefully over the opposite side of the clearing. The plane disappeared below the treetops for a time. Then it rose once and dropped again, not reappearing.

Rebo focused on a tall metallic cylinder on the opposite side of the clearing below the last sighting point of the glider. At the *coo-roo-coo* of a bird, he turned his head. In the piney woods behind them, a big-beaked green bird was perched on a tree branch. The bird flapped its wings rhythmically.

I am a murderer, Rebo thought. He became angry at the thought. *I don't need to think of such things! They are of no consequence to me!* He recalled chiding Namaba often for letting her conscience get in her way.

Namaba was saying something, but Rebo did not hear the words. When he became aware of her, she was pointing across the clearing at the big cylinder. "Let's see what it is," she said.

Minutes later, in fast approaching darkness, they were ransacking the *Amanda Marie*, tossing gear and supplies all over the cabin and out the open hatch.

"Odd food," Rebo said, biting into a chocolate bar, wrapper and all. "I don't like the covering."

"I don't either," Namaba said. She removed the wrapper from her candy bar and discarded it. "Better this way," she said.

As they reached a frenzy of consumption, fine, steamy mist poured from their noses and ears and their steam engine hearts purred at peak efficiency. Soon particles of food were escaping from the pores of their skin in the form of dark brown, powdery waste products. It was so dark now that they could barely see their way around the cabin, even with the aid of their glowing red eyes. They lay their bloated bodies down on the corrugated metal deck and went to sleep.

SEVEN

One of my great disappointments lay in the decadence of the Corker ruling class. Debauchery seemed imprinted in their Fruity souls.

> Comments made by Felix
> the Magician after
> abandoning Cork

While waiting for the castle's main gate to open, Javik looked beyond the old prunesayer to the Corkian sunset. The sky along the horizon was color-splashed, with a craggy ridge of clouds there resembling mountains. They glowed pastel pink, imitation mountains with dirty blue bases. Seconds later, like a chameleon, the range had become dirty white and silver. As voices called out from the guardwalk above, the sky and its clouds changed to dark gray.

"Who goes there?" a guard asked.

Prince Pineapple identified himself, then said to Javik with a smirk, "They can see me clearly, but always call out like that anyway. Consummate idiots!"

The heavy wooden gate cranked up, creaking and straining as it went. When it was fully open, Javik saw the mechanism behind the gate: large stone gears and ropes pulled by zucchini men slaves turning a wheel on the walkway above.

As the prince strode briskly into the castle, two Corker guards greeted him, saluting with a touch of their right thumbs to the center of their foreheads. Prince Pineapple duplicated the gesture.

"This way," Prince Pineapple said, looking down at his smaller Earthian companions. He hurried them across a gold-inlaid, white slate courtyard. The courtyard had a well in the configuration of a six-pointed star at the center, with a star-shaped frame of tomato and green bean vines surrounding it.

A marble-floored corridor beyond that had, at every doorway, two Corker guards holding electric sticks. They stood nearly motionless, moving their moist purple mouths only a little to suck at grain alcohol tubes.

Rounding a corner with the prince, Javik focused on elegant carved double doors directly ahead.

"The king's court," Prince Pineapple said.

The doors swung open as they neared, activated by rubber supermarket-door pressure pads at their feet. The court was full of Fruit people of every variety, chattering idly in a crescendo of idiocy. These people were dressed gaudily, with ornate pompadour leaf wigs in all the pastel colors. All sported white gloves, and many peered haughtily through monocles. To Javik, they looked like overdressed characters from an AmFed cartoon movie.

When the prince and his guests entered the room, the court grew quiet, with the members moving to the walls and talking in hushed tones. This exposed a purple and gold strip of synthetic Persian carpet at the center of the room. Puffing his chest out theatrically, Prince Pineapple strutted down the center of the carpet toward an unoccupied, gilded throne which rested on a wide platform.

A tinny bell rang from somewhere in the room.

"King Corker has been notified," Prince Pineapple said, stopping in front of the throne. He removed his helicopter beanie.

Two scantily clad peach girls pranced out from side doorways at each side of the throne. They pranced on tiptoes to the front of the throne, then began an undulating belly dance. It was an exotic display of potbellies and synchronized, pulsating folds of fat.

"Delectables from the king's harem," Prince Pineapple said.

The peach girls circled one another, trailing sheer black veils from their fingertips. Then they spread their pudgy legs and stretched back, swaying their arms gracefully. One of the girls had difficulty with this maneuver. Struggling to bend her back and touch her forehead to the floor behind her, she lost her balance and tumbled over.

Javik suppressed a smile as the peach girl staggered clumsily to her feet. The performance was bad, so bad in fact that he wanted to turn off the videodome switch. If only one had been handy!

"Yay mish-mish!" a Corker guard yelled, raising his electric stick high in the air exuberantly.

"Yay mish-mish!" all the men in the court yelled. Prince Pineapple joined in halfheartedly.

"What does that mean?" Javik asked. He shook his language mixer pendant. It seemed to be operating, but was not translating these words.

"Oh, what a peach!" Prince Pineapple said, surprised at the question. "I think it's one of your Earthian languages."

"Mmmm!" another Corker guard yelled. "Juicy Fruities!"

"Mmmm!" all the court's men yelled. "Juicy Fruities!"

Looking around, Javik noted that all the men in the court except Prince Pineapple were watching the peach girls with lust-inflamed eyes. The prince seemed almost not to notice them, and to Javik he had the appearance of one deep in thought, shouldering some great burden.

What foolishness, Prince Pineapple thought. *What a complete and utter sham!* He glared at the base of the throne.

"All kneel!" a casaba melon doorwoman called out.

The peach girls stopped dancing abruptly and fell to their knees at each side of the throne.

Following the others in the court, Javik and Evans knelt. Javik watched out of the corner of his eye as the king entered through one of the side doors.

Just then, Wizzy flew out of Javik's pocket and alighted on Javik's shoulder. "Took a little snooze," Wizzy announced too loudly. The words echoed around the room. He yawned in a loud, mouthy moan, stretching his lumpy body.

"Shhhh!" Javik whispered.

King Corker was a very large grape man in a ruffled white blouse and tight red pants, with scaly, grenache purple skin and six stubby legs like the other Corkers. But King Corker was much larger than other Corkers, perhaps twice their size. He wore an oversized grain alcohol backpack, and with one pudgy hand pulled the pack's plastic tube out of his mouth. Syrupy black liquid dripped from the tube down the front of his ruffled blouse. He appeared unconcerned about this.

As the peach girls undulated their thick arms in welcoming gestures, King Corker padded across the platform on red slippers. When the king hopped on his throne, Javik was intrigued at how neatly his six legs stacked on top of one another as he sat. The king sucked on his alcohol tube and stared down dispassionately with his black button eyes at Javik.

Prince Pineapple rose, pulling Javik and Evans up with him. "Visitors from Earth, Sire," he said, staring at the floor.

He doesn't even meet the king's gaze, Javik thought. *This prince is not to be trusted.*

"From Earth? From Earth?" King Corker said. "There is mirth from Earth?"

Prince Pineapple did a high backflip at the royal rhyme, clicking his heels as he went over. Everyone in court followed suit, even ladies in petticoats, like a mass automatic reaction—with the exception of Javik, Evans, and the king.

"Tell me a story," King Corker said petulantly, looking at Javik with a pouting smile across his wide mouth.

"You mean about why we're here?" Javik asked.

"Suffering souplines!" King Corker exclaimed angrily. He glowered at Prince Pineapple. "You didn't inform them that I like stories?"

"Uh, sorry, Your Majesty," Prince Pineapple said, obviously flustered. "I . . . uh . . . was overly concerned about the gar-bahge." Under King Corker's increasingly ferocious glare, Prince Pineapple leaned close to Javik and said in a cracking voice, "Tell him your funniest story. King Corker loves to laugh."

"Oh!" Wizzy squealed, jumping high in the air over Javik's shoulder and then landing back on the shoulder. "I like to laugh, too! Ha-ha-ha! A-ha-ha-ha-ha-hee!"

Javik winced.

"Shush, Wizzy!" Evans whispered. "Not now!"

King Corker appeared on the verge of exploding into anger. He drummed a forefinger impatiently on the arm of his throne.

"Does he mean a joke?" Javik asked, looking sidelong at Prince Pineapple.

"Anything. But make it quick. It's rude to keep funny things from our king."

"Well," Javik said, scratching the back of his neck, "here's one I heard a few weeks back. Once during the Atheist Wars,

General Ishmael Roberts . . . he was the founder of our American Federation Space Patrol, Your Majesty." Javik paused, expecting a nod from the king.

King Corker scowled. He sucked at his alcohol pack.

"Hurry!" Prince Pineapple whispered. "Get to the punch line!"

"I was just giving him a little background. Aw, Cha-rist!" Javik sighed, then resumed his story: "General Roberts was asked by a neighbor in his condominium building about the placement of key AmFed warships in deep space. It was a thoughtless question, touching upon highly classified information. Anyway, General Roberts leaned close to the questioner's ear and asked, "Can you keep a secret?'"

Javik glanced around the court, assuring himself that all ears were tuned in, hanging on his every word.

"Yes?" King Corker said, pursing his moist lips like a spoiled child about to receive another gift.

"Hurry," Prince Pineapple said nervously.

"You can't hurry a story," Javik snapped. "Timing is the whole thing. Anyway, Your Majesty, this neighbor was very eager, and he said, 'I sure can, General.' So General Roberts smiled and said, 'Well, so can I.'" Javik studied the king's face.

King Corker did not crack a smile. He sat motionless, appearing confused at the tale.

The silence of death permeated the court.

Javik shuffled his feet.

"I warned you, get to the punch line," Prince Pineapple said in a desperate tone. "Please!"

"That was it," Javik said. He shrugged, then glanced at Evans.

She shook her head and rolled her eyes upward.

Prince Pineapple covered his face with his hands. Cautiously, he peered through stubby fingers at the king.

King Corker's jaw had fallen in incredulity.

"Try another one," Evans urged. "One of those bawdy barroom stories."

"I thought the king might prefer something more highbrow," Javik muttered.

"That was an awful story," King Corker said. He thought for a moment. "So awful that it was funny." He laughed uproariously.

A floodgate of laughter broke loose across the court. This became a tittering of glee that died down when the king stopped for a breath and then started to roll again when the king resumed laughing.

Such fools, Prince Pineapple thought. *This court is full of mindless puppets.*

"Ho!" King Corker said. "Very clever, Earthian. And now I will tell *you* a story."

The court fell silent. Everyone leaned forward so as not to miss a word of the king's tale.

"Shall I tell a riddle or a joke?" King Corker mused, gazing playfully at the ceiling.

A watermelon man in a bright gold buttonless suit hurried to the king's side. The watermelon man flipped a large gold coin in the air, caught it in one hand, and pressed it against the back of the other hand. "A riddle, Sire," he reported. "Lord Abercrombie wants a riddle."

"Our planet God has spoken!" the court intoned. Javik saw Prince Pineapple's lips move, but no sound came from them.

I have a good pineapple brain, the prince thought. *We have no need for Decision Coins. Look at our pitiful king, consulting with a melonhead.*

"Very well," King Corker said, watching the watermelon man hustle to a position along the wall. "A riddle: Why can't Vegetable Underground troops go on a break for longer than five minutes?" He chuckled.

I have heard this story so many times, Prince Pineapple thought wearily. *And we're always expected to laugh.*

Javik looked around, then back to the king. King Corker looked like a fat, purple man about to burst with mirth.

A wave of tittering rolled through the court.

"Gosh," Javik said with a silly grin. "I don't know that one."

"Any longer," King Corker said, "and they'd have to be completely retrained!" He spit the words out with an exploding laugh, then howled with glee to the point where tears ran down his scaly cheeks. The peach girls dabbed his face with tissues. This must have been very cheap tissue, for little pieces of it stuck to the king's skin.

As Javik looked on in amazement, the entire court fell into a pandemonium of laughter. Fruits held one another up and repeated the punch line endlessly. "Did you hear that?" they asked. "The V-U's would have to be completely retrained!"

"Ah, ha-ha! Oh boy!" they said.

"That was a good one!"

"Those stupid Vegetables!"

After the peach girls stepped away from King Corker, he looked at Javik and asked, "Did you like my story, Earthian?"

Javik laughed halfheartedly and heard Evans do the same. "Very much, Your Majesty," he said. "It was hilarious."

"We hate Vegetables here, Earthian," the king said. "They are stupid, foolish creatures."

"Vegetables are dumb," the court chanted.

"And bitter, bitter, bitter," the men of the court yelled with deep voices.

"But Fruits are sweet," the ladies responded.

"Fruits are neat," everyone said.

The court grew silent. Then the peach girls fluttered out a side door, trailing their black veils.

"We have a saying here," King Corker said. Raising a forefinger in the manner of a Freedom Studies instructor, he added, "And it is very important." His head bobbed from the profound truth of this as he said, "'Once a Vegetable, always a Vegetable.' There is no hope for them, Earthian, except as servants."

Javik nodded.

King Corker sucked on his grain alcohol tube, dripping brackish ooze down his chin. A glazed, drunken look came over him. "I watched your ship come down," he said. He raised a hand, then dropped it.

Two watermelon men moved quickly from their wall positions to the sides of the king's throne. Upon reaching the throne, one of them flipped a Decision Coin, then whispered in the king's ear. Then the other watermelon man flipped a different coin, and he too leaned over to pass along a bit of wisdom to the king.

King Corker nodded, then waved both of them away.

"Our planet God has spoken!" the court intoned.

"Curious-looking creatures, these Earthians," King Corker said, looking from Javik and Evans to the prince. "Suppose I shouldn't say that. They do resemble the way Lord Abercrombie looked before his transformation."

"That wouldn't be *Winston* Abercrombie?" Javik asked, looking into the king's black button eyes.

"One and the same," King Corker replied irritably.

"Earth criminal!" Wizzy exclaimed.

"What is that on your shoulder?" King Corker asked. He spit a ball of phlegm into a brass spittoon. The spittoon rang.

"An embarrassment," Javik said, reaching for Wizzy.

Wizzy jumped away, hovering in the air. Javik grabbed for him, but the little comet flew just beyond his reach.

"Abercrombie came here to recycle," Wizzy said, glowing red. "A terrible crime. The Sayerhood came to return him for justice, you know. But they never found him."

"Wizzy, we don't care about all that!" Javik barked. "Now come back here!"

But Wizzy flitted away, just beyond Javik's grasping fingers.

Javik glanced at the king nervously. King Corker's face was a dark shade of angry reddish purple. He leaned forward on the throne, apparently having difficulty formulating a sentence. Little sentence bursts came out: "That thing . . . is not . . ." He tugged at the tube of his grain alcohol pack. The tube came off, squirting dark liquid all over him. "Get this off me!" he thundered.

The watermelon men moved quickly to his aid, pulling the backpack off their foundering king. His white lace shirt was a mess, completely soaked in black ooze. Under different circumstances, Javik might have thought this a comical sight. But there was nothing funny about the moment.

"I sense danger from Abercrombie," Wizzy announced, oblivious to the king's discomfort and rage. "He hates Earthians now, especially Uncle Rosy. And wants revenge for his failure."

"Silence!" Javik said.

"But isn't this your assignment, Captain Tom?" Wizzy asked, his voice an intolerable singsong. "To find any dangerous conditions and report them to Mission Control?"

"This is not the time or the place," Javik said. He lunged unsuccessfully at Wizzy.

"Enough!" King Corker thundered. "I will not tolerate disruptions!"

"You'd better control that thing," Prince Pineapple whispered to Javik.

Javik nodded. He inched toward Wizzy.

Undeterred, Wizzy said, "Winston Abercrombie was the AmFed Garbage Thrust Commandant. More than a decade ago—"

"You asked me about emotions," Javik said in a gentle tone, inching closer to Wizzy. The court was ominously silent, making Javik's words seem loud. "I want you to feel one now," he said. "That emotion is *fear*."

"Fear?" Wizzy said, moving out of Javik's range. "What is that?" He glowed red as he searched his memory banks. "Ah, here it is: 'apprehension concerning one's physical well-being.'"

Javik lunged for Wizzy while he was thus occupied and caught him. Feeling the intensity of all eyes in the court, Javik said, "I'm sorry." He stuffed Wizzy into his jacket pocket. "We obtain data from the device . . . but it's not functioning properly now." He felt his face flush hot with blood.

Wizzy became silent as Javik zipped his pocket shut.

"Check that thing out," King Corker said to Prince Pineapple.

"Yes, Your Highness." Prince Pineapple extended his hand to Javik. "Give it to me," he said.

"Gladly," Javik said. He unzipped the pocket and handed Wizzy over. "This thing's more trouble than it's worth."

While Prince Pineapple studied Wizzy, Wizzy glowed bright orange, becoming too hot for the prince's sensitive fingers.

"Ow!" Prince Pineapple said angrily, letting go of Wizzy. "It's hot!"

Javik shook his head in dismay.

Wizzy flew around the king's throne, then became dark blue and returned to alight on Prince Pineapple's shoulder.

"It's okay," Javik said. "He's not hot now."

Prince Pineapple looked warily out the side of one eye at the lumpy object on his shoulder. It was rather heavy.

Wizzy did not move or make a sound.

"Now," King Corker said, looking first at Javik, then at Evans. His eyes flared. "You are here about the gar-bahge, I presume." Javik noticed the affected pronunciation again. Apparently it was done to make trash sound cultured.

"Yes, Your Majesty," Javik said. "We're very sorry about it. The President of our American Federation of Freeness has asked me to extend his personal apology."

"Yes, yes," the king said impatiently.

"He has authorized me to send cleanup crews."

"Cleanup crews?" King Corker said, surprised. His eyebrows lifted in astonishment. "What on Cork for?"

"Why, to clean up the garbage . . . to take it away."

"We don't want it cleaned up!" the king said, glaring at Prince Pineapple. "Didn't you explain anything to him?"

"We didn't discuss the crisis in great detail, Sire. I thought you might prefer—"

"We want more gar-bahge, Earthian!" King Corker howled, directing a scalding glare at Javik. "Is that clear?" He thumped a clenched fist on the arm of his throne. "We want *more!*"

"I—I didn't expect . . ." Javik was stammering. "No one thought . . . I mean . . ." He looked desperately at Evans for support.

She looked away.

"We have a serious shortage of gar-bahge," Prince Pineapple said, looking at Javik. "In the past there was always enough for all. Our stores were full. There was plenty for Lord Abercrombie. But now, even the royal gar-bahge is threatened."

"How terrible," someone in the court said. Then a murmuring followed: "How terrible. How terrible."

"When can we have more gar-bahge, Earthian?" King Corker asked.

"Uh, I wasn't authorized to . . . uh, I mean . . ."

"An *underling,*" King Corker muttered. "I do not deal with *underlings.*"

"I have an idea," Javik said. "Why don't you manufacture new things, then smash the stuff around? You know, make dents, scratches, mangles, and rips."

King Corker's eyes widened. "You must be daft, Earthian. Imported gar-bahge is the only thing to have. Can't you see that?"

"Uh, sure. Then maybe I could arrange for more garbage. I'll go back to Earth and see."

"Go back?" King Corker smiled cruelly. "You aren't going *back,* Earthian. I know of such tricks, you see. You would bring warships."

"Oh no," Evans said hurriedly. "We wouldn't think of that!"

"No," Javik said. "We're from the government, and we're here to help you."

"One of the three biggest lies in the universe," King Corker said, recalling a sheet of paper in his royal funny file.

Javik's mouth opened in shock. He shuffled his feet.

"Your Decision Coin," King Corker said, looking at Prince Pineapple.

With Wizzy still on his shoulder, the prince fumbled in his pockets. Eventually he produced a large golden coin like the ones used by the watermelon men.

"Give it to the Earthian captain," King Corker instructed.

Prince Pineapple obeyed, then glanced sidelong at Wizzy.

Wizzy's cat's eye dimmed drowsily, so that it was only halfway open.

Javik studied the coin. Despite its size, it was very light in weight. Probably made of an alloy, he surmised. On one side was the bust of a human man's face bearing a stern, fatherly expression. Javik recognized it as Winston Abercrombie. Around Abercrombie were the smiling faces of Fruit people. The word "YES" was engraved in Corkian below the bust.

"Lord Abercrombie," Prince Pineapple said in a low tone.

Javik turned the coin over. The other side depicted a cluster of Vegetable faces surrounding a carrot man in a baseball cap. Below that was engraved the word "NO."

"And Brother Carrot," Prince Pineapple whispered. "The Evil One."

"Flip it," King Corker said.

Javik hesitated. "But what . . . ?"

"Flip it!"

Javik shrugged and tossed the coin high in the air. It clanged to the floor and rolled around at his feet.

Prince Pineapple looked at the coin. Then he retrieved it, while Wizzy used magic suction to cling to his shoulder. "Yes, Your Majesty," he said, stuffing the coin in his pants pocket. "It decided yes."

"Our Planet God has spoken," King Corker said reverently.

Then the court intoned, "Our Planet God has spoken."

It was a wondrous, charmed moment for everyone except Prince Pineapple and the visitors from afar.

"To the games!" King Corker shouted. Smiling, he looked at Javik and Evans, adding, "One Manno, one Wommo."

Prince Pineapple looked sadly at the watermelon advisers who stood nearby, recalling a time not so long before when King Corker had listened more to him. Until court politics turned against the prince. *Now I am Number One Adviser in title only,* he thought. *And soon he will take the title. What do*

I care anyway? This foolishness is not for me.

"Did you hear me, Prince Pineapple?" the king asked.

"Yes, Sire. But I wonder if . . ." Prince Pineapple stared at the ground, then looked past the king at the wall.

"What are you trying to say?"

"I just wonder if another course of action might not be appropriate."

King Corker was displeased. He balled both hands into tight, pudgy fists. "Another course of action?" he said. "You question the Decision Coin?"

"No, but perhaps we did not need to flip it."

Wizzy released a loud snort. He was sleeping fitfully on Prince Pineapple's shoulder.

Prince Pineapple hesitated, then said, "The Earthians are our guests, Sire. Emissaries from another planet."

"So what?"

"I'm not sure they should be enslaved, Your Majesty. There might be repercussions."

Enslaved? Javik thought. *In this place?* He sneaked a glance at his service pistol, holstered on his hip.

"Such as?" King Corker asked. "We already have a shortage of gar-bahge. What could be worse than that?"

Wizzy snorted again, then fell into a buzz saw of snoring. He tipped a little on the prince's shoulder.

Javik shook his head. "That damned Wizzy," he muttered.

"Stop it!" Prince Pineapple said to Wizzy, giving Wizzy a shove.

Wizzy clung to his perch and snorted again. Then he grew silent.

Prince Pineapple looked at the king, saying, "Enslaving them might destroy our last hopes of getting more gar-bahge. It could *force* Earth to send warships."

"You argue with me? And with the coin?"

Prince Pineapple bowed nervously. "No, Sire. I am merely advising you. I thought that was my function here." *I'm pushing it,* he thought. *Shouldn't do that, especially in public.*

"The decision has already been made. There is a declining Earthian population here, with no means of reproduction. We once had eight hundred and fifty thousand of them. How many remain?"

"Less than fifteen thousand, I believe."

"Closer to ten. The games take their toll. How will we be entertained when the games are over? Answer that one, *Adviser*."

Prince Pineapple hung his head.

"Take them!" King Corker ordered. "Now!"

"Yes, Your Majesty," Prince Pineapple said. He bowed obediently. This time, Wizzy fell off the shoulder.

"Aargh!" Wizzy grunted as he hit the floor. "Can't anyone take a nap around this place?"

Prince Pineapple retrieved Wizzy, then grabbed Javik's arm. "Come with me," he said.

"Like hell!" Javik said. He placed a hand on his holstered service pistol.

"You will be given an opportunity to survive, Earthian," King Corker said. "They are games of skill."

"And what are these games?" Javik asked, keeping his hand against his gun handle.

"You will learn soon enough," King Corker said. He motioned, and six bulky pear man guards surrounded Javik and Evans. A pear man put his hand on Javik's pistol, but Javik pushed the hand away.

"We'll take that," the pear man said. Then two pear men held Javik's arm while another reached for his gun.

Javik fought back, but was pushed to the floor. "Evans!" he yelled.

But Evans remained motionless. "It's no use," she said.

Javik was nearly squashed under a mass of Fruit flesh. He lost the gun. Struggling to his feet afterward, Javik glared around. King Corker was staring at him with cold, black button eyes.

"They are Earth games," the king said. "You should find them familiar."

Lord Abercrombie's fleshy half was tired, and he decided to go to bed early. Wearily, he rose from the black satin cushions of his throne and floated out of the main chamber.

He went down one box-lined passageway, made a left, then took another left. Soon he stood in the doorway of the Servicing cavern. He saw the blue linguistics meckie being worked on by two black and white repair technician meckies.

"I want that science program and anything else you have on geology, magnetics, astronomy, and disaster control," Lord

Abercrombie said in a loud voice.

The repair technicians stopped working and listened while Lord Abercrombie spoke.

He continued, "Program the whole works into that yellow meckie in the corner."

"Yes, Lord," one of the repair technicians said.

"And tell it to report to me first thing in the morning."

Lord Abercrombie turned and went to his bedroom chamber.

EIGHT

Some thoughts are never spoken.
These are among the most important

*Quotations From Uncle
Rosy,* page 18

Javik and Evans were separated when they left the king's court.
Four pear men pushed and dragged Javik down a long, dimly
lit corridor. The walls, ceiling, and floor were polished agate
stone in varying shades of amber and brown. Javik slipped
twice on the smooth floor, then took shorter, more careful steps.
A hunger pang shot through his midsection.

Reaching a wide spot in the corridor, they stopped. One of
the pear men slid open a rectangular metal lid on the floor,
revealing a dark compartment below. Javik heard the dull whir
and thud of machinery. He smelled rubber.

"In here," the pear man said.

Javik struggled, but the bottom-heavy Fruits were stronger
than they looked. They forced him through the opening.

Javik fell a short distance after they let go, slamming his
head and shoulder against a hard rubber surface. Realizing that
the surface was moving slowly, he guessed he was on a conveyor. Machinery whirred loudly, and now the rubber smell

was very strong. Faint illumination from the hatch opening faded. Looking up, Javik saw the lid slide back over the opening, leaving only a thin halo of light there. Soon he lost sight of the halo as the conveyor carried him away.

Another odor touched his nostrils next, a repulsive odor. "It stinks in here!" he mumbled. He shuddered at the realization of what it was. *Decaying flesh,* he thought, recalling a number of burial details on which he had served. And he recalled the odor of the creature in the Davis Droids.

Crouching in the darkness, Javik tried to think of his next move. The holster on his hip was light, evidence that it was empty. The rubber floor stopped now, falling silent. He heard a thunderous crowd roar above, and felt the floor shake.

Something rustled nearby, behind and to the left.

Javik whirled to face that direction, clenching his fists and extending them.

Then he heard other rustlings, from other directions. "Manno," he thought someone said, from his left.

Then he heard it again, a clear monotone: "Manno."

Javik recalled the King's words: *"One Manno, one Wommo."*

The sounds drew closer, and the disgusting odors became intolerably strong.

Javik crawled to his right, then sensed breathing on that side. They were all around him. Terrified, Javik curled into a defensive, fetal ball.

"Manno!" they yelled in monotones.

"Manno!"

"Kill the Wommos!"

Javik twitched at each utterance, expecting to feel humanoid hands on him at any moment. His body was rigid, and he felt the tautness of his arm, leg, and chest muscles. His heart was like a sledge inside: Boom-da-dee-boom! Boom-da-dee-boom!

"Get back!" Javik yelled. "Stay away from me!"

"Manno?" a raspy voice asked. "You are Manno?"

Slimy hands pawed at Javik in the darkness. He pushed them away, but they returned: wet fingers caressing his face and body. The fingers of many creatures, pressing all around.

Javik lashed out with his feet and felt his boots strike home against flesh and bones. The creatures fell back but returned, like an encroaching sea which could be stalled but never defeated.

A narrow band of light hit the side of Javik's face from above. Then the band of light widened. Looking up, Javik squinted as a lid slid open, clanging metallically. He heard thunderous crowd noises outside.

"One more pilot," a tenor voice said from above. Faces covered the opening. "Get the new Earthian. The one with no wounds."

Before Javik could react, a lariat snapped down and slipped expertly under his armpits. The lariat tightened around his body and pulled him to the surface. Javik thrashed at the rope as he was pulled up and out of the hole. He felt a sharp shoulder pain as he was dumped roughly on the ground.

A Corker removed the lariat, smiling at Javik with moist, purple lips.

Rising to one knee, Javik found himself on one end of a great stadium filled with cheering Fruit people. It was night, and the stadium was ringed with bright floodlights. The other end of the stadium was open, with two parallel strips of flood-lighted gray concrete extending into the distance. Far down the track, Javik noticed that the lanes narrowed to one. The Fruit spectators were colorful and demonstrative, waving their arms excitedly and hurling empty grain alcohol packs in all directions. Vendors hawking new packs worked the aisles.

Javik took a deep breath. He was hungry and tired, with the burning eyes and drifting consciousness of a person in need of sleep. A fine, stinging dust blew across his face. He felt a sneeze coming on. "Ah . . . ah . . ." It did not come. Having no tissue handy, Javik depressed one nostril to blow phlegm on the ground. He repeated the procedure with the other nostril.

"I think it's an Earthian," a Corker on his left said. Javik did not look in that direction.

"Different from the others," observed another.

"Cleaner looking."

Javik focused on two large auto carriers parked in pools of light at the near end of each concrete strip. One carrier was pink and black, the other blue and black. Cars painted in the same manner as their respective carriers roared down ramps from each carrier simultaneously, one from each carrier, then streaked side by side along the track—a pink and black car on one strip, a blue and black car on the other. He saw the cars vie for position as the lanes merged to one. The blue car shot in front at the junction, then went into a weaving pattern.

Lances of flame shot from the front of the trailing pink car. Gunfire peppered the air.

"Damn," someone said.

The blue car exploded in a high ball of blue flame. Javik stood up to see the car crash off the track against a low rock wall. A glowing orange capsule shot straight up from the crash scene. Then a white parachute opened over the capsule, guiding it back to Cork. Still glowing orange, the capsule drifted closer to Javik. He saw that it was a cage, with shimmering, orange-hot bars. Inside, the dead Manno pilot was stretched straight out and spinning slowly, like a pig on a spit.

What the hell? Javik thought.

"You saw it folks!" the public address man announced. "Another Manno loss!"

Pink balloons fluttered over the Wommo auto carrier to celebrate the victory. The Wommo fighter car pilot slowed her car at the other end of the track, then took an exit ramp to the left into a pink and black pit area.

"Never get in front," a Corker guard said to Javik. "You've gotta lay back."

"Listen to him good, Manno," an avocado man said, looking at Javik with seedy, dark green eyes. He nudged Javik's sore shoulder, causing Javik to grimace.

"He'll learn fast," the Corker said. "If he doesn't want to be a toastie."

Jeheezus! Javik thought.

"Who cares?" someone behind Javik said. "Let him roast."

I care, Javik thought. *But should I? Maybe this is as good a way to go as any.*

He watched the giant auto carriers exchange places, rolling by one another efficiently and rapidly. Javik was surprised at how mobile the big units were. Within moments each carrier was set up at the opposite track. Two cars rocketed down the ramps now, hitting the tracks side by side.

"You see that, Earthian?" the avocado man asked. "You can't go too fast or too slow. Too fast and the parallel car nails you from behind. Even if you get away, there's no glory in it. Too slow and another enemy car is on your track, coming right up your ass."

"Over here," a Corker said. "We need another pilot. He'd better . . ." The ensuing words were drowned out in crowd noises and an explosion on the track.

"Darn!" someone said. "There went another one."

"They're beating the hell out of us today."

"Glad I don't have to go out there."

Two beefy Corkers pulled and pushed Javik to a table attended by a very round orange man. Without a word, the orange man pushed a blue and black jumpsuit and a helmet across the table toward Javik.

Javik slipped the suit on over his Space Patrol outfit. The suit was a couple of sizes too big. The helmet fit poorly too, being designed for bulbous-headed humanoids. He heard radio chatter across built-in earphones.

He was about to ask for better-fitting headgear when a Corker shoved him roughly, saying, "This way." Javik was escorted to the Manno auto carrier, a massive warship standing in a bright pool of light. The blue and black carrier was long and three-tiered, with a hodgepodge of fighter cars on all levels. Each car had a large-caliber gun mounted on the roof, with machine guns on the front and rear fenders.

Javik was taken up a side walkway and assigned to a dented and bullet-riddled squareback on the lower level. A large black Corkian numeral "5" was on the door. Since the door was welded shut, Javik had to remove his helmet and pull himself in through the open driver's window. He slid into a torn black vinyl bucket seat. The seat squeaked as his weight settled into it. This placed him in a black-barred cage. Javik knew he would roast there if he lost. Nervously, he fingered the strap of the helmet on his lap.

Outside, a cheerful public address announcer called out action for the spectators. His voice was throaty.

It smelled of oil in the car. The instrumentation looked primitive to Javik, with rudimentary gauges for speed, tach, and other mechanical functions. A black pole suspended from the roof to his right had three white buttons on it, marked clearly: "TOP," "REAR" and "FRONT." *The guns,* he thought.

Locating the fuel gauge, he saw it waver. *What does this thing run on?* he wondered. *Probably alcohol of some sort.* He did not detect a telltale odor. After figuring out the braking and acceleration system, he rested his foot on the accelerator pedal.

A Corker leaned in the window and told Javik to press the "START" button. Javik moved away to keep dark fluid on the fellow's mouth and chin from dripping on him. "Watch for the green light on the track," the Corker said. "Then hit 'TAKE-OFF.'"

Javik touched the starter button and heard the engine roar to life like a rudely awakened beast. The headlights flashed on automatically. The car rumbled roughly and hesitatingly at first, then began to smooth out. As Javik looked down the black stripe on the car's hood, he felt the change in the engine's rhythm. Another car was in front of him, and beyond that a traffic signal flashed red.

"You're coming up, Manno," a weak voice reported from Javik's left. Glancing in that direction, Javik saw an old and wrinkled lettuce man slave. The man's body was light green and white, with white eyebrows and a crown of white fuzz. There was no neck: the body was the head and vice versa.

Javik nodded. He gunned the engine. Noticing a shoulder harness for the first time, he pulled it across his chest and snapped it into place.

"They race and fight on Earth highways like this?" the old slave asked. "Just like the promoters say?"

"I guess so. This sure as hell is exaggerated, though. We don't mount guns on cars back home. They're carried in glove compartments." He thought of the autocar signboards by which Earth drivers could exchange epithets. Feeling tense, Javik decided not to mention this. He used a sleeve to wipe perspiration from his forehead.

The slave grunted.

A Corker guard on the ground below yelled at them: "Cut the chatter! Pay attention to the games!" The guard purchased a new alcohol backpack from a passing vendor, paying for it with discarded Earth candy bar wrappers.

"It's Manno against Wommo!" the public address man announced. Javik heard sucking sounds over the speaker system and surmised the announcer was a Corker.

Waves of ovation, roars, and catcalls rolled through the stands.

Javik touched an unmarked console button to see what it was. Nothing happened. He checked several other buttons with the same result.

"Disconnected," the old slave said.

"What a heap," Javik said. He smelled exhaust from the car just ahead. Then the other car roared down the ramp and into combat, leaving a puff of black smoke across Javik's vision.

When the smoke began to clear, Javik saw the car explode in a distant ball of blue flame. An orange capsule shot up, then sprouted a parachute.

"Haven't seen a Manno victory all day," the slave said.

Inhuman games, Javik thought, seeing the traffic signal flash red. *Men against women, playing on the conditioned rivalries between Earth sexes.*

He snapped on his loose-fitting plastic crash helmet. Over the built-in earphones he heard nervous chatter as the Manno fighter car pilots communicated with the carrier's control tower.

"Okay, Ladykiller Five," the control tower said. "You're up next."

Javik was daydreaming, recalling some of his more memorable pleasure dome visits.

"Ladykiller Five, you there?"

Five, Javik thought, drifting back to awareness. *That's me.* "Here," he said into a microphone in front of his mouth.

"Blow that Wommo fighter car away, buddy."

"Right," Javik shook his head in disgust. *This is an important mission?* he thought. *I'd rather be ridin' a garbage shuttle.*

"Watch your blind spots, Ladykiller Five," the tower said. "Keep the other car in front of you all the time. Or rocket ahead to a Manno safe zone. That's a blue and black wall at the side. You can hide behind it, then pop out and blast the Wommo car when it passes."

"Don't we get any practice?" Javik asked.

Sardonic laughter filled the earphones. Then: "You've discovered the gun buttons?"

"Yeah." Seeing the traffic signal flash yellow, Javik held a finger close to the "TAKEOFF" button. *Not too fast*, he thought. His heart began to beat faster.

"You aim the gun bar by rotating, pushing, and pulling it."

The traffic signal flashed green.

Javik hit the "TAKEOFF" button and felt the accelerator under his foot depress. The car roared ahead, thumping as it bounced off the ramp to the pavement. G-forces threw him against the bucket seat. The helmet strap pulled at his chin. He grimaced from the stress.

This piece of shit moves out! he thought. But the car felt loose under him. Something rattled in the rear.

Peripherally, he watched a pink and black Wommo car on

the track to his left. It dropped back.

Javik tapped the accelerator to free it from takeoff mode. His car slowed, drawing even with the other car. He could see the pilot, a bulbous-headed Wommo humanoid in a pink and black jumpsuit. She glanced at him nervously. *Very young*, he thought. *Maybe only a kid.* He adjusted his helmet with one hand.

Machine-gun fire peppered the hood and broke his windshield.

No more lapses, he thought, grabbing the gun bar. It was cool. *She means business.*

A voice crackled across his earphones. "Fire on her, Ladykiller Five. What are you waiting for?"

He pulled all three triggers at once, and saw the red and yellow flash of his guns on the front fenders. *Wrong way*, he thought, turning the bar. He saw the fender guns turn toward the Wommo car. Noticing the guns on his car's right side raising higher than his car body, Javik felt a small sense of relief. The maneuver permitted his guns to fire over the car without the embarrassment of self-destruction.

The lanes were merging into one, and Javik hit the brake pedal. A bullet whistled by his nose, lodging with a thud in the parachute pack overhead. His fighter car slowed, but not enough. *I'm ahead of her*, he thought. *She's experienced!*

Javik's car hit the single lane first. Turning the wheel, his car spun into gravel on the shoulder. Then he swung across the lane and went into a weaving, elusive pattern. He heard the staccato rat-a-tat rhythm of machine-gun fire from the pursuing fighter car. At the loud boom of a big gun, he felt numb. Nothing hit.

Looking in his rearview mirror, Javik turned his guns and tried to zero in on the other car. A bazooka shot from his big gun hit the track to one side of the enemy car, not close enough to do any damage. He moved the bar a little and fired the big gun again. This one was a direct hit.

In his mirror he saw the Wommo car explode in a pink ball of flame. He heard the whoosh of the pilot's cage as it ejected. A distant, throaty voice announced the event over the loudspeaker.

Javik breathed a sigh of relief.

But then an urgent voice crackled across his earphones: "Get out of there, Ladykiller Five! Punch it!"

In his rearview mirror, Javik saw another Wommo fighter car approaching fast. Its headlights grew larger and brighter as it neared.

He floored the accelerator pedal. His car jumped ahead. Then he pressed the bazooka button. The shot missed, exploding off the track.

A blue and black Manno pit area came into view on his left. He took the exit at full speed, then hit the brakes. The car squealed and shimmied. Then a deceleration hook beneath Javik's fighter car grabbed catchers on the pavement, throwing him against his shoulder harness. The car slowed and stopped.

Dozens of smiling humanoid Mannos ran to Javik's car and pulled him out.

"Nice going!" they said in their monotone voices, patting him on the back. "You kept us from being shut out today!"

Javik was speechless. He wanted to be far away from there.

They lifted him and carried him on their shoulders, chattering all the while in their dull voices about it being party time. The stench of unwashed, decaying bodies was almost unbearable to Javik. Cold night air blew across his face, and for the first time he realized he had been perspiring.

I'm a hero, Javik thought, unenthused. *Whoopee*.

NINE

Two objects can be the same and
different at the same moment.
If you doubt this, compare an
apple and an orange.

                  One of the Timeless Truths

Earlier, after Prince Pineapple watched the pear men guards escort Javik and Evans out of the king's court, he turned to face King Corker.

"That will be all," King Corker said. He rose and padded out via his side door.

Prince Pineapple remained where he was. Holding Wizzy up to eye level, he said, "I hope your captain does well."

"Eh?" Wizzy said, lifting the lid of his cat's eye to peer through the clear agate dome on top of his body.

"I was hoping that your captain does well. Tonight. In the games."

"What do I care?"

"I just thought—"

"Pipe down, will ya? I'm so tired I can hardly keep my peeper open! A growing comet needs his rest, you know."

This remark suprised the prince, for he had no idea up to that time that Wizzy was anything other than a talking mechanical device. But the prince said nothing of this, remarking instead in a gracious tone, "Of course. You can explain all that to me later in my apartment. It is quiet there, a place where you can rest."

Wizzy did not respond.

Prince Pineapple felt Wizzy shudder on his palm. Then Wizzy emitted a gentle snort. Soon he was fast asleep, snoring and wheezing.

Prince Pineapple snuggled Wizzy against his belly and thought of the day's strange events. He considered discarding Wizzy somewhere outside, but decided against this. *The king must not be alerted in any way,* he thought. *I make my move tonight—Wizzy or no Wizzy.*

Deep in thought, the prince carried Wizzy out of the castle and along the narrow trail that led to his apartment near Sacred Pond. Low Vesuvius shrubs lined the trail, with occasional roots across the path that he had to step over. Cork's three synchronized suns were dropping quickly below the level of the horizon, casting yellow-orange tones against a swirling cloud layer to the west.

He climbed a low hill, from the top of which he could see Sacred Pond. The scroll bubble was barely visible, giving off low light in a fog mist at the center of the pond. Giraffe-necked trail lights flickered on as the suns disappeared from view. Prince Pineapple shivered, and for the first time became aware of Wizzy's warmth against his stomach. Wizzy glowed faintly red in the diminishing daylight. Unknown to the prince, Wizzy was in the midst of a data retrieving dream.

Wizzy's an odd gadget, Prince Pineapple thought.

Wizzy whistled like a teapot, then chuckled in his sleep.

The Sacred Scroll of Cork, Prince Pineapple thought, watching the bubble appear brighter as the abyss of night enveloped it. *I must try for it tonight. While Wizzy is asleep.*

It occurred to the prince that Wizzy might be dangerous to him, sent by Lord Abercrombie to prevent him from learning the secrets of the Magician's Chamber. Abercrombie had the secret and wanted to keep it for himself. Or Wizzy might be an agent of the king: an elaborate setup.

I must be on guard, he thought.

Later that evening, Prince Pineapple sat in a rocking chair in the darkened bay window of his apartment, looking down on the black murkiness of Sacred Pond. The scroll bubble was not visible from here, being completely enshrouded by fog. In the yellow light of a giraffe-necked trail light below, he saw sheets of wind-driven rain pounding the waters along the shore. At the edges of the lamp's upside-down bowl of light, curls of thick fog drifted like ghosts agitated by the light.

He glanced at a gold and brown pillow which lay on the floor in a slice of light coming in from the bedroom. The pillow was imitation Persian, with just the proper combination of rips and worn threads to make it very valuable. Wizzy was asleep there, his lumpy body swelling and subsiding with each breath he took.

Prince Pineapple turned to look back out the window. *Like a blanket over the pond,* he thought. *The fog rolls in each night like a blanket.*

He envisioned the Sacred Scroll of Cork sleeping peacefully at the center of the pond, untouched by Fruit hands. His pulse quickened, and he felt hot pineapple juice rushing through the veins of his neck. His head throbbed.

He closed his eyes in an attempt to reduce his juice pressure. *This is not the way I want to go,* Prince Pineapple thought, thinking of the recurring nightmares he had of dying from a burst juice vein. *"Keep calm," Lord Abercrombie tells us in our dreams. "Let a Decision Coin reduce the pressure . . . reduce the pressure . . . reduce the pressure . . ."*

Touching a finger to one side of his temple, he felt the throbbing subside. He grew calmer, dropping his arm to his lap.

I'd better go now, he thought, watching the rain. *Doesn't look like the weather will break.*

The prince rose and tiptoed past Wizzy. But in his haste, one of Prince Pineapple's feet caught on a tuft of carpet. He fell roughly, causing a lot of noise. He swore under his breath.

Wizzy stirred. His lumpy body stretched one way, then the other. This was a molecular transformation possible only in the Realm of Magic. Any scientist will tell you that cold stone is not pliable.

"Can't you keep quiet?" Wizzy asked angrily. He tipped his cat's eye toward Prince Pineapple.

The prince was struggling to his feet, cursing himself for his stupidity. "A thousand pardons," he said.

"None of which are accepted," Wizzy said. "I feel terrible . . . aches in every chem-bond of my body." He sniffled, then felt something strange taking over his respiratory system. "Ahh!"

he said, breathing in deeply. "Ahh . . . ahh . . . ahh-choo!"

Shaking his head sadly, Prince Pineapple muttered, "He'll never go back to sleep now."

"What did I just do?" Wizzy asked.

"Huh? Oh. You sneezed."

"Sneezed?" Wizzy glowed red, searching his data banks. "I have a cold?"

"Perhaps." The prince leaned against a wall.

"Do you have anything to treat such a condition?"

"Aspirin. But you have no mouth. Besides, you're a mechanical being, not at all similar to me or to a human being."

"You're laboring under a misapprehension," Wizzy said, changing to a deep shade of blue. "Use a knife to scrape powder from the aspirin tablet. Sprinkle me with it."

Prince Pineapple left the room for a moment, returning with a knife and an aspirin tablet. He did as Wizzy requested, kneeling over him and scraping fine white powder over his dome.

Wizzy glowed orange and became molten, thus absorbing the aspirin into his magical system. "Thank you," he said, cooling down and changing color again.

"Go back to sleep," Prince Pineapple said.

"With all the commotion around here? Are you kidding?"

"I'll be quiet. I think the sleep would do you good." He straightened and folded his arms across his chest, looking down at Wizzy.

"Since when are *you* my guardian? Everyone's always telling me what to do."

"I was only . . ." Prince Pineapple paused in mid-sentence. He sighed. "Well, I think *I'll* take a nap anyway." He returned to the bay window rocker, pulled a knitted blanket off the chair back, and slid into the chair. He covered himself and closed his eyes.

"Hrrmph!" Wizzy groused. He buzzed halfheartedly around the room. Then, as Prince Pineapple watched with one narrowly opened eye, he settled back on the pillow.

Prince Pineapple shifted to get more comfortable.

"You want to hear about me?" Wizzy asked. "I'm a baby comet, you know."

"Some other time. Let me rest." He kept one eye open narrowly, trying to conceal it at the edge of the blanket.

"First you wake me up and then you want *me* to be quiet while *you* sleep? That's a fine thing to do."

Peripherally, Prince Pineapple looked out the window at the diagonal sheets of wind-driven rain. He heard trees squeak together from the force of the storm. *Sacred Pond will be rough,* he thought. *Maybe the wind will subside.*

"Funny thing about you," Wizzy said. "I pick up thought waves from humans. But from you, nothing."

"You can read thoughts? Unspoken thoughts?" He sat up in the rocker, staring full-faced at Wizzy.

"Not yours, dear Prince. Nor those of your brethren. Perhaps you have no brains."

"No brains?"

"Well, not much in the way of brains anyway."

Prince Pineapple leaned forward, dropping the blanket to the floor. His eyes were bird alert. "Not much in the way of brains, you say? That may be true of the others, but I'll have you know I am in possession of a marvelous brain."

"I wouldn't be so sure about that. My red star crystal sensors are quite sensitive—although not yet fully developed. You'd think I would receive something from you if you had a decent brain. Just a hum, mind you . . . or a few garbled thoughts."

"I am capable of more than garbled thoughts!" Prince Pineapple jumped up and paced the room. Presently: "Lord Abercrombie tells us to use Decision Coins for all matters. If my brain is damaged, it is from disuse."

"That is possible. Entirely possible. Now why don't you relax? I'll tell you a little about how I came to be here."

Prince Pineapple sat on a shabby brown and yellow couch against one wall. "And how will I comprehend such things?" he asked. "Not having a decent brain and all."

"You do sound rather intelligent. Perhaps my sensors need adjustment. I'm sorry if I offended you."

The prince glowered, thinking, *Maybe he'll talk himself to sleep. I have a good brain. I use it all the time.*

The Orgy Building comprised one large, rectangular room with bead curtain doorways at each end. The room was full of partying humanoids when Javik was shown in by a Manno teammate. Nearly everyone in the room wore an electroplated purple badge, signifying conspicuous bravery back on Earth in the face of a disintegrating product. The bulbous-headed Mannos and Wommos swarmed around drunkenly, filling up nearly every square centimeter of space available. There was no music. Despite this, many partyers twisted their hips, swaying to unheard tunes while clutching drinks in tall glasses. It was like an Earth party in some ways, but distorted.

"After you've eaten from the kill," the Manno at his side said in a characteristic monotone, "find a Wommo bitch and take her in one of the fornication rooms along the wall." He pointed through the crowd at a row of red doors set very close together along the opposite wall. As Javik gazed across the room, he became aware of movement overhead.

The ceiling of the room was tinted glassplex or heavy glass, substantial enough to support a throng of Corkers and other Fruits above. They kneeled and peered down at the Earthian party, their eyes open fully in frenzied fascination. Most of them were gathered over the fornication rooms, where they pushed and fought for better views.

"They enjoy watching all our Earth games," the Manno said. "Fruits don't engage in our form of sex, you know. They grow in orchards and vineyards. When they're ripe, they simply fall off."

"No fun in that," Javik said, smelling what he thought was roast pig. If spoken to an old acquaintance, these words might have given the impression that Javik was his old womanizing self. But Javik did not feel the words he uttered. They came automatically, as if from a politician's voice tape. He was hungry and angry, hopelessly out of synch with his surroundings.

"Excuse me," the Manno said. "I just spied a delectable, if you get my drift." He sauntered off, wading into the crowd like a bee going for pollen. Soon Javik lost sight of him.

The room was divided into Manno and Wommo sides, with blue and pink banners designating each camp. On each side were banquet tables covered with red and white checkered picnic cloths. The tables held barred cages from the fallen fighter cars of the day, with the dead and unfortunate pilots spinning inside on spits. The cage bars were black now, having cooled. As Javik watched, tackle sets over each table lifted off the tops of the cages, exposing the humanoid roasts. The spits stopped turning.

To Javik's horror, the throngs moved in on the humanoid food, tearing off jagged hunks of cooked flesh which they stuffed in their mouths. Animal sounds shook the room: growls and snarls, sighs and grunts of satisfaction. The tables rocked as hungry humanoids pulled at the roasts from all sides.

"You'd better hurry," a Manno at Javik's side said. "We only got one kill today."

Javik only stared. Hunger pangs tore at his stomach. Cannibalism. It was beyond belief.

"Say," the Manno said, moving in front of Javik to look at his face. "You got our kill!" The Manno limped as he moved, and carried a deep gash across his abdomen. Black letters stamped on his forehead indicated that he was a Product Failure victim.

Javik looked away.

The Manno grabbed his arm, pulling Javik toward the Manno banquet table.

"Wait," Javik said, his voice feeble. He offered little resistance.

"Hey, guys!" the Manno yelled as they neared the swarm at the table. "Save a piece for this guy. He got our kill."

Stepping to one side so that Javik could get through, the Mannos greeted him with smiles that dripped meat juice. They patted him on the back and pushed him forward. Javik's hunger-starved nostrils tried to convince his brain that the strong aroma was roast pork. Then he saw it close up: a shredded female body with great pieces of cooked brown flesh torn away. The body was more dead than the dead, for it had died twice: once on Earth and again on Cork. Javik told himself that it should never have lived, if this was to be the end of it all.

"Eat," someone said, thrusting a piece of breast meat into Javik's quivering hands.

Javik held the meat unsteadily, staring at it in horror. This was being forced on him. He had to eat it. That made it all right, he told himself. A dull hunger pang tugged at his mid-section.

The Mannos turned their attention away from Javik now, resuming their demonic gluttony. The animal sounds increased.

Javik's mouth was filling with saliva. The fluid gushed in, anticipating his first bite. He wanted that meat. He needed it. He lifted the succulent piece close to his lips, nearly touching them.

"Go ahead," a familiar female voice said.

Looking to his left, Javik saw Evans smiling at him. In one hand she held a bone with shredded meat hanging from it. Dark red meat juice ran down her chin and over the front of her

Wommo jumpsuit. She chewed and swallowed, smiling and staring at Javik all the while. Her smile fit the occasion. It was satanic and all-knowing, seeing every frailty Javik had. Evans did not need eyes. Her smile saw it all.

"Eat," she said.

Javik heard a *clunk* overhead. Glancing up, he saw a cluster of Corkers looking down at him from the level above. "I'm like a zoo animal," he said.

"Don't be silly," Evans said. She nibbled at the bone.

Javik gagged. Looking down at the meat in his hand, his eyes widened at the realization of what he had almost done. He hurled the meat to the floor. "You think you know me, Evans?" he said, confronting her. "You filthy transsexual!"

Mannos scrambled on the floor to recover Javik's meat. Someone scolded him for wasting food. But he scarcely heard the words.

Evans's eyes narrowed to slits. The smile disappeared. "That was in my dossier?" she asked. "I had hoped they might leave it—"

"Get away from me!" Javik said.

Her all-knowing smile returned. "I know what you want," she said. "Let me demonstrate a fornication room for you." She nodded in the direction of the red doors.

"Shove off! Do you hear me, Evans? Shove off!" He felt his glands trying to convince him to accompany her. He seemed to be battling the inevitable. He craved Evans. He wanted to throw her down right there and enjoy her. His body screamed for her.

"No!" a voice thundered inside his skull. *"Not a transsexual!"*

"But who would know?" another interior voice asked.

"Give in," Evans said. Her voice seemed to come from Javik's own brain.

"Give in," another voice in his head whispered.

Javik steeled himself against the onslaught. "I'm not religious," he said, staring at meat juice drippings on one of his boots. His words were measured. "Never have been. But this seems . . . so evil to me."

Evans moved close to him. She pressed her short, buxom body against his. Her breasts were soft and inviting against his stomach.

He took a deep breath and moved away from her, bumping

into a Manno behind him. "You fit this garbage dump real well," he told her.

Her facial muscles slackened. Javik saw fear in her eyes.

"You're warped!" Javik screeched. "Everything here is warped! A cracked reflection of Earth!"

She laughed derisively. But it was a forced laugh.

Those Corkers are getting a good show, he thought. *Wait'll I start busting faces.*

"Hey, Manno!" a partyer shouted from the other side of the table. "Take it easy, teammate. We're here to have a good time."

Javik wished he had lost on the track that day. It might have been easier that way.

"Give in," Evans said. The smile was gone now, and she looked confused. Her gaze moved around nervously. Beads of perspiration clung to her forehead.

His body screamed for satisfaction. But now the scream met the high wall of Javik's innermost determination, his last line of defense. It had to hold and did. He felt the craving for Evans subsiding. Now he went to the attack and smiled, enjoying the look of hurt it caused on Evans's face.

"You got the kill today," she said. "The *only* Manno kill . . ." She was struggling to keep him in line. Her demonic smile returned for a moment.

He felt the corners of his mouth sag.

The hated smile took over her face again. It was a battle of words and expressions, with each side searching for the winning combination.

Another Earth game, he thought.

"You might as well enjoy yourself," she said. "While you can."

He wanted to knock that smile off her face. He wanted to see her dead. He wanted to throw her down and enjoy her. His glands screamed. He licked his lips.

"You can have some of our meat," she said, extending the bone to him. "We have plenty."

"I don't . . ." he said. He felt a torrent of angry words inside. He just shook his head.

She withdrew the meat. "We Wommos are good," she said, setting her jaw. "Better than Mannos. I'm glad I changed sexes!"

Javik's glare of hatred met a like glare from Evans. In that instant, he knew Evans would try to kill him if she went up against him on the track. She was no longer Co-Pilot Marta Evans. She was someone—or some*thing*—else. It scared him. It scared the living hell out of him.

She chewed at her upper lip while watching his every move.

Javik thought she was sizing him up for a fight. He had been in enough brawls to know the signs.

"Maybe I'll see you around," she said stiffly. She turned and walked away. Javik knew what "around" meant. It meant tomorrow, on the fighter car track.

He thought he heard the anger of more than one woman in her words. He was not even certain he heard anger. It was more a threatening undertone which made him realize what a remarkable source of competition the Corkers had tapped for their deadly games.

He watched Evans push her way through the crowd, moving into her netherworld, a place reserved for the unholiest of beings. Taking a drunken Manno by the arm, she pulled him toward the bank of fornication rooms. Overhead, Corkers scrambled to follow her.

I'm gettin' out of this zoo, Javik thought. *I'm gonna die as far away from here as possible. Someplace they can't use me.*

He battered his way through the drunken throng, feeling himself being drawn away by a welcome burst of inner morality. But he knew even that reservoir of strength would be short-lived without food. He told himself nothing would get in his way, and scarcely heard the Corkers overhead who scrambled to follow him.

At the Wommo banquet table, an ecstatic Wommo popped the eyeball out of a humanoid toastie. Tossing the eye high in the air, she caught it in her mouth. The Wommos cheered as she gulped.

Misshapen faces appeared and receded, gawking, smiling, and leering at him drunkenly. He called upon his last vestiges of pride to keep moving him forward.

"I've tasted Manno and I've tasted Wommo," a shrill-voiced Wommo said, singsonging the words. "The Wommo is sweeter, not nearly so chew-y."

Javik cursed softly, stumbling as he approached a bead curtain doorway. He readied himself for guards on the other side. *Lightning strokes,* he thought. *Short and fierce. Ten of those purple pudgies couldn't take me down.*

The bead curtain came into focus, swaying gently. The

beads knocked together with a dull, hollow sound. Javik took a deep breath.

Suddenly, three Corker guards spread the curtain, filling the doorway with their bodies. They pointed metal lances at Javik, but his trained eye saw the tips waver. And he noticed the drunken, rolling gaze of the big Corker in the middle. This one swayed way back. He had corporal stripes on his sleeves.

"Return to the party!" the corpulent corporal commanded. His voice was loose and throaty. He coughed and spit purple, bubbly phlegm on the floor.

Javik felt the blood drain from his face. *I'll kill these . . .* he thought. In the midst of the thought, Javik ducked under the corporal's lance and kicked him hard against the soft underside of his belly. The Corker grunted, tumbling over on his alcohol backpack with his lance pointed straight up in the air.

Seizing the vertical lance before the other guards could attack, Javik ran outside. A cool night breeze washed through his hair. The sting of a lance pricked the calf of his left leg. Jumping to one side, Javik swung back with his own weapon, knocking the guard's lance away.

The guard quick-footed backward, stopping when his alcohol backpack bumped the building.

"How about you?" Javik barked, lunging at the third guard.

This guard must have had more than the minimum issue of sense, for he dropped his lance and ran into the night as fast as his six stubby legs could carry him.

The big Corker corporal fought his way to his feet, with help from the other remaining guard. "Have you gone mad, Earthian?" the corporal asked. "Go back inside."

A droplet of rain hit Javik's cheek as he surveyed the area. He felt the night wind pick up. He was on the opposite end of the Orgy Building from the entrance he had taken. The building was one of three similar buildings fronting a dimly lit dirt carriage road. Across the road was a thick, dark section of piney woods.

"Did you hear me, Earthian?"

Javik's consciousness focused on the inverted bowl of stars over his head. He longed for his ship. Maybe he could clear the thruster tubes and fly it to a safe place on Cork for further repairs.

Excited voices snapped him to awareness. "Over there!" a

guard yelled. Javik saw two squads of Corker guards running toward him, one from each end of the road. They moved drunkenly, throwing yellow light on the ground with the lanterns they carried.

In the shadows of Prince Pineapple's apartment, Wizzy told of being dropped to Earth by his Papa Sidney. He described the subsequent adventures with Captain Tom Javik as well, and commented on their dislike for one another. Resting on a white coffee table doily, Wizzy tilted his cat's eye toward Prince Pineapple and said, "I wish I could be somewhere of my own choosing . . . streaking across the galaxy like Papa. I do not belong here."

Prince Pineapple leaned forward on the couch, resting his elbows on his lap and cradling his chin on his hands. This placed half of his face in the slice of light coming in from the bedroom. The wind howled outside. "Nor do I," he said. "I too am forced to do objectionable things."

"You have a papa?"

"There is but one papa on this planet: Lord Abercrombie. He leaves us virtually no free will. From ripening, we are trained to relegate even the simplest matters to Decision Coins." His voice grew bitter. "Our lives are but a series of coin tosses. I see no sense in it."

"Nice pun," Wizzy said.

Deep in his problem, Prince Pineapple was all seriousness. "As I told you," he said, "I have brains."

"I can see that," Wizzy said, wondering if pun recognition might constitute a valid intelligence test.

"We are told not to get too upset. Or we might burst a juice vessel. I'm angry enough now to let one blow wide open." The prince's face glowed crimson. He felt his juice pressure rising.

"Don't be silly," Wizzy said.

"I want to learn so many things," Prince Pineapple lamented.

"And I, too," Wizzy said. He rose half a meter above the doily, giving off a faint hum as he held position. "Is there no solution to your problem?"

"If only I had the Sacred Scroll," Prince Pineapple said. He worried for a moment, wondering if he should have revealed this. Then he sighed deeply, and his face grew a paler shade of red. He felt his juice pressure dropping.

"And what is that?" Wizzy asked, unable to read the prince's thoughts.

"Every magical planet has a Sacred Scroll. They were created thousands of years ago, describing the locations of all Dimensional Tunnels connecting the magical planets." He sat back, resting his hands on his lap. "On Cork, the scroll is protected by a magician's bubble at the center of Sacred Pond."

"Dimensional Tunnels," Wizzy said, glowing red as he searched his memory banks. "Also known as warples. Synthetic in nature. They crisscross the universe invisibly, permitting rapid travel between certain planets."

Prince Pineapple lifted his eyebrows in astonishment. *A most peculiar device, this Wizzy.* Then: "I need Cork's scroll," he said. "Do you suppose you might help me?"

"I would like to help you. I could check in on Captain Tom afterward, I suppose."

"Then row with me to the center of Sacred Pond. Help me pop the magician's bubble."

"That may not be so easy."

"We must go tonight. Already the other advisers are whispering against me."

"Do you know of anyone else who has tried to pop this bubble? Have *you* tried?"

"King Corker has blocked all attempts. He requires so much paperwork that no one has been able to obtain permission. I'm sure he wants the scroll for himself."

"I see." Wizzy settled back on the doily.

"Legend has it that the bubble can be popped only at night. And only with a dull instrument."

"Do you think the king has tried?"

"Of course. He would like to replace Lord Abercrombie. But I say we don't need a lord. Cork is a very ancient planet. According to legend, nutrients flowed from the soil before any lord appeared. That means they will continue to flow after the lord is gone."

"You want to throw Abercrombie out?"

"Yes, and then seal the entrance to his chamber, preventing anyone from getting in again."

Wizzy glowed red. "You might seal the chamber from the surface," he said. "But you can never seal the other side, the Dimensional Tunnel side."

"That is true. But at least I would accomplish something."

Wizzy flickered. "I'm losing my data base," he said. "Do you know how to get in?"

"No," Prince Pineapple looked away. A saying of unknown origin wafted across his consciousness: *"When you see what it is all about, there will be nothing left to do except to have a good laugh."* The thought puzzled him.

"Why do you expect to succeed when the king has failed?"

"It is only a feeling I have. That I am chosen, I suppose. Undoubtedly this is a common enough thought. But I must try anyway."

"And if you fail?"

"I will defect. This very night. Brother Carrot's Vegetable Underground could learn much from me. I hear he treats some Fruits rather well. I know all about Corker defenses."

"You have a boat to cross this pond?"

"Of course. Quite a sturdy little craft."

"I just thought of something. It's a rainy night. That's not a good time to venture out."

"But I have no choice. King Corker will order me into oblivion soon. Perhaps tomorrow."

"I do have certain magical powers," Wizzy said. "Though rather limited and unperfected. I could perish if I ever became very wet."

"Then stay in the apartment. It is yours. I have no further need of it."

"If I went with you, could you promise to keep me dry?"

"I would try. I could wrap you in plastic and keep you under my coat."

"But in a boat," Wizzy said, having second thoughts. He heard the wind and looked at the rain slanting against the window. "On a stormy night."

Prince Pineapple placed his palms on the couch, preparing to rise. "I should go," he said. "Make up your mind."

"We are alike, you and I," Wizzy said. "Controlled by others, sent off in circles to do inane things . . . as if we had no brains or wills of our own."

"Yes!" Prince Pineapple exclaimed, smiling as he locked gazes with Wizzy's cat's eye. "That's exactly right. Let's do this together. It will be a marvelous adventure."

"But some things confuse me," Wizzy said. "According to Papa Sidney, I'm supposed to help Captain Tom correct the damage caused by the evil anti-jobs criminal, Abercrombie.

But Papa was hurt by Job Support. They sent him to a therapy orbiter because that sustained more jobs than rehabilitation. Shouldn't my Papa have opposed Job Support? It hurt him terribly. Why did he continute to love the AmFed Way? Will I ever understand why?"

"That does sound peculiar," Prince Pineapple said. He settled back on the couch for a moment.

"Maybe Papa isn't so bright."

"But he has deep feelings. A wonderful sense of devotion. I can tell that from listening to you. He loves Earth and you."

"And he loves that idiot Captain Tom!" Wizzy exclaimed. "This love . . . You can help me to understand it?"

"Love is not something I can explain. It is something which comes over you, causing you to do strange things."

"Papa said that too."

"It is not a reasoning thing."

"Then how am I to know it?"

"It will affect you when you least expect it."

"I'm so confused."

"I felt love once," Prince Pineapple said. "For a lush young pineapple girl." He sighed. "But that was long ago. So very long ago."

Wizzy recalled the words of his papa just before dropping Wizzy to Earth: *"You must learn to control your emotions, but do not become callous in the process. Retain some vulnerability. This is perhaps the most important part of being alive."*

Prince Pineapple moved across the room. He flipped on a lamp. The room's darkness retreated, hiding in safe corners and under furniture. "I suppose I can wait a while longer," he said. "It can't get any worse outside."

A tree rubbed against the side of the building, followed by the crack of a branch. The branch thumped as it fell to the roof.

Wizzy alighted on the pineapple prince's shoulder. They went together to the couch. "I want to learn everything in the universe!" Wizzy exclaimed. "I want to experience everything in the universe!"

Prince Pineapple laughed as he made himself comfortable on the couch. "And I would settle for the knowledge of Cork."

"Maybe all the universe's secrets are here," Wizzy said, surprising himself with the statement. "Your goal and my goal may take us to the very same place."

"What do you mean?" Prince Pineapple asked, watching rain batter the bay window.

Wizzy shifted on the prince's shoulder. "I don't know," he said. "The words came out before I had a chance to think about them."

"You asked about love," Prince Pineapple said.

"I want to understand all my emotions," Wizzy said. "They seem to exert a great deal of control over me." His tone became excited. "Maybe that's what the words meant. Understanding my feelings may be a universal thing. I may not need to look elsewhere." The words floated across Wizzy's consciousness as if spoken by someone else.

"Could be. Be cautious of what you seek, however. Certain things are better left undiscovered."

"Such as?"

"Sadness. You won't want any of that. It's such a tragic thing. You don't want the death of a loved one, or loneliness." Prince Pineapple recalled his lost love. "These are not good feelings."

"I want them anyway."

"I don't think so." Prince Pineapple stroked Wizzy's back gently.

"But how will I ever know unless I try them?"

"Take my word for it. That should be enough."

Wizzy thought about this while wind-driven rain beat against the outside of the building.

They talked for hours like this, a pineapple prince conversing with a lump of stone on his shoulder. When the cracked plastic clock over the fireplace struck three, Prince Pineapple said they had to go.

"There is a break in the rain," the prince said. "We must hurry. It may not last."

As Prince Pineapple covered Wizzy with plastic wrap, Wizzy thought: *Plastic Is Fantastic*. The thought came to him involuntarily, a mantra from his father's life. "Don't wrap it too tightly," Wizzy said. "I need to breathe, you know."

It occurred to Wizzy that he had not actually agreed to accompany Prince Pineapple in pursuit of the Sacred Scroll. Not in so many words. Nevertheless, the decision had been made.

With guards approaching him from each end of the road, Javik's choices were limited. He dashed across the road into the woods, stumbling in darkness as the woods tangled him. Branches scratched his arms and face. Roots hooked his feet, sending him crashing to the ground. He closed his eyes and plunged forward, not knowing or caring where he was going. Just as long as he escaped.

Angry voices followed, calling out warnings and Corker curses. "You will starve, Earthian! Earthians need Earthians!"

"Death awaits you out there!"

"May the Lord God Abercrombie swallow you whole!"

This imprecation stuck in Javik's brain. *Abercrombie's a god here?* he thought. *Truly?* He pressed on, with more than a few misgivings.

Gradually the voices receded into the abyss of darkness in his wake. He slowed to a walk, holding his hands out in front of his face to warn of impending obstacles. A root caught his foot, but he pulled free without falling. Shallow scratches stung his face and arms. A shinbone throbbed. Pausing to reach down, he felt a flap of skin there. The pants were torn and wet with blood. It was not raining, but the waterlogged trees overhead dripped overflow on the back of his neck.

The ground was spongy here. He walked across stretches of clearing that lulled him into false security. Without warning, a branch would slap him rudely, or a root that apparently had life of its own would attempt to throw him down.

He could see very little, but had the impression that everything was purple: the trees, the ground, the air. Even the sky. He looked up often, occasionally catching a glimpse of a tiny star way out yonder twinkling faintly against a purple universe. He wondered if the color sensation was only in his mind, if it had something to do with the throbbing of his leg.

Javik felt sleepy. His footsteps grew labored. A hunger pang knawed at his stomach. He envisioned millions of grenache purple Corkers jumping over a fence of exaggerated height. Slowly and gracefully their chubby bodies floated in the stratosphere to clear the fence. He yawned.

I've got to stop somewhere, he thought. *Sleep. I need sleep.*

But a misty rain pelted his face, appearing suddenly like a cold slap. Now Javik was really miserable. He could not lie down in the rain. If only he could find an overhanging rock or log for shelter.

A branch scratched across his face. He cursed. His cheeks and forehead burned.

Pushing another countless branch out of the way, he stepped

up a little incline, unable to see anything but a great wash of purple across his brain. The ground changed. It became smoother underfoot, like compact dirt instead of the mottled forest floor. The misty rain had become a hard drizzle. He rubbed his eyes.

Off to the right and left, he saw flickering yellow lights. The didn't look like Corker lanterns. More like trail lights. He was on a trail.

"Which way?" he asked. These words were the first spoken in quite a while, and seemed to rush out of his stomach like bad food. He tasted acid. Javik had lost his bearings, with no idea which way to turn. It occurred to him that a Decision Coin would be handy. This was no time to have to think. He wanted to lie down.

A mixture of euphoria and fear struck him at finding the trail. What if he turned the wrong way and it led him back to the Corkers? What if both ways led to the Corkers?

Following his instincts, he turned right. Presently he walked under the yellow light of a giraffe-necked trail light. Beyond that he passed into purple blackness, with another speck of yellow light visible in the distance ahead. Soon he was past this lamp and in purple blackness again. This pattern continued until he reached an illuminated clearing.

The clearing seemed to be illuminated by a glow from the sky. The sky here was not purple. It was luminescent and pale white, far less intense than daylight. The faint shadow of his body stretched across tall grass on the ground.

The clearing grew lighter, and Javik began to distinguish terrain colors: pale green grass stalks dotted with tall-stemmed white flowers that had bright red centers. A powerful gust of wind shoved the flowers over in unison, like rows of cheerleaders. The rain stopped.

A blinding flash of green light filled the sky. Javik slammed his eyes shut. They ached. He felt his pulse quicken. The wind blew harder and louder, nearly toppling him.

Then the noise, wind, and light subsided, allowing Javik to open his eyes narrowly. High in the sky, an emerald green fireball veered heavenward, trailing three misty golden plumes. The plumes changed to silver.

Javik gasped. "A comet!" he husked, feeling the words rasp like sandpaper against his throat.

The Great Comet flashed high over Javik's head, staying so far away that he could keep his eyes open narrowly.

He smelled sulfur, reminding him of the terrible fire the year before on the therapy orbiter of St. Elba. He thought of Sidney Malloy.

The comet circled and repeated its maneuver. This time Javik noticed it was heading in a ten o'clock direction from the way he was facing.

A sign? he thought. *It went the same direction twice.*

The comet hovered overhead now, just low enough to illuminate the clearing.

Javik ran across the clearing in the direction the comet seemed to have indicated. Reaching the woods, he found an unlighted trail. As he walked briskly along the trail, he found that it had trail lights but they weren't operating. The pine tree tops made eerie profiles against green light from the sky.

The light moved with Javik, keeping his way dimly lit.

Feeling a rush of strength and excitement, he broke into a full run. Presently, Javik reached another clearing. The comet was still high overhead, hovering there like an emerald green personal sun.

Squinting to look into the Great Comet's brightness, Javik thought he saw the faint outline of a round face in the nucleus. The outline was gray, like that of a light charcoal sketch. Then it gained definition. It was a distantly familiar face. Javik was not certain. He rubbed his eyes and shook his head. He closed his eyes.

"Sid!" he yelled before opening his eyes. The realization hit him like a Bu-Tech thunderbolt. "Sid! Sid Malloy!" His eyelids snapped open as if mento-controlled.

Javik ran out in the clearing with his hands stretched to the heavens. Beyond the face in the comet, the stars seemed to burn brighter now, like reflected bits of silver on a black velvet cloth.

The face in the nucleus smiled, exposing a row of bright white teeth. It gave Javik the impression of an epic scale videodome toothpaste commercial. He didn't wonder how a comet could have teeth. He accepted it. This was not a moment to question such things.

As Javik stood in awe with his face turned to the eerie light above, he thought of Wizzy. *He spoke truth to me,* Javik thought. *Everything Wizzy said was true!*

"Sid!" Javik yelled. "Speak to me, Sid!"

There was no response. The gray lines of the face became

black, and the face took on a kindly, cherubic-cheeked expression.

"Skywrite something!" Javik pleaded. "Like you did over Earth! Come on, Sid! Say something to me!"

The Great Comet moved laterally. Javik ran to follow it. He reached the crest of a little hill, giving him a view of the entire clearing. He saw a wide path framed with AmFed garbage cannisters. Several hundred meters from that, a familiar profile jutted into the air.

"My ship!" he said. "The *Amanda Marie!*"

Javik watched the comet. It became bright orange, from its flaming nucleus to the tip of its misty tail. The face remained visible in the nucleus, but it was less defined now, a faint circle of cadmium yellow. The comet rose gracefully, then dipped like a hawk diving for its prey.

My God, Javik thought. *So this is where Sid went.* He shielded his eyes from the light. The backs of his hands became warm as the comet neared. Then they grew cooler and the light receded.

Through his fingers, Javik saw the Great Comet hovering high overhead, still orange but with a scolding expression on its face.

"Sid!" Javik yelled. "What's the matter, Sid?"

The face faded. The comet rose steeply in the sky, blowing a great wind across the clearing. It took a lateral course now, moving close to the horizon of the planet. The clearing grew darker.

Javik shivered.

Soon the comet was a distant speck. Then it dropped out of sight below the horizon. For several moments, glowing orange particles from its tail remained in the sky. They sparkled like the dying embers of a fireworks rocket. Then it was dark. Purple dark.

Wizzy was at the window of Prince Pineapple's apartment. "There!" he exclaimed. "Did you see the comet? Going away fast?"

"That was your papa?" Prince Pineapple asked, pressing his face against the glassplex. "I can hardly believe it!"

The Great Comet became a speck of orange light, then disappeared below the horizon.

Minutes later, Prince Pineapple ran into the Stygian blackness outside, carrying Wizzy under his coat against his belly. Although Wizzy was loosely wrapped in plastic, the prince leaned forward as an extra measure to keep rain from hitting him. In his haste, Prince Pineapple nearly slipped and fell.

"Careful!" Wizzy squealed as he was jiggled about. "I could fall and roll into the pond!"

A trail light at Sacred Pond's edge provided enough illumination for the prince to locate a shelter for Wizzy. Selecting a thick shrub next to the path, he leaned over and placed Wizzy under it.

A cool, wet breeze blew across Prince Pineapple's face as he straightened and surveyed the area. Curls of fog shifted on the surface of the water. He felt the wind shift on his face and saw the change in the curls of fog. Water lapped against the shore. *The rain's holding back,* he thought. *Maybe luck will be with me.*

He stepped off the path into shadows, clearing brush away where he had hidden the pram. It was a small craft, but rather heavy for its size. He dragged it to the shore, then returned for the oars.

As he passed Wizzy, the little comet squealed, "I felt a drop of rain! Check my wrap!"

"Impossible," Prince Pineapple said. "It's not raining at all." He tossed the oars in the pram, then went for Wizzy.

"You took your time," Wizzy gruffed as the prince lifted him. "Each drop takes a portion of my strength. Oh, to be in deep space, where there is no atmosphere and no water!"

Wizzy had better help me, Prince Pineapple thought as he stepped in the pram, *or I'll drop him in the deepest part of Sacred Pond.* He placed Wizzy beneath the aft bench.

Moments later the little boat was cutting slowly across the pond's choppy, foggy surface. Wizzy heard the dipping of the oars in water and the thump of waves against the hull. And he heard the dull clunk of wood against wood whenever an oar slipped from its oarlock; Prince Pineapple would curse whenever this happened, but soon would be back at his task. In a distorted vision through the plastic wrap, Wizzy could see Prince Pineapple from the belly down, leaning forward and back as he pulled at the oars.

"Whatever you do," Prince Pineapple said, "don't say anything that rhymes. It would force me to flip backward, head over heels. That would capsize this little boat."

"Like you did in court?" Wizzy asked, choosing his words carefully.

"Exactly like that."

"You can't control it?"

"I have tried. Dear me, but I've tried! It's instinctual with us. Our muscles pull us right over."

"You might have warned me about that earlier."

The pineapple prince disregarded this remark. Soon he was grunting with each pull at the oars and panting heavily. After a while he had to ship the oars in order to take a rest. He wiped his brow. Just then the boat rocked violently.

"What's going on?" Wizzy squealed.

"It's getting rough out here."

"I can tell that."

A wave washed over the gunwale, splashing cold water on the plastic wrap over Wizzy. Some leaked through and touched him. This sent the little comet into a state of panic. "Save me!" he cried out. "Save me!" Wizzy glowed bright orange now and scooted through Prince Pineapple's legs to a dry forward portion of the deck.

The prince turned to watch Wizzy. "The plastic wrap!" Prince Pineapple said. "You're glowing like a coal! It's melting all over you!"

Wizzy paled to yellow. "That burst of heat dried me off," he said. "But there's a limit. Bursts like that use a lot of energy. I presume you brought more plastic wrap?"

"I did not."

"I wish I hadn't come on your ridiculous voyage!"

"Remember all those things we have in common," Prince Pineapple said. Angrily, he resumed his struggle with the oars. He was fighting a strong current now, and had to row just to remain in one place. A floating log bounced off the side of the pram's hull, sending a dull, disturbing shudder through the boat.

Prince Pineapple watched the log disappear in the current aft of his boat. He was straining to the breaking point; his hands were burning from his effort.

A light rain started. This caused Wizzy to cry out in terror and seek the farthest reaches of shelter under the forward bench.

Rain mixed with perspiration ran down Prince Pineapple's face. Because of the current, he took quick breaks of only a few seconds to wipe his face.

All the while, Wizzy complained with each wave that washed aboard and with each increase in the intensity of precipitation. It was raining steadily now, and the prince turned to see Wizzy glow bright orange, drying himself. Finally, in desperation, Wizzy suction-perched on the underside of the forward bench, clinging there like a fat fly on a ceiling.

"I feel dizzy," Prince Pineapple said.

"Then turn back!" Wizzy said.

"Never!" Prince Pineapple rowed harder now, drawing strength from his deepest reservoir of energy. Images of the Sacred Scroll of Cork danced across his half-closed eyes.

Something heavy landed on his belly, then pushed its way under his coat. "I'm losing strength," Wizzy said. "Keep me in here. Keep me dry...." The voice faded.

Prince Pineapple considered returning to shore for Wizzy's sake. "Do you still want me to take you back?" he asked.

Wizzy did not respond.

Now Prince Pineapple thought of the perspiration on his underclothes. Soon this wetness would soak through and meet the encroaching outside moisture from waves and rain. There would be no dryness then. He reminded himself of his priorities. Wizzy was expendable. The scroll was not.

Just at the moment when Prince Pineapple felt he could row no more, the waves subsided and the rain stopped. He shipped his oars and took deep breaths to restore himself. An eerie low light radiated across the surface of the water. The pond was like glassplex here, and there was a purple luminescence just below the surface.

"What's going on?" Wizzy asked. He poked his nucleus out from under the coat.

"I don't know. It's different here. And I feel the boat moving forward, as if it's being pulled by something. It's not an opposing current now."

"The rain is gone!" Wizzy said happily. He ventured into the night air for a little spin, being careful only to fly above the boat. His tail was yellow orange as he flew, and it cast a sparkling reflection on the water that had accumulated in the boat bottom. Soon Wizzy alighted on Prince Pineapple's shoulder. There he glowed orange for a moment to dry the fabric of the coat.

Overhead, Prince Pineapple saw stars burning more clearly than he could ever recall having seen them. Two synchronized

Corkian moons passed over them quickly, momentarily casting their warm glow across the water. Then the moons disappeared beyond the horizon of fog.

"I have seen the magician's bubble out here," Prince Pineapple said. "On clear days. According to legend, my scroll is trapped in the bubble."

"*Your* scroll?"

"A slip of the tongue."

Squinting his cat's eye, Wizzy saw a yellow glow in the fog off their starboard bow. "I see something out there," he said.

"Where?"

"Off the starboard bow."

"Where? Where?"

"It's impossible to miss!"

"I don't see it!"

"Well I see it clearly," Wizzy said. "The fog's clearing. We're drawing nearer. Yes! It's a bubble—floating just above the surface of the pond."

"Must be a spell on me," Prince Pineapple muttered thoughtfully, "caused by Lord Abercrombie's soil nutrients every time I recharge. I am permitted to see the bubble from afar, but once I draw near..."

"Could be a magician's trick, all right."

"We're going directly toward the bubble?"

"Yes. And I see something inside. A rolled parchment."

"The Sacred Scroll!" Prince Pineapple said. "How far?"

"Less than fifty meters."

"Tell me when we're close enough to hit it with the oar handle. Something dull will pop the bubble, according to legend."

"Don't rely on that legend. It may have been planted in your pineapple brain by Lord Abercrombie."

"There's nothing wrong with having a pineapple brain."

"I didn't say there was. But your legend smacks of trickery to me."

"Then forget the oar. Do it your way. You with all the knowledge of the universe."

"We'd better stop bickering," Wizzy said. "It's just ahead now."

Prince Pineapple felt the boat slow.

"Almost there," Wizzy reported, perching himself on the bow seat. "We'll go right under it."

The bubble was bright yellow and perhaps half as big in circumference as the length of the pram. Inside the bubble, floating freely, Wizzy saw an old-looking rolled parchment tied with brown cord.

When the bow of the pram slipped beneath the bubble, Wizzy glowed the hottest white-orange he could and smashed against the underside of the bubble. He bounced off a soft surface. Then he tried again, bouncing off again.

Seeing where Wizzy was attacking, Prince Pineapple thrust forth his oar handle. He felt it strike something soft. Then there was a loud clap of thunder. A lightning bolt in front of Wizzy's eye sent him scurrying for cover beneath the prince's coat. The oar clattered to the deck of the boat.

Prince Pineapple began to see something where the oar had struck: the broken image of a rolled, yellowing parchment, bound with brown leather cord . . . unidentifiable letters on the parchment with an "X" over them. The image faded to invisibility.

"I saw it!" Prince Pineapple said. "But now it's gone!"

Venturing out on the prince's lap, Wizzy said, "We're dead in the water. You just have to reach out and take it. Would you look at that! It says 'Torah' on the scroll, but that's been crossed out. The bubble's gone now. You blasted it with the oar."

Prince Pineapple reached for the place he had seen the scroll. He felt something there: stiff paper. But he withdrew his hand suspiciously without grabbing hold. "Too easy," he said.

"Probably a discarded religious document from Earth," Wizzy said. "Torah . . . that was sacred to one of their religions."

"This cannot be," Prince Pineapple said. "The Sacred Scroll of Cork predates the arrival of Earthian gar-bahge."

Wizzy glowed red, calling upon his data banks for assistance. "I think it's the original scroll, all right," he said. "With fake markings added by Abercrombie to confuse anyone finding it."

Prince Pineapple extended both hands, wrapping his fingers around the parchment. The paper was rough to his touch and cool. He pulled it to him, pressing it against his belly. "I have it!" he said. "I have it!"

Wizzy flew to one side of the prince and watched him bend

over the scroll, like a fleshcarrier parent sheltering its child.

A bright vision flashed across Prince Pineapple's brain. He saw Lord Abercrombie clutching the scroll in much the same way. In fast forward, he watched Abercrombie cross a series of obstacles: desert...ice...swamp....It went too fast for further details. In his vision, the prince saw Abercrombie immerse his entire body in the soil—in a rock-walled cavern somewhere beneath the planet's surface. Then he saw the scroll fly back on its own, returning to Sacred Pond. Distantly, Prince Pineapple heard a voice. The image faded.

"Snap out of it," Wizzy said. "Let's get this boat moving."

Prince Pineapple tucked the unseen scroll inside his coat and buttoned the coat all the way up. In a daze, he located the oars. Soon he was guiding the pram back the way they had come. "That sure was easy," he said.

"Your troubles have just begun," Wizzy said.

TEN

The females of every fleshcarrier
planet claim to have special
powers. On Earth, it is
known as "woman's intuition."
Morovians call it "yenta." Uni-
versally, it causes females to nag.

Excerpt from the expeditionary
notes of Sevensayer Arnold

Javik made his way across the purple-dark clearing carefully,
trying to recall his ship's location from the momentary flash
of the comet. His belly ached with hunger, a gnawing sensation
that increased with each passing moment. There was food on
the ship. He looked forward to it.

After a good deal of probing with his hands and with the
tips of his boots, he encountered something on the ground which
rustled like gortex. He knelt and picked it up, recognizing it
by touch as a survival pack. All the pack's normally full pockets
were open and empty.

He muttered a curse. His foot came in contact with a cello-
wrapper, then another. Then a small pile of them. All were
empty.

"Someone's been here, damn it. And I'm hungrier than hell!"

Bemoaning his misfortune, Javik located the Tasnard rope
he had left dangling from the side of the ship. He wrapped the

rope around his chest and under his armpits, then mento-commanded it. The rope lifted him gently up to the corrugated metal surface of the entry platform. The hatch was open.

He smelled something peculiar as he entered the cabin, something unlike any odor he had ever before encountered. It struck him that it was a dull odor, if an odor could be dull. His nostrils flared as he sniffed the air. He still could not see anything, but the sensation of purpleness was gone.

An animal? he wondered. *It's not an offensive odor.*

Javik stood motionless for a moment, listening to night sounds. The mournful howl of a wolf drifted across the clearing, followed by what sounded like an owl's hoot. Then he became aware of something alive on board, breathing deeply and roughly, as a large man or animal might do. He detected separate sounds.

There's two of them in here, he thought. *Asleep with full bellies.*

Cork's two synchronized moons moved overhead in their rapid night passage, lighting the clearing with a cool harvest glow. Feeling exposed in the doorway, Javik dropped silently to the deck. When the moons had passed, he rose and crept stealthily across the cabin.

Can't risk a light, he thought, pushing debris on the deck away carefully with his foot. *Maybe I can find Blanquie's automatic pistol.*

The rumbling breathing changed in cadence. Javik froze. Only one of them was breathing deeply now. The other was chugging rapidly, like a steam engine. Presently, the rapid breather joined the other in a symphony of deep breathing.

Javik emitted a sigh of relief, then tiptoed aft. He dropped to all fours, feeling along the corrugated metal floor for the sleeping compartment hatches. Feeling a fine powder on the surface, he paused to lift some to his nose. It smelled dull.

Now his groping fingers touched one hatch cover and, just aft of that, another. Still farther aft, he touched a third. This was Blanquie's, the one he wanted. Javik mento-spun the little wheel that controlled the hatch, and heard the wheel's metal parts grind too loudly.

A sleeper stirred, causing the ship to move.

Something heavy, Javik thought.

The deep breathing resumed its cadence.

Carefully, Javik lifted the hatch. It creaked, but did not disturb the sleepers. Then he dropped his legs over the edge into the compartment, probing down for the first rung of the ladder. He reached up and dropped the hatch cover without locking it, then descended to the floor of the compartment. A loose object was on the floor. His foot found it, sending him down with a thud that shook the ship.

He took a deep breath, listening with every pore and nerve of his body.

"Ahunga!" a deep, loud voice said from above. This translated across Javik's language mixer pendant as: "What in the Moro Hell?"

Javik tried to mento-lock the hatch, but felt no click in the back of his brain. *That gun had better be in here,* he thought. He mentoed on the light, feeling the brain click that told him his implanted mento unit was functioning. Corner ceiling lights flashed on, casting stark white shadows around the compartment. He tried mentoing the hatch lock again, but got no response.

While Javik searched the compartment, he heard an angry voice and a good deal of commotion in the cabin above.

Crash! Something fell up there. The shattering of glassplex followed.

"Over there!" another voice said from above. This voice was not nearly so deep as the other, and sounded female to Javik. "A light!" the voice said.

They spoke in a peculiar language, translated to Javik by the language mixer pendant around his neck. He touched the pendant for a moment, then mentoed off the compartment lights.

They saw a ring of light around the hatch, he thought.

"Now it's gone!" the female voice said.

Javik groped in the darkness, opening cupboards and drawers. Finally he located the service pistol in a drawer, wrapped in a cotton shirt.

The voices and movements were directly overhead now. "I saw it here someplace," the female voice said.

Javik checked the clip of the automatic pistol. It was loaded. He crouched in a corner, staring up at the pitch-black ceiling of the sleeping compartment.

"This thing opens," the deep voice said. Javik heard the hatch mechanism turn.

If only I could mento the main cabin lights from here, Javik thought. *Then I could see them when the hatch opens.*

The hatch creaked open. The voices were near now. Javik saw four eyes above, glowing in the dark like red coals.

Not human, Javik thought. *That's for sure.* His pulse quickened.

"In here," the deep voice said.

"You're going in?" the other asked.

Javik felt the floor shake as one of the intruders descended the ladder. Whatever it was moved athletically and heavily, with no hint of clumsiness. The odd, dull smell touched Javik's nostrils again.

"Here somewhere," the deep voice said from inside the compartment with Javik.

Javik held his breath for a moment that seemed like an eternity. Then he mentoed on the compartment lights. "Freeze!" Javik shouted as the lights went on. He trained his gun on the intruder.

Rebo coiled back on his haunches, staring at Javik with smoldering, startled eyes.

Javik was equally startled upon seeing a three-legged, hairy creature wearing a black leather jacket. Rebo held his long knife in one hand. He shifted it to the other menacingly, staring all the while at Javik with red, pupilless eyes. He took a step in Javik's direction.

"Back!" Javik ordered.

Rebo took another step forward.

Javik aimed the gun at the pillow on Blanquie's bed and fired. An orange flash shot out of the barrel, whacking a laser bullet into the pillow. The pistol crack was deafening.

Terrified, Rebo dropped his knife and leaped for the hatch ladder. He pulled himself up smoothly to the cabin level, then reached back to close the hatch.

Seeing what the creature had in mind, Javik fired again. A bullet grazed Rebo's fingers, creasing and stinging them. He cried out in pain, then withdrew his hand. Javik heard him lumbering away.

Javik climbed out of the sleeping compartment and mentoed on the main cabin lights. He saw two of the three-legged creatures standing near the open main hatchway. The creatures froze where they were as Javik leveled his gun on them. Near them, a layer of light brown powder covered the deck.

Following Javik's gaze, Namaba glanced down at the powder.

"What is that stuff?" Javik asked.

"Our bodily wastes," she replied. "Excreted through our pores after we ate."

"Powdered shit," Javik said, angrily. "On *my* ship!"

"Who are you?" she asked.

"I'll ask the questions here," Javik said. He touched a deep scratch on his forehead.

"Very well," Namaba said.

"Quiet," Rebo snapped, turning his jutting head to glare at her.

"It looks like you ate everything I had," Javik said, looking at the one he judged to be female. "Two months' rations!"

"Our boilers were low," Rebo said, answering for her.

Javik motioned aft with his pistol. "Move back there," he said. "Sit on the floor so I can think."

Namaba and Rebo followed the command, loping past Javik warily. Javik noted that the larger creature kept eyeing the open sleeping compartment hatch.

"Try for that knife and it'll be the last move you make," Javik said. "This thing packs a big wallop."

"Do as he says," Namaba said. "Your knife is no match for his thunder piece."

Rebo glared at Javik.

"We are Morovians," Namaba explained. "I am Namaba, daughter of Heroista the Alchemist."

"And I am Rebo, son of Montenegro the Prisoner." His eyes flashed defiantly.

"What are your last names?" Javik asked.

"Last names?" Rebo said. "What is a last name?"

"Well, my name is Tomas Patrick Javik. That's a first name, a middle name, and a last name."

"Three names for one person?" Rebo exclaimed. "How curious!"

"It helps to distinguish me from everyone else. There are only so many names to go around."

"Your people have little imagination," Namaba said. "We have thirty-two billion inhabitants on the planet of Morovia. Every one with a different name."

"Sometimes a duplication occurs," Rebo said. "By accident. But the Name Bureau always finds it and issues a decision concerning who gets to keep the name."

Javik located an empty survival pack and began scouring the cabin for food and survival gear. He found a box of space matches, a half-eaten bio bar, and a penlight. Kneeling, he searched a pile of rubbish on the deck. "Ah," he said, locating a tiny tube the size of a roll of candy. "The lightweight tent." He tossed it in the pack. Questioning Namaba and Rebo as he searched, Javik learned of their remarkable journey to Cork.

Javik stuffed a package of dehydrated apples and two bio bars in his pack. "What were you on Morovia?" he asked.

"I was a very important leader," Rebo said, "in charge of an entire territory of inhabitants."

"That doesn't explain much," Javik said. "What's the emblem on the backs of your jackets?"

"The Southside Hawks," Namaba said. "Our club."

"I'm club president," Rebo said.

"Punks," Javik said. "We've got punks on Earth, too."

"We're not punks!" Rebo said, bristling.

Javik swore at each empty food wrapper he found. He kicked the base of the magna-scope console, glaring at the Morovians. They sat motionless. "Did you guys have enough to eat?" Javik asked with a sarcastic whine. "I oughtta kill you."

"We're very sorry," Namaba said. "We thought your ship was abandoned."

"That's quite correct," Rebo said. "How were we expected to know? There was equipment all over the place, you know."

"Funny," Javik said. "Both of you speak kinda elegantly— not with big words, but not like gang members either."

"Everyone on Morovia speaks this way," Namaba said. "We are renowned for having large vocabularies. That has no bearing on intelligence, of course. We use many words we don't understand."

Javik located a leaking, smashed container of water capsules. "Shit," he said. Only two of the clear little capsules were undamaged, so he placed them carefully in his titanium pillbox, returning the box to his pocket.

"What do you plan to do with us?" Rebo asked.

"I'm going to try to get this ship going," Javik said angrily. He eyed a shattered land compass on the floor. "And you're getting off." He found two collapsible plastic water pods, ten-liter size, and stuffed them in the pack. *I'll need these,* he thought.

"Take us with you," Namaba said. "Take us back to Moro City."

"Yeah," Rebo said. "There's an airfield just outside—"

Javik laughed boisterously. Seeing a holster on the deck, he retrieved it and strapped it on. "If this ship takes off," he said, "and that's a mighty big 'if' with all the hull damage, it's not going very far. I just want to get it to a safe place where I can work on it." He holstered the pistol, gazing at Namaba's eyes. They burned soft red, with no pupils. He looked away.

Chee-rist! Javik thought. *I'm attracted to her! Why? First a transsexual and now a three-legged beast! I've been away too long!*

"Why do you look at me so?" Namaba asked.

After a moment of silence, Javik's gaze flitted to Rebo. Rebo was giving him a hard stare, possibly because of Javik's interest in Namaba. *This one could be dangerous,* Javik thought. He dropped the survival pack on the science officer's chair.

"Can you go to Moro City after repairing your ship?" Namaba asked.

"This ship isn't going anywhere near Moro City," Javik said, rummaging in the pack. The salivary glands in his mouth gushed as he found a bio bar. He tore the cello-wrap off and bit away a corner of the bar. It was honey sweet, and he savored it.

Four red eyes watched as Javik ate. Rebo licked his lips.

Sternly, Javik motioned toward the open main hatch. "Get out," he said in a low, even tone. "And make it fast."

Rebo and Namaba scrambled for the circular hatchway. Namaba let herself down the Tasnard rope hand over hand, followed by Rebo.

As Javik watched, the Morovians lumbered across the clearing. Soon they were out of range of the light cast by the *Amanda Marie*'s open hatch.

Javik mento-flipped on a spotlight to watch them. He followed their path by mento-directing the light, dogging their every move. The Morovians glanced back nervously as they ran, continually trying to elude the beam of light. But Javik kept it on them until he saw them enter the woods.

Javik ate half of the bio bar, then wrapped the rest hurriedly. He knew he should not have eaten even that much, despite the gnawing ache of hunger across his midsection. There was no telling when he would find more food.

After switching off the spotlight, Javik noticed four red eyes looking toward him from the woods, burning in the darkness like hot embers in a firepit.

"We should have rushed him," Rebo said. From his crouched position with Namaba just inside the woods, he glared across the clearing at the *Amanda Marie*. The ship's spotlight flashed off. Rebo pushed a small pine tree branch out of his way. It cracked.

"But the thunder stick," Namaba said, her voice a nervous, shivering whisper. "We could have been killed!"

"A bluff," Rebo said. "It just made noise."

"And your yenta tells you that?" Her tone was sarcastic.

"I have no yenta," he said, irritably. "And neither do you."

"All Morovian women have yenta," she said. "And mine tells me he would have killed us. He is very intense."

"Pshaw!"

"But I sense goodness in him—a potential friend."

"I don't know...."

"I'll tell you something else, Rebo. You're different here— not the same ruthless gang leader I knew on Morovia. My yenta tells me this, too. You know it to be true."

There was no response. Rebo shifted on his haunches.

"It's true, isn't it?" she prodded.

"Yes," Rebo said. "I am different, and it confuses me."

A giraffe-necked light cast the short shadows of Prince Pineapple and Wizzy as they disembarked from the pram at the edge of Sacred Pond. Prince Pineapple kick-shoved the boat out on the water, clutching the scroll under his coat with one hand.

From his perch on the prince's shoulder, Wizzy said, "The rain has stopped. "Let's have a look at the scroll."

As Wizzy glowed white to provide light, Prince Pineapple pulled the scroll out and unfurled it, holding one hand at the bottom edge and the other at the top. This seemed peculiar to the prince, for while he felt the stiff parchment paper between his fingers, he could not see it.

"Wrong side," Wizzy said, seeing a heavy "X" across the

sheet. "Rather a poor job of Torah fakery on Abercrombie's part," he muttered.

Prince Pineapple flipped the scroll over, pulling it close so that Wizzy could read it more easily. The paper crackled.

"It's a map," Wizzy said. "It says in one corner to look for three-dot trail markers."

"Three dots," Prince Pineapple said. "Magical signs. Yes, I have seen such markings."

"We're to take Baker Road from Sacred Pond, to Avenida Five. Thence to All Souls Hill and across Dusty Desert."

"The Badlands," Prince Pineapple said, his tone reflecting disappointment. "I feared as much."

"There's a Bottomless Bog shown here," Wizzy said. "And a place called Moha. Are you familiar with those?"

"Moha sounds familiar. Can't quite place it. There's a short-cut to All Souls Hill. We will pass your ship." He rerolled the scroll and secured it with the cord. Removing his coat, he placed the scroll and the coat on the ground. "I should recharge now," he said. "A long journey awaits us."

Wizzy did not comment on this. *I haven't actually agreed to remain with the prince*, he thought. *But he does need me to read the scroll, and Captain Tom doesn't want me around. . . .*

Twenty-five minutes later. . . .

Prince Pineapple leaned forward with a newfound sense of purpose as he walked, for now he had the Sacred Scroll of Cork. Wizzy was on his shoulder, brightly lit to show the way. They were crossing through the carriage parking lot of the shopping center, passing dimly lit stores whose windows displayed discarded Earth household gadgets. Prince Pineapple knew the stores would be bare soon. Lord Abercrombie would demand all gar-bahge for himself. It was inevitable.

Pausing at the corner of the center's largest building, the prince whispered, "Dim your light. I hear something."

Wizzy darkened.

Prince Pineapple looked around the corner, then scampered back to a dark doorway. "Corker security patrol," he whispered.

Two guards walked past, making loud sucking sounds as they worked at their grain alcohol backpack tubes. Had the guards been attentive, they would have seen and apprehended

Prince Pineapple. Fortunately, they did not turn their heads.

Five minutes later, Prince Pineapple and Wizzy had reached the safety of a shortcut path through the woods. It was a little-used way without lighting, so Wizzy glowed brightly again, concentrating his light forward.

Many roots and stones were embedded in the ground, and in places the path was difficult to locate because of the lack of traffic. Prince Pinapple took the wrong way once, and it was nearly ten minutes before he realized his mistake. He back-tracked, finding the correct path.

"We're going around Corker Stadium," the prince said. "Can't risk going out there. Too many guards."

Presently they reached a wider path, with trail lights glowing yellow. Wizzy dimmed to conserve his energy.

"We were on this trail yesterday," Prince Pineapple said. "Your ship is just ahead."

Wizzy recalled his papa's instructions concerning remaining with Captain Tom. But Javik had been cruel to him. *He doesn't want anything to do with me,* Wizzy thought. *Surely Papa will understand.*

Prince Pineapple took a fork in the path, stepping onto a wooden bridge. Wizzy heard the cadence of the prince's feet on wood boards and the squeal of a raccoon.

Returning to his thoughts as they left the bridge, Wizzy wondered if he might have been more pleasant, despite Captain Tom's attitude. He turned this over in his mind several times. No answer leaped out to salvage him from the dilemma. At times, Prince Pineapple would say something to jar Wizzy's concentration. And Wizzy tried to think of other things. But each time a nagging question returned: *Should I go back for Captain Tom?*

"Light!" Prince Pineapple said. "Give me light!"

"Huh?" Wizzy said. "Oh." He glowed brightly.

They had reached the end of the trail, arriving at a wide clearing. The cool gray light of dawn washed across the sky, showing distant treetops on the other side of the clearing.

Wizzy recognized this place. The ship was here somewhere. He slanted his cat's eye, gazing in all directions. The beam of his light moved as he scanned.

"That way," Prince Pineapple said, pointing ahead and to the right.

Now this guy's giving me orders, Wizzy thought. *First Papa, then everyone else*.

Wizzy was directing the light beam the wrong way, causing Prince Pineapple to trip. "Pay attention!" the prince snapped, stumbling over something.

Wizzy directed his beam ahead of Prince Pineapple. They made their way to the center of the clearing.

Suddenly, Prince Pineapple dropped to a prone position on the ground. Wizzy fell from his shoulder, tumbling in cool, damp grass. "Dim it," Prince Pineapple said.

Intent on escaping the dampness of the grass, Wizzy did not respond. He found a dry area of dirt on which to sit.

"Dim it, I said!"

"Oh," Wizzy said, darkening. "I thought you said, 'Damn it.'"

"Someone's on your ship," Prince Pineapple said, pointing across the gray light of the clearing.

Now Wizzy saw it too—the *Amanda Marie* with its cabin lights blazing. And someone standing in the lighted hatchway. "One of the guards you posted?" Wizzy asked.

"I doubt it. They wouldn't stay all night."

"A scavenger, then?"

"Nothing of value there yet. The ship is far too new."

"Maybe it's Captain Tom!" Wizzy said, surprised at the excitement in his voice.

"Could be," Prince Pineapple said, rising to his feet. "We'll give it a wide berth to play it safe." He skirted the ship now, angling toward a craggy hill across the clearing with Wizzy dark on his shoulder.

Wizzy saw the profiles of mountains against the dawn sky. Deep grays in the sky were giving way to pastel pinks and blues, like an artist mixing colors on his palette. "We're going up there?" he asked.

"Right. We'll have to scramble through the woods with no trail for a while. The trailhead's too close to the ship.

Wizzy was curious about who was on the ship. "But what if it *is* Captain Tom?" he asked.

"And what if it is?" Prince Pineapple said, his tone worried. "Remember how he treated you, Wizzy. He doesn't want to see you."

"I suppose you're right."

A distant, brilliant flash of orange in the sky caught Wizzy's attention. A Great Comet swooped down gracefully, then veered up and away. Within seconds it was a far-off speck, no more noticeable than a bright star. "Oh!" Wizzy exclaimed.

"What's the matter?" Prince Pineapple asked.

"There!" Wizzy said, casting his gaze toward the retreating comet. "It's Papa Sidney!"

"I don't see anything."

"It's almost out of sight now. But it *was* Papa! I know it!" Wizzy thought for a moment, then: "He was telling me to stay with Captain Tom."

"Don't be ridiculous."

Wizzy lifted off from the prince's shoulder, flying in a holding pattern there.

Prince Pineapple continued on for several steps, then turned. "Come on, Wizzy. We've a long way to go."

"I have to find Captain Tom." Wizzy glowed orange. A bright yellow tail flared from his nucleus.

"But the scroll! I can't read it without you. I can't even see the damned thing."

"I'm sorry, but I must do as Papa says."

Prince Pineapple hung his head dejectedly, sensing there was no way to change the little comet's mind. Removing his beanie, he gave the helicopter rotor a spin. When he looked up, Wizzy was gone, streaking across the clearing toward the ship.

Wizzy changed course once to look back at Prince Pineapple. The prince was barely visible in the low light, a solitary, shadowy figure standing there. Then the prince replaced his helicopter beanie on his head, taking a few hesitating steps toward the craggy hills. He picked up his pace and began to walk briskly.

He's going anyway, Wizzy thought. *The fool!*

Wizzy thought he saw Prince Pineapple wave to him. But the visibility was not good, and Wizzy thought it might even have been an obscene gesture.

When Wizzy reached the ship, Javik was standing in the circular hatchway with his hands on his hips. Javik's legs were spread, and the position of his body gave the impression of a person blocking the entrance. His head moved from side to side in negative fashion. He was not glad to see Wizzy. "What do you want?" Javik asked.

"I came to help." Wizzy noticed scratches on Javik's face.

"You can help by staying the hell out of my way!"

Wizzy bristled at the remark. Perching on a large rock near the base of the *Amanda Marie,* Wizzy saw the sky open up with pale blue color as the new day arrived.

"Even if you were worth a damn," Javik said, "which you definitely are not, there would be nothing for you to do here. The ship has big problems."

"How bad?"

"I just checked all systems. The ailerons are heavily damaged, with two flaps totally useless. Most of the rocket tubes are plugged. Hell, this thing went through a bad dust storm, then was rolled on the ground and tossed in a hole."

"Couldn't we make the parts with the metalworking equipment onboard? We could shape wall and floor pieces into ailerons."

"I'm surprised you understand that," Javik said. "We'd need too much time. Corkers will be here soon, looking to take me back."

"Why don't we go with Prince Pineapple?" Wizzy asked. He told of the prince's quest for the Magician's Chamber occupied by Abercrombie. Javik listened intently, and Wizzy thought he saw his expression brighten for a time. "It's supposed to be a rough journey," Wizzy said. "Rougher than a cob, from the looks of the scroll map."

Javik turned and went in the cabin. Wizzy followed, and watched Javik's angular form slump into the captain's chair. Through the windshield beyond Javik, Wizzy saw the tangerine orange ball of a Corkian sun just above the treetops.

.Wizzy flew to the dashboard and set down there. "Why don't we go with the prince?" he asked.

"And what will you do if I don't?" Javik asked, smiling thinly.

"I'll stay with you, of course."

"Because Papa said? Is that why?"

Wizzy's yellow cat's eye looked perplexed and angry at the same instant.

"I saw the comet," Javik said. "It passed overhead just before you arrived." The cabin grew quiet for nearly a minute.

Then Javik kicked the base of the instrument panel. "Damn this ship!" he said.

"Remember your mission," Wizzy said. "Find anything unusual and report back. Wouldn't that be something if you could learn more about the arch-criminal, Abercrombie?"

"I know enough about this friggin' planet! All I want now is a couple of pleasure dome maidens, a table full of food, and at least three days of uninterrupted sleep."

"But Abercrombie is nuts. Prince Pineapple says so, anyway. Abercrombie must hate Earth because of what Uncle Rosy did to him. What if he tries to break this planet out of orbit?"

"And send it toward Earth?"

"Right."

"Too farfetched. It'll never happen." Javik kicked the instrument panel base again.

"Maybe not. But you can't stay here."

"You're right about that, Wizzy. And I'm not going back to those games."

"Then you'll go with Prince Pineapple?"

"'These are not problems,'" Javik muttered, recalling a schoolboy mantra. "'They are opportunities.'"

"What?"

"Nothing. Yeah. I'll go." With a rush of energy, Javik lunged to his feet. Locating the survival pack he had filled, he glanced around the cabin for anything he might have missed.

"Do you have a tent in there?" Wizzy asked, recalling the dangers of water for him.

"You think I'm stupid or somethin'?" Javik barked. He unsnapped a gortex bag from the wall and stuffed the bag in his pack. "Stay outta my way as much as possible. You got that, Wizzy?"

Wizzy burned orange with anger, becoming so hot that Javik saw smoke under him on the plastic dashboard. Wizzy smelled the burning plastic and cooled down. Had Wizzy been human, he might have bitten his lip at that moment. For he did not say anything in response.

When Javik and Wizzy reached the hatchway, they saw Prince Pineapple standing below, looking up at them. "I had a thought," the prince said excitedly. "Maybe we could all go together—on your ship."

"Everyone wants my ship," Javik said. "But it's a no-go.

If I could get it running, I'd blast outta here so fast it would . . ."
He sighed, adding: "I'll go with you, Prince. On foot."

"Wonderful!" Prince Pineapple exclaimed.

Javik wrapped the black and white Tasnard rope around his
chest and under his armpits, then mentoed it.

"You won't regret this," Prince Pineapple said.

The Tasnard rope carried Javik gently to ground level. Wizzy
flew down in a streak of yellow light.

"I already do," Javik said, looking at Wizzy. Javik mentoed
the Tasnard rope. It curled neatly into his open palms. He put
the rope in his survival pack.

Wizzy flew in a short, angry circle.

"Let's see your scroll," Javik said, looking at Prince
Pineapple.

The tall pineapple man unbuttoned his coat and handed the
parchment to Javik.

"You can't see this?" Javik asked, accepting the scroll. "Not
at all?"

"No." Prince Pineapple's tone was tense. He did not like
having to depend upon anyone. "Lord Abercrombie placed a
spell on me," he said. "I'm sure of it."

"Well, I can sure see it," Javik said. "It shows a steep path,
gaining thirty-three hundred meters in elevation over a distance
of nine kilometers. Water at two points, one near the top. Then
a high desert, fifty-two kilometers across. Icy Valley on the
other side."

"Icy Valley," Prince Pineapple said. "I have heard of it.
Magicians created it, according to legend." He looked past
Javik, not meeting his gaze.

After looking over the prince's rather thin and worn coat,
Javik removed his wardrobe ring and handed it to him, saying,
"Put this on."

Prince Pineapple tried the ring on each of his stubby fingers,
finally settling on the pinky of his left hand. That was the
smallest of the lot.

"Now remove your coat," Javik said.

"What on Cork for?"

"Just do it," Javik said, looking nervously across the clearing. All three Corker suns were above the treetops now, filling
the clearing with light.

Prince Pineapple dropped his coat to the ground, placing
the scroll on top of it.

Javik held the prince's hand and stared at the rectangular turquoise stone on the wardrobe ring. He mentoed it. The stone glowed bright turquoise blue. Then an orange thread darted out of the ring, pausing in midair for a moment like a snake about to strike.

Prince Pineapple jerked his hand.

"Just stay still," Javik said. He gripped the prince's hand tightly. "This won't hurt a bit."

The orange thread sped up, down, and around Prince Pineapple's left arm, then did the same on the other arm, went around the neck and around the torso. A closed plastic zipper appeared down the front. Within seconds, Prince Pineapple was wearing an orange vari-temp coat. Through a similar procedure, he received a pair of matching pants, which stitched their way over his purple and black checkered shorts.

"That outfit will work better in all temperatures than what you had," Javik said. He retrieved the wardrobe ring and used it to obtain his own similar outfit.

"Magic?" Prince Pineapple asked, touching the sleeve of his new coat in awe.

"Naw," Javik said, lifting his survival pack from the ground. "Just Bu-Tech."

Prince Pineapple removed his red helicopter beanie with its bright yellow plastic rotor. He held it against the coat. "Are you sure this doesn't clash?" he asked.

"Oh no," Javik said, recalling the bright purple outfit the coat and pants covered. "You look great, Prince."

Prince Pineapple pursed his lips in a serious manner and looked at Javik. Then the prince donned his beanie and turned toward the trailhead. Soon he was leading the way up a rugged path that skirted a rockslide.

"Watch your step," Prince Pineapple said. "I have been to the top once, and there are perilous places—narrow stretches of mountain goat trail with steep dropoffs."

Wizzy flew at the rear, flaring a bright green tail which intermittently changed color as he gained control over it. A thick mist rolled down from the gnarled, gnome's-cap rocks above. Soon they entered the mist. The trail became steeper, putting a noticeable strain on Javik's Achilles tendons. He stopped to stretch the tendons, jogger-style, then caught up with the others.

* * *

Lord Abercrombie rolled over on his narrow four-poster bed, pulling the imitation down blankets over his face. Reflected morning sunlight had traveled to his bedroom via an elaborate network of mirrors, throwing the room into cheerful white light.

He was on his flat side now, with his invisible magical side penetrating the mattress and bedsprings. At the whir of an approaching meckie, Lord Abercrombie looked through the mattress and bed frame with his magical visual sensors.

It was the yellow meckie, the one Abercrombie had ordered programmed with scientific data. It was dented, stocky, and rivet-covered, with a yellow light pulsating on top. It had no face, and one arm dangled at its side in disrepair. "Are you awake, Lord?" the meckie asked. His voice was deep and metallic.

"I am now," Lord Abercrombie said grumpily.

"I was told to report to you first thing in the morning, sir."

"That didn't mean in my bedroom." He peeked out from under the covers with his human eye. "I meant in the main chamber."

"Oh. Excuse me, Lord." The meckie turned to leave.

"As long as you're here, tell me about planetary magnetics. Can that be spoiling my magic, and my other disaster control efforts?"

"Definitely, sir. The linguistics meckie was in Servicing when I received my program, and she filled me in on your concerns."

"Oh? Well, I suppose that's all right."

"I went to the surface last night and did a little homework on planetary magnetics. While you slept."

Lord Abercrombie sat up and put his pillow between the small of his back and the headboard. Reflected sunlight slanted across his covers from a ceiling mirror. He didn't say anything.

"I spoke with a magical tree up there, Lord. It's an old oak, about five hundred meters east of the entrance slab."

"I know the tree. It's one of the history-keeping places of the Council of Magic. But it would not tell me anything— other than its age and galactic serial number."

"Maybe it let its guard down a little for me," the meckie said. "It was a beautiful evening last night, with harvest moons making their passage every hour. I spoke with the tree about the weather. You know, sir—small talk."

"You're here to describe chitchat with a tree?"

"There's more than that. He's not a bad sort, actually. Just following orders. He's tens of thousands of years old, you know."

"I can imagine."

"Anyway, he said the weather used to be more stable—less stormy. Then the magicians came around and started stirring things up."

"The others tried disaster control too?"

"Apparently. I didn't ask for details. Anyway, the tree mentioned something about Cork being out of whack magnetically. Everything is okay until somebody tries to fool with Mother Nature. Then the monopoles go crazy."

"Monopoles?"

"Subatomic particles, Lord. Responsible for magnetism."

Lord Abercrombie's human eye became bird alert. "The reverse rain—it's caused by a magnetic imbalance in the planet?"

"Uh huh. The planet and its atmosphere function as a single unit."

"Did the tree say anything else?"

"No. I tried a number of direct questions after that, but it closed up the trunk hole it had been using as a mouth and wouldn't say another word."

"Good work. Now what? How can I be more effective?"

"Well, Lord . . . Do you mind if I sit down?"

"No. Go ahead."

The meckie hopped on a side chair, retracting its wheels to form a flat surface under its body. Its defective arm hung loosely at its side. "I've been thinking about this planet, Lord. I think the magnetics are shifting all the time. Pulling one way, then another. Those little monopoles travel in packs, kinda like schools of fish."

"You mean through the dirt?"

"Mostly through iron and other elements in rock."

"Oh."

"You moved a couple of rocks with magic, didn't you, Lord?"

"You *have* done your homework."

"My theory is that you moved them when the monopoles were somewhere else, or at least when they weren't present at full strength."

"So I should strike when the little buggers aren't around."

"Precisely." The meckie's dome light pulsed erratically, then resumed its regular pattern.

"And how do we determine where the little bastards are?"

"No way of telling that. They're not detectable by any equipment I know of."

"What do they look like?"

"Invisible."

"That's just great. So we keep trying, eh? And if we're lucky . . ." Lord Abercrombie paused reflectively.

"That's about it, Lord."

"Thank you. You may leave now. And get your arm fixed."

After the meckie left, Lord Abercrombie lay back in bed and pulled the covers over his half head. *Maybe I can find some of those monopoles when I'm soil-immersed,* he thought. *I'll wipe 'em out.*

Rebo and Namaba shivered as they crept out of their hiding place in the woods. They moved a few steps into the clearing toward the *Amanda Marie,* then stopped and looked around, their red eyes darting nervously. Over the craggy hills to their left, a thick, dirty white mist rolled toward them.

"The creature with the thunder piece went that way," Namaba said, pointing.

Rebo did not say anything.

They took a few more steps, then stopped again to check for danger. All seemed clear, and Rebo nodded to her that it was safe. He bolted for the ship, with Namaba in close pursuit.

Reaching the ship, they found that the rope no longer dangled over the side. So Namaba positioned herself near the base, leaning forward and exposing her backside to Rebo in leapfrog fashion. It was a maneuver they had practiced often in Moro City.

Rebo took a long, loping run for her back, then used her as a springboard to leap to the deck level of the ship. Finding another rope in the cabin, he secured it and dropped it down for her.

The cabin was in disarray, with scraps of cello-wrap and equipment strewn everywhere. Sunlight slanted in through the open hatch, sending the cabin's night shadows retreating for their secret day places.

Namaba began searching for food.

Rebo climbed down into the sleeping compartment hatch

and found the knife he had left there. His feet were cold on the metal floor. He stood looking at the shiny knife blade for a while, recalling the previous evening's confrontation with the two-legged creature.

I ran away, he thought. *In Moro City, I would have fought to the death. But he did have a powerful weapon....*

While Namaba moved around noisily on the upper deck, Rebo continued his thoughts. *I didn't want to kill!* he thought. *It wasn't fear that stopped me.* But Rebo was not certain of this, unaccustomed as he was to reasoning things out.

He slipped the knife into its sheath on his coat, then noticed a ruby-red, octagonal pendant on the floor. Picking it up, he saw that it was multicolored, with geometric-shaped faces on it. The mechanism beeped and flashed a green light. Rebo kept the device and took it with him to the main deck level. It was bright in the cabin now, forcing him to squint.

"No food," Namaba said, approaching him. "It's all gone." She stood with her back to the sunlight, casting a hulking shadow at Rebo's feet.

"I found a nice necklace for you," Rebo said, placing the pendant and chain around her neck. It beeped.

"Pretty," she said, watching the device's light flash from green to red, then back to green.

Rebo rummaged in a pile near one corner, locating a handful of dried pear pieces. They searched together for a while, not finding anything more. "You take this," he said, extending his paltry bit of food to her.

She looked surprised at this, but accepted his offer.

"What's wrong?" Rebo asked.

"Nothing," she said, chewing the dried pears in one mouthful. "Only..."

"Only what?"

"You've never been this thoughtful," she said. She swallowed.

"Whattaya mean? I pulled you outta that laboratory fire and took you under my wing in the Southside Hawks. Wasn't that *thoughtful*?"

"You needed a woman," she said. "It was a prestige thing."

"Aw, get off that, will ya?"

"Just forget I tried to compliment you," she snapped.

"Listen," Rebo whispered. "Did you hear that?"

Looking across the clearing, they saw hundreds of Fruit

people approaching. All were wearing three-piece suits and suit dresses. All carried briefcases.

Rebo was first to the rope, but he stepped aside and helped Namaba down.

"Hurry," she said, waiting for him at the bottom.

Two Fruit men were only a few meters away now, running at breakneck speed. As Rebo and Namaba fled, one of the Fruits, a kiwi man with fuzz all over his round little body, yelled, "Wait! We want to speak with you about your legal needs!"

Rebo and Namaba hurried toward the hill trail they had seen the creature with the thunder piece take. But the kiwi man was very fast and caught up, running alongside Rebo. The big Morovian gave the fuzzy fellow a stiff cuff, sending him rolling away. Business cards flew out of the kiwi man's pockets.

Now the other fast Fruit caught the Morovians. This fellow was a very speedy and especially seedy variety of lemon. He too ran alongside Rebo. "We are lawyers!" the lemon man yelled. "Here to represent the Earthian slave, Javik! The police are not far behind!"

The pendant hanging from Namaba's neck beeped.

Rebo heard the distant, mournful wail of sirens. Looking back, he saw four police chariots with bright silver badges on the sides being pulled across the clearing by teams of carrot men.

"Police?" Rebo said, alarmed. He slapped a business card out of his face.

The lemon lawyer clutched at Rebo's fur. "Maybe you need a lawyer too," he said. "I could use the work."

Rebo gave the sticky yellow fellow a massive cuff, sending him spinning and reeling away. Then the Morovians picked up their loping pace. Four other lawyers caught them anyway and clutched at them, pulling their fur so hard that it hurt. One tore the pendant off Namaba's neck. The pendant beeped, then was trampled underfoot.

Rebo and Namaba used their forelegs as weapons now, laying waste to the quartet of clamoring lawyers. "Faster!" Namaba said. "We've got to get away!"

Although he had no idea what lay ahead on the steep trail into the hills, Rebo knew he had to go that way. Visions of police chases in Moro City flashed across his mind as he and Namaba reached the trailhead.

Their feet struck a rocky surface. The trail became steep quickly, skirting a rockslide. Ahead, Rebo saw a bend in the trail with a large rock outcropping over that point. Beyond the bend, wisps of fog curled invitingly, offering security for the pursued.

"Adarka!" a police bullhorn blared.

Rebo did not understand the word, and did not realize the function of the pretty pendant which lay on the trail far behind them. But the authoritative sound was enough to make him pick up his pace. Glancing back, he saw thousands of lawyers at the trailhead, falling behind as they fought with one another for position.

"Adarka!" the police repeated.

When the fleeing Morovians reached the trail bend, Rebo looked back again and saw purple-uniformed police officers struggling to get past the clog of lawyers.

Rebo and Namaba rounded the bend, stretching their legs to climb a steep, rugged trail. The trail moved into thin fog now, skirting a dry creekbed. Then it leveled out for a time. But soon it rose steeply once more, cutting around gnarled trees that clung to the rocky hillside. Soon the din of police and lawyers could be heard no longer.

They galloped more slowly now. "We've got to find food soon," Namaba said, glancing back at Rebo. "Our boiler pressures will be low after all that exertion."

Prince Pineapple, Javik, and Wizzy were traversing a narrow switchback trail, still going up sharply. The path was hard and rocky at this point, but curiously enough there was soft forest soil only a few steps to one side. It appeared as though someone had intentionally selected the most difficult route. Ahead of Javik, Prince Pineapple's stubby legs moved rapidly, pulling him forward with unaltering, powerful steps.

Feeling warm and drained from the exertion and only half a bio bar back at the ship, Javik wondered how the soft-looking pineapple man could keep up such a pace. And only the day before, the prince had been so weak. *He's had another recharge,* Javik thought.

The rugged path seemed to grow steeper and more rocky with each step. Javik saw no end to it. Gnarled pine trees along the trail sparkled in streaks of sunlight that filtered through the fog.

"You won't believe what's on top," Prince Pineapple said as he stepped over a jagged, fallen rock. "A high desert, with no way around it. There's sheer cliffs all around, making this the only approach."

The trail cut into woods now, offering some shade. The ground beneath their feet was softer here, with more moisture and less rocks.

"We'll need to find water soon," Javik said. I finished the only water capsules I could find. Brought along a couple of collapsible plastic containers we could fill."

"I remember a creek along here somewhere," Prince Pineapple said. No sooner were these words spoken when he stopped and pointed a quivering finger at a tree. "Three dots!" he exclaimed. "Sign of the magicians!"

"We're on the right trail," Wizzy said, inspecting the dots closely. They were raised and white, in the form of a triangle. "The dots don't actually touch the tree," Wizzy said. "They float just off the surface. Portable dots, I guess."

"No time to concern ourselves with that," Prince Pineapple said.

They continued on the trail, and presently Javik heard running water. At first it was only a distant, welcome murmur. Then it became louder, sounding like the flow of autocars on a New City expressway.

"Strange how it's so green and wet here," Prince Pineapple said, stopping at a viewpoint and looking at the ridge ahead. "But just beyond that ridge..."

Javik looked back. There was no movement downtrail. Much of the mist had burned off now, condensing in the rays of the Corkian suns. The clearing from which they had started was visible far below, with the *Amanda Marie* glinting in sunlight.

Wizzy flew by him.

Squinting, Javik made out movement around the ship: thousands of tiny, shifting specks that had to be Fruit people. *Got out of there just in time,* he thought.

"It's like another world on top," Prince Pineapple said, continuing on and leaving Javik behind. The prince's words became more distant. "I was there once, you know, but turned back. It's so desolate. This time there'll be no turning back."

Javik quick-stepped to catch up with the others.

Wizzy circled Javik as he arrived, then flew at Javik's side. "Why does Sid want us together so badly?" Javik asked, turning his head toward Wizzy. "For your good, or for mine?"

"For both, I'm certain," Wizzy said. "I as his son and you as his closest friend."

"His *closest* friend?" Javik's blue eyes opened saucer wide. "But I didn't even see the guy for twenty years before our reunion!"

"Time doesn't always erase deep feelings," Wizzy said. "Besides, Papa Sidney sees things on a universal scale now. Twenty years is but a moment to him."

"I think you're starting to understand love, Wizzy," Prince Pineapple said.

After a while they reached a place where a narrow band of running water crossed the trail. Stopping here, Prince Pineapple removed his helicopter beanie and said, "I'm going to recharge. There's a good spot for you to get water off the trail." He set his cap on a rock and trudged off.

Javik removed his survival pack, feeling a twinge from his shoulder. He knelt on the ground and searched in the pack, pulling out two collapsible water pods. Afraid he might get his automatic pistol wet, he unsnapped the holster from his belt and placed it on top of the pack.

Prince Pineapple was seated on the ground now, opening his folding shovel. Javik passed him, reaching a little waterfall that cascaded down the hillside into a pool. After splashing water on his face and drinking, he began filling one of the pods.

Wizzy circled over the prince's head, looking down on his leafy green headdress. Ceremoniously, Prince Pineapple wrapped one bare foot with the barbed nutrient-transmitting cord. Soon the foot was inside a little hole he had dug.

Javik watched Prince Pineapple too, while filling the second water pod. He saw contentment on the prince's face now as nutrients from the rich soil flowed into his pineapple body. Prince Pineapple had a dreamy far-off expression, with half his face in sun and half in shade. Javik thought again of the videodome commercial. This prince was another distortion in this garbage-distorted world, like an Earth videodome fantasy come to life.

With the three travelers thus engrossed, and with the camouflage sound of running water, none of them noticed two hairy, black-jacketed creatures approaching from below. Talking as they rounded a switchback in the trail, Rebo and Namaba did not see Javik's survival pack until Namaba nearly stumbled over it.

"The thunder piece!" she said, seeing the gun.

Javik and Rebo saw one another at the same instant. Javik dropped the water pod in the pool and ran for his pack, thinking he might be able to frighten the creatures by running directly toward them.

Instinctively, Rebo grabbed the service pistol. Remembering how Javik had held it, he gripped the handle, pointing the barrel at Javik.

Javik stopped cold. "Be careful with that thing," he said, hearing strange but understandable words cross his lips as the language mixer did its job. He was less than a meter from the business end of the barrel. It looked very large.

I see how to use this, Rebo thought, eyeing the trigger. His forefinger inched toward it. Then he stopped. For the first time in his life, he consciously questioned ways which once had been automatic for him. He felt guilt for past killings, especially for the old flower vendor.

Wizzy was in action now. He streaked toward Rebo in a blur of orange light.

Javik was a little quicker. Seeing Rebo hesitate, he slapped the gun away.

Then Wizzy hit Rebo hard on the side of the head, knocking the bulky three-legger hard to the ground. Rebo rolled on his stomach with a moan, exposing the grapple bird insignia on the back of his coat.

Javik retrieved the gun, noticing that Namaba was making no effort to get it. "Over there," he said to her, motioning toward Rebo with the pistol barrel.

Namaba moved to Rebo's side.

Rebo sat up, rubbing the side of his head with one hand. His head moved slowly in a circle, with his eyes clamped shut. His hair-framed face was contorted in pain. Then his eyelids lifted slowly, revealing dazed, dull-red eyes.

"Lucky for you I was here," Wizzy said. He was dark blue now, hovering in midair at Javik's eye level.

"Whattaya mean?" Javik snapped. "*I* knocked the gun away!"

"That guy's a lot bigger than you. He would have smashed

the hell out of you before you got to the gun."

Javik pursed his lips thoughtfully. "Maybe," he said grudgingly.

"Look at my body!" Wizzy exclaimed. "I've grown since yesterday. I feel it. Do you see any difference?" Wizzy stretched his yellow cat's eyeball, trying to get a glimpse of himself. But he couldn't even see his tail.

"You look lumpy again," Javik said, smiling thinly as he studied Wizzy. "Pebbles and dirt are stuck all over you."

"Always critical, aren't you!" Wizzy snapped. "For your information, Captain Tom, the dirt and pebbles make me stronger. I'm gaining strength every day."

"Sure, sure." Javik looked away, seeing that Prince Pineapple was finishing his recharge.

Wizzy glowed bright, molten orange. The lumps on his body became smooth and liquid, sparkling in the sunlight. Then he cooled to a glistening hue of dark blue.

Prince Pineapple walked up, buttoning his shovel to his belt. "Had a little trouble, I see," he said.

"Thanks for helping, Your Highness," Javik said, sneering.

"I only just noticed," Prince Pineapple said, sputtering with surprise at the remark.

"Finish filling those water pods, will ya?" Javik said to the prince. "I need to think about our guests for a moment."

"I am a prince of Cork," Prince Pineapple announced haughtily. "I do not fetch water."

"Now look," Javik said, turning his gun halfway toward Prince Pineapple. "I don't have time to . . ."

Wizzy flew to Prince Pineapple's side, saying, "Captain Tom is throwing his weight around. Let me help you with the water, Prince."

"Maybe just this once," Prince Pineapple said, reassessing the situation. Scowling, he turned and went with Wizzy toward the little waterfall.

Javik watched Namaba as she knelt and cradled Rebo's head on her lap. Her red eyes had an intriguing softness to them. The light brown face was delicate and hair-framed, remotely simian, with light brown hair on her body that glistened golden in the places where sunlight touched it. Although she wore a black jacket matching Rebo's, the only other article of clothing was a yellow ribbon with black polka dots secured to the mane of her long neck. Catching Javik's intense gaze, she looked away shyly.

As Javik had nearly finished filling the pods before the interruption, it did not take Wizzy and the prince long to complete the task. Prince Pineapple filled the second pod, and Wizzy capped it, sticking the cap to his underside with suction and then spinning it securely over the pod opening.

"Whee!" Wizzy said as he spun.

When they returned, Javik was still looking at Namaba. Glancing up at Prince Pineapple as the prince brought back one of the pods, Javik said, "They're going with us. I don't want to lug that water and a survival pack across the desert."

"No argument by me," Prince Pineapple said. "That water's heavy." He went for the other pod.

"But what will they eat?" Wizzy asked, hovering at Javik's side.

"I'm not sure we need to be concerned with that," Javik said. He secured his holster to his belt and slipped the gun into it. Then he fumbled in the survival pack. Locating a roll of nylon cord, he said, "Maybe we'll use 'em till they drop."

Namaba looked at Javik in a way that made him regret the statement. It was a scolding expression, the reproachful look a child might receive from its mother.

Javik looked away uneasily, wishing he had not snapped at everyone. He was tired and in a mean mood, feeling that events were slipping from his control, and with a hunger pang knawing incessantly at his belly. He cut off a length of cord. "This will secure our water pods to that big guy," he said.

As Prince Pineapple returned with the other pod, Javik focused on the shovel and nutrient cord attached to the prince's belt. *Maybe,* Javik thought. *Maybe I could* . . . Javik resolved to wait until the last possible moment before making such a radical decision—the moment when there were no more scraps of food in the pack.

Early that afternoon the travelers reached a high wall of closely fitted granite stones. Prince Pineapple said this comprised a portion of the rock bowl holding Dusty Desert. A howling wind blew on the other side of the wall, filling the air above them with particles of grit.

"According to legend," Prince Pineapple said, "this was

once a great high lake. But it dried up long ago, leaving only sand and dust."

"Dust?" Wizzy said. "I understand the sand, but the dust—that is another matter, beyond my geologic knowledge."

"Don't worry your lumpy nucleus about it," Javik said. "We have to cross this thing, whether you understand its origin or not."

"One must seek to comprehend," Wizzy said. "One must always seek to comprehend."

Prince Pineapple found a way of scaling the wall, stepping in narrow rock chinks with the sides of his shoes. Reaching the top, he removed his beanie and knelt to protect himself from the wind.

Javik followed, then dropped his Tasnard rope over the edge to bring up the water pods. After this, he dropped the rope back, mentoing it to help Namaba and Rebo up. Javik kept his distance from the Morovians, and always held one hand near his holstered pistol.

The howling wind subsided now. Javik looked out on the desert, watching dry, powdery dust and sand swirl in little whirlpools. A number of red, yellow, and blue AmFed garbage cannisters were scattered about, half buried.

Prince Pineapple walked the wall to Javik's left, searching for a way down to the desert floor. A mottled black and gray rat dashed across the top of one of the prince's shoes. It paused nearby, staring up at him with beady, bulbous little eyes. Then it scampered down the wall to the desert, disappearing in a mound of dusty soil.

Prince Pineapple knelt and looked over the edge where the rodent had descended. "Here's a good place," he said, stuffing his helicopter beanie in his back pocket. Finding a foothold, he lowered the other leg carefully, locating a second chink to support his weight. Soon his leafy headress was below the top of the wall.

The wind picked up again as Javik descended.

When all were gathered at the bottom, Wizzy surveyed the great expanse of Dusty Desert, rolling his cat's eye gaze around in awe. "We have to cross *that?*" he asked.

"Only an early obstacle," Prince Pineapple said. "There will be others. Some may not be shown on the scroll." *Moha,* he thought. *Now, what is that?*

They brought forth the Sacred Scroll and studied it.

"No headings shown here," Javik said. "We'll have to guess on a course." Glancing at the map and getting his bearings as best he could, Javik sighted across the desert along his outstretched arm. "Off that way, I'd say."

While Prince Pineapple put the scroll away, Javik mentoed his wrist digital to activate the land compass feature. "Three-five-two," Javik said. "That's our course."

Prince Pineapple kicked at a clump of sandy dirt.

"I'll carry your shovel and barbed cord now," Javik said, touching the prince's arm.

"Wha-what?" Prince Pineapple's scaly brown face took on the twisted countenance of surprised rage.

"I'm in charge of this mission, and I've just given you an order."

The prince glared down at Javik. "*You're* in charge? Wherever did you get that idea?"

"You question my authority?" Javik asked, his tone menacing. He placed one hand on the handle of his automatic pistol and looked up at the prince with his best icy stare. Javik knew the stare was fear-inspiring. Once, someone had called it a "death stare." It was the sort of thing that could send women and small children scurrying for safety.

Prince Pineapple was no match for the death stare. His gaze flitted away nervously. "But why must you have my nutrient kit?" he asked. "Surely you don't intend to attempt a charge on yourself?"

"It has occurred to me. But I'm not ready to take that risk. Not until the food's gone."

"You feel this will control me in some way, then?" Prince Pineapple stared at the ground as he spoke. He sniffed the warm odor of sun-drenched dust.

Javik smiled stiffly. As Wizzy and the Morovians watched, Javik gripped Prince Pineapple's arm.

"Ow!" Prince Pineapple said. Angrily, he pulled away and removed the shovel, cord, and sheath.

Javik secured them to his own belt.

They covered their mouths and noses with scarves, then ventured out on the desert, with everyone walking ahead of Javik. This was at his command, for he was feeling increasingly alienated from everyone in the group. Javik's feet slipped often in the mixture of sand and dirt. He wondered why. It should be less slippery than sand alone.

Aw, to hell with the answer, Javik thought. *I'm getting like Wizzy.*

Hearing Javik's thoughts with the red star crystal embedded in his nucleus, Wizzy studied a bit of gritty sand adhering to the agate dome over his eye. *Let me see,* Wizzy thought. *Intermingled face-centered cubic crystals and young, rich latosol . . . an odd combination of old and new geology.*

Wizzy's thoughts were interrupted when a cloud of gritty sand enveloped the group, blocking out all three suns. Soon they were a struggling column, with Prince Pineapple pushing ahead and the others lagging behind.

Javik began to fall back more than the others, owing to his hunger-weakened state and to second thoughts he was having concerning the wisdom of what they were doing. Soon he stopped and waved his arms. "We'll have to go back!" he yelled. "We can't cross this wasteland on foot."

"Press on!" Prince Pineapple screamed over his shoulder.

Javik tasted dusty dryness through the scarf. His lips were parched.

Rebo and Namaba fell back, joining Javik. Then, reluctantly, Wizzy abandoned the prince too. "I'm having trouble flying in this stuff," Wizzy said to Javik.

Now the pineapple prince turned angrily, glaring back at the others across the top of the dirty scarf covering his nose and mouth. "Leave me my nutrient kit, then," he demanded.

"Not a chance," Javik yelled. He glanced at his wrist compass, turning his body until he faced the return course. The wind blew a flap of his scarf open, exposing his mouth. He resecured it.

Rebo shifted the water pods on his back. Namaba pulled one of them lower to distribute the weight more evenly.

They started back, leaving Prince Pineapple alone and angry. The prince remained steadfast, and soon Javik could not see him any longer. Then the prince emerged from a swirling, dark cloud, trudging angrily and kicking up a lot of his own dust. He caught Javik and the others just as they reached the desert edge, at approximately the same place from which they had begun.

Prince Pineapple's eyes were aflame with anger. For the first time, he stared Javik down. "Why did you . . . ?" he sputtered.

"I don't know if we should go on," Javik said, reactivating

his blue-eyed death stare to win the battle of glares. "I mean, is it really worth it?"

"How can you ask such a thing? With so much at stake?"

Rebo set the water pods on the ground thoughtfully. "Prince Pineapple," he said. "Why do you want this Abercrombie so badly?"

"Someone has explained the Magician's Chamber to you?" Prince Pineapple asked, surprised.

"Yes." Rebo nodded in Wizzy's direction.

"Then you know I must rid Cork of the devil Abercrombie. He is evil."

"And replace him with yourself?" Rebo asked.

"Certainly not! We'll throw him out together and seal the entrance."

"We have no stake in your planet," Rebo said. "None of us do, except you."

"That's not entirely true," Javik said, recalling his mission. "You've got some points, though, Rebo."

Rebo motioned Javik to one side and then whispered, "This prince is a bad one. Too haughty. And he has shifty eyes."

"He's not so bad," Wizzy said, flying up and overhearing the remark.

Javik remained away from Rebo and kept one hand near his holstered pistol. "What makes you think I trust *you?*" Javik asked, looking at Rebo.

"That pineapple guy is just using you," Rebo said. "He needs you and Wizzy to read his damned scroll. You have no use for him."

"You're a smart one, eh?" Javik said. "Used your brains back in Moro City, did you?"

"Had to," Rebo said. "Or I'd have been dead a long time ago."

Glaring at Javik and Rebo, Prince Pineapple started to say something. His lips parted. But he decided not to speak. Seeing a shady spot next to a curving protrusion on the rock wall, he retreated to be by himself.

Namaba moved in to eavesdrop on Javik's conversation with Rebo. She picked pieces of grit out of Rebo's fur with her long fingers. After a while she said, "My yenta tells me we should continue. We must cross this desert."

"How?" Rebo asked.

She shrugged.

"Yenta?" Javik said. "What's that?"

"A very powerful form of intuition," Wizzy said, glowing red to retrieve the answer from his storehouse of knowledge. "Morovia is one of the planets where a more refined form of this phenomenon can be found."

"We don't need a galactic travel commentary," Javik said.

"Wizzy is correct," Namaba said, looking at the little comet. "My mother once explained it to me in much the same words. How did you know?"

"I too have yenta," Wizzy said. "A variation on yours."

"But aren't you male?" she asked.

"That is my hormonal inclination."

"The guy can't even say yes or no," Javik gruffed. "He's worse than a New City bureaucrat."

"Morovian men have no yenta," Namaba said.

"Forget this yenta stuff," Rebo said. "I think we should go back. Call it common sense. That desert is too much for us."

"My yenta tells me there is a way back to Morovia on the other side of the desert."

"Do tell," Rebo said.

Namaba looked at Wizzy, asking, "Do you know of any basis for my feeling?"

Wizzy glowed red. "Hmmm," he said. "Well, here's a little something. The entrance to the Corkian Magician's Chamber is adjacent to this end of the Dimensional Tunnel. Offhand, I'd say you got here through the Dimensional Tunnel."

"But we landed far from that," Rebo said. "Near Captain Tom's ship."

"Abercrombie used meckie-dug tunnels and a sacrifice hole to divert you," Wizzy said. "There's a labyrinth of passageways beneath us."

"I saw his metal men digging the sacrifice hole," Prince Pineapple said.

"They're called meckies," Javik said.

"There you have it," Wizzy said. "The lady with the yenta is correct. The way back to Morovia is across this desert."

"I don't know," Rebo said. He brushed dirt off the thigh of his foreleg. "Why do you oppose me now, woman? Have you forgotten your obligation to me?"

"A yenta cannot be denied," she said softly.

"You're ungrateful!"

"I have repaid you many times over, Rebo. And don't forget

about the reward. I could have turned you in to the police."

"You considered that?"

"Everyone in your precious club did. Don't kid yourself."

Javik looked back across Dusty Desert, thinking how similar it was to a sea—so treacherous and storm-tossed, with ripples of gritty sand like dehydrated, time-frozen waves.

The argument subsided.

As if in answer to Javik's thoughts, a great desert sailing ship emerged from the dust, showing its prow and forward mast. Three gray sails were puffed full with air.

Namaba yelled something. Javik did not make out the words. Soon all of them, including Prince Pineapple, were standing beside one another, looking out at what they presumed to be an apparition.

But if it was an apparition, Javik found it to be extremely detailed, with three masts of billowing sails, full rigging, and bright orange banners on top of each mast. Men scurried about on the deck and clung to the rigging.

Fruit men, Javik thought as the ship neared. Then he saw a massive carrot man in a baseball cap and a number of smaller carrot men.

Struts on each side of the ship had been fitted with balloon tires to roll the craft along the desert, and Javik counted the struts: eight to a side. As the ship drew closer, Javik heard it creak, and he picked up the wind-tossed shouts of the crew. Dust-encased lettering on the bow spelled out the Corkian equivalent of *Freedom One*. Javik read this easily, using the language mixer pendant hanging from his neck.

"A schooner," Wizzy said, glowing red. "Rather ancient by Earthian standards."

The crew released lines to slacken the sails, and the *Freedom One* slowed, drawing up parallel with the wall. Four apple men dropped a wooden gangway. Unfortunately, they forgot to secure the upper end, and it clattered to the ground.

"Idiots!" the big carrot man yelled. "Can't find decent slaves anymore!"

Prince Pineapple stepped back, showing fear on his face. "Brother Carrot!" he husked. "With *Fruit* slaves!"

Another gangway was located and let down properly. Brother Carrot loomed at the top of the gangway. "You folks need a ride?" he asked boisterously, tugging at the brim of his cap. Javik saw that it was not a baseball cap after all, but was instead a black captain's cap with gold braid on the brim. He towered over the surrounding Fruits and Vegetables. An oversized folding shovel and nutrient cord were strapped to his waist.

Prince Pineapple tried to conceal himself behind Rebo, but was spotted.

"I see one of you knows me," Brother Carrot said with a broad smile. "And who are you, Mr. Pineapple?"

"Prince Peter Pineapple," the prince answered, showing his face. He straightened and stepped out from behind Rebo.

"Ah," Brother Carrot said, walking slowly down the gangway. "So you're the one. The missing adviser."

"News travels fast," Prince Pineapple said.

"An army does not progress without intelligence," Brother Carrot said. The wooden gangway shook under the weight of each step he took.

"You plan to attack King Corker?" Prince Pineapple asked.

"I am like you," Brother Carrot said, reaching the ground. "An enemy of the Fruit king."

We are not alike! Prince Pineapple thought, using good judgment to curb his tongue. *No Vegetable is the equal of a Fruit!* "These are . . . uh . . . my friends," he said. He introduced Javik and the others to the Vegetable Underground leader, giving a brief summary of their backgrounds. He did not give any details on Wizzy other than his name, being uncertain as to how the Vegetable leader would respond.

Rebo loped close to Brother Carrot and looked directly into his black button eyes. They were about the same height. "You have a gang, pal?" Rebo asked.

"A gang? Well, a very large gang, you might say. It's called an army."

"Same thing," Rebo said. He leaned close to Brother Carrot, speaking in a low tone. "I can be of use to you, pal. And Namaba, too. We know about fighting."

"That so?" Brother Carrot said, showing mock interest.

"We could use a ride across the desert," Javik said. "Isn't that right, Prince?" he added, looking at Prince Pineapple with a teasing smile.

"Uh, yes," Prince Pineapple said uneasily.

"You want to be in my army too?" Brother Carrot asked, looking at Javik.

"Thanks, but no. I've had my share of combat." He rubbed the scar on the bridge of his nose.

"I don't need volunteers anyway," Brother Carrot said. He looked at Rebo. "Thanks for the offer."

"Sure," Rebo said.

"The ride is yours," Brother Carrot said. He turned and stepped up the ramp, adding, "Umfira ti-ta."

The language mixer on Javik's pendant beeped. He shook it, scowling at a red trouble light on the device. The light blinked green. "What did you say, Brother Carrot?" Javik asked.

"Come aboard," Brother Carrot said, waving expansively with one arm.

The language mixer was working now.

As Brother Carrot led them up the gangway, Javik held back and said to Wizzy in a low tone, "What do you read on this carrot guy? Is he a friend?"

"No signal received," Wizzy replied. "I tried, but there don't seem to be any brain waves."

"Vegetables have no brains," Prince Pineapple muttered out of Brother Carrot's hearing range.

"There was no signal from you, either, Prince Pineapple," Wizzy whispered.

"There's something wrong with your apparatus, then," Prince Pineapple huffed.

Javik suppressed laughter.

"Enemies of the king!" Brother Carrot said as he reached the deck of the ship. "So many enemies!" He broke into sing-song: "A foe of King Corker is a foe of . . . Oops! That didn't work, did it?"

In the captain's cabin, Brother Carrot introduced the group to Captain Cucumber, an amiable dark green chap who didn't say much. The captain smiled a lot, deferring often to Brother Carrot when questions were asked.

Javik watched Rebo and Namaba move to a corner at one end of the long cabin. There they rested on their haunches and listened intently while the others talked.

Brother Carrot was a dominating figure. When he rested his frame on a spindly-legged sea couch, the couch's legs bent. "We have thirty freedom ships like this," he said proudly.

"Imagine that!" Prince Pineapple said.

Javik thought the prince's tone was patronizing, but Brother Carrot seemed not to notice.

"For the past week," Brother Carrot said, "we have sailed

the desert sea, learning its treacherous ways, charting dead-heads and the like." He smiled, and his black button eyes glowed as he looked at Javik. "Quite a few of your Earthian gar-bahge cannisters are buried in the sand out there. They make navigation tricky."

"I can imagine," Javik said humbly. He and Prince Pineapple were seated on oak side chairs.

"My army of thirty thousand men crosses Dusty Desert tomorrow," Brother Carrot exclaimed.

"But King Corker has no idea," Prince Pineapple said, leaning forward with his eyes open wide in astonishment.

Brother Carrot laughed, and his laugh filled every corner of the room. It was boisterous and surprisingly good-natured for a man having his extensive responsibilities. "Your King Corker has never had any sort of an idea." he quipped.

Prince Pineapple smiled. "True," he said. "Oh, so true! Decision Coins are his crutch."

Brother Carrot removed his cap and brushed dust from it. "Prince Pineapple," he said. "My sources tell me you have been in disfavor with the king for several months now."

Prince Pineapple scowled. "Your sources are correct," he said. "But should you divulge military secrets to me? The disfavor story might be a ruse."

"King Corker can do nothing now, even if he knows. Events have been set in motion. Big events. My carrot men are fierce fighters, you know. Each is better than twenty-five of the king's royal guardsmen . . . those fat, drunken slobs."

"Your brethren are well known for their strength," Prince Pineapple said. Suddenly he raised his rear end and reached in his back pocket, pulling out a rather mangled helicopter beanie. "Thought I'd lost this for a moment," he said, noting that the yellow plastic rotor had been broken from his sitting on it.

"Too bad," Javik said. "You broke it."

"This just adds to its value," Prince Pineapple said. "Honor prevented me from breaking it intentionally, of course. But the way it happened was quite acceptable."

Javik watched the prince don his beanie.

Brother Carrot's eyes flashed ferociously in Prince Pineapple's direction. "You think of my carrot people as good slaves," he said. "But I'll free them. I'll free every last Vegetable in captivity."

"Good luck to you, sir," Javik said.

Brother Carrot ranted for several minutes now, saying something about a powerful Fruit Doom bomb that he was going to use against King Corker. Javik tried to ask him about the bomb on two occasions, but each time was unable to get in a word. Presently, Brother Carrot looked at Javik and asked, "Where are you folks going?"

"Can you drop us off at the edge of Icy Valley?" Javik asked.

"I'd be happy to," Brother Carrot said. His eyes continued to flash from his anger over the Vegetable enslavement. "But I don't recommend that way. Go farther west, to the meadowlands. The way is much easier there, and there are many quaint Vegetable villages."

"Uh," Prince Pineapple said, groping for words. "The Earthian here wants to go a different way. He has been sent to check on the gar-bahge situation."

"I see," Brother Carrot said. "Very well, then. I will take you to Icy Valley."

"This Fruit Doom bomb," Javik said. "What is it?"

Brother Carrot darkened. "A terrible thing," he said. "But I must use it to prevent further battle casualties, you see. It will shorten the war."

"How does it work?" Javik asked.

"Classified," Brother Carrot said, smiling thinly. He sat back and focused his eyes on Javik.

This is not a suitable occasion to use my death stare, Javik thought. He looked away.

ELEVEN

Nothing worth attaining is
ever easy. If it seemed easy
to you, you're not there yet.

One of the heretic, anti-
Job Support thoughts
banned by Uncle Rosy

"Get under way!" Captain Cucumber shouted, speaking into a brass, wall-mounted tube near Javik. The captain read from a chart spread across a dark-stained table: "Heading, forty-eight degrees, twenty-six point seven minutes north latitude, one hundred five degrees, fifteen point four minutes west longitude."

Javik heard running feet on the deck overhead, and the voices of mates barking instructions to the crew. Soon the schooner began to move. Then it picked up speed, and wind could be heard howling through the rigging. It was a creaky ship, and it built up a cadence of noises as its balloon tires carried it across the dusty wasteland.

"Your Fruits call my people the Vegetable Underground," Brother Carrot said, looking at Prince Pineapple with a bemused smile. "But that's a misnomer. We are not underground. Nor are we rebels. The Vegetables are a different people, a sovereign nation. We would live in peace with King Corker, but he insists on enslaving my people."

Prince Pineapple rose nervously and walked with some difficulty to a porthole, holding on to bolted-down furniture and handrails as the ship pitched. Through a haze of dust and sand he saw that they were riding the face of a dune, rising along the sandy giant at a sharp angle.

"Hold on!" Captain Cucumber yelled.

The *Freedom One* powered over the top of the dune and headed down the other side. Prince Pineapple felt acceleration.

"Quite a ride, eh?" Brother Carrot said.

The dunes in the distance looked like great ocean waves to the prince. He recalled a trip across the Purple Sea when he was a child, a vacation cruise with the most important pineapples of the day. Those were better days.

Seated on the floor in the corner, Rebo was watching a fly crawl along the floor. It jumped over a ridge in the pegged wood, then took a big hop toward Prince Pineapple.

Seeing the fly out of the corner of one eye, Prince Pineapple smashed it with one foot. "Miserable fruit fly!" he cursed.

Brother Carrot snickered.

"Now why'd you have to do that?" Rebo asked.

"Because I hate fruit flies!" the prince thundered. "That's why!"

"Poor little fellow," Rebo said. "He couldn't have harmed you. Not a big strong pineapple man like you."

Prince Pineapple looked away haughtily, peering out the porthole again.

"It's a survival thing with him," Brother Carrot explained. "Fruits are trained from infancy to kill fruit flies. Slaves are always leaving them on my ship."

Wizzy flew to the couch and set down on a cushion next to Brother Carrot. "I see you keep many Fruit slaves," Wizzy observed, looking up at the carrot man's ruddy, orange face. "Only moments ago, however, you were criticizing King Corker for the same practice."

"This thing you introduced as Wizzy," Brother Carrot said, looking calmly at Prince Pineapple. "What is it, precisely?"

Before Prince Pineapple could answer, Wizzy piped up, "I'm a little comet, Your Excellency, from far across the universe."

"I know nothing of comets!" Brother Carrot exclaimed, proud of his ignorance. "You are strange creatures...all of you."

"Come here, Wizzy," Javik said. "Leave Brother Carrot alone."

Brother Carrot placed a large hand on Wizzy, saying, "I've decided to answer your question, little fellow. The Fruits took the first slave. We merely retaliated."

"But where does it stop?" Wizzy asked. "And who can be sure which side took the first slave? You have firsthand knowledge of this?"

"Really!" Brother Carrot said haughtily. "This is a truth which my people have always known. How dare you question our ways?"

Javik snatched Wizzy away before the argument worsened. "My apologies, sir," Javik said. "The little fellow here is not overly bright. We'll explain it to him later."

"Put me down!" Wizzy said.

"Okay," Javik said, placing Wizzy on a side table. "But don't ask any more questions."

"That's right," Brother Carrot said, glaring at Wizzy. "You've got a lot to learn." Brother Carrot sat back, seeming to realize for the first time how angry he had become. His face broke into a wide smile. The boisterous, friendly laugh returned.

"I'm going topside," Javik announced, stepping cautiously across the deck as the ship rocked. "Is that okay, Brother Carrot?" he asked, lunging for a dark-stained railing on the two-step staircase leading to the door.

"It's a mite dusty up there," Brother Carrot said. "But go ahead."

"I'll be back soon," Javik said. "I want to see how this ship works." As his foot touched the first step, he caught Namaba's gaze. He heard the wind outside. The ship creaked.

While Javik watched, Namaba rose from her haunches and loped to his side. She kept the gaze of her soft red eyes on him as she moved.

Javik stepped back and drew his service pistol. "Get back over there," he snapped.

"I want to talk with you," she said. "Alone."

Looking beyond her to the corner, Javik saw Rebo sitting on his haunches there. Rebo's expression was troubled. "All right," Javik said to her. He motioned her ahead of him.

In the corridor outside, Javik slid the cabin door shut. With the pistol, he motioned to the right.

Namaba led the way down the long, dark-stained corridor,

loping on three legs in the Morovian way. Bright brass light standards clung to the walls, casting yellow light on Namaba as she passed. Javik smelled linseed oil.

At the end of the corridor, Javik motioned Namaba aside and swung open a heavy door leading to the deck. The door squeaked noisily. Hesitating, he watched dust swirl along the deck and heard the crewmen and their overseers shouting back and forth. The ship attacked the face of a fresh dune, throwing a thick cloud of dust and sand across the deck toward Javik. He slammed the door shut.

"We'd better stay in here," Javik yelled, raising his voice to be heard over the noise outside. Feeling something in his eye he tugged at the eyelid.

Namaba looked at him with sparkling, innocent eyes. "I don't care where we go," she yelled. "But I need to talk with you."

They moved down the corridor to a quieter place. With his gun still drawn, Javik looked intently at her. She was taller than he, and easily twice his weight, with light brown hair around her face that shone golden in the light of a nearby light standard.

"What is it you want?" Javik asked, blinking to clear his eye.

"Why did you bring us?" she asked. "Just to have Rebo carry your water? Is that all? We can't survive without food."

"Maybe I didn't think it out too clearly," he said, his voice wavering. He stared at the floor.

"Well it's high time you did," she snapped. "Our lives are at stake."

Javik stared past his pistol barrel at the pegged oak deck. He heard Namaba chug-breathing, and saw the base of her hairy forepaw on the deck. He did not look up, feeling unable to meet her gaze.

"We have to eat," she said. "You can't leave us to die somewhere along the trail."

Slowly, Javik raised his gaze to meet hers. "I haven't done you any harm," he said. "There was no food for you back there."

She looked away. Then: "There are animals in the woods of this planet. We could hunt."

"You mean kill something and cook it?" Javik asked, his face twisted at the revolting thought.

"You have a thunder piece. I assume it kills."

"I couldn't eat that sort of food," he exclaimed. "It would have to be processed, blended, strained, and stabilized first."

"You'd eat it," she said, "if you had no choice."

"I'll share what little food I have with you," Javik said.

"The contents of your pack are but a snack to us," she said, glaring at him. "You're just stumbling around, aren't you? Do you expect to find a restaurant out here, with nice clean plates and tablecloths?"

Javik considered gaining the offensive by criticizing her for stealing his food from the ship. But that was history and unchangeable. Her voice carried an unmistakable scolding tone, but had an underlying softness that intrigued him.

God help me, Javik thought, *but, I think she's attracted to me.* It was inevitable. Women just had to get close to him.

In the captain's cabin, Prince Pineapple stood at a porthole with Wizzy hovering at his side. The ship was surfing across the face of a dune wave, pitched at such an angle that the prince had to hold a brass wall handle.

"Your Captain Tom doesn't trust me," Prince Pineapple said. "That's why he took my nutrient kit."

"It does give him a degree of control," Wizzy said.

"You agree with what he did?" The words were clipped, angry.

"Not necessarily. But I can see why he feels as he does. I have read his thoughts. He believes you want the Magician's Chamber for yourself, that you will do anything to gain power."

"How preposterous! Wherever did he get such an idea?"

"He saw something he didn't like in your eyes. You rarely meet his gaze. And he heard the wrong inflection to your voice. Insincerity was the word he used in thought."

"What sort of evidence is this?" Prince Pineapple gazed at Wizzy until Wizzy's cat's eye focused on him. Then the prince looked away.

"A commander needs no evidence. He is responsible for his mission and for the welfare of his party. He makes decisions."

"That sounds like an army training manual excerpt," Prince Pineapple observed tersely.

"Not entirely," Wizzy said. "I've seen something of this as well. Any observant being can see the nervousness or guilt in your eyes. It's in your mannerisms, too. You seem . . . uncertain."

Prince Pineapple shook his head in dismay. *Can it be?* he wondered. *Do others see something I'm not aware of myself? No. I can't believe it.*

While the prince thought, Wizzy gave advice on what he should do to get back in Javik's good graces. This struck Prince Pineapple as peculiar, considering Wizzy's own shaky status with the leader of their expedition. The drone of Wizzy's voice was starting to give Prince Pineapple a headache.

"Leave me alone," Prince Pineapple said, pushing Wizzy away from the window.

During his next soil-immersion period, Lord Abercrombie searched for monopoles diligently, trying to find the subatomic particles that allegedly were causing him so much trouble. They were nowhere to be found. But Lord Abercrombie knew they were there. He tried magically inducing two rockslides, a flood, and a forest fire, all without the tiniest hint of success.

If I ever find a pack of those little buggers, Lord Abercrombie thought, *God help them!*

After a while, he turned his attention to activity on the planet's surface, using his billions of visual and auditory sensors. He saw the *Freedom One* crossing Dusty Desert. It made him angry.

Prince Pineapple wants to replace me, Lord Abercrombie thought. *Add him to my list of enemies. Right up at the top with the monopoles. And Brother Carrot with his army of blithering Vegetables. I've always worried about him. Can't forget Javik, either. He's Uncle Rosy's emissary.*

Furiously, Lord Abercrombie pulled himself out of the hole. "They're all against me!" he muttered, blowing dirt off his wardrobe ring. After mentoing the white stone on the ring, a dry shower cleaned every pore on his fleshy half. Using the turquoise stone next, he watched and felt a white caftan with a blue scroll sleeve thread its way over his half body. A black satin slipper wrapped itself around his foot, and a thistle half crown attached itself to his skull.

"I can see some of my enemies," he said. "I hear them, too—plotting against me and against my Corker allies. But what can I do? Hardly anything while buried. One tiny rockslide is the grand total of my magic."

He kicked a tuft of dirt. The dirt crumbled.

Moments later he stood before an instrument panel in the

Disaster Control Room. "Three of the bastards on one ship!" he said, his voice reflecting fury and frustration. "Maybe I can get all of them at once this way . . . if those monopoles stay out of my way."

He touched a green console button, then slammed down three adjacent brown toggles. "Sector one-one-six," he said, speaking into a microphone. "Three hundred k.p.h. winds . . . from the southwest, heading two-eight four."

"Confirmed," a computer voice reported.

Meckies at stations around the room tapped keyboards to coordinate the attack.

"Don't fail me," Lord Abercrombie said, coaxing the old equipment.

"Two fifty," a meckie reported.

Lord Abercrombie closed his eye and prayed softly.

"Three hundred, sir," came the next report. "Approaching the desert sailing ship. Impact estimated at four minutes."

"Hot damn!" Lord Abercrombie exclaimed.

"All systems working," another meckie said.

"I'm going into soil immersion," Lord Abercrombie said, turning to leave. "I want to enjoy this firsthand."

"Trouble, sir," a meckie said. "That reverse rain again."

Lord Abercrombie leaned over and moaned, "Oh no!"

"Equipment shorting out, sir."

Sparks flashed from all the consoles in the room.

"So close," Lord Abercrombie said, feeling ready to cry. He straightened and barked a command: "Shut down all systems!"

Hurriedly, the meckies did as they were told.

Abercrombie stepped back as the console near him continued to spark. At times like this he felt like giving up on the Realm of Flesh. But Magic offered no more prospect of success.

The rolling whine of an emergency siren sounded from the tunnel outside their door, along with the loud whirs and clanks of approaching meckies. Soon the room was full of meckie technicians, searching for a loose piece, a pulled wire, or anything else that might have caused yet another failure.

But Lord Abercrombie sensed this search would do no good. *This planet is cursed*, he thought. *Someone has made it uninhabitable for beings like me.*

"Hit 'em with anything we've got left!" Lord Abercrombie shouted. "Try wind, earthquakes, anything!"

It was midday, with three synchronized Corkian suns blazing overhead. As Javik stood with his companions at the edge of Dusty Desert, he felt cool in his vari-temp coat. The coat fluttered in a light wind. Behind them loomed the wall of closely fitted granite stones that formed this far side of the bowl holding the desert.

"That rain was really something," Rebo said. "Came right up out of the desert. Damndest thing I ever saw."

"I've seen it before," Prince Pineapple said. "It's become rather commonplace on Cork."

"We've seen it too," Wizzy said, hovering nearby. "When our ship was approaching the planet."

Brother Carrot waved from the deck of his desert schooner as it pulled away. "Good luck, my friends!" he yelled. Javik heard him say something after that, but the words were lost in the wind. The *Freedom One* picked up speed, cutting through rapidly moving clouds of surface grit.

"Nice fellow," Namaba said.

Prince Pineapple searched the wall for a place to climb.

"I don't think Fruits and Vegetables are so different," Wizzy said, perching on a wall stone near Prince Pineapple. "Brother Carrot carried a folding shovel on his belt, just like yours. He had a barbed cord, too."

"Pshaw!" Prince Pineapple said, finding a foothold to begin his ascent. "Fruits are superior. Everyone knows that. We grow on trees and high vines, while Vegetables grow next to the dirty ground." He climbed partway up the wall.

Wizzy glowed red as he retrieved data from his internal storehouse.

Prince Pineapple neared the top of the wall. "There is no comparison," he said. He lifted himself to the top of the wall and stood with his hands on his hips, looking down at the others with an air of superiority.

Wizzy flew up to hover in the prince's face. "What about strawberries?" Wizzy asked. "They're Fruit, and they grow along the ground."

"A strawberry is *not* Fruit!" Prince Pineapple exclaimed. "What an odd notion!"

"Enough of this," Javik said, climbing the wall by the same route Prince Pineapple had taken.

"You're wrong, Prince!" Wizzy said. "Extremely wrong! And what about green beans? They grow on high vines, which would make them as good as any Fruit."

"Preposterous!" Prince Pineapple thundered.

Reaching the top of the wall, Javik stepped between them. "Stop this!" he snapped. "Some of us do not have time to stand around arguing. Unlike his Royal Hind Ass here, my food source is not unlimited."

Prince Pineapple scowled ferociously.

Wizzy added Javik's expletive to his own stored arsenal.

Namaba and Rebo scaled the wall without help from Javik's Tasnard rope. As Namaba reached the top, she gave Javik a scolding smile.

He looked away. "All right," he said. "Let's find the trail and get a move on."

When they had descended the other side of the wall, Javik told Prince Pineapple to bring out the scroll.

"Idiots," the prince muttered as he handed over the scroll he still could not see. "I am surrounded by idiots."

Javik knelt on the ground, where he spread open the scroll. "We're here," he said, pointing to one side of the Dusty Desert.

To Prince Pineapple's eyes, it looked as though Javik were pointing at the ground. "Draw me a map in the dirt," the prince demanded, "so that I may see too."

Hurriedly, Javik used a stick to scratch out a portion of the scroll map on the ground. "Here's the Dusty Desert," he explained as he drew. "And Icy Valley. Just beyond that is a forest. We'll camp there."

"The valley must be behind us," Prince Pineapple said, turning and pointing at a misty area between two snow-covered hills.

"Tomorrow we cross Bottomless Bog," Javik said. "If these distances are correct."

"Where's that Moha shown?" the prince asked. "Something disturbingly familiar about that name."

"Here," Javik said, making a mark in the dirt.

Just then, a ferocious wind roared across their position, obliterating the dirt scratchings and nearly tearing the parchment from Javik's grasp.

"Lord Abercrombie is angry," Prince Pineapple said. "He will not let us pass without a fight."

"You think he caused that wind?" Javik asked. "Naw. There's no weather control here."

"We will see," Prince Pineapple said, groping for the scroll he could not see.

Javik released the scroll and watched the prince roll it carefully. Namaba tied it with the piece of leather cord. When the Sacred Scroll of Cork was safely secure beneath his coat, Prince Pineapple turned away from the wind, taking the path that led toward the misty valley.

Javik removed his vari-temp coat and stuffed it in the pack. He felt the warmth of three suns on the back of his neck as he followed the others. Javik imagined tiny solar nutrients entering his body, and tried to convince himself that his strength was returning. But this was a ruse. He knew he was declining, and had a frightening thought: What if the whole planet was against him?

Can such a thing be? he wondered. Javik felt that forces were whipsawing him—doing with him whatever they wished.

He felt the suns cool, and looked back. Clouds were moving in from behind. Ahead, curls of fog were approaching, running out of the valley to greet them. A shiver ran down the back of his neck and through his shoulder blades. He stopped to put the coat back on.

When Javik caught up with the others, Rebo and Namaba were zipping up their heavy club jackets and pulling the collars around the lower parts of their long necks. Prince Pineapple stood to one side of the trail, apparently expecting Javik to assume the lead. Wizzy hovered nearby.

"You lead," Javik said to the prince. "Then the Morovians."

Prince Pineapple frowned and stomped ahead, negotiating a narrow, rocky path that sloped gently downward from the desert plateau. They passed a number of AmFed garbage cannisters here, and at Javik's suggestion these were given a wide berth.

"Many are radioactive," he told them.

Swirls of fine, light gray mist curled ahead of them like a graceful, supernatural life form that was beckoning to the travelers. What was in the valley beyond? "Come see for yourself," the mist seemed to say.

From the rear, Wizzy saw Prince Pineapple disappear into the mist, followed by the others.

"The ground's frozen," Javik said, feeling his footsteps crunch. A dull, aching pain pulled at his belly. *Gotta find more food,* he thought, glancing at the folding shovel which rode on his hip. Gastric juices filled his mouth as he focused on the nutrient cord wrapped around the shovel handle. He swallowed.

"Something strange about this mist," Wizzy said.

I agree with that, Javik thought. *But there's also something strange about Wizzy . . . and the others.* The recurring video-dome commercial flashed across his weary mind. He saw ten pineapple men dancing in a chorus line, then ten Wizzies, then ten three-legged Morovians.

"Can't see two meters ahead," Prince Pineapple said, walking very slowly. His foot slipped on a pebble, causing him to fall against a rock wall he had not noticed in the fog. He stumbled, trying to regain his footing.

"Watch it!" Rebo said, catching Prince Pineapple by the arm. "There's a dropoff on your right."

Prince Pineapple leaned against the wall, breathing deeply from the sudden fright. "Wonder how far down," he said.

"Just be glad you can't see it," Javik said, catching up with the others.

The trail dropped steeply now. Soon the prince slipped again and came very close to going over the edge.

"I'll lead," Javik said. "And if any of you have any funny ideas about hitting me over the head, remember this: I have the nutrient kit, which may be our only hope for food. I'll fall over the edge. You can count on it. And in this fog, who knows if you'll ever find me?"

"We get the message," Namaba said.

Javik used his wardrobe ring to fit himself with a pair of brown ski gloves. Then he did the same for Prince Pineapple and the Morovians.

"You oughtta toss those jackets over the edge," Javik said to Rebo and Namaba, seeing that they were shivering. "Let me fit you with something functional."

"We'll manage," Rebo said.

"I'll take you up on that," Namaba said. She tossed her black club jacket over the edge of the cliff. Rebo glared at her.

Javik fitted her with a lemon yellow ski outfit. It surprised him more than a little to see the clothing follow her irregular form perfectly, giving her pants, a jacket, and a hooded top.

Resuming their course, Javik guided a gloved hand along the rock wall and probed ahead with one cautious step at a time, not committing the weight of his body until he was sure of his footing.

After an hour that seemed much longer, Javik felt run-down. Stopping on the narrow trail, he shared a bio bar and dried apple pieces with Rebo and Namaba. "Maybe we'll find food after we get out of this valley," Javik told them.

"He expects to find a restaurant out here," Namaba said. "I think we'd better learn to hunt."

"I haven't seen that many wild animals around," Rebo said.

"There are very few animals on Cork," Prince Pineapple said. "This is explained in one of our legends, which says that—"

"Hang your legends!" Javik snapped.

"We'd better figure something out soon," Namaba said, looking at Javik, "or that shovel on your hip will be used to bury us."

Javik closed his pack and put his arms through the straps to pull it on his back.

A short distance down the trail, they dropped underneath the fog. Now, less than thirty meters below, they could see the snow-and-ice-covered valley floor, stretching into the distance like a placid white lake.

"It's clearing," Javik said, glancing warily at the others. The trail became less rugged, dropping gradually. As Javik negotiated this section, he looked back often and remained well ahead of the others, fearful that he might catch a heavy rock on the back of the head.

Reaching the valley floor, Javik saw that the foggy mist formed a rather uniform ceiling all the way across the valley. The terrain was almost perfectly flat, permitting him to see a distant rock wall. It struck him as unusual that snow and ice would be on the valley floor but not on the trail they had just traversed.

When the balance of the party caught up, Javik scrutinized the scroll again. "We're here," he said, pointing to a spot on the parchment. "At the base of the cliff trail. Another trail should be somewhere over there." He pointed across the valley to his right, approximately along the line of a nearby path formed by small animal tracks. Javik counted four sharp toes on each track. He wondered what sort of an animal it was, and if he had the nerve to kill one and eat it. Looking up, he saw Namaba staring at him.

Wizzy flew in the direction Javik had designated. "There's a pretty good trail here," he called out, hovering over a slight rise in the terrain.

When Javik and the others reached the trail, Javik found it to be a trough of ice, perhaps a meter below the level of the surrounding terrain. Fresh, powdery snow lay on the ground all around, but there was none in the trough. Here the brown earth was visible beneath a thin layer of ice. As Javik stepped down to the trail, he felt the ice crackle under his feet. He kicked at the ice, lifting a slab and exposing a section of ground.

"Can you explain this, Wizzy?" Prince Pineapple said, stepping into the trough next to Javik.

Wizzy glowed red, but came up with no answer. "I'm sorry," he said. "It's a mystery to me."

Javik knelt, removing one glove. He dug in the soil with his bare hand. "Ground's warm," he said.

"Magicians have passed this way," Prince Pineapple said.

The travelers set out single file on the trough trail, led by Wizzy and Prince Pineapple. "Kinda pretty here," Wizzy said, tilting his yellow cat's eye toward the prince.

Prince Pineapple did not respond.

"I said—"

"I heard you," Prince Pineapple said curtly. "Just keep your distance."

"You still sore at me?" Wizzy asked, hovering near the prince's face.

Prince Pineapple pushed Wizzy out of the way and trudged past him.

"I'll find a friend somewhere else," Wizzy said.

"I'm hungry," Namaba said, looking back at Javik.

"There isn't much food left," Javik said.

"We've got to eat," she said. "It's that or die."

"I'm hungry too," Javik said.

"Then let's finish off what's left," Rebo said, loping along the trail and looking back at Javik.

"There's two bio bars left," Javik said. "And some dried apples. I'll split it all up now. You can do what you want with yours."

This was agreeable with the Morovians, so Javik stopped

and opened his pack. The remaining food was divided. Then Javik wrapped his portion and returned it to the pack, while the Morovians gulped theirs.

"Don't ask for any of mine," Javik said.

Noticing some crumbs on the trail, Namaba fell to her knees and pressed her face against the ice. She scoured the trail with her tongue until all the stray crumbs had been retrieved.

Javik watched her intently as he pulled on his pack. Glancing up the trail, he saw Prince Pineapple and Wizzy waiting.

"Thank you," Namaba said as she stood up.

Javik nodded. "Water anyone?" he asked. He held his mouth under the spigot of one of the water pods on Rebo's back, filling his mouth. He shut off the spigot and straightened, holding some of the water in his mouth.

He swallowed slowly, watching the Morovians drink. Seeing Rebo take too much, Javik stopped him.

"But all the snow around," Rebo said. "We could melt it and drink it."

"Might be contaminated," Javik said.

Rebo put his mouth to the spigot again, disregarding Javik's instructions.

"Enough!" Javik barked, giving Rebo's large head a stiff shove.

Rebo straightened and met Javik's gaze. They stood two meters apart, with their gazes locked, portending mortal combat. Rebo was first to look away. Then he looked back at Javik, saying, "I could take you now, before you had a chance to pull that thunder piece near your hand."

"I doubt it," Javik said. The fingers of his gun hand twitched.

"I'm very fast for my size," Rebo said.

"He's telling you the truth," Namaba said.

Javik's mouth became a thin, steely line. His lips parted, and terse words crossed them: "We're in this together, Rebo. You understand that, or you would have tried to take me earlier."

Rebo smiled, revealing iridescent blue teeth. He extended his forepaw to Javik. "You're a pretty tough little guy," Rebo said as they clasped hands.

Javik knew he was taking a chance. But he couldn't keep looking over his shoulder. He would have to sleep sometime. Studying Rebo's face, he saw deep lines framing the undersides of the eyes, lines formed in the worries and battles of another world.

"I was a killer once," Rebo said as their hands separated.

"That was on a different world," Namaba said. "And besides, those times are dead." She looked at Javik. "Rebo is not the same here."

Javik looked at Rebo again, noticing a scar on the side of his head and a nick out of one of his wide, cuplike ears. This was not a killer. Not any longer. He was a potential friend. Javik was sure of it.

"Hurry up!" Prince Pineapple yelled, glowering.

Javik caught Namaba's gaze before they resumed their course. "Those morsels of food won't last us long," she said.

Thirty minutes later they reached the rock wall at the opposite side of Icy Valley. A short search produced two trails within a hundred meters of one another, each taking a different route up the rock face.

Javik studied the Sacred Scroll of Cork. "I only see one trail here," he said.

"Maybe it doesn't matter," Prince Pineapple said. He took several steps up the nearest trail, then stopped and screamed.

Javik dropped the scroll and drew his service pistol. "What is it?" he yelled, running toward the prince.

Prince Pineapple was roaring back down the trail. "Look behind me!" he squealed. "On the trail!"

"Where?" Javik said. "I don't see anything!"

"Paula!" Prince Pineapple said, near hysterics as he reached Javik. He buried his face in his hands.

"What are you talking about?" Wizzy asked, joining them at the trailhead.

"Paula Pineapple," the prince said. "The girl I almost permied. She's on the trail holding a huge cleaver. She threatened to cut me up into little pineapple squares."

"But there's no one there," Wizzy said.

"That's right," Javik said. "Take a look for yourself."

Prince Pineapple pulled one hand away from his face and looked back up the trail. "I still see her," he insisted. "She's going to kill me if I take that trail."

"Nonsense!" Javik said. "I'll show you." He holstered his gun and hiked up the trail, taking big, confident steps.

As Prince Pineapple watched in terror, the image of the pineapple girl faded. Then the image disappeared in a puff of mist. Suddenly, Javik stopped and drew his gun again. He backed down the trail.

"What is it?" Prince Pineapple called out. "I don't see her anymore."

As Javik retreated, he kept his eyes glued on a beautiful dark-skinned girl who stood in the center of the trail, holding an automatic rifle. The barrel was pointed directly at Javik. He knew the girl. It was the one he had almost permied—the one from the astro-port so long ago. He had left her because of the uncertainties of war.

Reaching the trailhead, Javik explained what he saw, stuttering. Then he asked, "How? H-how could she be here? We're on the opposite side of the universe from Port Saint Clemente."

"We don't see anything," Namaba said.

"I'll try it," Rebo said. While Javik watched, Rebo loped up the trail, approaching the dark-skinned girl who still stood on the trail holding a rifle. As Rebo neared her, the girl's image faded and disappeared in a puff of mist.

When this happened, Rebo stopped in his tracks. Then he turned and loped down the trail.

"What happened?" Javik asked.

"I saw Namaba," Rebo said. "She was blocking the trail, holding a long switchblade in each hand." He looked back. "She's still up there."

Namaba's dark eyebrows arched in surprise. "Me?" she asked. "How could that be? I'm here."

"Magicians at work," Prince Pineapple said. "Or Lord Abercrombie."

"Do you see the pattern?" Rebo asked, looking at Javik.

"You love Namaba, don't you, Rebo?" Javik asked.

Rebo nodded, catching Namaba's troubled gaze.

She looked away.

"In each case," Javik said, "we are threatened by the one we love most in the entire universe."

"Exactly," Rebo said. "The image of Namaba on the trail is fading now."

"Let's try the other trail," Prince Pineapple suggested.

The others agreed. Prince Pineapple led the way up the second trail, stepping slowly and cautiously at first. The trail became steep and narrow. Soon they were in mist again, on a cliff trail similar to the one that had led them into Icy Valley. With each step, Prince Pineapple expected to confront Paula Pineapple again. But she did not appear. They increased their pace and began to make good progress.

But then Wizzy flew to the front and squealed, "Wait! I think we're going the wrong way!"

"What?" Prince Pineapple said, stopping.

Javik and the others made similar surprised comments as they stopped.

"Someone wants us to go this way," Wizzy said, "It's too easy."

They talked it over. Generally, it was conceded that Wizzy might be right. But Javik was less convinced than the others. "Maybe it's just the opposite," he said. "Whoever is orchestrating this knew we would have doubts. Maybe we were expected to stop and turn back."

"How do we decide?" Prince Pineapple asked.

"Your Decision Coin," Javik said.

"Don't be silly. Abercrombie controls that."

"I don't agree," Javik said. "I'm in charge here, and I say flip it."

Prince Pineapple shrugged and produced his large gold coin.

"The 'yes' side and we take this trail," Javik said. "The 'no' side and we take the other."

Prince Pineapple flipped the coin, being careful to keep it from falling over the cliff. It rolled a little ways and lodged against the rock wall at one side of the trail.

"It's 'no,'" Javik said, retrieving the coin. He handed it to the prince.

"Then we take the other trail," Prince Pineapple said.

Javik smiled. "Wrong," he said. "We do the opposite. Abercrombie does control that coin. He wants us on the other trail."

Prince Pineapple shook his head in confusion. "I don't know," he said, stuffing the coin in his pants pocket.

"I'm sure of it," Javik said. "Let's go."

Lord Abercrombie was soil-immersed, permitting him to see and hear the activity on the trail. *I don't control Decision Coins,* he thought. *They're strictly chance.*

He concentrated on breaking a large rock outcropping just over the heads of the travelers. It was already cracked from natural conditions, and should not require that much effort. But no incantation, prayer, or command could convince even the smallest chunk to break away.

Two days ago I induced a small rockslide, he thought,

frustrated. *Now, whenever my enemies are vulnerable, I can do nothing.*

Lord Abercrombie was more dismayed than angry. He had experienced so many failures that the latest installment came as no surprise. He felt this attitude probably contributed to his failings. The magnetic imbalance of Cork could not be responsible for everything. But he was helpless to change, and felt himself falling into the great cosmic crevasse populated by losers. He wondered why attitude suddenly seemed so essential to magical success. Attitude was supposed to be a psyche thing, a concern for super-achiever fleshcarriers. It should not belong in a magical situation. Maybe it had something to do with his being caught between realms: Things were getting muddled from his indecision. Or maybe it was something deeper, an overlapping between the realms of Flesh and Magic.

Lord Abercrombie's tympanic sensors picked up a cracking sound. A tiny piece of rock broke free from the outcropping and bounced down the cliff face, falling harmlessly on the trail next to Javik. It was such a small piece that none of the intended victims noticed it.

Oh, well, Lord Abercrombie thought. *It was something, anyway.* Helplessly, he watched Prince Pineapple lead the way up the correct trail.

As the travelers resumed their journey, the ground began to shake. Javik heard a low rumble, which grew louder.

"Run for it!" Wizzy squealed, looking up the cliff with his cat's eye. He could not see very far in the thick mist. "I hear a rockslide."

"Uptrail," Javik yelled, seeing a domed rock shelter just ahead. "Under that big rock."

They ran and flew for their lives, taking shelter under the domed rock. An avalanche of jagged rock thundered by them, bouncing off the side of the cliff. From the safety of their shelter, they heard the rocks land angrily on the valley floor.

When the noise subsided, Javik ventured out cautiously. The mist was becoming dark gray now, and he knew why. "We must hurry," he said. "It will be nightfall soon."

Still soil-immersed, Lord Abercrombie was raging at the latest turn of events. *So close!* he thought. *I almost had them!* Then he wondered if he had caused the slide or if the rocks would have fallen anyway. After all, the outcropping had been cracked long before he took notice of it.

I have to assume I did it, he thought. *I can't give up now.*

Javik led the way up the trail, sidestepping a number of small rocks in the way. "Don't step on any of this loose stuff," he said.

Beyond the slide area, the travelers began to move quickly, trying to reach a suitable campsite before dark. They glanced up often, fearing the mountain would cut loose again.

We're moving deeper into Lord Abercrombie's web, Prince Pineapple thought. *He is all around us, ready to swallow us at any moment.*

Night was descending rapidly, spreading its purple-black Corkian mantle across the cliff trail. It took away what little visibility the fog had left for them, forcing them to travel slower and slower. Wizzy's white glow worked as a fairly decent light for a while, but he had trouble keeping it lit. Perhaps it was due to the full day he had already had, with many occasions to call upon his data banks. Finally he asked to be carried. Grudgingly, Javik placed him in a pocket of his vari-temp coat.

The intense darkness made the prospect of another rockslide terrifying to Javik. If he heard it coming, where would he flee? Surely such a catastrophe would send some and perhaps all hurtling over the edge.

It was dark and windy when Prince Pineapple insisted on a break. For some time before that, Javik had noticed that the prince had been dragging his steps. By the time he called out, Prince Pineapple had slipped to last in line.

"Tell him to be careful with this," Javik said, passing the folding shovel and nutrient cord to Namaba. As she passed it on down the line, Prince Pineapple said he had heard the command, and that it was an unnecessary thing to say.

Every muscle in Javik's body wanted to sleep. But this was no place to pitch a tent. An icy wind cut across his legs. He considered donning a pair of vari-temp pants with the aid of his wardrobe ring, but decided against it. Too much energy required to mento it. He probed with his gloved hands for a place to sit. The ground was cold under his bottom.

Javik heard Namaba and Rebo find their own places to rest. Their breathing was labored, coming in short, staccato bursts, like steam engines with just enough poop left to go straight to the garbage launch facility.

The clunk and clang of Prince Pineapple's shovel rang out from downtrail.

"Maybe we can sleep here," Namaba suggested. "Right on the trail."

The idea had some appeal to Javik, and even made a certain amount of sense. It might be safer than stumbling around in the dark. But no one seconded the motion.

She did not repeat her suggestion.

Soon they were back at it, straining their muscles nearly to the breaking point. Prince Pineapple was a hot dog now with the fresh charge. Generously, he offered to carry the water pods and the survival pack. These were turned over to him. Even with this added weight, the prince surged far ahead of the others, often going so fast that he had to stop and wait for them to catch up.

It was a night of nights, the sort of monumental struggle one never forgets. With each step, Javik thought the trail grew steeper and more rocky. The wind bore down on them from uptrail, the worst possible direction, often forcing backward steps. If only it would blow from behind! Such a wind would help them to the top.

But the wind god, or whoever was in control of such matters, was not on their side.

Javik did not mention his thoughts. They only brought to mind Lord Abercrombie and the suggestion that he might be working against every move they made. Javik tried to convince himself that Abercrombie did not exist, and that even if he did exist, he could not control the wind or rockslides. But with each attempted step, Javik grew less confident of this.

Sometime in the early morning hours they stumbled onto a high plateau. The mist disappeared here, and Javik saw two harvest moons dropping below the horizon. A blanket of stars twinkled overhead, a cool blanket which offered welcome psychological warmth. Javik felt physically warmer here as well, as the wind had died down, going to one of the hiding places for such phenomena.

"You wanna camp here?" Prince Pineapple asked, coming back down the trail. With the moons behind him, Javik could not see his face.

"Yeah," Javik said.

In waning moonlight ahead, Javik saw the ghostlike outlines of treetops, framed majestically against the Corkian sky. Somewhere nearby a river ran, making its night journey with the moons. They were on soft soil now, at the edge of a forest. The moons disappeared below the horizon.

Javik took Wizzy out of his pocket and awakened him. "Give me some light," Javik said.

Wizzy did not complain, despite being so tired that he could barely keep his peeper open. He glowed bright white.

Prince Pineapple moved in close to watch. He moved around to stay warm.

Javik searched in the pack until he found the tent tube, a tiny roll no larger than a package of Lifesaver candies. Locating a flat spot on the ground, he set the tube down. "Stand back," he warned.

Everyone moved away from the tube.

Javik mentoed it. *Come on, brain,* he thought, knowing there was no manual way to pitch the specially packed, lightweight tent. *My mento unit had better be operable.* He felt no pain around the implanted mento unit.

The gortex tent popped open like fast-forward photography on an inverted, ugly flower.

Prince Pineapple gasped and stepped back. "Oh!" he said.

The tent stood taller than Javik and was at least four meters square. In Wizzy's flickering light, four curved, interlocking corner poles of expandable titanium appeared and stabbed through eyelets at each corner of the tent fabric. Then eight stakes hammered into the ground all around like a short burst of machine-gun fire. The door flap unzipped and flopped open, a final indication that the unit was ready for occupancy.

"Amazing," Prince Pineapple said. A light went on inside as he poked his head in. "It even has beds!" he exclaimed, seeing three single beds, completely made up. He heard a fan whirring.

"This is nothing," Javik said, his voice weary. "The Earth-use models have full appliances, even videodome units. That makes for a heavier package, of course—nearly a quarter of a kilo instead of this little one-hecto baby."

"Sure looks like magic to me," Prince Pineapple said.

A short distance away, Rebo and Namaba found a place on the ground where they cleared away the rocks, twigs, and pinecones. "Do you have enough space?" Rebo asked, selecting a spot for himself. The river was loud here.

"I'm fine," she said. Namaba lay on her side, with her head on one arm. In the light cast through the open tent doorway, she watched Javik enter the tent.

"Where did Rebo and Namaba go?" she heard Javik ask.

"I think they're over toward the river," Prince Pineapple said.

Rebo lay down on the ground where he could see Namaba's glowing red eyes. "You said I was different," he said. "And I agree. There have been great changes in my brain. With this yenta you say you have, Namaba, can you explain it?"

"Your words are not so harsh," she said. "And they are slower, evidently spoken from a calm soul. I see it in your eyes, too, Rebo. They are softer and more compassionate."

"Softer? You mean I am no longer a man?"

"No, silly! I just mean that you're nicer now. More considerate."

"Then let's get married," he said. "When we return to Moro City."

"A meteor shower!" Javik yelled, poking his head out of the tent.

Namaba and Rebo sat up and watched a sky full of burning embers plummet to Cork. One large chunk caught Namaba's attention. It disappeared below the treetops, and she heard it hit the ground.

"Only about fifty kilometers off," Javik said.

The sky grew dark again, revealing the backdrop of stars.

"You might return to your old self back home," Namaba said, lying back down beside Rebo. "Your gang was always first, and I was just a possession."

"I've given that a lot of thought," Rebo said. "I'll be leaving the Southside, finding honest work."

"I like the sound of that," she said. "But I can't forget the way you were. If only I had met you now."

"I can't forget my other self, either," he said, showing sorrow in his tone. "The image of that old flower vendor still haunts me."

"Yeah. That was a terrible thing."

"Rebo! Namaba!" Javik yelled. "You guys okay over there?"

"We're fine," Rebo said. But he did not feel fine. The tank in his steam boiler stomach was in a knot.

"I'm afraid it's too late for us," she said. "I've known the other Rebo."

"But I won't ever see the Hawks again! I promise," Namaba saw his eyes narrow to dim slits. Then they closed, evidently in prayer.

"No," she said. "I'm sorry, but no."

Presently, Rebo heard rumbling slumber from the other side of the camp. He wished he could fall asleep so easily. But his mind churned. It was the new mind in the new Rebo, carrying thoughts that seemed never to have existed before.

He heard Namaba turn to her other side. During the next hour, Namaba turned over many more times while Rebo lay awake. But this was no consolation to him. He wanted to share happiness with her, not turmoil.

TWELVE

The planet naturally attracts space debris, much of it radioactively and ionically charged. When this is combined with a basic magnetic imbalance, the place becomes inhospitable to the pure energy waves required by a magician. Magic still works there, but only erratically.

> Conclusion of the magicians'
> task force assigned to Cork,
> sixty-seven centuries before
> Abercrombie's arrival

As Javik slept, Lord Abercrombie left his soil-immersion chamber and floated just above the surface to the Disaster Control Room. There he supervised work on the old earthquake and flood machine. This was comprised of a long bank of cracked CRT screens and discolored computer keyboards along one wall, manned by six dented meckies. As he entered the room, he heard squeaking, whirring, and synchronized rattles as the meckies tried to get the equipment going.

"Anything?" Lord Abercrombie asked, expecting to receive the usual long list of problems.

"We're flooding the ancient riverbed on the east edge of Dusty Desert," a soprano-voiced silver meckie reported.

"Eh?" Lord Abercombie said, moving to the meckie's side. He rubbed his human eye and then studied the water table gauges to one side of the CRT screen. Not believing the readings, he slammed the butt of his hand against them. The needles jumped only a little, returning to their original position. "I don't believe it," he mumbled. "How long has this been working?"

"Three and a half hours, Lord," the silver meckie said.

"And no sign of the monopoles?"

"Not so far. We're concentrating all the spring waters for thousands of square kilometers—raising them to the level of the desert plateau."

"How long before we get a rip-roaring flood?" Lord Abercrombie asked.

"Just a few hours, if everything holds together."

Still not believing his good fortune, Lord Abercrombie said, "Be careful not to get the flood going too soon. We want to catch Brother Carrot's entire fleet when they're in the middle of the desert."

"Yes, Lord."

Lord Abercrombie felt like jumping up and clicking his heels. There had been so many misfortunes, so many dashed hopes. Then he remembered that he only had one heel left. It didn't matter, anyway. He needed to keep a more even temperament, not becoming too euphoric during good times or too depressed during the bad.

It's not a loser's mentality, he told himself. *I'm just being sensible.*

"What about the monopoles?" the silver meckie asked. "They could get in our way if we wait for Brother Carrot. How about a hurricane where the army is now?"

"We'd have to shut down the flood to do that," Lord Abercrombie said. "Better not risk it. Let's keep what we have going."

Three midmorning suns cast their rays around the campsite as Javik opened the tent flap and stepped out. His feet and hands were cold. He wiped his nose with one sleeve, then stared at the bio bar in his hand. With gnawing, screaming hunger at his midsection, he lifted the high-energy bar to his lips. Slowly he nibbled at it, tasting the sweetness of honey and feeling the texture of reprocessed oat flakes on his tongue. When he was halfway through the bar, he considered saving a portion for Rebo and Namaba. Then he ate Rebo's allocation, following that with Namaba's.

I warned them, Javik thought, licking the corners of his mouth to retrieve the last molecules of sweetness there. Hearing running water, he walked past the sleeping form of Rebo and looked over the edge of a low embankment.

A small stream ran below his vantage point, sparkling cheerily in sunlight. On the ground nearby, Rebo stirred and stretched. Javik wondered where Namaba had gone. Then he saw her, in shade at the base of the embankment, leaning over the water. The stream was not as large as Javik had imagined it to be the night before. And it seemed quieter now. Oddly, the banks were wet by each side a good ten meters above the water level.

Rebo loped to his side, yawning.

"Look at that water level," Javik said. "It's dropped a lot recently. I'd say overnight."

"Huh," Rebo said, not showing interest. "Boy, am I hungry!" he said. "You got anything left in your pack?"

"No. You finished your share yesterday." Javik was still hungry, even hungrier than he had been before eating the bio bar. The bit of food had activated his appetite. In a big way.

Prince Pineapple walked up, asking for his nutrient kit. Javik gave it to him, then watched the prince trudge away sleepily, looking for a spot to recharge.

"We've gotta figure something out," Rebo said. "Can't go on without nourishment."

"Don't imagine you have many streams in Moro City," Javik said, returning to his own subject. "But they aren't supposed to drop like that. Not in such a short period of time."

Rebo was watching Prince Pineapple recharge himself on a patch of dark ground at the edge of the forest. The prince had one foot immersed in a freshly dug hole and his eyes were closed. In ecstasy, he leaned back on both elbows.

Javik looked too, wondering if the nutrient kit would work for him and the Morovians. To Javik it looked as though Prince Pineapple was receiving a form of sexual gratification. It was the way he leaned back, and the look of sublime pleasure on his pineapple face.

"Why couldn't we do that?" Rebo asked.

"I was just thinking the same thing."

They watched Prince Pineapple remove his bare foot from

the hole and wipe it with a moist-pak towelette. Glancing at Javik and Rebo nervously, he found his sock and slipped it on.

"I'm pretty damned hungry," Javik said.

"Same here."

Without another word, they walked toward Prince Pineapple, reaching him just as he was refilling his hole.

"We'll take that," Javik said, grabbing the shovel and barbed nutrient cord.

"You first?" Javik asked, extending the items to Rebo.

"Go ahead," Rebo said. "I'm not afraid, even if it kills you, I'd have to give it a try. We're different, you know, and it might only work for one of us."

Javik looked around for a place to dig.

"It won't work for either of you," Prince Pineapple said. He stomped on the loose dirt from his hole, packing it flat.

Javik dug at a furious pace, clanging the shovel on stones and throwing loose dirt in all directions. Some dirt landed on the prince's shoes.

"Watch it," Prince Pineapple said haughtily. "And don't damage my shovel."

"Get rid of him," Javik said. "Before I lose my temper."

"Beat it," Rebo said, showing no respect for the prince's royal status. He gave Prince Pineapple a mighty shove, causing him to stumble backward.

"Ruffian!" Prince Pineapple said.

Wizzy flew up just then. "You shouldn't do that," he said. "A prince of Cork deserves our respect."

"I can take care of myself," Prince Pineapple huffed. He stalked off in the direction of the tent.

"Wait!" Wizzy squealed, flying behind the angry prince.

Prince Pineapple paid no heed to Wizzy.

"I'd like us to be friends again," Wizzy said. "We have too much in common to be at one another's throats."

"You have no throat," Prince Pineapple said coolly.

"It was a figure of speech."

"But I have shifty eyes," Prince Pineapple snapped, still stalking away. "You can't be friends with someone like that."

"Let's talk about it," Wizzy said.

"There's nothing to discuss," the prince said, raging. "And I don't need any friends."

Wizzy stopped following, and let the angry prince go his

own way. Prince Pineapple found a log on which to sit and sulk.

Sadly, Wizzy flew off to be by himself. He missed his friend and thought back upon their wonderful conversation in the prince's apartment. *My first friendship,* Wizzy thought, alighting on a tree branch. *It didn't last very long.*

A chubby yellow bird chirped cheerily on a nearby branch.

"You wanna be my friend?" Wizzy asked.

The bird had a short beak, with nervous, beady eyes. It looked at Wizzy curiously, then chirped again and flew away.

"Guess not," Wizzy said. He tried to cheer himself by remembering his Papa Sidney's strong friendship with Captain Tom. *I'll find a friend,* he thought. *Somewhere in this great big universe, there's a friend . . . just waiting for me to find him.*

Wizzy circled the campsite. Spotting a worm crawling along the ground, he landed in its path and glowed a friendly shade of lavender. Unimpressed, the worm crawled around him.

"Oh, well," Wizzy said.

Just then the chubby yellow bird dived at the worm, snatching it in its beak. A startled Wizzy watched the bird fly off and disappear in the woods.

"Maybe that's the way to get a friend," Wizzy said. "Just swoop down and carry one away." Resolving to give this more thought, Wizzy flew down to the creek, hovering over Namaba as she washed.

"That was great!" Javik said after his recharge, leaping up from the hole. He felt nourished and sexually gratified at the same time, a wonderful completeness he had not experienced in recent memory.

"Pretty good, huh?" Rebo asked.

"*Pretty* good? It made the whole trip to Cork worthwhile, that's all!" Javik knelt and removed the barbed cord from his foot.

"Say," Rebo said, looking at Javik closely. "The scratches are gone from your face. So's the scar you had on your nose."

"That so?" Javik said. He rubbed his forehead, the bridge of his nose, and his cheeks. They were smooth.

Rebo was hesitant to attempt the charge. "I'm not like you," he said. "This could still kill me." He took the cord from Javik and wrapped it around one paw. Timidly, he extended the paw toward the hole Javik had used. It touched dirt. He put his weight on the paw. There was a slight tingling. Rebo's red eyes flashed around nervously.

"Anything?" Javik asked. He brushed off his own foot and put on his sock and boot.

Rebo shifted his paw around in the hole. "My skin's kinda thick," he said. "So I barely feel the barbs." He shifted his foot again. There was no change in the sensation.

"Try a new hole," Javik suggested. "Maybe that one's used up for a while."

"Huh?" Rebo said, glancing at Javik. "Oh, yeah. Thanks." He stepped out of the hole and used the shovel to dig a fresh one. Soon he was recharging too. It worked so well that steam shot out of his ears in frosty puffs against the cool morning air.

"That *was* good," Rebo said as he finished. "What a meal!"

"Did you feel anything else?" Javik asked, keeping his voice down.

Rebo thought for a moment. "Yeah," he said. "Now that you mention it. Kind of a noppi noppi feeling."

Javik's language mixer pendant did not translate this expression, but no explanation was required. "A guy could set up one hell of a resort here," Javik said. "Folks would cross the universe to enjoy some of this. It even heals cuts and scars."

Javik noticed brown powder forming all over Rebo's body, blowing off in the wind and getting on his black club jacket. *Bodily waste,* Javik thought, picking up the dull odor again. *Not so distasteful as human wastes.*

Rebo smiled broadly. "Ah!" he exclaimed.

"I'd better fill the water pods," Javik said. He retrieved the nutrient kit and connected it to his belt.

Recalling that Namaba was at the creek, Rebo's smile faded. "I can get it. Wait. Do we even need water now? With the nutrient kit working for us?"

"The charge might wear off quickly," Javik said. "And what if something went wrong with the nutrient kit?"

"Yeah, I guess."

"Stay here and fill those holes," Javik said. "You can push the dirt back with your paws."

Rebo did as he was told.

Javik returned to the camp and lifted the partially full water pods and the survival pack out of the tent. Stepping safely away, he mentoed the habitat into a tight little ball.

What a terrible death, he thought, *if I ever mentoed this thing shut while still inside.* Javik had heard of a camper getting squeezed into a tight little roll, but wondered if it was just another folktale.

Moments later, Javik put the tent roll in the pack. Leaving the pack there on the ground, he took the water pods and trudged down a short bank to the river.

Namaba smiled when she saw him. "I was waiting for you," she said, securing the yellow and black polka dot ribbon to her mane.

Javik told her the marvelous news about their new source of nutrition, omitting the prurient details.

Namaba wiped cool water across her face. "That *is* good news," she said. "I'll recharge too, when we return to camp." She noticed Javik's scratches were gone, and commented on this.

"The recharge," Javik said. "Some kinda wonder cure."

Standing at the top of the embankment, Rebo watched Javik and Namaba. He heard their muted words and saw them smiling at one another. Namaba's laughter cut through the chill morning air like a knife piercing the center of Rebo's steam engine heart. He focused on the holstered thunder piece worn by Javik. But his thoughts of harming Javik were short-lived. Rebo felt ashamed for having them.

Namaba watched Javik as he knelt on a flat stone and filled the pod. He capped it and reached for the other pod.

"Do you remember the two trails?" she asked. "Back at Icy Valley?"

"Yes." Javik suppressed a burp from the recharge.

"If I had gone up the first trail," she said, "I know whose image I would have seen there."

"Sure. Rebo's."

As Javik looked at her, a soft smile formed on her lips. "I would have seen *you,*" she said.

"Me?" Javik fumbled with the second pod's lid. He noticed the river level was still dropping, leaving only a few centimeters of water in some places.

"I love you," she said.

Javik forgot about the water level. Feeling his heart kick, he set the full plastic pod on a rock and stood up. Taking a deep breath, he gazed downstream. The river, which was now a creek, reached a bend several hundred meters away, a place where sunlight sparkled cheerily on the water. Two ruby red birds flew close to the water at the bend. Their wingtips touched the water, spraying mist.

"How can you be so sure?" he asked. "We've hardly spoken."

"Morovian women know such things instantly," she said. "We feel love this way. It only takes a glance to know. Or a touch. She moved close to Javik and clasped one of his hands in hers. "We have yenta, you know."

Namaba's grasp was firm. She had light brown hair on the back of her hand. Her palm and fingers were cool from the stream, but Javik felt them warm quickly in his grasp.

Javik compared Namaba's feelings with what Wizzy had told him about Sidney Malloy. *Sid considers me his best friend,* Javik thought, *though I've only seen him twice in twenty years. Now this. These things don't fit the normal pattern. You can't have a friend you hardly ever see, or a lover you barely know.*

"I will tell you a love poem," she said, looking into his deeply set blue eyes. "One my mother taught me. . . ."

Javik did not remember the words. It was something about a Morovian maiden whose soldier went off to battle far away. He died on a far-off battlefield while she waited in Moro City, pining away beneath a flashing V.D. clinic sign. It was a sad poem, with words that lilted and drifted across the sun-sparkled water.

He felt her grip tighten.

Javik looked up at her. She was a head taller and much heavier, but Javik did not give this much of a thought now. He saw a tear roll down her cheek.

"I always cry at that story," she said, brushing the tear away with her free hand. Then she pressed her lips against Javik's, rubbing gently from side to side.

Her lips were surprisingly soft to him. He kissed her in the Earth human way that he knew.

The ways of Earth and Morovia were different, so they took turns trying the new techniques. It was a union across the heavens, two different life forms finding common ground. Javik felt it was an important moment. Not just for himself and Namaba, but in a larger, cosmic sense.

"You have been with many women," she said. Javik did

not hear jealousy or anger in her tone. It was simply an undeniable statement of fact.

Javik's entire love life flashed across his eyes. The old life of pleasure-dome maidens and girls in every astro-port had died. He would never return to it. He knew Namaba should seem even more unusual to him than the transsexual, Evans. By all rights, he should be repulsed by Namaba. But his feelings were far from revulsion. He needed constancy, someone on whom he could rely. He wondered how Morovians made love.

"Do you think we might share a child?" she asked, apparently sensing his unspoken thought.

Javik smiled. "We will see," he said.

They walked hand in hand up the embankment, each cradling a full water pod in one arm. As they entered the campsite, Javik thought Rebo was going out of his way to avoid them.

Rebo rested on his haunches off to one side, busying himself by picking things out of his fur. He seemed preoccupied and sad.

Peripherally, Javik saw Namaba as she looked at Rebo. She used to go to him at times like this, helping him to clean himself in the Morovian way. But Rebo was on his own now. Javik knew she had decided this. The touch of her lips and the grip of her hand had told him so.

Far across Dusty Desert from Javik and his party an ancient riverbed was full. Moments later, from his soil-immersed position, Lord Abercrombie watched the waters roll across the desert, over ridges of pebble and sand, returning the place to its former watery state. Desert palms were uprooted or immersed in a high wall of water.

"Heh, heh, heh!" Lord Abercrombie's laugh reflected the turn in his fortunes.

Nothing can stop a flood, he thought. *It's on the way.* He wondered if monopoles could swim.

"What was that?" Brother Carrot asked. "A low roar? Do you hear it?" He stood at the bow of the *Freedom One* as the big desert schooner crossed the face of a dune. Twenty-nine other ships laden with eager Vegetable troops followed Brother Carrot's lead craft.

Captain Cucumber stood next to him. "I hear something too." He peered across the desert.

"It's getting louder," Brother Carrot said. "Must be the wind."

Suddenly a wall of water appeared, bearing down on them at high speed. Brother Carrot and the captain ran for the passageway. Just as they closed the door behind them, the water hit.

The *Freedom* rolled to one side. It became dark in the passageway.

"We're going over!" Brother Carrot said, scrambling to find a handhold in the passageway. He grabbed a hand railing. "My beautiful fleet!" he moaned. "My beautiful army!" He heard his men belowdecks as they clamored in confusion.

The cucumber captain was not so fortunate. Unable to find a handhold, he slid on the pegged floor the full length of the passageway. This left him in a jumbled position on the other end, against a cabin door. "My ship!" he moaned. "My beautiful ship!"

Water seeped in as the ship was consumed, getting Brother Carrot's shoes wet. The ship began to rock gently now, and the din of rushing water quieted. Brother Carrot felt the ship right itself and float upward.

"We're floating!" Brother Carrot exclaimed.

At the other end of the passageway, the captain was struggling to his feet. Holding the handrail, he sloshed his way slowly back to Brother Carrot. "You're right," he said, a hesitant smile on his cucumber face.

"You mean this thing was designed to float?" Brother Carrot asked.

"Sure. We took extra time and sealed the hulls."

"Idiot! We could have launched our attack earlier!"

"But this flood, sir."

"We would have missed the flood. Can't you understand that?"

"Yes, sir."

Sunlight streamed in the passageway portholes as the *Freedom One* bobbed to the surface. Brother Carrot peered out a porthole and was overjoyed to see other ships bob up. Some had broken spreaders or masts. All had torn sails and rigging in disarray. Two AmFed gar-bahge cannisters popped to the surface below his porthole.

"Nine, ten . . ." Brother said. "There's eleven, twelve . . . I count fifteen ships on this side."

He ran to the hatch and slid it open. Knee-deep water rushed in. He waded out, reaching the gunwale on the ship's starboard side.

Men were streaming across the decks of the *Freedom One* now, lining the rails on each side of Brother Carrot. Hearing the chatter of his crew around him, Brother Carrot watched men filling the decks of the other ships in his battered fleet.

Dusty Desert was gone now, having been replaced by a lake that stretched across the entire rock-lined bowl. Waves lapped gently at the hull of the *Freedom One*. The ship rocked.

Brother Carrot removed his familiar black and gold cap, waving it in the air. Boisterous cheers rang across the water as the soldiers on each ship saw him. The men on his own ship cheered too, and patted their leader on the back.

"All accounted for," Captain Cucumber shouted. "I count twenty-nine other ships."

"Signal each of them," Brother Carrot said, replacing his cap on top of his leafy head. "Have the rigging repaired in breakneck time. That means I'll break the captains' necks if it isn't done. We'll float across now."

"But none of us have necks, sir," Captain Cucumber said. "Eh?"

"Our heads and bodies are one, sir."

"Then I'll find a way to separate them. Hop to it!"

Using sensors in each grain of sand, piece of dirt, and drop of water on the planet's surface, Lord Abercrombie saw and heard this activity. *Damnit!* he thought. *I didn't expect this at all. Who'd have imagined it? Those blasted ships float!*

Lord Abercrombie knew he could not remain halfway between realms any longer. It was becoming too much of a strain. *I must commit myself,* he thought. *But to what? A coin flip. That's what I need. I'll find someone on the surface who is flipping a coin.*

Using his visual sensors in a patch of grass, Lord Abercrombie found King Corker standing there, trying to decide whether or not to attend the games at Corker Stadium. This was a small grassy area on one side of King Corker's courtyard. Bending his blades of grass to look upward, Lord Abercrombie saw a castle guard tower silhouetted against a cloudless sky. A purple Corker banner on the tower fluttered in a light breeze.

"Bring me a Decision Coin!" King Corker thundered.

A watermelon man aide scurried up.

Okay, Lord Abercrombie thought. *Here's my question: Do I commit myself to the Realm of Magic?*

"Should I go to the games?" King Corker said to the aide. "Or should I languish in my harem?"

"You must select a yes or no question, Your Highness," the watermelon man said.

"Oh, King Corker said. "You're quite correct. Very well, then. You pick one."

Fools! Lord Abercrombie thought. *Hurry up!*

"Should King Corker go to the games?" the watermelon man said. He flipped the coin, then caught it on one palm and slapped it to the back of his other hand. "It says yes, Your Highness."

"I would have preferred the harem," King Corker said, "but bring me my carriage."

I have a trip to make too, Lord Abercrombie thought.

"But he was not anxious to make the commitment to magic. He would do it the following day, after trying a few more events with the disaster control machinery. The monopoles were staying away, Abercrombie reasoned, and he could have a last fling in his fleshy form.

The path through the forest was easy to follow, with three-dot magical markings on a number of ancient trees and rocks. Prince Pineapple walked briskly ahead, almost out of sight of the others. The continuing confrontation between him and the rest of the party was leaving scars.

Sunlight filtered through high pine boughs, making intricate webs of light over Javik's head. Walking beside Namaba that morning, Javik watched Wizzy spend his time flying through the high, sunny boughs. The little comet's body and tail sparkled in the slender strands of light that touched them.

Spending a good portion of the morning up there, Wizzy would yell such things as, "It's incredible up here! The rays are so symmetrical, so delicate!" Then he would streak along the beams of light, forming parallel streaks of light with his tail.

"I'm seven days old today!" Wizzy squealed at one point. "And I feel great!"

Once, Javik scolded Wizzy for being light-headed. "Don't be so silly," Javik shouted. "We have important problems, such as figuring out how to get back to Earth. You're not helping at all."

"Can't one be happy and have problems?" Wizzy replied, alighting on a high branch.

"No!" Javik yelled.

This activated the soap box orator in Wizzy's personality. While a bird warbled sadly in the background, Wizzy gushed philosophy, saying he was starting to understand happiness at long last, that it was to be found wherever you were, despite any problems you faced. "Every situation has bits of happiness," Wizzy said. "They should be discovered wherever they are hiding and nurtured."

"I wish I'd never brought him," Javik said, leaving Wizzy behind, still discoursing. "He's out of his mind."

"It's beautiful here," Namaba said. "Like pictures I have seen of places on Morovia. Country places."

"You've never been outside the city?"

"Never before."

"I'm looking forward to seeing Morovia with you," Javik said. "I hope the Dimensional Tunnel will take us there, and not somewhere else."

"We'll have a wonderful life there."

"First I have to check on Abercrombie," Javik said.

"What do you mean?"

"If he's a threat to Earth, I've got to get him out of the Magician's Chamber. That may mean killing him. If he's no threat, I'll leave him there."

"You didn't mention that before. I thought Abercrombie was the prince's concern."

"I've been thinking about it. I'll probably never see my ship again, meaning there's no way to return to Earth. I was called a patriot once. That's what some folks said, anyway. There was a Colonel Peebles, though. He criticized me for making independent decisions. So I hit him in the face. I hit a lot of people in the face."

"And you want the honor back?"

"Sure. Wouldn't anyone?"

"I wonder if it's worth the danger," she said.

"I don't know," Javik said. "All I know is I have to do it."

They fell silent.

Presently the ground became soft and moist, and the travelers made impressions in the soil as they walked. Javik heard and felt the suction of his heels as he lifted them to make each step. The red top of an AmFed garbage cannister was visible in deep mud off the trail to their left.

Wizzy dropped from the treetops now, gliding gracefully across the path in front of Javik. "End of the forest," Wizzy called out. Then he raced ahead along the path, disappearing over the crest of a little hill.

Prince Pineapple followed Wizzy, showing his broken helicopter beanie last as he too disappeared over the hill.

Javik was next to reach the crest. Here the sunlight was much stronger, with only a few slender trees on each side. At the bottom of a little hill a great swampy area stretched as far as he could see. He smelled decaying vegetation. Patches of brackish, green moss and other plants floated in the dark water. Skirting the edge of the water, tangled bushes seemed shadowy and threatening, even in full sunlight.

"Bottomless Bog," Prince Pineapple said, looking back at Javik.

As Namaba and Rebo caught up, a mosquito buzzed in Javik's ear. He swatted it away.

Bottomless Bog was a stupefying thing, appearing every bit as wide as the great Dusty Desert. But the bog seemed even more foreboding. It was dark, dank, and mysterious.

Wizzy flew back and buzzed nervously near Javik's ear. Thinking he was another mosquito, Javik nearly cuffed him, withdrawing his hand just in time.

A slender, straight line ran down the center of the bog. Prince Pineapple identified this, saying, "According to legend, that is a single log. In ancient times, trees grew in the area now comprising the bog, trees which were as high as these cliffs." He looked up.

High, polished cliffs stood on two sides of the bog, reflecting the bog's dark surface on their mirror faces. The cliff tops were immersed in clouds, extending so far up that Javik could not see how high they were.

"And how deep is the bog?" Wizzy asked.

"Bottomless," Prince Pineapple said.

Wizzy cast a fearful cat's eye gaze at the bog. "Bottomless?" he said. "But it looks shallow."

"It isn't," Prince Pineapple said.

"Just a minor obstacle, Wizzy," Javik said, sneering. "Remember your philosophy. Find happiness in each situation."

Wizzy glowed an embarrassed shade of red.

"I wonder if we could go around," Javik said, swatting another mosquito. He looked at Wizzy, adding, "You're energetic today. Fly around those cliffs and see if there's a way for us."

"Are you kidding?" Wizzy said. "I'm beat now. Maybe tomorrow."

Scowling, Javik said, "If you hadn't played in the forest all day, you might be able to make yourself useful."

"I'm not at your bidding!"

That's telling him! Prince Pineapple thought.

"Let's have a look at that scroll," Javik snapped, glancing at the prince.

Slowly, Prince Pineapple brought forth the Sacred Scroll of Cork from under his coat. He extended it to Javik.

"Come on," Javik said. "Don't play games with me."

"Games?" Prince Pineapple asked.

"Reach back in your coat and get me the scroll."

"It's here. In my hands."

Javik's eyes flared angrily. Then a look of shock crossed his face. "I don't see it," he said. His fingers darted forward and touched an unseen parchment held by the prince. "I can't see the damned thing anymore!"

"Nor can I," Namaba said. She looked at Rebo.

"Nothing there," Rebo said.

Prince Pineapple thought for a moment, then said, "We have all recharged now. Lord Abercrombie's spell is on each of us."

"I can see the scroll," Wizzy said sassily. "And I'll read it to you, Captain Tom . . . if I so choose."

"You'll read it," Javik said. "Remember what papa said."

"Spread it open," Wizzy snapped.

Javik and Prince Pineapple held the scroll open, deciding not to place it on the moist ground. Wizzy hovered in front of it, his yellow cat's eye slanted at something no one else could see. "Uh huh," Wizzy said. "Uh *huh*."

"What does it say?" Prince Pineapple asked anxiously.

"We have to cross the log. No way around, according to a specific notation. An unnamed meadow is shown on the other side. Then we must pass between two white cliffs. At this point the scroll is marked 'Moha.'"

"Nothing on what Moha is?" Prince Pineapple asked.

"I looked for that when I could see the scroll," Javik said. "There's no detail at all."

"Beyond Moha," Wizzy said, "it's only a short distance to the Dimensional Tunnel. It's adjacent to the Magician's Chamber entrance."

"We'd better start across," Prince Pineapple said. He tugged at the scroll.

Javik considered keeping it, but had another thought and released it. *No sense antagonizing him unnecessarily,* Javik thought.

"Be careful with my nutrient kit as you cross the log, Captain Javik," Prince Pineapple said. He placed the scroll back in its carrying place beneath his orange vari-temp coat. "If you lose it, all of us except for Wizzy will perish. That includes your girlfriend."

Javik nodded, pursing his lips. "Lead on," he said, pointing toward the log.

Prince Pineapple reached a flat-stone-covered path leading down to the point where the log touched the shore. Decaying moss clung to the sides of the log and floated in the water. Jumping on the log, Prince Pineapple looked back and said, "No rhymes, please! Can't afford a backflip here." He started across the log, unable to see the opposite shore.

Just as Javik reached the log, a thick swarm of mosquitoes surrounded him. He fought them off, but they were persistent. He felt his skin swell on the back of his neck and on his forehead.

"Goddamn bugs," Javik said. He fumbled in his pack. "And no repellent here!"

"They don't seem to bother Rebo or me," Namaba said. She was just behind Javik, and helped him swat the mosquitoes. "Our skin is pretty tough."

When the mosquitoes had eaten their fill of Javik, they flew off, skipping across the murky water. To Javik, they seemed gleeful as they left, frolicking away on full stomachs.

Namaba tested the log with her forepaw. The log didn't move.

Behind her on the shore, Rebo asked, "You okay?"

"I think so," she said. "It seems sturdy enough." She stepped on it carefully, balancing her two rear paws on the wide surface of the log. Then she took a little hop forward, pulling with her forepaw and pushing with both hindpaws.

"Watch for patches of moss," Prince Pineapple said, glancing back. "The wet stuff is slick." He was several meters ahead, moving cautiously.

Wizzy waited until last. Hesitantly he scooted along the log behind Rebo, just millimeters above the surface.

"Whatsamatter, Wizzy?" Javik called back, seeing Wizzy's trepidation. "You don't seem so chipper anymore."

"Don't tease him," Namaba said. She smelled stagnant water.

"Mind your own business!" Wizzy screeched. He had a funny feeling as he followed the others. Something was wrong in this place. Terribly wrong.

"Perfect!" Lord Abercrombie said, brushing dirt off his half body as he left the Soil Immersion Chamber. "Now let's try a nice little earthquake in Sector 114!"

Not taking time to dry-shower, Lord Abercrombie used his wardrobe ring to dress while he floated on air through the labyrinth of passageways. Following the circuitous route known only to him, he arrived presently in the Disaster Control Room. There he saw meckies working on one of the computer terminals. Parts were strewn on the floor.

"Just needs a minor adjustment," a silver meckie reported, his voice a less-than-reassuring mechanical whine. "Nothing to worry about."

"Hurry," Lord Abercrombie said. "They're crossing Bottomless Bog. *The end of my fleshy self is near*, he thought. *This would be a nice way to go out*.

"Another hour at most," a gold-plated female meckie said. "We'll finish in plenty of time."

Lord Abercrombie floated around the room nervously while the meckies continued their work. He knew it would take all the remaining hours of daylight for Prince Pineapple and his group to cross the bog—at least five to six hours. *I'll drown that motley bunch in the bog*, he thought. *Then tomorrow, before my permanent soil-immersion, a nice quake-induced rockslide to bury the Vegetable army on the trail*.

King Corker's open French brocade carriage sped along Avenida Seven in bright afternoon sunlight, pulled by one hundred of the strongest carrot men in the realm. The king was late for the games. He sucked impatiently on his grain alcohol tube.

"Faster!" the king yelled, his voice a drunken gargle.

The white-suited cantaloupe coachman cracked his whip over the blinder-fitted carrot man team, urging them to greater speed.

Snap! Snap!

Now the coachman brought his whip arm way back to get a good lick at the team. The tip of the whip caught King Corker's backpack tube as he sat in the rear, pulling the tube right out of his mouth.

"Fool!" King Corker yelled.

The coachman glanced back nervously as the coach took an exit leading to Corker Stadium. "Sorry, Your Majesty," he said.

King Corker rubbed a sore upper lip. He muttered angrily, glaring at the crowd as his coach entered the stadium. The crowd roared their support for his royal personage.

"Whoah!" the coachman bellowed, hauling back on the reins. The coach screeched to a stop in front of the flag-draped royal box.

Two watermelon man aides ran forward. They helped King Corker down.

"Damn fool driver!" King Corker said as he was escorted to his box seat. He pulled his backpack tube forward to look at it. The tube was bent. "Get this pack off me," he ordered, refusing to sit down. "And bring me another."

One aide removed the royal alcohol pack while the other ran for a new one. "My driver did it," King Corker fumed. "With his infernal whip."

"Shall we tweak his nose, Sire?" the aide asked.

King Corker considered this while the other aide fitted him with a replacement pack. "Yes," the king said. "Then twist his ears. And don't forget to cut five centimeters off his nutrient cord. He won't be so careless again."

As the king took his seat, he saw a bright flash on the horizon, beyond the gray concrete fighter car track. Realizing it was a comet, King Corker felt his heart palpitate. His breath became short. He took a deep breath, feeling his heart pounding wildly.

The comet's nucleus was bright red, the color of Earthian

blood. It had a threadlike, golden tail that stretched across the sky.

"Bad omen," a woman said behind King Corker. She was a member of the royal court.

Others in the stands whispered nervously, concealing their words from the king's ears.

King Corker knew what they were saying. A comet like that always brought evil tidings, often portending the death of a king. He watched the comet swing wide and then speed away. It disappeared below the horizon.

King Corker lifted one arm weakly, signifying that the games were to begin. A bright blue starter flare flashed over the track, in line with the last sighted position of the comet's nucleus.

Seeing the flare, Marta Evans hit the red super-accelerator toggle on her dashboard. Her pink and black fighter car sped down the ramp of the Wommo auto carrier, bumping as it hit the pavement. It was a hot afternoon.

Out of the corner of her eye she saw a blue and black enemy fighter car running with her on the parallel track. Two hundred fifty meters ahead, the simmering tracks merged. She had played this Earth game six times now, with six enemy kills.

I'm good, she thought. *Damned good!* She licked her lips, anticipating how good the toasties would taste at their evening orgy. She tasted perspiration salt on her lips.

Her car shook.

"Piece of crap car," she muttered. "It's not steering right."

She noticed ripples in the pavement ahead. Her car dipped and rose, screeching as its underside slammed into each peak and valley.

Earthquake! she thought. Instinctively, she hit the brakes.

But before her car could slow appreciably, she and the parallel car arrived at the merge point simultaneously. They exploded in pink and blue balls of flame. Two glowing toasties shot skyward. Then white parachutes flowered, supporting the toasties as they dropped to Cork.

In his earthquake-damaged royal box, King Corker pulled himself out of a heap of rubble. Large portions of the grandstand had been destroyed, and his subjects cried out in pain from wherever they lay. One of the king's watermelon man aides lay on his face nearby, mortally wounded. He had been split asunder, and his black seeds were all over the place. The other aide was nowhere in sight. Survivors streamed out of the stands, running wildly to get away from the stadium.

Having remained in the Disaster Control Room for the earthquake, Lord Abercrombie saw the results flash across a digital CRT screen. "Oh, no!" he moaned. "We hit the wrong sector! We're wiping out our allies!"

"We're sorry, Lord Abercrombie," the meckies said in unison. They milled around nervously, awaiting an outburst from their lord.

"It's not entirely your fault," Lord Abercrombie said, feeling compassion for the dented and scratched meckies who had tried so hard for him. "If only I had decent equipment!"

"Do you think the monopoles did it?" one of the meckies asked.

"How the hell do I know?" Lord Abercrombie said. He bemoaned his misfortunes for a full five minutes, then recalled his decision to soil-immerse himself in the Realm of Magic the following day. It was beginning to look like a very wise decision.

Wanting a last fling in the Realm of Flesh, Lord Abercrombie set his loyal meckies to work yet another time. They worked feverishly, searching for that precise combination of tachyon laser signals that would shake Bottomless Bog.

Fifteen minutes later a meckie reported a tremor in Sector 221, a region five hundred kilometers from the bog. "Strength zero point two three, Sandlin scale," the meckie said.

"That's closer," Lord Abercrombie said, heartened. "Not very large, though. Try again. Stronger and closer."

The next quake was ten times as powerful. Unfortunately, it was also ten times as far away.

"Keep trying," Lord Abercrombie urged. "We've got it going now, and I'll shake the whole planet if I have to." He wondered how long the aging equipment would hold together—machinery that had been knocked down on Earth, containerized, and catapulted across an entire universe.

But fortune smiled on Lord Abercrombie this time. A sizable tremor shook Bottomless Bog. Prince Pineapple was less than fifty meters from shore when he felt the log move. Looking back, he saw ripples rolling across the dark water, hurling themselves against the log. The log was quite narrow at this point, having tapered significantly.

"Look out!" Wizzy squealed. "Waves!" Feeling too weary to fly, he dropped to the surface of the log and held on with magic suction.

Frantically, Prince Pineapple motivated his stubby legs and scrambled for the shore. He made it.

Javik and Namaba fell to their knees on the log and tried to hold on. The log began to whip, first one way, then the other. They crawled to safety with no time to spare.

Rebo was not so lucky. He was on a more slippery section and was having trouble keeping his balance. From the shore, Javik saw that the water pods on Rebo's back were getting in his way.

"Dump the pods!" Javik yelled.

Rebo pulled off the roped-together plastic containers and dropped them in the bog. They floated. Then, on all three knees, he started to crawl for shore.

Suddenly the log snapped just behind Rebo, sending him and Wizzy in opposite directions on different pieces of wood. Rebo began to lose his balance. He held on precariously for a moment, then fell in the water with a splash.

"Help!" Rebo yelled. Slimy, decaying vegetation filled his mouth. His voice gurgled, "Hellup!"

Javik found the black and white striped Tasnard rope in the survival pack. "Swim!" he yelled. "Swim for shore!"

"I don't know how!" Rebo yelled, floundering in the water. Steam shot out of his ears from the exertion.

"Help him!" Namaba said. "Oh, Tom, help him!"

Javik mentoed the Tasnard rope. It flew toward Rebo, but fell far short, plopping in the thick water. "Not enough line," Javik said.

"Oh God!" Namaba said.

Wizzy had been carried quite far away on the other section of the log. He glowed orange-hot, attempting to dry away any water that touched him. Swampy water ran across the surface of the log, hissing when it hit Wizzy's superheated surface.

Feeling a survival-inspired burst of energy, Wizzy rose straight up in the air, hovering above the log like an autocopter. Bright silvery-purple particles shot out of his rear, forming a short tail of intense light. Far across the water, Wizzy saw Rebo drowning. And he saw the unsuccessful shoreside effort to save him.

Wizzy's first instinct told him to fly for shore. Already he had been weakened by the water, and he was not certain how much strength he had left. His strength had shown a troublesome proclivity for appearing and disappearing without warning.

But he recalled Javik referring to him as useless. This haunted him. Without further ado, Wizzy streaked toward Rebo.

"Look!" Namaba said, pointing at the ball of light speeding across the surface of Bottomless Bog. "It's Wizzy!"

Javik stood motionless, watching.

Wizzy made a soft landing on top of Rebo's head, which was the only dry spot he could see. "Stay calm," Wizzy said. "I'll try dragging you to shore."

Wizzy used magic suction to grab hold of Rebo's fur. "This may hurt a little," he said, tugging at the fur on top of Rebo's head.

"That's all right," Rebo said, grimacing from the pain. "Go ahead."

Wizzy pulled hard. Rebo began to move through the muck, but thick patches of dead plant life in the water made the going difficult.

"He's doing it!" Namaba said.

"Good going, Wizzy!" Javik yelled.

But Rebo thrashed his arms and forepaw, splashing slimy water all over Wizzy. This sapped the little comet's energy in a matter of seconds. Soon he could not glow orange-hot to dry himself and could not pull any more.

Javik mentoed the Tasnard rope and it plopped in the water, just short of Rebo. "Try to reach it!" Javik yelled.

Rebo thrashed more now, trying to reach the rope. This covered poor Wizzy with more water.

"I can't . . . hold on!" Wizzy screamed. He let go of the fur on Rebo's head and rolled down Rebo's neck into the water. He sank out of sight.

Rebo managed to grab hold of the rope. It was slippery with slime, so he wrapped it around one arm. "I've got it!" he said.

Javik mentoed the Tasnard mechanism, ordering it to bring Rebo in. But it only responded weakly, not enough to move the big Morovian. "Too much goo on it," Javik said. "Help me pull."

Prince Pineapple, Namaba, and Javik pulled the line in. Moments later, Rebo crawled ashore. On his knees in soft ground and gasping for breath, Rebo looked up at Javik gratefully. "I am your servant now," Rebo said. "Morovian honor dictates it."

"Wizzy!" Prince Pineapple bellowed, looking out on Bottomless Bog. "Wizzy!"

Thinking about what Rebo had said, Javik unwrapped the Tasnard rope from him and mentoed it to locate Wizzy. The tip of the rope flew lethargically out to the place where Wizzy had disappeared and sank in the bog. Javik felt it go limp in his hands. Slowly he pulled the rope back. Wizzy was not attached to it. Javik repeated this procedure a number of times. It became apparent that the effort was useless.

"Wizzy's gone," Prince Pineapple said. "The water..." His voice trailed off in sadness.

"I know," Javik said. He felt disheartened too, and this surprised him. He wished Wizzy would pop out of the water and say something annoying. In his mind's eye, Javik saw Wizzy again in the treetops, chasing streaks of sunlight. And he recalled their angry words. This had occurred only hours before.

Javik turned his back on Bottomless Bog. Ahead stretched a gentle flowered upslope, with jagged white cliffs in the distance. The shadows of approaching night stabbed across the cliff faces.

He heard a rustling noise at his side. Then he felt Namaba's hand in his. She squeezed him reassuringly. "I love you," she said.

THIRTEEN

When you see what it is all about, there will be
nothing left to do except to have a good laugh.

Quotation from Judao-
Buddhic novel (22nd Century Earth)

Wizzy tumbled through murky green water that was faintly
illuminated by daylight above. After several seconds in the
water, he became aware of the fact that he was not lung breathing any longer, having discarded that antiquated system of
oxygenation in favor of a higher physical state. His papa had
told him this would happen. Wizzy was not sure when the
transition had occurred, but knew it was a good sign. It meant
he was becoming more like Papa Sidney every day. But this
was only a tiny bit of cheer in Wizzy's great chasm of gloom.

The daylight overhead dimmed as he dropped deeper into
Bottomless Bog. The water grew cooler. Most of Wizzy's
strength was gone now, having dissipated soon after the water
completely enveloped him. He knew there was no fighting
back. He might as well conserve his remaining energy.

But for what? he thought.

A net of vegetation on the bog lake's false bottom supported
him for a second. Then it tore away, and Wizzy resumed his
descent.

Wizzy closed his cat's eye, with the dim hope that this might conserve a small bit of strength that would be useful later. But he knew the bog was too deep. Even with that extra dab of energy, it was foolishness to imagine ever pulling himself out.

The water became pitch black now. He despaired. Wizzy felt the entire universe crushing in around him, forcing him down and pressing him into a deep, permanent sleep.

I'm only seven days old, he thought. *It isn't fair.*

Wizzy wondered if he would become a simple, ordinary rock, undistinguishable from any other. Or would he retain his precious consciousness? He knew most if not all of his remaining strength would dissipate in the continued exposure to water. But how fast would it occur? Would it be only seconds from now? Was this his final thought? Perhaps he would become a storehouse of cosmic information, keeping all the data he had accumulated as a growing comet and adding to that all the information from sitting on the bottom of a bog for millions of years. A multitude of questions raced across his brain as he tumbled deeper into Bottomless Bog.

It occurred to him now that the bog might really have no bottom, as its name suggested. Perhaps he would tumble forever, with unanswered thoughts such as these continually cropping up.

It has to have a bottom, he thought. *This is a planet. The bog can't be deeper than . . . but it is a magical planet.*

His thoughts warped now, reaching beyond the limit of his young brain's capacity. He pictured a bog passing through the entire diameter of the planet: two bogs on opposite ends of the globe, connected at their deepest points. He might tumble to the center of the planet—and then? Would he continue up and out the other side?

No, he thought. *Gravity would pull me back to the center. I don't have enough momentum.*

If the bog was magical, this line of reasoning had no merit. Magical things did not follow any of the accepted laws of physics.

Wizzy felt a crosscurrent move him. He thudded against a rock wall, then dropped again. *The shoreline,* he thought. *I was close when I slipped and fell. Must be a straight dropoff.*

With a distinct *plop* that sounded clearly in Wizzy's tympanic sensors, he landed on a soft bed of decaying plant life. He sank slowly. Finally he reached a muddy bottom where his descent stopped.

I'm on the bottom, he thought, feeling an undefined emotion. *There is a bottom!* He felt mud oozing over him, covering him entirely.

Wizzy returned to the thought of resting for millions of years on the bottom. He pictured it all in his mind: Someday in the far future the bog would dry out. The once muddy bottom would become parched and cracked. Snows would come and go. Seasons would change. Winds would blow across the land, ultimately turning the mud to a fine powder that would blow away. Layer after layer would erode, finally exposing Wizzy.

His mind rolled at such a thought. It was a pleasing thought. Three suns would warm him once again. Stars and harvest moons would grace his evening. Comets and shooting stars would flash overhead.

Would his magical powers of flight return then, once he had dried out? Or had they been lost forever? He assumed the powers would return. After all, a few million years meant nothing in terms of the universe. He knew Papa Sidney would not pull him out, for Wizzy would not learn anything that way. Patience. That was what Wizzy needed. He would wait for the inevitable drying out.

He felt better in his world of thought until a troubling realization struck him: What if his magical flying power never returned?

Now he envisioned Cork shifting on its axis. Heavy rains would come, drenching the once parched soil. Trees and other green plants would spring from the ground, spreading their seeds in the wind to form duplicates of themselves. Ultimately a period of decay would return. The water table would rise. Many of the plants would die. Once again the area would become a bog.

If all this occurred, would Wizzy be able to escape before the water descended upon him? Or would he be paralyzed, condemned through all eternity to be buffeted by the elements?

Maybe I'm dying here in obscurity, Wizzy thought. *Becoming part of the planet.* He knew it was this way with other life forms: In death, their remains became one with the soil, one with the cosmos.

* * *

Namaba scrambled up a little hill to a knoll. Nightfall was approaching fast, with gray light turning to deeper, darker shades.

"We can camp up here," she said. "The ground is firm, and we can watch for Wizzy."

When Javik and the others reached the knoll, they agreed that it was a suitable place. A meadow of scarlet flowers extended up a gradual rise above them. In the distance, the hulking shadow of a cliff wall rose. It appeared impregnable to Javik. He searched in the fading light for the crack in the cliff that marked the pass they would have to find. He couldn't see it.

"What a beautiful meadow!" Namaba exclaimed.

"Quite a contrast to the bog," Rebo said.

Namaba looked at Rebo and smiled. "Yes," she said. "Quite a contrast. The bog is how you used to be, Rebo. Dark, murky, and treacherous."

"And the flowers? That is how you see me now?"

Namaba smiled softly. "No, you macho Morovian," she said. "But you're closer to them than the bog."

Rebo looked perplexed.

Javik took Prince Pineapple aside and said, "Listen, Prince. I'm going to have to ask you to sleep outside the tent tonight. I'll bring your bed out." Javik scratched the mosquito bites on his forehead.

"I have seen Earthian fornication rooms," Prince Pineapple said with a huff. "I know what you and Namaba have in mind."

"You don't understand at all," Javik said. "All you've seen is the physical side. It is more than a mere game."

"I doubt that."

"I need the time with Namaba," Javik said. His voice was firm. "We don't know what will happen tomorrow. That beautiful meadow may be treacherous. And who knows where it leads?"

Prince Pineapple set his jaw and stared up the hill. Two synchronized moons were making their first nightly pass over the cliffs, rising rapidly into the sky. Stars rushed out now, as if switched on by a planetarium master.

"I'll put your bed out," Javik said.

Prince Pineapple did not respond.

Javik turned and walked away. The issue was settled. Prince

Pineapple would sleep outside, whether he liked it or not.

"Let's put the tent here," Namaba said. She cleared away rocks with her forepaw.

Rebo was nearby, clearing a place on the ground to sleep. She saw him look at her sadly. Then he looked away.

As Javik mentoed the tent, he thought of Wizzy's disappearance. Now no one could read the scroll. *Things are not going well*, he thought.

Then he caught Namaba's tender gaze and recalled Wizzy's philosophy of finding happiness in unlikely places. The red glow of her eyes intensified. She smiled, revealing iridescent blue teeth.

"Maybe Wizzy wasn't such a bad guy," Javik said, watching the tent stake itself.

"You're sorry you didn't get along with him better, aren't you?" she said, noticing puffy mosquito bites on Javik's face and neck.

The tent flaps opened.

"In a way," Javik said. He dragged out a bed for Prince Pineapple, placing it well away from the tent. When Javik returned, he brought his survival pack with him. "I can feel sorry about Wizzy now," he said, "when he isn't here. But his blasted personality . . ."

"We all wish some things could be changed," Namaba said. "But we can't dwell on them."

"I know." Javik stepped into the tent and mentoed on the overhead lights. As they filled the enclosure with white light, a ceiling heater fan began to whir.

Hesitantly, she followed.

Javik arranged his orange vari-temp coat, gun, and other gear on a pop-up table in one corner. When this was finished, he looked at Namaba. She was just inside the doorway but looking out, apparently not certain what she wanted to do.

"It is pleasant in here," she said, feeling warm air from the heater fan.

Javik mentoed the tent door. It zipped shut with a noise that startled Namaba.

She moved away from the door.

Looking at Javik uneasily, she removed her yellow vari-temp coat and pants. "There are things I wish could be changed too," she said. "I didn't stop Rebo from killing an old man back in Moro City. Rebo feels terrible about it now too. It was senseless." Moisture glazed over her soft red eyes and filled her eyewells.

"I thought you said not to dwell on unchangeable things," Javik said, moving close to her.

"That is true," she said. "But some things should not be forgotten."

"Let's live for now," Javik said. He took her hand and led her to one of the beds, where they sat down.

"I will try," Namaba said.

"I don't know how Morovians make love," Javik said. He half stood to reach her mouth and rubbed her lips with his the way she had shown him. "But I'm willing to learn."

Namaba kissed Javik in the Earthian way. Then she pulled away. "There has to be a way to do it," she said. "Maybe your method and mine are not so different."

"I want you to carry my child," Javik said. "Don't laugh at me." He kicked off his boots.

"I'm not laughing." She gazed at him tenderly. "Children are the common ground of two souls, however different they may be."

Javik smiled impishly. "You're as bad as Wizzy," he said. "Spouting philosophy."

She laughed. "I suppose you're right."

Javik thought about Namaba's laugh. It was rich, warm, and honest. A spontaneous thing. He wished he could hear it more, that they might enjoy a lifetime together. There were so many things he wanted for the future. He mentoed off the lights, leaving the heater fan on.

Namaba's red eyes and iridescent blue teeth formed purple spectrums on the tent walls, reminding Javik of the purple darkness of the Corkian night. He glanced quickly at his digital watch, then pressed his mouth against hers. *I couldn't have timed this more perfectly if I'd tried,* he thought. *Only five more seconds.*

Javik's clothing disintegrated in a puff of dark smoke, leaving him wearing nothing but his wrist digital and his wardrobe ring.

From his position on the ground outside, Rebo heard them making love.

"I didn't know there was a position like this," Namaba said.

"Three legs do have an advantage!" Javik exclaimed.

Rebo heard Namaba's steam engine heart chugging loudly. He moved out of hearing range and cleared a new place to sleep.

After Javik and Namaba made love, he donned pajamas and fell asleep on his own bed. He slept for less than an hour, however, before stirring and half opening his eyes. An eerie red glow illuminated the interior of the tent.

Javik sat straight up and snapped open his eyes. The first thought in his sleep-addled brain was fire. Then he saw that the glow came from Namaba's eyes, which were wide open. She was lying face up on her bed. The heat fan whirred.

"Namaba," Javik whispered. "Then, a little louder: "Namaba!"

She did not move or say anything.

"You awake?"

Still no response.

Namaba's breathing sounded deep and regular to Javik. He wondered if that was the way all Morovians slept. But her eyes gave off a glow that disturbed him, preventing him from returning to sleep.

Javik swung his feet off the bed and crept through red light to the door. He mentoed the door, causing a mosquito net to unzip. The outside tent flaps flopped open, letting in cool air. He flipped on a penlight and tiptoed barefoot across the campground, intending to see if Rebo slept the same way.

"Ow!" Javik whispered, stubbing his toe on a rock or a twig. Pain surged through his foot, then subsided as he neared Rebo.

Rebo was asleep on his side, snoring deeply. Javik moved around to see his face. Rebo's eyes were closed.

Perplexed, Javik returned to the tent. He lay awake for a while, finally drifting into troubled slumber. He dreamed of a black widow spider. In his dream the spider's face was Namaba's, and it had her same soft voice and pleasant ways. He and the spider made love, after which Javik fell asleep. While he was asleep in the dream, the spider hovered over him. Suddenly, as he lay helpless, the dream spider sprayed paralyzing gas on him. Then the spider's jaws opened wide. It was going to devour him!

Javik tried to wake up. But he could not move, could not breathe. A great weight was on his chest. He smelled a dull odor.

Javik sat bolt upright for the second time that night. Perspiration stuck to his clothing and poured down his brow. He wiped his face on a sheet and threw all the bedding off.

He swung out of bed, removed his service automatic from the corner table, and placed the gun next to his pillow. He did not sleep again that night.

At dawn Javik dressed and left the tent. He stood looking uphill at the first stretch of meadow they would cross that day. Dew-kissed scarlet flowers sparkled as the first bits of daylight touched them.

Entranced, Javik walked past Prince Pineapple's bed and selected a rock. There he sat and watched as Cork's three suns began their daily march across the sky. A wash of red against the distant white cliffs became orange, then gold with streaks of pale blue. The colors reminded him of Sidney's comet. They were pure and changed in the blink of an eye.

Feeling tired, Javik slid the shovel and nutrient cord out of the belt carrier. Then he set about digging in the soft, loamy soil. The shovel clanged against a rock. This caused Prince Pineapple to stir and turn the other way on his bed.

Soon Javik's bare right foot was wrapped in the barbed cord and immersed in cool, moist soil. His foot tingled. Juices flowed up his leg to the rest of the body. Thinking of Wizzy as he recharged, he gazed dreamily across the camp toward the glistening, dark bog. There was no sign of life there. He could see one part of the log where it had split and recalled poor Wizzy there, clinging for his life.

I miss the little fellow, Javik thought. *I'd like to give him a swift kick, but damnit, I miss him.*

Javik spent extra time recharging, and this helped make up for some of the sleep he had lost. Afterward he noticed the mosquito-bite bumps on his face and neck were gone.

He left the shovel and cord on the ground and walked down to Bottomless Bog. Javik looked out at the split log ends and across the murky, vegetation-soaked water. There were no ripples, no mosquitoes, no signs of life whatsoever.

When Javik arrived back in camp, he saw Prince Pineapple swinging grumpily out of bed. "Damned lumpy mattress," the prince said. He stretched, then rubbed a crick in the back of his neck. "Bedding's damp too."

"Did His Royal Hind Ass wet the bed?" Javik asked.

Nearby, Rebo opened one eye. He sat up on the ground and rubbed his hands through the fur on top of his head.

"Certainly not!" Prince Pineapple huffed. "I was referring to dew upon my covers."

"I'm sure Rebo would trade his spot for your comfortable bed," Javik said. "He slept on the ground last night."

"Ruffians belong on the ground," Prince Pineapple said, casting a wary, disdainful glance at Rebo.

Rebo lunged playfully at Prince Pineapple, stopping short.

Prince Pineapple jumped back, then realized that Rebo was only kidding around. "Hrrumph!" the prince said.

Javik laughed, forgetting for a moment about his problems and aches.

Namaba emerged from the tent. Smiling at Javik, she said, "New day, old day. Gone is gone." Seeing a surprised look on Javik's face, she explained quickly: "Traditional Morovian greeting."

"Oh," Javik said. "I thought you were talking about my mosquito bites."

"Gone after a recharge?" she asked.

"Uh huh. I went down to the bog afterward. No sign of Wizzy."

Namaba detected hostility in Javik's eyes as he looked at her. She moved close to him and asked, "You are angry with me?"

"You did keep me awake last night," he said. "Your eyes . . ."

"Their glow disturbed you? I'm sorry, Tom. I was awake all night, you know."

"But I spoke to you. There was no answer."

Nearby, Rebo was winning an argument with Prince Pineapple over who would recharge first.

"I was deep in thought," Namaba said. "Thinking of this new land and of our new love. A Morovian in a thought trance cannot hear anything. It is when all of our physical senses are shut off."

Javik rubbed the bridge of his nose where the scar used to be. It was smooth.

"This place!" Namaba exclaimed, gazing out at the meadow that sloped above them. "It's so beautiful!"

Javik agreed.

"If only we could stay here," she said.

"You mean, just pitch a tent and live in the meadow?"

"Sure. Why not? We could use the nutrient cord for food."

"But what if Rebo and Prince Pineapple don't want to stay? We're all on one cord."

"Couldn't we divide it?"

"I don't know," Javik said. "Wouldn't want to chance it."

After everyone had recharged, Javik was packing his gear for the day's journey. He heard Rebo call his name from somewhere in the meadow. "Captain Tom! Come look at this!"

Javik walked briskly, following the sound of Rebo's voice. Over a little hill he found Rebo standing in the midst of flowers and scattered rubble. An AmFed garbage cannister lay nearby on its side, split open from head to tail.

"Is this from Earth?" Rebo asked. He stood with his hands on his broad hips, looking up at Javik.

Javik nodded.

"Ooh!" Prince Pineapple said, coming up behind Javik. "What beautiful gar-bahge!"

"I think it's a goddamn mess," Javik said, sniffing a peculiar, metallic odor. "We'd better be careful. I don't see any nuclear material down there at first glance, though."

Javik made his way down the hill of scarlet flowers, followed by Prince Pineapple.

As they arrived, Rebo held up a blue tintette. "What's this?" he asked.

"Put it in your mouth," Javik said. "See if you can find a match and light it."

"It's a bomb? An Earthian suicide technique?"

Javik laughed. Looking up the hill, he saw Namaba loping toward them. "You smoke it," Javik said, looking back at Rebo. "Here, give it to me."

"Nice selection of imported gar-bahge here," Prince Pineapple said, picking through the rubble. "Here's a clock, a Charlie Choo-Choo lamp, and a couple of Batman comics."

"What's going on here?" Namaba asked.

Javik placed Rebo's tintette in his own mouth. "Anyone got a light?" he asked.

No one stepped forward.

"Well, I wanna do this right," Javik said with a bemused expression. "I'll be right back." He ran up the hill.

"How strange," Namaba said. She picked up three tintettes from the ground—one blue, one yellow, and one red.

"Put them in your mouth," Prince Pineapple said.

Presently, Javik returned with a tin of lightweight matches. "That's the way," he said, seeing Namaba with three tintettes in her mouth. "You'd be a super consumer on Earth."

"I'm doing it right?" she asked.

"Pick one," Javik said. "It will be easier."

She kept the red tintette, discarding the others.

"I'm gonna take some of this stuff with me," Prince Pineapple said, loading his arms with junk.

"Put that down for a minute," Javik said. "Prince, you and Rebo put tintettes in your mouths too. We're all gonna have a smoke."

When all had tintettes firmly grasped between their lips, Javik told them to gather in a close circle. "You've done this before, haven't you, Prince?" Javik asked, as he struck a match.

"Oh, sure," Prince Pineapple said.

Javik lit the tintettes, then doused the match. "Watch me," he said, taking a deep puff. He let out a big puff of bright blue smoke.

Rebo took a shallow puff. "Ugh!" he said, coughing. "I'm your servant now, Captain Tom, but this is asking too much!" he discarded the tintette.

Prince Pineapple puffed and coughed too.

Seeing red smoke curl out of Namaba's nostrils, Javik said, "That's it! I think she's got it!"

"What's the purpose of this?" she asked, gagging. She had an aghast expression. Her eyes rolled upward.

"I'm not much of a smoker myself," Javik said. "It's not a good habit to have in the cockpit."

"Earthians enjoy this?" she asked, picking a piece of tobacco out of her teeth.

"It's a leading pastime," Javik said.

Namaba shook her head in disbelief.

"Look, Namaba," Javik said, taking her arm and leading her up the hill. "There's something I've always wanted to try. We see it on home video all the time."

She looked at him inquisitively.

"Bring your tintette," he said.

They walked up the hill of scarlet flowers. The sky was blue and young, an intense, vibrant blue that has been known to grace the skies over lovers. The sweet, delicate aroma of mint touched Javik's nostrils whenever he kept the tintette away from his nose. He felt sublime.

Reaching a flat section of meadow at the top of the hill, Javik began to skip, sort of a jerky slow motion.

Namaba let go of his hand and laughed. "You look so silly!" she said. "What are you doing?"

"I've seen it on home video," Javik said. "It's in magazines, too, and on billboards. We're lovers, don't you see? Frolicking in a meadow with tintettes dangling from our mouths. It's the AmFed Dream. And we found it clear on the other side of the goddamn universe!"

Namaba took a puff of her tintette and tried to skip. But this turned out to be more of a jerk-hop, owing to her third leg. She coughed, puffed, and laughed, trailing red smoke behind her.

"Slower," Javik said. "Do it slower."

"But why?" Namaba asked, stopping and looking at him curiously.

"Because that's the way it's done on home video."

She skipped in slow motion, with movements that alternated between near grace and total clumsiness.

"Better," Javik exclaimed. He caught up with her and blew smoke in her face.

Namaba took this as a challenge. Gleefully, she inundated his face in smoke.

They had a short battle like this, then held hands and were off together, slowly skipping and jerk-hopping across the meadow.

"Hey!" Prince Pineapple yelled to them. "What are you doing?"

Javik envisioned a camera panning in on them as they frolicked in the flowers. He and Namaba were the stars of a videodome commercial, watched in more than three hundred million homes.

"What a commercial it would be," Javik exclaimed. "Me and a three-legger!"

Namaba stopped and looked at him with a hurt expression. "You're making fun of me?" she asked. She was breathing hard, with little puffs of steam coming from her ears and nostrils.

Javik smiled. He stretched up and gave her a little peck on the lips. "I was just being silly," he said.

They walked back toward Rebo and Prince Pineapple. At the sight of the prince, Javik was reminded of his recurring thought. Prince Pineapple so resembled a videodome cartoon character, and now the tintettes. . . . Javik discarded his tintette.

"Hurry!" Prince Pineapple yelled. "We've a long way to go today." His arms were full of salvaged garbage.

"Hey," Javik said, turning to Namaba. "Remember how silly Wizzy was yesterday in the woods?"

"We've found our moment of happiness," she said, flipping her tintette away with surprising expertness. Namaba looked down at Javik. Her eyes sparkled.

This is no goddamn dream, Javik thought. *And I'm glad it isn't.*

They stopped, and their lips touched in the Earth way. Javik hardly heard Prince Pineapple as he continued to yell at them. Javik and Namaba were in their own little world. He wanted it to last forever.

Brother Carrot stood in morning sunlight on the foredeck of the *Freedom One,* watching his troops disembark. His fleet bobbed in gentle waves next to the granite wall that comprised the limits of the new lake. Carrot soldiers clattered down wooden gangways to the top of the wall. From there they climbed freestyle to the ground.

"Kill the Fruits!" Brother Carrot bellowed, using a megaphone.

His men cheered.

When the *Freedom One* had been unloaded, Brother Carrot strode triumphantly down the gangway, waving his black and gold cap.

His troops shouted and cheered their adulation.

Lord Abercrombie watched helplessly while the Vegetable army marched on the Corker stronghold. After causing so much earthquake damage with his disaster machine, Lord Abercrombie was disaster-shy, afraid to make things worse.

It was mid-morning when Brother Carrot led his men past Javik's ship. Rays of sunlight glinted off the undented portions of the ship's titanium body. Brother Carrot felt warm from the exertion of the brisk march down from what had once been Dusty Desert. He loosened his collar.

"To victory, lads!" he yelled in the megaphone. "Send the Fruits to their gory, juicy beds!" Looking back, he saw six black and gold uniformed carrot colonels who marched in front of six columns of rifle-carrying carrot men. Each colonel sported a black and gold cap like Brother Carrot's, except the colonel's caps had much thinner strands of gold braid on the brims.

The colonels passed Brother Carrot's message on down the lines, using their own, smaller power megaphones.

Boisterous hurrahs rose from the ranks.

Between Brother Carrot and the colonels, fifteen of the strongest, meanest carrot men in the Vegetable army pulled a towering wood and plastic catapult. Beside that rolled the Fruit Doom bomb trailer, pulled by six carrot men. The Fruit Doom bomb was big, round, and black—a deadly sphere that Brother Carrot knew would annihilate his enemies. Being a live bomb, it buzzed loudly.

Brother Carrot smiled at the thought of King Corker's demise. Then he turned and thundered, "There is plunder ahead, lads! Plunder for all!"

"Plunder!" the colonels announced to the majors, not quite as loudly as Brother Carrot.

"Plunder!" the majors yelled in unison, their megaphoned voices not as loud as those of their superiors.

And so the message went down the lines, until the corporals had their opportunities too. "Plunder!" they squealed gleefully.

Bawdy cheers ran through the ranks.

The army narrowed to double file, negotiating a trail through the woods. Then it widened to six columns again as it emerged on the other side.

The earthquake-ravaged remains of Corker Stadium loomed ahead beneath a cerulean blue sky. Corkers and other Fruits in their path fled the advancing juggernaut. Some of the more foolish Fruits sat regally in their carriages, commanding carrot man slaves to pull them to safety. A dark cloud passed in front of the suns, throwing Corker Stadium into shadow.

A hundred meters to his left, Brother Carrot watched a team of six carrot man slaves unharness themselves, leaving a pudgy casaba man stranded in his carriage. The casaba man was furious, and he shook his fist at them, shrieking, "Back to your stations! Back to your stations!"

Brother Carrot waved his cap triumphantly.

His troops cheered.

The six freed slaves waved to Brother Carrot and shouted their support. Then they overturned the carriage, sending their pudgy former master fleeing for his life. Shouting boisterously and waving clenched fists, they ran to join their brethren in the Vegetable army.

More slave teams joined Brother Carrot as he marched through the Corker shopping district. The slaves brought stones, clubs, and anything else on which they could lay their hands.

The burgeoning army entered the expressway now, marching by abandoned Fruit carriages and the bodies of Fruits who had been killed by their slaves. Brother Carrot pushed down the brim of his cap, shielding his eyes from the suns.

They rounded a turn, bringing the rocky fortress of Corker Castle into view. Brother Carrot saw Fruits streaming across a drawbridge, entering the castle through the main gate. Purple Corkers lined the walkways and ramparts, their weapons glinting in the sunlight.

"There it is, lads!" Brother Carrot yelled, waving his cap once more.

His men cheered again, and a thunderous cheer it was. For now the ranks were swelled with thousands of freed slaves.

They passed a green expressway sign that read "CORKER CASTLE—NEXT EXIT."

Now Brother Carrot increased the marching tempo, and his men quick-stepped up the exit ramp. Ahead, the castle drawbridge was being closed. Those Fruits who were not able to get sanctuary fled in all directions.

"Onward, lads!" Brother Carrot urged.

Rifle shots rang out from the castle and echoed down the valley. Then a Corker cannon roared. The cannonball arched and landed short of Brother Carrot, off to his right in a banana grove.

A gunnery officer caught up with Brother Carrot, saying, "We should set up here, sir. We're just out of range of their guns."

"Halt!" Brother Carrot boomed to his colonels.

The command echoed down the columns, and finally the army ground to a halt.

"Over here!" the gunnery officer barked, motioning to the carrot men in charge of the catapult.

The catapult squadron positioned the big wooden siege machine on a flat parking strip. Outriggers were cranked down. Then the Fruit Doom bomb was wheeled over and loaded onto the catapult's sling.

"Carefully, men," Brother Carrot said. "Load it carefully!"

Rifle and cannon shots continued to ring out from the castle. One cannon ball rolled close to the empty bomb trailer and bounced off a fir tree.

"Hurry men," Brother Carrot yelled. "That was too close."

"Ready, sir," the gunnery officer reported.

"Aim carefully," Brother Carrot said to the gunnery officer. "We'll only get one shot."

"Better move it a quarter of a degree left," the gunnery officer said, standing next to the siege machine and eyeballing the target. "And raise it just a hair."

Carrot men spun positioning dials as the gunnery officer spoke. A platform holding the catapult arm shifted.

"There!" the gunnery officer shouted.

"That's it?" Brother Carrot asked. He heard the bomb buzzing.

"Yes, sir."

"Then let 'er go!" Brother Carrot shouted.

The gunnery officer moved a toggle on the side of the catapult, causing the long mechanical arm to snap forward. The Fruit Doom bomb arched toward Corker Castle, spinning slowly in the air. To Brother Carrot, the projectile seemed to travel in slow motion. He knew it was a terrible weapon to use. But it would prevent Fruit and Vegetable deaths in the field.

"Oh, no!" someone said. "It's going in too low!"

"No," the gunnery officer said, stretching and using body motions to urge the bomb a little higher. "I think it'll just barely . . ."

Brother Carrot covered his face with his hands.

The Fruit Doom bomb arched just over the castle wall, landing in the courtyard. A mushroom-shaped black cloud rose over the doomed castle.

This brought a tremendous cheer from the Vegetable troops.

Brother Carrot peeked between his fingers.

"On target, sir," the gunnery officer reported.

When the bomb hit, King Corker was standing on a balcony overlooking the courtyard of his castle. He was in the middle of shouting a command to the captain of the Corker guards when a warning trumpet sounded.

Before anyone could react, the courtyard was swarming with voracious, razor-toothed fruit flies. King Corker had only half turned toward his room when the flies caught him. He died a terrible death, his flesh consumed in a horde of frenzied attackers.

The screams of dying Fruits filled the air.

From the other side of the moat, Brother Carrot heard the screams. Five minutes later, a pervasive, deathly silence settled over Corker Castle. Brother Carrot knew it was over. He felt bad about it, but knew it was something that had to be done.

After another five minutes, Brother Carrot gave the command to turn on the Mother Hummer. When his men were slow to react, he snapped angrily, "Faster, men. We don't want flies killing all the Fruits in the valley. Who would do our work for us?"

Two soldiers jumped now, flipping switches on the sides of the bomb trailer. A large, clear plastic funnel rose out of the trailer bed. A loud drone-whir filled the air, throbbing and pulsating with that one sound no tiger fruit fly could ignore.

A steady stream of flies left Corker Castle now, making a straight course for the trailer. They disappeared into the funnel.

"Beastly little creatures," Brother Carrot said to his gunnery officer.

"Yes, but cross-bred with herpes stock to perfection!"

"War is hell," Brother Carrot said, watching the last flies enter the funnel. Looking up with moist eyes, he saw slaves all along the castle walkways. Some lowered the purple Corker banner. Most of the slaves were carrot men, but Brother Carrot spotted occasional cucumber, lettuce, and cabbage people.

Five plump tomato girls from King Corker's harem appeared on one wall now, waving white lace and squealing so loudly that Brother Carrot could hear their words from across the moat. "Long live Brother Carrot!" they said. "Long live Brother Carrot!"

While Brother Carrot watched, the drawbridge was lowered. Then he brushed dust off his uniform and called all the officers forward. "This is our moment in history, lads!" he told them.

Soon after that, Brother Carrot led a company of men along the short, curving section of road that led to Corker Castle.

The men had grown quiet, and Brother Carrot knew why. Each of them had imagined this moment for so long, in so many waking and sleeping dreams, that now they could only savor it with their eyes.

Layers of puffy white clouds moved rapidly across the sky. To Brother Carrot they looked like the fleeing ghosts of fat little Corkers. He smiled.

The smile hardened when three dead banana men came into view. They were laying face up in a grassy planting area at the center of the road. Most of their flesh had been torn away by the savage fruit flies.

"See that?" Brother Carrot said to the company colonel as they passed. "Good slaves. We could have called the flies back a little earlier."

The colonel nodded and murmured in solemn agreement.

They reached an uphill straightaway now, with high English hedges on each side, the last stretch before reaching the castle. Brother Carrot felt his pace quicken. The men chatted excitedly in low tones. Freed Vegetable slaves cheered wildly and waved brightly colored cloths from the castle walls above.

The drawbridge was only a few steps away when a wrinkled old prune woman in a frumpy brown dress stepped through an opening in the hedge. Stopping at the side of the road, she leaned her chin on a carved wood cane and stared up at Brother Carrot. She had a most curious expression on her face. Brother Carrot judged it to be a combination of sadness and bemused tolerance. He wondered how she had survived the Fruit Doom bomb.

"Greetings, Brother Carrot," the old woman said in a throaty voice. "And greetings to your lean, hungry warriors." She used one hand to smooth her dress.

Brother Carrot raised his right arm, causing the procession to stop. The old woman was terribly wrinkled, and her skin was a pale plum shade. The eyes were unmistakably sad, Brother Carrot decided. And the mouth was mildly amused. "How long have you been here?" he asked.

"All the time," she rasped.

"Why didn't the flies get you. Are you a magician? Or a witch?"

The old woman laughed. It was a wheezing, choppy laugh, like the strainings of an engine that didn't have long to run.

"What would flies want with an old prune lady?" she asked. "My skin has lost its sweet bloom. It is old and leathery."

Brother Carrot stared at her.

"I am Priscilla the Prunesayer," she said. "Once I was a lovely young plum, easily the fairest in the land."

"And now you tell fortunes?"

She straightened for a moment, then leaned on the cane again. "That is correct."

"And what is mine, old woman?"

"Why, the same as King Corker's, naturally."

"You mean I will die?" he asked.

"We all die sometime," Priscilla the Prunesayer said.

"That wasn't what I meant," Brother Carrot said. He stepped close to her, intending to grill her militarily with questions.

The old prune woman closed her eyes, and a serene expression crossed her face. Then she tottered for a moment.

Brother Carrot reached out to steady her, but she slumped to the ground.

"I think she's dead, sir," the company colonel said.

As Brother Carrot looked down on the prunesayer's body, thousands of Fruits fled the area. Many ran up the trail toward the lake that covered Dusty Desert. Others crossed the western grasslands. Still more reached the eastern seashore and took to boats.

Two who escaped by boat were Matteo and Nacho Pear. They used their own sailboat, not at all a large craft—less than eight meters in length and sloop rigged. Matteo and Nacho had sailed it often to the small unnamed island they saw now across the strait, on picnics and other happy occasions. This island was the first in a necklace of isles that stretched across the sea. Legend told them this. The brothers planned to hop from one landfall to the next, seeking refuge as far away as possible.

But never before had they sailed beyond the first island.

Feeling a strong wind against his face, Matteo pulled the mainsail halyard. He thought of the good times he and Nacho had enjoyed on this boat. A dark cloud structure bore down on them from the sea, bringing with it a chill wind and a misty rain. He secured the mainsail, then raised the jib.

The little boat began to pick up speed.

"I'll get even with those rotten Vegetables!" Nacho yelled.

He stood at the tiller, finding the best angle on the wind.

Matteo heard these words as he knelt in the bow, securing the bowline on a cleat. He saw the dark outline of the unnamed island on the horizon. "Death to the Vegetables!" he bellowed.

In less than a day Lord Abercrombie would soil-immerse himself permanently. There would be enough time to look over his recycling facility and meckies one last time.

For now he was soil-immersed in the usual half-committed way, knowing he would be back in Flesh in a matter of hours. With the visual and auditory sensors in each droplet of seawater, Lord Abercrombie heard the angry words of the pear brothers. He saw the lumpy form of Matteo as Matteo fine-tuned the rigging to get the most speed out of the boat. And he saw Nacho at the tiller, trying to steer a straight course in changing winds.

With countless sensors all over the planet, Lord Abercrombie eavesdropped on other Fruits as they vowed eternal revenge. All this triggered a moment of introspection in Lord Abercrombie. The past and future of his planet appeared before him like a magnificent, fluxing historical tapestry.

Vagabond Fruit armies made thrust after thrust against a fat and sedentary Vegetable kingdom. The Fruits were lean and oppressed, with all the power and fury of righteousness on their side. In fast forward across the tapestry, he saw the Fruits in power again, with wronged Vegetables hiding in the hinterlands plotting revolution. These Vegetables were led by Brother Carrot. The cycle repeated itself over and over in much the same pattern. Different faces appeared and disappeared. But the words and deeds were much the same.

Lord Abercrombie laughed at the timeless folly of the situation. Every pore of the planet echoed his laughter. Then the laughter became a storm of embarrassed rage, for Abercrombie came to understand the foolishness of his own paranoic fears. His laughing rage blew across the surface of Cork in a powerful, howling wind.

It was late morning, and Prince Pineapple walked briskly along the dirt meadow trail, well ahead of the others. Over one shoulder he carried a dark green gortex stuff sack Javik had let him use. The sack rattled, being full of treasures from the

AmFed garbage cannister. The jagged white cliffs ahead seemed just as far away now as when they broke camp. He quickened his step.

He became aware of distant, murmurous laughter. It seemed to bounce off the white cliffs, traveling on an angry wind across the scarlet flower petals of the meadow. He felt the wind pick up now, pressing the flowers around him against the ground. The laughter became loud. Menacingly loud.

Frightened, he turned and bolted back down the trail.

Javik saw Prince Pineapple running back at full speed, with his bag bouncing on his back and his pineapple face contorted in terror. "Run!" Prince Pineapple yelled. His black button eyes were wild.

Javik heard the laughter now. It grew louder as Prince Pineapple approached, becoming a thunderous, booming cacophany as the prince ran screaming by. Javik covered his ears. He and the Morovians fell to the ground.

Looking back, Javik saw Prince Pineapple trip and fall.

The laughter grew fainter now. Soon it was gone.

"What the hell was that?" Javik asked. He became aware of a pain in his right hand. Namaba had been squeezing it too tightly. She was wearing the lemon yellow vari-temp coat and pants he had given her.

Namaba released her grip. "I don't know," she said.

Prince Pineapple crawled back with his bag, joining the others. "Is it gone?" he asked.

They increased their pace after that, walking so hard toward the cliffs that Javik felt a muscle pain in the front of one thigh. Late morning became midday, then mid-afternoon. Three Corkian suns baked the travelers and withered the flowers along the trail. Perspiration covered Javik's body. He wiped his brow often with moist-pak towelettes.

Heat waves simmered in the distance. Javik shielded his eyes with one hand to look at the white cliffs ahead. "That bog has to be way behind us," he said. "But I'd swear those cliffs were not one step closer than this morning."

Prince Pineapple fell to the ground in a heap. "Let's rest," he said. "A little nap...a recharge..." He was lying in a bed of flowers asleep as the last word crossed his lips.

"Sounds good to me," Javik said.

"Hand me that shovel and cord," Rebo said. "I'd like to recharge and go on ahead a ways."

Javik unhooked the nutrient kit from his belt and handed it to Rebo. "You think something's just ahead?" Javik asked.

"It's his yenta," Namaba said acidly.

"I just feel a little restless," Rebo said, smiling crisply at Namaba. "And I don't claim to have any damned yenta."

Namaba sat back on her haunches and smiled apologetically. "Sorry I picked at you," she said. "I'm tired."

Rebo took the shovel and cord a few paces off the path and went through the now familiar recharging ritual.

Moments later, Javik saw Rebo's tripod form loping away on the trail ahead, framed against the distant white cliffs. Javik watched him for a while, then removed a tiny yellow plastic square from a side pocket of his survival pack. The square was smaller than a sugar cube. At Javik's mento-command, it flowered into a white sheet lean-to with three foam pads on the ground.

Manually, Javik moved the lean-to so that it afforded shade for Prince Pineapple. "Don't want any cooked pineapple," Javik said, winking at Namaba.

She smiled.

Javik and Namaba settled down for a nap on two of the pads, using the remaining shade of the lean-to. Before falling asleep, Javik asked Namaba about her mother. "She was an alchemist, wasn't she?" he said.

"Uh huh. I used to help her with her experiments. I caused the fire that nearly killed both of us, you know. If it hadn't been for Rebo happening along."

"I'll have to thank Rebo for that sometime," Javik said.

"No. That might be rubbing it in. Do you think he's jealous?"

"Yeah. But he likes you."

Javik grunted.

"My mother used to call me Nama," she said.

Javik was tired and silly. "Your mama called you Nama?" he said.

"Oh, you!" She tickled him in the side.

Hearing the rhyme in his sleep, Prince Pineapple did a powerful backflip, knocking over the lean-to and clicking his heels when he was airborne. He landed in an angry heap in the rubble of the lean-to. "What the hell?" he said, still not fully awake. Moments later: "Who said a rhyme!"

"Uh . . . sorry," Javik said. "You heard that in your sleep?"

"That's the most dangerous time, when my muscles are relaxed!" Angrily, he pushed the twisted lean-to away and curled up on the ground.

Javik straightened the lean-to and set up resting places under it again for himself and Namaba.

"You can call me Nama too," Namaba said, suppressing a giggle.

Javik stretched out on a pad next to her. "Are you sure?" he asked.

"I wish you would."

Wizzy lost all sense of time. His memories faded like the decaying thoughts of an old man. His attention span grew baby short. He was a rock now, condemned to sleep in a bed of slime.

Bursts of anger from the life remaining in him were drowned out in a muddy death that permeated every cell of his magical body. Like a dying fleshcarrier looking for a warm place to curl up and die, he burrowed deeper in the mud. Soon he reached firm, moist soil.

Then, in a quick, angry thrust of his remaining energy, he darted a short distance between two rocks, pushing soil behind him as he went. This blocked the short tunnel he had dug, preventing Bottomless Bog's slime from advancing through it.

Only barely conscious, Wizzy found himself in a tiny, dry underground chamber. He glowed a sickly shade of yellow, then flickered out. It was the quietest, darkest place in the universe.

FOURTEEN

Often it is a matter of degree. It is wrong, but not
that wrong; right, but not that right. It seems that
black and white are ideals, obtainable only by paint
pigments, and even there . . .

A Timeless Truth

It was nearly time for Lord Abercrombie's final soil immersion.
He moved from metal man to metal woman, inspecting his
meckies for the last time. Using a chamois cloth, he burnished
a brass "REBUILT" plaque here, flicked dust off a shoulder there.
It was a solemn occasion, with all the meckies standing in three
neat rows near Lord Abercrombie's throne.

Wearing a cardinal red caftan with gold scrollwork on the
sleeve and half collar, Lord Abercrombie glided to his throne.
He felt a final urge to sit upon it and look out at his underground
mechanical staff. The black satin cushions felt soft beneath his
half bottom. "I'm leaving soon," he said.

A blue female meckie rolled forward from the ranks, asking,
"You've made a decision, Lord?" This was the artistically
programmed linguistics expert, the one with the gargling voice.

"I have."

"Flesh or Magic?" the meckie asked.

"Magic. It may not be the correct decision, but at least it's
a decision. That's something, anyway."

"Good luck, Lord Abercrombie. What should I put on the
history wall?"

"I'll take care of that myself. If I turn into any sort of a decent magical planet, that should be a minor matter." Lord Abercrombie felt a tear welling up in his human eye. The thought of never seeing his recycling facility again was a burden. Then he remembered the visual sensors he would have when he became the planet. Still, it would not be the same.

The blue meckie rolled back into the ranks.

"You've all done your best," Lord Abercrombie said. "I want each of you to know that." He rubbed his eye.

"Goodbye, Lord," the meckies said in unison. They waved stiffly and noisily, clanking their metal arms.

Lord Abercrombie glided to the corridor. He heard mechanical voices behind him in the main chamber, and poked his head back in. The linguistics meckie was touching the arm of his throne, acting as though she wanted to sit upon it.

"Go ahead," Lord Abercrombie said, smiling softly in his half-faced way.

She started. Turning to face him, she said, "You mean sit on it?"

"Sure. Why not? It's of no use to me anymore." He turned and left.

As he negotiated the intricate maze of passageways leading to the Soil Immersion Chamber, Lord Abercrombie did not feel happy or sad. It was a numb, neutral feeling, possibly in preparation for the killing of his remaining fleshy self.

Minutes later, he dropped into the immersion hole with more than a little trepidation. Sitting down, he covered his fleshy leg with dirt. The soil was warm. He closed his human eye and visual sensors and lay back in the hole. Warmth greeted his fleshy half-backside.

In a flurry, Abercrombie used his hand to pull dirt over the rest of his exposed skin. His hand was last in. It remained outside for several seconds. Then it made a waving motion and pulled itself into the hole.

Goodbye, Abercrombie thought. *And hello*.

After a short nap, Javik recharged. He felt fresh. Returning to the lean-to, he nudged Namaba to awaken her. "We'd better get going," he said. "Should try to cover more ground before dark."

She sat up and yawned.

*   *   *

Namaba was just completing her recharge when she noticed Rebo loping toward them from uptrail.

"You've got to see this," Rebo shouted. "It's just up the trail."

"What's up the trail?" Namaba asked, handing the folding shovel and barbed cord to Javik.

"You've got to see it," Rebo said.

"You're not making any sense," Javik said.

Prince Pineapple stirred from his nap and sat up. "What's all the commotion?" he asked.

"Come with me," Rebo said, almost too excited to speak. He pulled at Javik's arm.

"All right, all right," Javik said. He secured the nutrient kit to his belt.

"Wait," Prince Pineapple said, rising to his feet. "I need a recharge."

"Hurry," Rebo said. "No one will believe this."

Javik tossed the nutrient kit to Prince Pineapple. "Make it quick, Prince."

While Prince Pineapple recharged, Javik mentoed the lean-to and pads. With a crisp snap, they popped back into the tiny yellow cube. Javik replaced the cube in a side pocket of his survival pack. Seeing an empty bio bar wrapper in the pack, he tossed it out on the meadow.

After Prince Pineapple was allowed an abbreviated recharge, they all went with Rebo. The meadow sweltered in the afternoon heat of three Corkian suns. Soon Javik was perspiring again. Waves of hot air danced ahead of them, blurring features on the white cliff.

At the rear, Prince Pineapple complained about the shortness of his recharge. His bag of junk clattered as he walked.

Rebo ran ahead, then waved and called for the others to hurry.

"Rebo's gone mad," Javik said. "His brain is sun-baked."

"I've never seen him like this," Namaba said.

"We'd better catch him," Javik said. "And make him lie down in the..." Javik stopped in mid-sentence. Rebo had disappeared!

"Where'd he go?" Namaba asked.

"Magic!" Prince Pineapple said.

They heard Rebo's voice now, but could not see him. It seemed to come from the trail just ahead. But the meadow was perfectly flat here, with no places that might conceal Rebo's large body.

"Rebo!" Namaba shouted. "Where are you?"

"A little ways up the trail. Keep going."

They walked cautiously, following Javik. He took each step with care, testing the ground before committing the weight of his body.

"There is magic in this meadow," Prince Pineapple said.

"Hey!" Namaba said, running into Javik's back.

He had stopped suddenly in front of her. "My foot!" Javik said. "Look at it!"

Namaba saw the back half of his foot. But the front was gone. When Javik pulled his foot back, she saw it in its entirety.

"An invisible barrier," Javik said. He reached back and took Prince Pineapple's bag of junk. While the prince protested, Javik threw the bag forward. It disappeared, landing somewhere with a loud clatter.

"Quit throwing things at me," Rebo said, still unseen. "That darn near hit me!"

Javik took a deep breath and stuck his face through. There was no physical sensation at all. He saw Rebo standing on a piece of white shale at the base of a towering cliff. Above, the sheer face of the escarpment was profiled against a deep blue sky. The scene was so awesome and so surprising that Javik felt a shortness of breath.

"Don't hold back," Rebo said.

Javik stepped through, followed by the others. A series of "oohs," "aahs," and "wows" followed.

"I told you it was magic," Prince Pineapple said. He found his sack of trash and swung it noisily over one shoulder.

"We were getting close to this cliff all day," Rebo said, "but didn't know it." He touched a triangular dot pattern on the cliff at his side, then pointed to Javik's left, where a trail ran between the cliff and the edge of the meadow. "More dots that way," Rebo said.

"We might have given up and turned back," Javik said, scratching his head. "And it was here all the time."

"What do you think, Prince?" Rebo asked. "Did the magicians create that illusion, or was it Lord Abercrombie?"

"I don't know," Prince Pineapple said. His black button eyes squinted as he stared up the face of the cliff.

"How far up the trail did you go, Rebo?" Namaba asked.

The yellow and black polka-dotted ribbon fell from her mane and fluttered away in the wind, unnoticed by her or the others.

"Not far," Rebo said. "Moha should be ahead, whatever that is."

"Moha," Prince Pineapple said, feeling a chill run down his back. "Something is coming back to me. A Moha is spoken of in one of our epics. It is a fearsome thing—a terrible monster."

"It would have been nice to know this earlier," Javik said, staring at the prince with his hands on his hips. "Don't suppose we have much choice now, though. No way to cross that bog again."

"What sort of monster is it?" Namaba asked.

"I don't know," Prince Pineapple said. "Didn't pay much attention to epics in school. It destroyed a Fruit army, I think."

"It is best not to hesitate," Rebo said, recalling his gang warfare days. "Sometimes the thought of a thing can be more terrifying than the reality."

They set out along the trail at the base of the cliff, looking for three-dot markings.

With the decision to commit himself, Lord Abercrombie changed rapidly. His fleshy half disappeared entirely. His mind became more expansive, capable of deeper, more significant thought. He was the planet Cork now, more than ever before. His face became the face of the planet that was exposed to the heavens.

With his visual sensors, he looked out upon the grays and blacks of night on one side of Cork. On the other side, he observed varying shades of color, from sky blues to the oranges, reds, and yellows of dawn and sunset. He told himself he was thinking about important things. Cosmic things.

I have a comparatively large planet, he thought. *Some are bigger than mine, but most are smaller. Earth is smaller!*

The comparison with Earth made him happy, for it seemed to him that he was more important now than Uncle Rosy or any other Earthian. It was a territorial thing: The guy with the most turf was superior.

Maybe this can be a stepping stone to something greater, he thought. *A method of conquering other worlds could occur to me.*

He rubbed the plates of two continents together to relieve

an itch. It was an automatic movement, and it surprised him.

Hmm, he thought. *Think I'll try that again.* He rubbed the continents together again in just the same way.

I'll bet I can wipe out Brother Carrot now, he thought. *And Prince Pineapple, too! I might have done it earlier, if I hadn't been afraid to commit myself.*

But this prospect did not appeal to him very much. It seemed beneath him, a trapping of his former self. Besides, with Abercrombie soil-immersed, the chamber entrance leading down from the surface of the planet was sealed.

A major planet does not concern itself with fleas, he thought.

So Lord Abercrombie concentrated on more important matters. On the night side of his planet, he saw deep space, with more stars and bright planets than all the grains of sand in his deserts. He wondered who out there might be plotting at that very moment to invade his territory via the Dimensional Tunnel.

I can't seal the damned thing, he thought. *Anyone entering the Dimensional Tunnel from another planet could land on my doorstep. Uninvited. Well, go ahead and try. I'll give you one hell of a fight.*

His paranoia raged anew, but on a much larger scale than before. He recalled having laughed at the foolishness of his own fears when he thought he had seen the Big Picture. His laughter roared across the surface of the planet then. But nothing seemed at all funny to him anymore.

A cloud of silver meteorites passed near Cork on the dark side, and Lord Abercrombie could see that they were going to miss him by a good fifty thousand kilometers.

This way! he thought, wanting more bulk for his surface.

But the meteorites went on their inconsiderate way, leaving a space trail of sparkling silver embers.

When the embers had died out, a flash of orange lit up the blackness of space. Something was approaching at high speed, growing larger and more brilliant with each passing second. Lord Abercrombie's joy overflowed, like the anticipation of a spider about to ensnare a tasty fly. It was a large orange ball, bearing down on him.

Nice meteor, he thought. *Come a little closer.*

Seconds later, Lord Abercrombie blinked his visual sensors. *Wait,* he thought. *It's getting too big. My God! It's huge!*

He began to wonder who was ensnaring whom.

The orange fireball became so bright that Lord Abercrombie could not keep his visual sensors open. At the last moment the fireball turned and went the other way. When Abercrombie next looked, through slit-wide sensors, he saw a great orange comet, with a long, translucent tail that stretched across the sky in a graceful, orange thread of light.

The comet swung around to Abercrombie's daylight side and headed toward him again. Again he was forced to close his visual sensors in the brightness. Abercrombie felt the comet sear through his atmosphere. He smelled sulfur and waited for the impact. Strangely, he felt no heat on his surface.

Sidney the comet swooped over Bottomless Bog, then returned and hovered there. The cadmium yellow outline of a face appeared across his flaming orange nucleus. Sidney smiled gently.

Be patient, Wizzy, he thought, looking down on the bog tenderly. *A million years is but a moment. You'll be free someday, my son. Then you'll do wondrous things.*

Lord Abercrombie tried to open all his visual sensors, but repeatedly was blinded by the brightness of the Great Comet. The comet irritated him. It hovered in his face like a giant, fat mosquito, and he had no arms with which to swat it.

Lord Ambercrombie searched his surface until he found a bank of visual sensors he could keep open. As chance would have it, these sensors were on decaying plants floating just beneath the surface of Bottomless Bog. He peered through the murky water of the bog, using the water as a fleshcarrier uses sunglasses.

He saw the smile on the face of the comet now, and it seemed to be smiling directly at the sensors he had open. *It knows I can't do anything,* Abercrombie thought. *It's laughing at me.*

Lord Abercrombie created a hurricane. It was quite a powerful hurricane, and it broadsided the comet, bringing with it a gathering of cumulonimbus clouds. This did not bother the intruder at all. The comet continued to smile.

It thinks it's superior to me, Abercrombie thought, fuming. *It's prettier, more mobile.*

Now Abercrombie built formations of towering, anvil-topped clouds around the sides of the comet. Bolts of lightning lanced into the comet. Thunder roared across the sky. Abercrombie attacked until he felt fatigue. Again, this did not faze the comet.

It must have a weakness, the frustrated planet thought. *But what could it be?*

Lord Abercrombie considered letting loose a torrential downpour on the comet. But he felt rock weary, and the thought of such an attack seemed ludicrous to him. The fireball was so immense that only part of it was in the planet's atmosphere; much of it extended into deep space.

Just before the appearance of the comet, Prince Pineapple insisted on another recharge. The charge he had received earlier that afternoon had been short because of all the excitement generated by Rebo. It needed augmentation, and he selected a spot along the trail at the base of the white cliff.

Prince Pineapple closed his eyes and went into a trance during his recharge, as he was wont to do. It was at the height of this ecstasy that the Great Comet appeared in the sky over this side of the planet.

When the sky flashed orange, Javik and the Morovians covered their eyes and dove for the ground. Namaba cried out that the sky was on fire.

"I don't think so," Javik said, unable to look. "My guess is that it's a comet or a big meteor. And it's awfully close."

They heard the pounding of thunder in the distance and wondered if this was the end for them.

Lord Abercrombie wanted the minerals, gases, and other materials in the comet. With them he would be infinitely larger, infinitely more powerful. A force to be respected in the universe.

I must move out of orbit, he thought, *if I'm going to make any sort of a showing in battle. Why isn't the comet attacking? Is it teasing me?*

Lord Abercrombie tried to move his planet out of orbit. "Uuumph!" he grunted.

Cork did not budge.

Now that would really be something, he thought. *To move around wherever I want, whenever I want.*

The thought of this so appealed to him that he tried again. Over and over he tried. But Lord Abercrombie did not budge one centimeter out of orbit.

Maybe I just need to try a little harder, he thought.

So he concentrated every bit of energy he had. The nutrients on Cork's surface began flowing to his core as Lord Abercrombie called upon them for support.

These nutrients are mine, he thought. *No more sharing them with fleas on my surface!*

Sidney the comet focused his attention on the meadow of scarlet flowers. He saw Javik covering his eyes and prone on the ground at the other end of the meadow, at the base of the white cliff.

My lifelong friend, Sidney thought. *May good fortune grace your steps.*

It troubled Sidney that Javik would have to die comparatively soon, limited as he was by the frailties of flesh. Sidney wished he could offer Javik the longer life of a comet or perhaps a small star so that they might spend more time together.

But it was only a passing thought, one of those space dreams that magical comets are known to have. Sidney looked back down at Bottomless Bog.

Lord Abercrombie felt the nutrients of living forms surge into his core. He was absorbing entire flowers, small trees, and shrubs, along with many Fruits and Vegetables who were recharging at that moment. Many of the hardier flowers on the planet held out against his gluttony, as did most of the large plants.

With one foot in the ground, Prince Pineapple was at the height of his recharge. It was that euphoric point where all the juices from the soil flowed at full force through his pineapple veins. With his eyes closed, he leaned back on both elbows and savored the moment.

Then he screamed. "Eeeeah! Eeeeah!" The skin on his exposed foot stretched nearly to the breaking point. Something powerful was pulling at it! He tried to open his eyes, but a blinding fire across the sky prevented it.

"Help!" Prince Pineapple shouted. "For God's sake, hurry!"

Javik followed the sound and crawled to Prince Pineapple's side. "What's wrong?" Javik asked. Shielding his eyes, he squinted to look at the prince. A cluster of flowers within Javik's narrow range of vision disappeared into the ground with a loud *fwwwp-pop* suction noise. He heard the pops of suction all around and saw the ground color lighten.

Prince Pineapple did not respond. He was unconscious. But his bare foot was moving sporadically, jerking like a bodily limb consumed with the throes of death.

I've got to get him out of there, Javik thought.

Flowers were disappearing beneath the surface at a furious pace now, leaving all the ground that Javik could see denuded.

Javik pulled on Prince Pineapple's arms. Then he realized that his hands were stuck to the prince. He could not pull them free and could not get Prince Pineapple out of the hole.

"It's got me too!" Javik yelled. "Knock me away, somebody! Use that survival pack I left on the rock!"

Since Namaba was closest, she felt with her eyes closed until she found the pack. Then she felt Rebo's firm grip on her arm.

"This is *my* duty," Rebo said. He took the pack and crawled rapidly over to Javik. Keeping his eyes closed, he swung the pack until it struck Javik.

"Harder!" Javik screamed.

Rebo gave the survival pack a mighty swing, knocking Javik free. Prince Pineapple remained stuck to Javik, so he too was knocked away from the hole.

"It's . . . the end of the world," Prince Pineapple said, rolling on the ground and moaning. He was short of breath.

"I think we're okay," Javik said, catching his breath. "If that's the comet, it's probably over the bog where Wizzy was lost."

They spoke without opening their eyes, like people in a dark room.

"You mean it's Wizzy's dad?" Namaba asked. She squeezed Javik's hand.

"That's what I'm thinkin'," Javik said.

"I was almost recharged," Prince Pineapple said after a while, beginning to breathe regularly. "Something started pulling on my foot . . . sucking on it. I might have been pulled underground."

"We're even now, Rebo," Javik said. "You're no longer indebted to me."

"My obligation did not end when I saved you," Rebo said. "That is not our way. It is a lifelong thing."

A furious rhythm came from the meadow now, drowning out all conversation.

Fwwwp-pop!
Fwwwp-fwwwp-pop!
Fwwwpop-da-dee-pop!
Fwwwp-pop-ditty-pop-ditty-pop-pop-pop!

In the next instant, the ground rumbled. Then everything fell silent. The sucking sounds stopped, and there seemed to be no life in the vicinity other than their own.

Lord Abercrombie exploded out of his immersion hole, bouncing off the rock ceiling of the cavern. Dirt flew everywhere.

His scream echoed through the passageway. "Eeeeah!"

Abercrombie floated back down in slow motion, supported by a parachute of magical air. His naked body was different now. It still was partly magical and partly fleshy. But now it was a mixture, with splotches of skin next to empty spaces . . . a knuckle here . . . a knee there . . . both thighs . . . two hands but only one arm . . . the top of his skull . . .

Gradually, all the fleshy places filled in. When Abercrombie landed, his body was entirely flesh again. In an awakening haze, he tried to crawl back in the hole. But unseen hands pushed him away, gently but firmly.

I'm rejected, Abercrombie thought. *The Realm of Magic does not want me!*

Wearing nothing but his wardrobe ring, he stumbled out of the Soil Immersion Chamber into the labyrinth of passageways. The maze had once been second nature to him. But now he walked aimlessly in wrong directions, tripping and falling often. He scraped his knees, shins, and arms on the hard, rocky ground. The pain made his sensation of rejection even more acute. Only fleshcarriers felt such pain.

Sidney the comet arched heavenward, leaving Cork and all its problems behind. As Sidney left the atmosphere and accelerated in the vacuum of space, he thought about how glad he was to have found his present life. It was a prize far greater than anything offered by Earth's Bureau of Freeness, an existence never before contemplated by an Earthian.

Sidney remembered wishing for a Bu-Free prize, and now

it struck him as funny. Tragically funny. He wanted to tell millions of Earthians how foolish they were to waste their lives hoping for such things. He thought of the problems on Cork too, and considered interjecting to set things straight.

Then he changed his mind. *I can't worry about that stuff,* he thought. *One comet can only do so much.*

Gracefully, he streaked across the starcloth of space at many times the speed of light.

"It's gone," Javik said, opening his eyes. He rose with the others and squinted to look around. The sky was pastel blue, with three Corkian suns just above the horizon. But there was no warmth from the suns. A chill wind blew dust over the desolate expanse that once had been a pristine meadow.

"My God!" Namaba exclaimed. "Every flower is gone!"

Javik shivered, despite having on the vari-temp coat. "Let's get out of here," he said. "There's death in the air."

The trail at the base of the cliff ran alongside the denuded meadow for a short distance. Occasional broken flower petals, leaves, and stems on the ground were reminders of what once had been. The three-dot markings were clear along the shale cliff here, and appeared more frequently than before—as if to reassure them that they were going in the right direction.

Walking ahead of the others, Javik harbored deep doubts. Even with the certainty of the markings, he was not at all convinced that this was where they should be. And as he glanced back at Namaba, Rebo, and the prince, he saw it on their faces too: wide-eyed expressions mirroring his own fear.

They skirted a sizable pile of loose rocks which had fallen across the path. Nervously, Javik looked up at the white cliff before returning to its base. The broken pieces of shale showed evidence of having fallen recently, with flat, unweathered surfaces.

After they had gone a little farther, Javik thought he heard low, chanting voices. He stopped and raised his hand. "Listen!" he said.

The others stood still. The only sound was a rattle from Prince Pineapple's bag of garbage.

"Shhh!" Javik said.

Somewhere a rock tumbled down the face of the cliff. Javik's gaze darted in all directions. "I don't hear it now," he said.

"Maybe it's the wind," Namaba suggested, "whistling over the rocks."

"Yeah," Javik said.

The trail rose up an embankment now, leading them to a high area which was not all that wide. Down a steep incline to their left a deep blue lake began to emerge beneath a curved section of trail. The lake sparkled in the late afternoon suns as if fine jewels had been encrusted just below its surface.

"I christen thee Jewel Lake," Javik announced. He made the sign of the cross, touching his forehead, shoulders, and chest.

"It gets narrower," Prince Pineapple said, pointing ahead.

The incline falling off to Jewel Lake became a sheer dropoff less than a kilometer uptrail, leaving them only a narrow trail. Above and to the right a stark white cliff looked out uncaringly.

That's a long way down, Javik thought.

When they reached the beginning of the narrow trail, Prince Pineapple found three black dots on the side of the cliff. There could be no doubt. Ahead the trail wound around a jutting portion of cliff. Javik heard low, chanting voices again, louder this time and unmistakable—voices that seemed to come from somewhere uptrail, or perhaps overhead. He craned his neck to look up, but saw only clouds moving against the sky along the top of the cliff.

"I hear it now," Namaba said. "Deep voices."

"Magicians," Prince Pineapple said. "Or their spirits."

"The wind, more likely," Javik said. He sighed and faced the precipitous trail. "Good sense tells me to camp here for the night. We're losing daylight and there's a flat spot back a ways . . . just wide enough for the tent. But I want to get away from this place."

The others agreed. As they started out with Javik in front, Javik heard Prince Pineapple reminding everyone to avoid rhymes. *I ought to wait for the worst dropoff and really lay one on him,* Javik thought. *Wonder if he'd hit the lake on the fly.*

"I know some good rhymes," Javik said. "Do you prefer Mother Goose or dirty limericks?"

"Neither!" Prince Pineapple squealed, plugging his ears with his stubby fingers. In his excitement, he dropped the bag containing his possessions. It clattered over the edge, gone forever. "Now see what you made me do!" he wailed.

"I'm sorry," Javik said. "I didn't mean to do that. Maybe we'll find another cannister ahead. Millions of them were catapulted."

"That was a particularly nice selection," the prince gruffed.

"Better the bag than you," Javik said.

Javik turned his attention to the trail. Footing was becoming more treacherous, with many loose pieces of shale. The windchant grew louder as they rounded a bend. Then, inexplicably, the noise died out. The lake had narrowed to no more than the width of a river below them, with portions of it in shade as the suns dropped.

"It's too quiet," Namaba said.

"I see the pass," Javik said. His voice was an excited whisper.

A split in the white cliff was clearly visible only a few kilometers uptrail. With blackened areas on each side of the divide, it appeared to have been cut out of the white shale by a bolt of lightning.

"We'd better pick up our pace," Javik said. "I don't want to be on this trail after dark." He began to quick-step.

"And the Moha?" Prince Pineapple said. "The monster of legend? You would rather share an evening with that?"

"My service automatic packs a hell of a wallop," Javik said. "It's a baby cannon."

"Maybe we should turn back," Namaba said. "It seems more sensible to face this Moha in the daylight."

"What does your yenta say?" Javik asked, slowing to a walk.

"It's been giving me trouble since we left the meadow. I get no indication now at all."

"Back a ways, all I could think about was getting the hell out," Javik said. "Now I'm not so sure I did the right thing." He paused and looked back.

Just then a cacophany of angry voices rose from the rear. Javik saw something bright red on the cliff just above Prince Pineapple. A group of tubby little creatures stood on a ledge up there. They shouted in froglike voices and waved their arms angrily.

Strawberry people? Javik thought.

Prince Pineapple looked up. "Outcasts!" he yelled. He ran uptrail to get away from them. A thrown rock glanced off his back.

Javik and the others ran until they were out of range of the hurled missiles.

"They live in caves up there," Prince Pineapple said, looking back. "I think we interrupted a sacred ceremony. That's why the chanting stopped. They're mutants that grow on the ground. His voice became a hiss as he added, "Like Vegetables."

"I remember your argument with Wizzy," Javik said. "But don't melons grow on the ground too? I saw several in the royal court."

"I'm not going to tell you a melon person is as good as any other Fruit," Prince Pineapple said. "We've all heard of melon-heads. But a melon is much better than a strawberry."

"How so?" Javik asked.

"It just is, that's all."

"I guess we're not turning back," Javik said, seeing strawberry people swing down to the trail on ropes. They gathered there, chattering excitedly in throaty, croaky voices that made them sound like a pond full of bullfrogs.

Prince Pineapple's mouth curled downward in revulsion as he looked at them. "Mutants," he snarled.

The strawberry horde moved closer. They took a few steps, chattered nervously, then took more steps. They appeared to be building up courage.

"Maybe we could block them off with a rockslide," Rebo suggested, pointing up the wall. "Aim your thunder piece about there, Captain."

"We may have to come back this way," Javik said. He began to run uptrail. "Let's go!" he said.

The quartet took short, quick steps, looking down constantly to keep from taking a misstep on the loose trail. Just centimeters to their left the sheer dropoff waited like a predator toying with its prey.

They didn't have to look back to know the strawberry people were in pursuit. Angry grunts and the scuffling of many feet told them this. A small rock glanced off the back of Javik's head. He heard Prince Pineapple and the others curse as they were pelted. Javik's implanted mento unit throbbed.

Javik broke into a full run. His feet skipped over loose slabs of shale. Some pieces fell from the trail toward the ribbon of blue lake far below. The trail began to drop down steeply now, and it was all Javik could do to keep from tumbling forward head over heels.

They ran down, ever down, in daylight that was fast becoming dusk. Javik's knees ached. Quick glances back told him the pursuers were slow, and he was relieved at this. The lake was far behind them now, and the trail widened. The sheer dropoff became more of a gradual incline across white granite.

With the strawberry people out of sight, Javik and his group were nearing the bottom. In shadows ahead, Javik saw the pass between the cliffs. Charred streaks along each side of the pass told a story only the planet knew. Layers of orange covered the sky.

They slowed to a walk, passing near a cluster of AmFed garbage cannisters. Prince Pineapple gave them a longing look, but did not ask to stop. One was split wide open, with government forms and pamphlets spread around. The other cannisters were basically intact, with only a few bright objects showing.

As they neared the pass, it became apparent that something on the ground was wedged between the cliffs. It was round and large, but somewhat difficult to see in the waning light.

"A big boulder?" Javik said, in a low voice.

"We'd better be careful," Prince Pineapple said.

The excited voices of strawberry people behind them caused them to quicken their steps. Javik was just about to bolt when he glanced back and saw that the pursuers were stopped on the trail.

"Mo-ha!" they chanted. "Mo-ha!"

"I told you," Prince Pineapple said, looking around nervously.

"Mo-ha . . . Mo-ha . . . Mo-ha . . . Mo-ha . . . Mo-ha . . . Mo-ha . . . Moha-Moha-Moha!" Faster and faster they chanted, sounding to Javik like the tape of an old-style train that Sidney Malloy had played for him once. It was one of the illegal things in Sidney's safe.

"The Moha is here somewhere," Prince Pineapple said. "The scroll said where the cliffs meet."

Javik started when dozens of long tentacles popped out of the boulderlike mound. "That's no rock," he said.

The quartet approached carefully, with their small complement of weapons drawn. This amount to no more than Javik's automatic pistol and Rebo's switchblade knife. Namaba and Prince Pineapple found heavy stones. The mound was less than fifty meters in front of them now, and in the dim light they saw eyes on the tip of each tentacle. The eyes had black pupils with white corneas. Each tentacle was poised, cobralike, and the eyes stared sullenly at Javik's group.

"Why," Namaba said, leaning forward to get a better look, "it's a . . . a potato! A giant potato!"

"Yeccch!" Prince Pineapple exclaimed, feeling disgust. "A Vegetable mutant!"

"Is there any chance it might be friendly?" Rebo asked.

"Not this monster!" Prince Pineapple said. "If I remember my epic right, it destroyed an entire Fruit army."

Rebo's dark eyebrows furrowed. "But should we assume . . . ?"

"You get close enough to find out," Prince Pineapple said to Rebo. "Then we'll know for sure."

"I'm gonna do that," Rebo said. He dropped his knife. Looking at one of the potato monster's eyes, Rebo decided it was sad. Rebo felt honor-bound to protect Javik from the monster, and he still felt love for Namaba. But he also felt something else: an inexplicable desire to understand the creature.

"Wait," Javik said, catching Rebo's arm. "One of those tentacles could strangle you. The eyes don't look friendly at all."

"Maybe he's just afraid," Rebo said. "A protective posture. I've seen it many times in gang combat." He looked at Namaba.

"My yenta is not working," she said. "It's been out since we passed through the magic barrier in the meadow." She thought for a moment, then dropped her rock. "I'm going with you."

"Don't," Javik said.

"I'm going," she said simply. It was the female tone of determination Javik had heard from Earth women, the mindset that could not be resisted by mortal man.

Rebo and Namaba approached the Moha. They walked slowly. "Don't show fear," Rebo whispered. From the hill far behind them, Namaba heard the strawberry people's chant: "Mo-ha! Mo-ha! Mo-ha!" With each step, Namaba's steam engine heart raced faster, pumping air and water through her system. She felt pressure building. Then it released as steam shot out of her cuplike ears. *Show no fear,* she thought.

Rebo extended his arms to the Moha in a friendly gesture. "Friends," he said in a soothing tone. "We are your friends."

The tentacles coiled back and looked to Namaba as if they were about to lash out. The Moha seemed to be waiting for them to get closer.

Namaba closed her eyes with each step, occasionally opening them narrowly to peer at the potato monster. Its lumpy skin was the rich brown color of the soil.

"Friends," Rebo repeated. "We are your friends."

Namaba squinted, afraid to see fully what was going to happen next. They were only a few steps from the Moha now, well within reach of its tentacles.

To Namaba's surprise, the tentacles relaxed and started swaying gracefully. She opened her eyes all the way.

Rebo laughed. "That's a good fellow," he said. "No one's going to hurt you." He stroked the Moha's side.

"Thank God," Namaba said. "I didn't think you could do it."

Rebo looked at her with eyes that burned from hurt. "You didn't? You came with me out of *duty*?"

"Well, you did save my—"

"You owe *me* nothing," Rebo said, still stroking the Moha. "That obligation is to the other Rebo, the one I left on Morovia."

Namaba was sorry she had not met Rebo later in her life. They had done too many bad things together. It all seemed so long ago. She had to have someone new, someone untainted by the terrible old memories of Moro City. She looked back at Javik.

Javik slid his service pistol back into his holster, then retrieved Rebo's knife. Seeing Prince Pineapple was still holding a large rock, Javik told him to drop it.

Prince Pineapple knew he had no choice—not if he wanted to reach the Magician's Chamber. Grudgingly, he complied. As he joined Javik, however, a thought struck him. "I am a Fruit," Prince Pineapple said. "And that is a potentially ferocious Vegetable. There are natural hatreds between us."

"Just don't call it any names," Javik said. "And no quick movements."

"If the Moha tries to strangle me," Prince Pineapple said, "will you use your gun against it?"

"Maybe," Javik said. He was not teasing the prince this time. Javik honestly was not sure what he would do if such a thing occurred. "Let's hope it doesn't happen," he said.

Prince Pineapple said a little prayer as he walked with Javik to the Moha. Rebo was being lifted high by one of the tentacles.

"Gently," Rebo said, stroking the suction-cup-covered tentacle. "Up and over." The tentacle lifted him to the other side, out of view of the others. "That's it," Rebo was heard to say.

Prince Pineapple and Javik were beneath the Moha's swaying tentacles now. The prince shook with fear. A Moha eye was just centimeters away, looking at him intently.

"Go with him, Namaba," Rebo yelled from the other side. "I'm safe on the ground now."

Soon all the adventurers, even a perspiration-covered pineapple prince, had been lifted over the top and deposited safely on the other side.

"He just needed a little love," Rebo said. "Most folks probably throw rocks at him."

They camped nearby for the night.

FIFTEEN

Five magician trainees were discussing the comparative storage capacities of a rock, a grain of sand, and an atom. All knew from their lessons that no correlation existed between size and storage capacity. But then a black-robed magician appeared, asserting that a rock afforded far more storage capacity and ease of data retrieval than its smaller brothers. Through a series of elaborate demonstrations, the magician proceeded to prove his assertion. At the height of his audience's confusion, he admitted it was all a practical joke, that he was not a magician after all. "Actually," he said, "I am a droplet of Markesian slime brought in on one of your shoes."

One of the Rejected Stories

As they broke camp the following morning, the suns seemed cheerier to Rebo. He was not certain whether they reflected what lay in store for the group, but felt some part of their brilliance had to emanate from what he had done the previous evening.

While Javik loaded his survival pack, Rebo looked back at the Moha. The Moha was not moving now, having withdrawn its tentacles.

Poor ugly, lonely fellow, Rebo thought. On the cliff trail beyond the Moha, there was no sign of the strawberry people. Rebo wondered if they had seen the Moha lift them over its back.

That will be the stuff of legends, Rebo thought. *They'll say we were magicians, of course.*

Although it amused Rebo to think of himself as the subject of a legend, he knew it was not an important thing. Namaba was the thing of most consequence to him now, but she no longer wanted anything to do with him. Hearing Javik and Namaba laughing together behind him, Rebo thought sadly, *Perhaps the suns sparkle for them.*

Beyond the white cliffs and across the denuded meadowland, Wizzy remained in the underground compartment he had dug with his last spurts of strength. As Wizzy awoke now, he had no idea how long he had been asleep. It might have been a million years. Or only a million deci-seconds. It occurred to him that time was virtually meaningless so far beneath the surface. No suns marked the passing of days, and there was no variation in the temperature. Without visible cycles of life and death, happiness and sadness were muted.

Wizzy felt only one reality: He was buried and forgotten.

So it was in this cold and lonely place that Wizzy stirred and opened his cat's eye. In the white glow light of his rested body, he surveyed the specks of dirt along the ceiling of the tiny chamber. The specks looked very large to him, since they were exceedingly close. He studied them in minute detail, noting a most unusual crystalline shape.

Insoluble silicon, he thought. *With aluminum, oxygen, hydrogen, iron, calcium, magnesium, potassium . . . so much in such a small space!*

Wizzy may have stared at this speck of soil for only a few moments. Or perhaps it occupied him for the better part of a thousand years. Eventually he did look away, for one can only stare at something like that for so long before losing interest.

He stretched and yawned, then stretched again. "Oh my!" he exclaimed. "I wonder what has happened above?"

Wizzy envisioned Javik and the others long dead now, among many skeletons bleached white on the surface and visited often by the suns, the wind, and the rain.

He cried out at this thought. The sob of a millennium nearly overwhelmed him. But Wizzy held his tears, fearing even mercuric moisture might harm him. Soon his sadness passed.

Then it occurred to him that he could call upon his data banks to see how long he had been buried. So Wizzy glowed bright red, filling his little space with a warm glow. *Let me see,* he thought. *How many millions of years was it?* His micro-miniature magical circuits brought forth the startling answer.

"Thirty-eight hours!" Wizzy said, bellowing so loudly that it made his tympanic sensors ring. "Can it be?"

He verified the data. It was correct.

Wizzy moved around a little bit in the cramped quarters, trying to find the most comfortable position. For a while, he lay upside down, then on each side, then again on his bottom. No position seemed particularly satisfactory.

He spent some time wondering what to do next. Then he realized that he had been burrowing into the soil overhead. Pieces of dry dirt were being displaced in this unconscious maneuver, moving down along the sides of his lumpy body and piling up beneath him.

He stopped moving, afraid to twitch for fear of breaking through into Bottomless Bog. *How long have I been doing this?* he wondered. *How far am I from the bog?*

Then he remembered how close he had been to the shore when he fell in, and recalled the straight dropoff he had bounced into just before hitting bottom. Maybe he was no longer directly beneath the bog. Possibly it was a natural survival instinct that had moved him, causing him to burrow laterally just enough to get under dry land. If that had happened, he only needed to rise straight up to freedom. Wizzy knew up from down, being able to sense the pull of gravity.

But what if I'm beneath a curved portion of the bog bottom? he wondered. There was only one way to find out. If he became wet again, he could burrow back down and go to sleep for another thirty-eight hours.

Now Wizzy made a conscious effort at burrowing upward. He moved slowly at first, afraid that he would break through the bog at any moment. After traveling a good two meters, Wizzy became confident and increased his speed. This led to another increase seconds later. Soon Wizzy was a molten orange fireball, rising upward at a high rate of speed. Encountering rocks in his path, he dodged the larger ones. The smaller stones embedded themselves in his malleable skin.

Wizzy exploded out of the soil into the clear, cerulean blue sky above Cork. Three suns undimmed by clouds warmed his body. He rose a thousand meters above the planet, then did a series of joyous loops, trailing white smoke behind him.

It's wonderful here! he thought. *A great time to be alive!*

Recalling the map on the Sacred Scroll of Cork, Wizzy flew over the barren land that once had been a meadow. *The planet has changed in a short time,* he thought. *There are no flowers on this portion.*

Fresh doubts struck him concerning how long he had been entombed. He felt strong now, perhaps too strong for having been asleep only thirty-eight hours. *Maybe my data banks have been damaged,* he thought. *And I've been asleep for a long time.*

In the distance, Wizzy saw a high white cliff. He flew toward it. After a while, he noticed that the cliff did not seem to be drawing nearer. He increased his speed.

A short time later he burst through the magical barrier and hit the face of the cliff. His momentum and bulk broke away large pieces of shale, and he tumbled to the ground among them.

Wizzy felt embarrassed as he emerged from the rubble, although certainly no one had witnessed his faux pas. He alighted on a flat piece of shale to think.

Something colorful on the ground caught his eye. It was black with yellow polka dots—a strip of cloth. A thought struck him, but he dismissed it immediately. It couldn't be that!

He moved closer to it.

The ribbon from Namaba's mane! he realized. It looked fresh and nearly new. It hadn't been there long.

On the cliff just overhead, Wizzy saw a three-dot trail marking. *They've been this way,* he thought. *Recently.*

Reaching the cavernous Dimensional Tunnel room, a nude, dirty, and thoroughly disheartened Lord Abercrombie tried to compose himself. Shivering in front of a wall mirror, he saw that his body was completely flesh, without a single magical void. *I may as well make the best of it,* he thought, seeing the reflection of his packed train of trunks in the mirror. *I can't stay on this planet.* The galactic wind howled behind him.

Wanting to freshen up for his Dimensional Tunnel trip, Lord Abercrombie mentoed his wardrobe ring and took a dry shower. The ring played its cheerful tune. It was a novelty for him to see electrolyzed dirt falling off the side of his fleshy body which had not been there only a short time before.

"It's fresh-up time!" Lord Abercrombie sang, following the tune played by the ring. "It's fresh-up time!"

He began to feel better.

At his next mento command, a bright yellow caftan with black braiding on the arms and neck stitched itself around his body, followed by white satin slippers and a full thistle crown. His powers were diminished now, but at least he looked more regal than before. He turned before the mirror, admiring each angle.

Petulantly, he decided to change the outfit.

At his mento command, the old outfit disappeared in a *poof* and everything except the standard-issue thistle crown changed. His caftan became bright purple with slender gold stripes. Gold slippers adorned his feet.

He turned in front of the mirror and decided that this looked very nice. But improvements could be made. So he changed the outfit. Then he changed again. A dazzling array of colorful caftans and slippers flashed in front of the mirror as Lord Abercrombie put on a one-man fashion show.

But none of them suited him to perfection. An inexplicable element was missing each time. So Lord Abercrombie made a ferocious, pouting face in the mirror and leaned towards the glass with his hands on his hips.

"None of these outfits will do for my trip!" he shouted. "None will do at all!"

The glassplex mirror became hazy. Then it rippled. Seeing his reflection distorting in the mirror, Lord Abercrombie stepped back, alarmed. Distant, cackling laughter echoed inside his skull. It grew louder. He threw his hands over his ears, but this did no good.

"Stop it!" he screamed.

His caftan, slippers, and thistle crown disintegrated in a small explosion that startled him. He had not mentoed this. Then the wardrobe ring slipped from his finger and flew across the cavern, disappearing into the blackness of the Dimensional Tunnel.

His brain reverberated with laughter. Red and white striped crew socks appeared on his feet, then disappeared. Next, a royal purple ascot wrapped itself around his neck, pulling itself tighter and tighter as the laughter continued.

"Guggg!" he said, gagging.

Now the ascot disappeared, leaving behind a red burn mark on Lord Abercrombie's neck. He rubbed it.

The laughing voices receded. All became quiet, with the exception of a slight, whistling wind from the Dimensional Tunnel.

"I didn't want to keep that ring anyway!" he exclaimed, laughing nervously. This became two short laughs. Then two longer laughs and a confident chuckle. Soon he was howling, with his nude body bent over in mirth.

"A-ha. A-ha-ha. Aha-ha-ha-ha-ha-ha-ha-ha-ha!" His glee bounced off the cavern walls and entered the Dimensional Tunnel, ending up who knows where.

Lord Abercrombie thought of his laughter reverberating across the universe. This struck him as so funny that he laughed even harder.

"Well!" he finally said. "This has been a good joke on me!"

He scampered into the outer passageway, intending to find something recycled to wear and a meckie to accompany him on the trip.

Before setting out that morning, Javik and the others found that they could again recharge. No one understood what had happened the day before, when Prince Pineapple and Javik had almost been sucked into the ground. They theorized that it had been a peculiarity of the meadow.

Everyone, even Prince Pineapple, said goodbye to the Moha and thanked him for being so helpful. Shortly after they set out for their final assault on the Magician's Chamber and the Dimensional Tunnel, Rebo ran back to pat the Moha again. There was no response from the potato creature other than a graceful waving of its tentacles, so no one was certain how much intelligence it had.

"I really liked that guy," Rebo said as he rejoined the group.

They turned uptrail, moving into agate country, with sparse and gnarled noble fir trees dotting the way. In all directions they saw massive slabs and hills of translucent, ochre-colored stone. Morning sunlight permeated the agate rocks, making them appear liquid.

Soon they reached a one-story oriental gazebo that had a wooden wall on the side facing the trail. The other side of the structure opened in a half circle. Eight neat stacks of dark brown fabric were spaced evenly around this half circle, under the shelter of the roof.

Javik found a sign on the inside of the wall, written in three languages, each of which he recognized with the aid of his language mixer pendant. "Interesting," he said. "It's in English, Morovian, and Corker."

The others gathered around and verified this.

Reading one of the versions, this is what Javik saw:

> THESE ARE THE EIGHT FOLDING PATHS.
> SELECT A PATH.
> PUSH IT OPEN.
> IT WILL UNFOLD BEFORE YOU.
> WALK ON IT.

No one knew which trail to select, so each unfolded two paths. They flip-flopped open into the distance like the binding displays of an encyclopedia salesman. When all were open, they found that one had three-dot markings every few hundred meters. The others were unmarked.

They set out along this path, with Prince Pineapple forging into the lead. "The Magician's Chamber is close," he said. "I know it."

Soon the path became a dirt trail. As they reached dirt, the cloth path folded up behind them, returning to the gazebo. On both sides they watched the other paths flop back as well.

After only a few more steps, Prince Pineapple was forced to stop suddenly, for a large wooden sign painted with white letters had sprung up in his path. This was printed in the three languages of the group.

"'Go back!'" Prince Pineapple said, reading the Corkian version. "'Wrong way!'" He scratched his head.

After a moment of thoughtful silence, Javik said, "I don't believe it, Prince. Go around."

Prince Pineapple agreed. "An Abercrombie trick," he said. He started around the sign.

But the sign moved to block his path.

Javik tried to go around the other way, but the sign split into two neat halves, with a wooden portion blocking both him and the prince.

Namaba and Rebo made attempts too. But now the sign

split into four pieces, with one in front of each of them.

"Do not be alarmed," an omnipresent voice said. "I am attempting to help you."

"Who said that?" Javik asked, startled.

The quartet backed away from the sign pieces, gathering together a short distance back.

The sign pieces drew themselves together again.

"Many months ago," the voice said, "Lord Abercrombie sent his meckies to the gazebo. They switched the paths around. You need to move over two paths to your left."

"You are not Lord Abercrombie?" Prince Pineapple asked, one eyebrow lifted inquisitively.

"Certainly not. I am a magician's helper, left here aeons ago to watch over the area. This is a galactic park, you know. I'm sort of a park ranger, you might say."

"You are invisible?" Namaba asked.

"No more than you, dear. I am the beautiful rock to your left."

Namaba looked down and saw two medium-sized agates on the ground. She touched one. "Is this you?" she asked. The rock was smooth and sun-warmed.

"Certainly not! That is a common agate. I, on the other hand, am a history stone—a repository of all the legends and data concerning this quadrant of the starfield. Now Abercrombie is washed up, rejected by the Realm of Magic."

They gathered around the stone and looked down at it. This rock looked no different from any other in the vicinity. It was about the size of Javik's hand, yellow ochre in color.

Prince Pineapple felt a rush of excitement at the thought of Lord Abercrombie being rejected by the Realm of Magic. For the first time the prince consciously considered the possibility of stepping into Abercrombie's place. Before this he had felt only generalized anger, a desire to throw Abercrombie out. Now he felt something entirely different. He wanted to be lord.

They were right about me, Prince Pineapple thought, looking at each of the others. *They saw it in my eyes.*

Javik looked at him.

Prince Pineapple looked at the talking agate and asked, "How do we know we can trust you?"

The agate laughed, its voice seeming to come from all around. "You don't. But then, what choices do you have?"

Javik lifted the stone and stood up with it. "I could toss you in a ravine," Javik said. "There's one just over there." He nodded to indicate direction.

"I could place barriers in your way to prevent it," the agate said. "I'll tell you what, though. If you want to take this trail, go right ahead."

"You won't stop us?" Prince Pineapple asked.

"No. But do you really think that would be wise, Prince Pineapple? Do you, Namaba?"

"It knows our names!" Namaba said, surprised. She looked around.

"Someone around here knows our languages, too," Rebo said.

"This could all be Lord Abercrombie's doing," Prince Pineapple said. "We've all recharged. He knows everything about us now from the connection."

Namaba wrinkled her hair-framed face into a frown. "I think my yenta is working again," she said. "It tells me we should trust the agate."

"You're certain?" Javik asked. He leaned over and put the stone back where he had found it. "We don't have much to go on," he said, rubbing his tongue across his lower lip. The lip was chapped.

"I think I agree," Rebo said. "This agate might have threatened us, or tried to bluff us with its magic. It didn't do either of those things."

"Do you mind if we continue on this trail a little ways?" Namaba asked, leaning over the agate, "and then make our own decision?"

The sign disappeared. There was no response other than this.

Namaba loped ahead to where the sign had been, then passed beyond. "Let's take the other trail," she said.

All agreed, and they set off across a field of rock. Here they encountered occasional long-stemmed yellow flowers that had six round petals apiece. Javik picked a flower and used a piece of twine to secure it to Namaba's mane. "This will replace the ribbon you lost," he said.

Glowing bright pink with a yellow tail, Wizzy skirted the base of the white cliff, following the three-dot trail markings.

He flew above the blue lake, which narrowed to a ribbon of water, then paused at the beginning of the precipice trail. From there he passed the cliff dwellings of the strawberry people. Three of them ran out to watch him as he flew by.

Wizzy was a good deal larger now than he had been, and his translucent tail extended a good five meters behind his nucleus. This must have been quite a sight for the outcast strawberry people, especially following so closely on the heels of the episode with Javik's party.

Wizzy left the strawberry people in the wink of a cat's eye. He swooped low over the Moha now, passing through the opening in the cliffs. This agitated the Moha, and it waved its tentacles wildly. One tentacle passed harmlessly through Wizzy's gaseous tail.

Reaching the eight folding paths, Wizzy nudged them open. In doing this, he clumsily destroyed the gazebo with the fire from his nucleus. Fortunately, a foresighted magician had treated the cloth paths with flame retardant.

While the gazebo burned, Wizzy checked each path. Quickly he located the one with three-dot markings. Streaking along this path, he reached the dirt area so rapidly that the magical agate did not have time to warn him.

"Wait!" the agate called out. "Not that way!"

But Wizzy was so far uptrail that he did not hear the agate.

With Prince Pineapple trudging ahead and Rebo bringing up the rear, Javik and Namaba walked beside one another holding hands. At first the lovers found this difficult to do, owing to the markedly different cadence of their steps. Namaba's gait was more of a lope, with her head bobbing up and down, while Javik walked erectly and smoothly in the Earthian manner. After a kilometer or so, they found a middle ground, with Namaba moving more smoothly and Javik herky-jerking it.

"We'll be married in Moro City," Namaba said. "My minister can do it." The light brown fur on her mane was gold-tinged from the sunlight.

"Where would I work?" Javik asked, squinting. "Is there a Morovian Space Patrol?

"We have an Air Guard," she said. "But Morovian ships are more primitive than yours. And we have nothing to compare with the technology in your wardrobe ring."

"That's not technology," Javik said with a wink. "It's magic."

She smiled.

"I don't mind if the place is a little backward," Javik said. "Just as long as we're together." He thought about how sappy his words might have sounded to him once. But it struck him that the really important things in life were sappy.

Catching up, Rebo said, "It won't be easy for you on Morovia. I'm not saying that out of jealousy. Most folks will be afraid of Tom."

Namaba's eyes flared. "They can all go to Morovian Hell."

"It's easy to say that," Rebo said. "But you'd better think it over carefully. They'll think Tom is a freak."

"Then I'll make my living touring the planet," Javik said flippantly. "We'll make enough money off freak shows to build a rocket and get the hell out of there."

"We're not doing any sideshows," Namaba said. "You're no freak. A Morovian on Earth would face the same situation. You're different, that's all. We'll prove to people that different is not bad." She squeezed his hand tightly. "We'll make them understand," she said. Her lips were a thin, determined line.

"Good luck to both of you," Rebo said. "Maybe I can help, when we all get back—if the Dimensional Tunnel works out the way we hope."

Namaba glanced back at Rebo and saw sincerity in his eyes. They glowed a soft shade of red.

"Say," Rebo said, looking at Namaba. "Do you remember Jamaro? Remember how he came back all deformed after the Hoka Wars?" His expression became troubled as he realized he had placed himself into a hole.

"Jamaro returned with only two legs," Namaba explained, glancing at Javik.

"Pretty horrible, eh?" Javik said.

"I used a bad example," Rebo said, biting nervously at his lower lip. "I was just thinking I could work with those kinda guys—you know, in therapy."

Javik thought of Sidney.

"Sounds fine, Rebo," Namaba said. "You'll do fine. All of us will!"

"We have wars on Earth, too," Javik said. "I was good at that game. Seems like a long time ago, though." He reflected upon the Atheist Wars, when he and Brent Stafford swaggered across half the star system. "Hell, I'd be a young general now if I'd been able to keep my nose clean."

Seeing Namaba looking at him curiously, Javik forced a laugh. "Guess I'm pretty funny, eh?" he said. "Someday, Namaba, we'll be gray-haired, sitting in rockers on our front porch. A little Morovian kid'll be sitting on the steps, and I'll be starting to tell a war story. You'll say, 'Not that one again!' Or maybe you'll smile softly and leave, knowing I've changed the story with each telling, making more of myself than there really was."

"'Anything worth saying is worth exaggerating,'" Namaba said, nodding her head. "That's what Grandma used to say."

"Sounds like your grandpa told his share of tall tales."

Namaba laughed. "Maybe that little Morovian kid will be our grandchild."

"That'd be somethin'," Javik said. "Yessir. That'd be somethin'!"

Engrossed in the conversation, Javik suddenly realized they had fallen far behind Prince Pineapple. He could just see the top of the prince's helicopter beanie beyond a rise in the path. Then Prince Pineapple turned and ran back toward them. When the prince's face came into view, Javik saw that he was shouting something. The words were lost in the wind.

"Looks like he's found something," Rebo said.

They picked up their pace and moments later found Prince Pineapple standing over a pile of sun-bleached bones.

"A Yanni tribal burial ground," Prince Pineapple said, brimming with excitement. "With long goat bones in a triangular pattern."

"There's a significance to that?" Javik asked.

Prince Pineapple looked full in his face with the expression of a scolding Freeness Studies instructor. "Triangle . . . three dots."

"Oh, sure," Javik said. "A magical sign. What do you think it means?"

"It's a sign that we're close," Prince Pineapple said.

"Speaking of signs," Namaba said, pointing uptrail. "I see another one."

As she spoke, a wooden sign was rising slowly from the ground beside the trail just a few meters ahead. When it was all the way up, she saw it rested on two legs and was red with white lettering.

Javik walked up to it and read. It was printed in English:

DIMENSIONAL TUNNEL
2 KILOMETERS

Javik stepped aside so Rebo and Namaba could read it. Now it changed to Morovian. When Prince Pineapple read it, the printing became Corkian.

"Three languages again," Javik said.

They set off, and soon were out of sight of the sign. Minutes later they heard rapid footsteps approaching from downtrail. Turning their heads, they were surprised to see the sign running after them. Two arms had sprung from the edges of the sign-board, and its legs had big, clumpy feet. Jumbled letters were shaped in the form of a cherubic, smiling face.

As Javik's jaw grazed his boot tops, he watched the sign run by and plant itself in the ground a few paces uptrail. The sign's arms folded in and melded with the board. The facial letters formed English words. The feet disappeared, leaving two rigid board legs planted in the ground. Here is the message Javik saw:

DIMENSIONAL TUNNEL
1 KILOMETER
Approach at own risk.
Strong galactic currents.

They continued on their way. A few minutes later the sign again rushed past. This time it planted itself in front of a large flat stone and began to glow like a New City neon sign. There was a new message:

DIMENSIONAL TUNNEL
LAUGH TO ENTER

They searched the base of the flat stone, looking for a tunnel or a doorway. Seeing nothing, they looked at one another and shrugged.

"Guess we'd better laugh," Prince Pineapple said.

So they laughed.

And laughed.

And laughed some more.

Their laughter echoed off the rocks, trees, and shrubs around them. They laughed so hard that the sign broke into uncontrollable giggles. Its lettering became a muddled, unreadable mess.

With tears in his eyes, Javik saw two humanlike puffy white clouds drop feet first from the sky. They were not very large as clouds go, being perhaps twice as tall as Javik. But they were quite muscular. Ceremoniously, with stern expressions on their puffy faces, they took positions on each side of the giant slab of stone.

"It's under the rock!" Prince Pineapple said.

Javik wiped tears from his eyes and cheeks.

Using its little finger, one of the clouds lifted a corner of the slab and peeked under it. "Oooh!" the cloud squealed, dropping the slab. "A big worm touched me!"

"Oooh!" the other cloud said.

"Oooh!" the sign said. And the sign jumped completely out of the ground, landing in a clump of bushes.

Now the clouds leaped high in the air and were carried off by the wind. Soon they had floated out of sight.

The sign crawled out of the bushes and ran downtrail. Soon it was gone too, leaving the travelers in a most bewildered state.

Just then Javik heard a faint little chuckle. He didn't know where it came from. Looking at the solemn and confused expressions of his companions, he knew they hadn't done it.

You must realize that this was perhaps the tiniest chuckle in the Aluminum Starfield. It might have been trapped beneath a pebble and then kicked free by someone's foot. Or maybe it was simply a slow echo, having just completed its bouncing journey from surface to surface.

Whatever the scource, it was just enough of a chuckle to complete the required amount of laughter. As Javik looked at his companions, he became aware of a creaking noise. It came from the large slab of rock.

"It's moving!" Namaba exclaimed.

Sure enough, the stone was lifting like a megalithic hatch, creaking higher and higher until it fell over the other way on its top. It might not have creaked so much if only someone had been there to oil its magical hinges. Unfortunately, there was a decided shortage of magician's helpers in this part of the universe.

Moving to the edge, Javik saw steps leading down from all sides of a square hole. It resembled an inverted, hollow pyramid. In a wild flight of fantasy, he envisioned a pyramid rocket landing here and plowing into the ground. It was a preposterous thought, causing Javik to wonder if a magician was playing tricks with his mind.

Prince Pineapple started down the steps.

"Hold it, Prince," Javik said, grasping Prince Pineapple's arm firmly. "I want you to wait here." Javik released the prince.

"What do you mean?" Prince Pineapple asked. "We were going to get rid of Abercrombie together."

"I'm going to see what Abercrombie's been up to," Javik said. "If he's no threat to Earth, I'll leave him and enter the Dimensional Tunnel with Rebo and Namaba."

Prince Pineapple's black button eyes opened wide in shock. *"Leave him?* You can't do that!"

"I'm not going to get rid of him for you," Javik said. "I've never trusted you." Javik removed his Tasnard rope from the pack and mentoed it. The black and white striped rope looped around Prince Pineapple's arms and torso, pulling his arms tight against his body. Javik pulled the struggling prince to the surface.

"Now see here!" Prince Pineapple said. "You can't—"

"Shut up," Javik snapped. He mentoed the rope again, instructing it to tie the prince to a nearby willow sapling.

The Tasnard rope curled out of Javik's grasp and dragged Prince Pineapple to the tree. It tied him there in a standing position.

"Earthian bastard!" Prince Pineapple said. He pulled at the rope and kicked, but it held him fast.

"That'll keep you on ice," Javik said. He turned to Namaba. "Stay here," he said. "It might be dangerous."

"I agree," Rebo said.

Namaba leaned down and gave Javik a kiss on the mouth. "I'll watch the prince," she said.

"And this is one tough lady," Rebo said.

Namaba half smiled. Her eyes were full of concern for Javik and Rebo. "I should go with you, Rebo," she said. "My Morovian obligation . . ."

"You can help by staying here," Rebo said. "Keep an eye

on Prince Pineapple. We can't have him getting in the way."

"All right," she said softly.

Javik and Rebo stepped carefully into the hole. The upside-down pyramid was larger than it appeared to be, and soon Namaba saw their forms diminishing in size as they proceeded. She lost her sense of perspective. For a moment she thought they were climbing up the steps.

With her back to Prince Pineapple, Namaba did not see that the Tasnard rope was beginning to slip. Something in the bog had damaged the rope's delicate mechanism. Quietly, Prince Pineapple removed the rope from his arms and torso, pulling it over his head. He pulled a long goat bone out from under his coat. It was sharp on one end, having been broken in the indeterminate past.

They plan to leave me on the surface! the prince thought desperately.

Javik and Rebo reached the base of the hole now. Namaba watched as Javik leaned down and looked inside a square, black hole. He jumped into it, followed by Rebo.

Prince Pineapple swung the bone mightily, hitting Namaba on the side of her skull and slashing her skin sack with the sharp portion of bone. It was a mortal blow.

A loud sound of releasing steam came from Namaba. Her body took off like a discharging balloon, looping in the air and wetting Prince Pineapple's face and clothing with steam. Soon Namaba's body was no more than an empty, hairy bag of flesh. It dropped to one side of the entrance.

The Sacred Scroll of Cork fell from Prince Pineapple's coat, unnoticed by him. He leaped down the steps with the zeal of a fanatic, carrying the long goat bone. "It's mine!" he said. "The Magician's Chamber is mine!"

Wizzy's path brought him to a Vegetable village by the sea. Here tiny white stucco houses clung to hillsides and to cliffs overlooking the blue water. Over the center of town, Wizzy looked down on a cobblestone square thronging with thousands of Vegetable people.

Glowing kelly green from his flaming nucleus to the tip of his wispy tail, Wizzy dipped low over the square. He heard the excited conversation of the people.

"Did you hear the news?" a voice said. "Brother Carrot is victorious."

"Wonderful!"

"Death to the Fruits!"

"Things will be different now!"

While Wizzy had grown to many times his original size, he still was not such a large comet. At first only a few Vegetables noticed him over their heads. Gradually, however, the word was passed and fingers began to point. Soon, Wizzy had become the center of attention.

"I must have taken a wrong turn somewhere," Wizzy mumbled. He felt embarrassed. His nucleus changed to a bright shade of crimson, and his tail matched that.

In the next hour and a half he retraced his flight carefully, finally arriving back at the burned-out gazebo. Flying slowly along each of the eight folding paths now, Wizzy encountered a wooden sign which had sprung up in his path.

Wizzy burst right through it.

"You foolish fellow!" the magical agate yelled after him. "Come back here!"

Sheepishly, Wizzy returned and spoke with the agate. Wizzy had his faults, but he knew the truth when he heard it. Shortly he was on the correct path.

How stupid of me, Wizzy thought as he sped along the path in a bright green blur. *All that wasted time.*

"Curious fellow," the magical agate said, watching Wizzy flash in the distance. The agate felt warm in the rays of three suns. Now, as it grew quiet once again, he drifted off to sleep, his history storehouse just a little bit richer.

With weapons brandished, Javik and Rebo dropped to a rocky passageway surface. The passageway walls were gray stone, dimly lit from unseen sources. Rebo's eyes glowed bright red, casting an eerie light. Seeing darkness in one direction and light in the other, they walked toward the light.

It was cold here, so Javik paused to mento on a pair of vari-temp pants, matching his orange coat. "You want anything?" he asked, looking at Rebo.

"Naw. I'm fine." Rebo was cold, but decided he didn't need more than his club jacket.

The passageway opened into a wide, well-lit cavern. One wall of the cavern faced a series of clear glassplex tubes.

"This place looks familiar," Rebo said.

Moving around a stocky pillar, they came upon a gray rock

throne with black satin cushions. Junk sculptures made of scrap pieces of metal, plastic, and glassplex flanked the throne.

"Of course," Rebo said, touching a throne cushion. It was smooth and cool. "The half-faced creature sat here."

"Half-faced?"

"Namaba and I were in those tubes out there, going around and around. Then we landed next to your ship." Rebo's red eyes darted around nervously. "He's here somewhere."

"Abercrombie? You think it was Abercrombie?"

"I don't know. But he was very angry with us."

On the other side of the chamber they found another passageway. They moved from light to dark in this passageway, not speaking. It was very quiet. It was colder here, and Javik saw Rebo shiver.

"You sure you don't want something to wear?" Javik asked.

Rebo did not answer. He moved ahead of Javik, extending his knife in front of him in the low light of the passageway. Rebo glanced back often as they proceeded, revealing fear in his face. Presently they came upon a side cavern full of silent machinery. Meckies were piled near the doorway. Nothing moved in the room.

"I thought I heard something," Javik said, pointing up the passageway.

Rebo listened intently for a moment. Then he shrugged his big shoulders. "I don't hear anything."

"I don't hear it now," Javik said. "Let's go on."

They passed dozens of other caverns similar to the first. Inside each it was the same: meckies piled motionless near the doorway and not a gear moving anywhere.

Soon the passageway widened like a funnel opening and grew lighter. They rounded a turn and were in another cavern. This cavern had three mirrored walls. The fourth side was black, with no wall visible. Javik heard wind noises in the room and felt cold through his vari-temp clothing.

Judging from the shadows, Javik decided this cavern was illuminated from above. There was a considerable amount of light where he and Rebo were, contrasting with the darkened fourth side of the room. Oddly, however, when Javik looked up he saw only dark gray rock with no source of illumination. A long train of trunks was in the center of the cavern. Javik saw something move behind one of the trunks.

"You there!" Javik barked, dropping to his belly and holding the gun out with both hands. "Step out where I can see you!" Unnoticed by Javik, the folding shovel and barbed cord slipped out of their sheath and fell to the ground.

A human figure wearing dark coveralls emerged from the shadows. This was a bearded man, much shorter than Javik, stepping forward with his arms folded across his chest. Javik heard Rebo's heavy breathing at his side.

"I've been expecting you," the man shouted. He walked toward Javik. His beard was dark, of indeterminate color.

"Stay back," Javik said. "Keep your distance."

But the man came closer. He was not armed, and appeared harmless enough to Javik. "I was just about to go on a trip," the man said, nodding toward the trunks. "Everything is packed."

"You're Winston Abercrombie, aren't you?" Javik asked, looking closely at the man's eyes. They were widely set and large. Javik stood up, still aiming the gun.

"That is correct," Abercrombie said. His voice was distant and unconcerned. It almost seemed to come from the wind that howled around them. A phosphorescent, pink label on his shoulder flashed this message:

100%
recycled
material

"It's the same man," Rebo said. "But his face . . . It's complete!"

Abercrombie unfolded his arms and gestured toward the blackness behind him. "That, gentleman, is the famous Dimensional Tunnel." A smile touched the corners of his mouth, then dropped to steely hardness.

"I am from Earth," Javik said, gripping the gun handle too tightly. He felt perspiration on his palms. "Sent to investigate the garbage situation . . . and your disappearance."

"But I have not disappeared," Abercrombie exclaimed. "Do I look invisible to you?"

"No."

"I'm quite visible, quite fleshy now." He laughed. It was a piercing, cackling laugh. The laugh of a crazy man.

"I think you'd better come with me," Javik said, motioning with his gun barrel.

"Come and get me," Abercrombie squealed. He stepped back into shadows.

"Hold it!" Javik snapped.

Rebo followed Abercrombie.

Javik moved forward now too and saw Abercrombie stepping backward, approaching the blackness of the Dimensional Tunnel. Abercrombie cackled with laughter.

Rebo was close to him now, but stopped short when he saw the edge of the tunnel just a few steps behind Abercrombie. "Be careful!" Rebo warned.

"I know where I am," Abercrombie said. "I don't like to travel without luggage, but we do as we must."

Rebo switched his knife to his other hand and reached out until his fingertips nearly touched Abercrombie.

"Let him go," Javik said.

"I'm five times the size of this little feller," Rebo said. "You want to question him, don't you?"

"Yes, but . . ."

Javik stopped when he saw Rebo grab one of Abercrombie's arms. Rebo towered over Abercrombie and was many times his bulk. Rebo pulled.

But Abercrombie did not budge. He smiled diabolically.

Rebo dropped his knife and grabbed hold with both hands. He dug his paws into the ground and pulled again.

Abercrombie still did not budge. "Heh-heh-heh!" he cackled.

"Let go of him!" Javik shouted.

But it was too late. In one ferocious flip, Abercrombie pulled Rebo over his shoulder and hurled him into the Dimensional Tunnel.

"Aaaiy!" Rebo screamed. Then he was gone.

"I have the strength of fifty," Abercrombie said, approaching Javik. "You are in my domain."

Javik pulled the trigger. The gun jammed. He turned and ran, with Abercrombie in pursuit. Javik knew why Abercrombie was so strong. He was insane.

"This is *my* chamber!" Abercrombie squealed. "*Mine*, Earthian."

Suddenly, Javik dropped to his knees, turned, and fired. This time a flash of orange flame shot out of the gun barrel. A thundercalp reverberated off the walls.

The laser shell hit Abercrombie square in the shoulder. He

fell to the ground, unconscious.

Javik tied Abercrombie's hands and feet with mento-produced strips of heavy cloth from his wardrobe ring. Then he brought the first-aid kit out of his pistol handle and caulked Abercrombie's shoulder wound.

Since Abercrombie was a small man, Javik lifted him easily over one shoulder. When he reached the passageway, Javik saw Prince Pineapple running toward him at full tilt, waving a long, sharp bone. The big pineapple man had the same crazed expression as Abercrombie, and was approaching fast.

"What are you doing down here?" Javik shouted. "I told you . . ." He ducked. The bone whistled by his ear. Javik dropped Abercrombie to the ground and reached for his gun. Then a thought struck Javik and he screamed, "There was a young lady of Rhodes! . . . Who sinned in unusual modes!"

Prince Pineapple did a high backflip, landing neatly on his feet. "Damn you!" he said.

Javik continued: "At the height of her fame! . . . She abruptly became! . . . The mother of four dozen toads!"

The angry prince did a double backflip.

Then Javik attacked with more dirty Irish limericks, sending the hapless prince backflipping into the distance of the corridor. Javik heard his rhymes echo, and surmised this would keep Prince Pineapple occupied for a while.

As Javik reached down to lift Abercrombie, he thought of Namaba. He walked rapidly. Then he broke into a full run. Reaching the base of the inverted pyramid, he lifted Abercrombie up to the lowest step. Then he crawled up and again lifted Abercrombie's limp form over his shoulder.

Javik sprinted up the steps. Reaching daylight, he called Namaba's name. There was no answer.

"Namaba!" he repeated. "Namaba!"

Then he saw it on the top step at the opposite side of the pyramid: a tiny bag of fleshy fur with a yellow flower attached to it. He dropped Abercrombie on the ground and ran to her. "Namaba!" he moaned. "My God!"

Something creaked, but Javik paid it no mind.

"My love!" he wailed, overcome with grief. Javik knelt over her deflated, lifeless body and took the flower from her mane. He pressed it against his nostrils. It still smelled sweet. She had been alive only minutes ago.

A loud creak caused him to look up. The stone was dropping! A shadow had moved halfway across the opening.

Javik's mind raced. *In or out?* he wondered. *Shall I take her and jump in the Dimensional Tunnel?*

The stone lid continued to drop. It was three-quarters shut. Javik was completely in shadow.

But she's dead, Javik thought. *I couldn't live on Morovia without her.*

At the last possible moment, Javik grabbed Namaba's body and rolled into the sunlight above.

With a loud *plop* the stone dropped over the opening. Dust rose from the area.

Javik did not want to move. He lay on his back with Namaba against his chest. The warmth of three suns caressed the backs of his hands. Namaba's body was light, without substance. He wondered how someone so alive and so vibrant could be reduced to this.

A tear ran down his cheek.

In the settling dust, a parchment rose silently skyward, unseen by Javik. It was beginning its journey back to Sacred Pond. But Wizzy saw it when he flew up. And he saw Javik lying on the ground holding Namaba's body.

"Captain Tom!" Wizzy squealed, streaking down in a bright green flash. "Captain Tom!"

Far beneath the surface of Cork, Prince Pineapple was lying on the ground, recovering from a nearly fatal attack of backflips. In a daze, he staggered to his feet. He ran one way, then the other, searching every passageway, every cavern. No one else was there. Locating the base of the pyramid steps, he stared up into darkness.

His head throbbed. He needed time to think.

Rebo wished he had accepted the vari-temp clothing when Javik offered it to him. He was cold. Damned cold. Freezing air rushed at him through the vacuum of an immense, universe-wide tunnel. Storms of gray and blue raged across his brain. Pinpricks of cold stabbed him. It was so cold that he felt hot. He remembered feeling this before, after falling into the maw of the Parduvian flytrap.

His body rolled into the shape of a three-legged fetus, just as it had before. Then it straightened, and he saw twinkling stars in the shadowy blue distance. The blues, greens, and browns of planets appeared and receded. Great suns came and went, blinding him with their intensity.

But the suns were cold. He wanted to get warm more than anything else. His brain became foggy.

Short visions of Namaba's face flashed in front of him like props in an amusement park tunnel, then splintered as Rebo hurtled through them.

Now he was a fetus again, spinning, spinning, spinning. He was a baby, newborn and ready to start his life.

I can still be useful, he thought. *It's not too late.*

He tried to shout this thought. It was pure truth and needed to be heard. But his voice made no sound.

In his muddled mind's eye, he envisioned a ward full of disabled war veterans. Inexplicably, all the veterans were children, as if they had gone to war before growing up. Rebo was on a platform, delivering a motivational talk. Everyone respected and loved him.

The tunnel became a great ocean wave, contracting and swelling. It pulled him forward. Inexorably, painfully forward. His brain became the ocean wave, pulling him back to Moro City. He wanted to go back. There were important things to be accomplished.

He broke free of the water and ran through the tunnel in immense, loping strides—strides that carried him millions of kilometers at a time. Eternity pressed in on him. He had to hurry.

He sensed warm yellow and orange colors in place of the grays and blues. His body tingled as the cold dissipated through his pores. His frantic strides became slow-motion easy, with his muscles pulling him forward in tremendous, smooth bursts. He felt sleepy, and a calmness came over him.

Rebo remembered the magical meadow, wishing he had been the one to frolic with Namaba. It might have been that way . . . might have been that way . . . might have been . . .

A red flash tore across his eyelids, and he was hot. Intensely hot. So hot that it seemed cold. He shivered, then felt his body temperature normalize.

Rebo opened his eyes. A scowling Morovian police officer stared down at him.

"I got one!" the police officer yelled. "It's one of those Southside Hawks." He pushed Rebo over roughly and cuffed his hands.

Rebo saw a brass plaque just centimeters from his face. It read: "PARDUVIAN FLYTRAP."

I'm back, he thought. *Back!*

The police officer stood him up.

"Listen to me," Rebo said. "I must tell you something."

"Plenty of time for that in court," the officer said. "They'll pop you certain for what you did to that poor old guy."

Rebo felt the officer's grip tighten on his arm. Uncontrolled rage twisted the officer's face.

No one will believe me, Rebo thought. *I've changed, and no one will know.*

EPILOGUE

Maybe Hoover was right.

Graffiti on New
City park bench

Wizzy buzzed low over the prone, face-up form of Javik. "Captain Tom!" he said. "You okay, Captain Tom?"

Javik sat up dejectedly and placed Namaba's body on the ground next to him. He mentoed for a soft terry-cloth bathrobe, and a white one wound its way around his arms and torso. Then he removed the robe and wrapped Namaba's body in it. His movements were gentle, reverent.

"She's gone," Javik said. He stared at the survival pack, which lay nearby on the ground. *Sleep*, he thought, thinking of the tent and beds inside.

"God, I'm sorry," Wizzy said.

"I loved her," Javik said. "Prince Pineapple's gone too. He went crazy." Javik brightened for a moment as he focused on Wizzy. "You're larger," he said. "And your tail..."

Wizzy flew in a little circle.

Javik ducked to avoid the gas of Wizzy's tail. "That's a nice shade of green, too," Javik said.

Abercrombie started to regain consciousness. His eyes blinked. Still tied at his wrists and ankles, he rolled over from his back to his side.

"I have a much better color selection than before," Wizzy

296

said. "Many more nuances of the spectrum, with still others waiting to be discovered."

Javik's face darkened. "Where the hell have you been, anyway?"

"I know what you're thinking," Wizzy said, glowing light red to study Javik's thoughts. "If I'd been here earlier, Namaba might still be alive."

"It crossed my mind," Javik said. He lifted Namaba's wrapped and lifeless form and carried it to a shady place beneath a pine tree, overlooking the big rock slab. He reached for the folding shovel on his hip, planning to dig a grave for her. But the shovel wasn't there.

"Something wrong?" Wizzy asked.

"The shovel and barbed cord," Javik said, looking around. "Must have dropped them someplace."

With Wizzy's help, they searched the entire area. Nothing was found.

"Where was the last time you saw them?" Wizzy asked.

"I'm sure I had them before entering the Magician's Chamber." He looked at the rock slab. "Damn, I hope we don't have to open that again. I've gotta find that stuff or I don't eat."

"I can dig a hole," Wizzy said. He flew to the spot Javik had selected and burrowed approximately a meter and a half into the soil, throwing dirt out in a pile beside the hole.

Javik did not say anything. He lifted Namaba's body and placed it gently in the hole. Not knowing any religious words, he stood there for a minute, looking down at her and crying. Then he knelt and pushed dirt over her, packing it down with his boots afterward.

"I think you expected too much of me," Wizzy said, hovering nearby. "After all, I'm only a little over seven days old. And I've tried to help you."

"Big deal," Javik said. He looked around for a marker, settling on a sizable agate.

"I think you could have shown more appreciation," Wizzy said. He watched Javik grunt as he pushed the agate to the grave site.

Javik horsed the rock until he had it in place. "Maybe it's a magical agate," Javik said. "Someone for her to talk with."

"Uh huh," Wizzy said.

I've lived more in these few days than in my whole life before that, Javik thought, staring down at the gravestone. *And now I've died, too. Prince Pineapple killed both of us at once.*

"I still don't understand all the emotions," Wizzy said. "I've made progress, though. You're experiencing sadness now."

Javik searched the area until he found a yellow flower like the one he had given Namaba. Digging up the entire root system with his bare hands, he took it back and planted it over her body.

It's done, he thought.

Looking around, Javik did not see Wizzy. Then something bright green flashed in the sky, catching his eye. It was Wizzy, sparkling in the sun and streaking away. Approaching Wizzy from deep space and growing larger by the moment, Javik recognized the Great Comet, burning white-hot, with a wispy, smoke-white tail.

Hearing the roar of rocket engines behind him, Javik looked back. An AmFed space cruiser with full para-flaps extended was setting down by the rock slab. A cloud of dust rose overhead.

"How'd they find me?" Javik mumbled. He tasted dust.

Then he looked skyward and knew the answer to his question.

"Goodbye!" the Great Comet wrote, making a trail of smoky letters across the blue sky.

"Goodbye!" Wizzy wrote, in smaller, more uneven letters.

Javik smiled as he squinted to watch the comets swoop high overhead, like a pair of fighter plane pilots. It was a joyous maneuver, shared by a proud parent and a proud child.

"Hey, fella," Abercrombie shouted, getting up on one elbow. "You're gonna be a goddamn hero, bringing me back and all. You know that?"

Two crewmen appeared in the open main hatch of the space cruiser.

"Yeah," Javik said, showing no enthusiasm. Wearily, he went to Abercrombie and removed the heavy cloth from his ankles.

They trudged together through the dust toward the waiting cruiser. The crewmen waved and yelled something.

Maybe I was a little hard on Wizzy, Javik thought.